THE INEVITABLE SPRING

BOOK 2 OF THE

THE DESTROYER'S WRATH

N. P. COOPER

A catalogue record for this work is available from the National Library of Australia

FOR ALL THOSE AUTHORS WHO INSPIRED ME WITH
THEIR OWN WORKS. EVEN IF THEY NEVER KNEW.

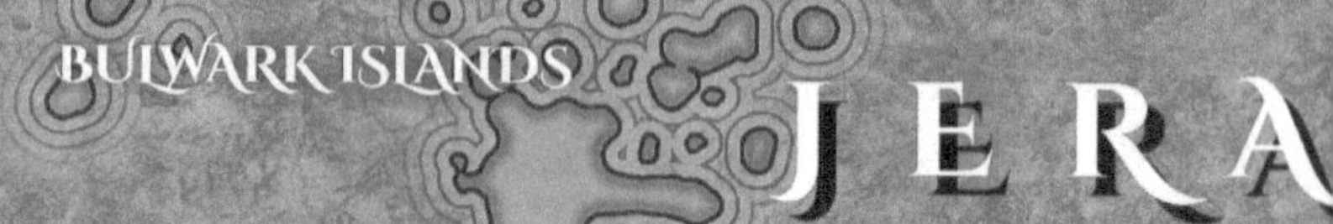
BULWARK ISLANDS
JERA
GREAT NORTH OCEAN
NORTHWATCH
HARVERNESS CRATER
ASMERE
NESTARN
ICE RA
KARVER
DARK IRON MOUNTAINS
MIRALTHRALL
STONEKEEP
CORDOVA
CLEARBROOK
DANAREL
MIRALLYN RIVER
HILLCREST
RAILAIN
LAKE PRISTINE
HEARTLAND'S GATE
SEAL COVE
GREENTREE LAKE
ROLLING HILLS
THE BONE COAST
LAKETOWN
CLIFFSIDE
MIDLAN
WESTERN PORT
GUILTOWN
SOUTH
WESTERN WATERS
THREE SEAS
TO AVSAN
SEA

ON
TO JERANAH
N
HENMAR'S POINT
CLAIREMONT
THE JADE COAST
ARA
MOUNT WHISPERWIND
TERRALIV HOMELAND
CONCLAVE CITY
PERESET
GRANDELL
JEPHSTAT
MIDWAY
DAMERETTE
RIVER
THE WRAITH WOODS
CARUEL
FOX HEAD LAKE
RIVER'S BEND
CAMAR RIVER
ARAMAR
TO SUNSET ISLES
EA
THE EMERALD SEA
ARBORIT HOMELAND
EASTERN WATCH
SILVERTOWN
OAKVIEW
AIDEN'S INLET
SEA OF DREAMS
'S LANDING
ISHES
MARASDAN

WINTER

The further west, the stranger things get.
Common Jeranonian Saying.

PROLOGUE

GREENTREE LAKE

Dark clouds blanketed a sky which had once been bright and clear.

It was the tail end of a short, hard winter and a chill wind was busy bending the long grasses of the Sammorand plains low towards the east.

A horse trudged up the dirt track which was all its far-flung destination deserved. Water was going to fall from above soon, of that the horse was certain as a biting gust of wind caused it to shiver despite the day's exertions.

A tiny insect landed on its nose, and the horse snorted as it shook the pest off. The increasing number of such irritants most likely meant that winter was finally losing its icy grip.

A familiar hand patted the horse on the neck. It looked around at the smaller two-legs riding atop its back. As always, the two-legs perched on a thing which smelled like cow that helped it keep its balance.

The two-legs was making noises at another two-legs also atop a horse nearby, but none of the sounds were familiar, so the horse continued walking.

If it had understood, it would have known the human was asking how much further it was until they came in sight of Greentree Lake, the most western village within Jeranon's domain.

For many years there had been disturbing rumours about this place. If they were to be believed, Greentree Lake was involved in everything from cannibalism to collusion with the nations beyond the Dark Iron Mountain Range. All one had to do from here was look up to see those jagged, snow-shrouded peaks slashing at the sky as the squad approached their eastern foothills. Foothills on which Greentree Lake sat perched. Aside from perhaps Angara, Greentree Lake was likely the single most isolated township in all of Jeranon. It was the kind of place almost no one had cause to visit unless on an errand of the most urgent sort.

The small group of soldiers still wore the green and brown colours of the king's army for all the good it did them. For the hundredth time that day, the officer in charge tugged absently at the insignia of Miralthrall's College of the Arts, which now overlaid the king's coat of arms on the chest of each man's uniform. He had no idea when Nereth had found time to have their spare uniforms altered, but despite there being no other modifications, it was as though the garment no longer fit correctly.

Hassan sighed and let the uniform be. He had never been one to pay much heed to rumours and gossip. Nevertheless, the sheer barbarism of some of the tales Jarl had told him on the way here warranted a certain level of caution.

At forty-five years of age, Hassan was a seasoned campaigner. He'd fought and even led many successful battles for his king over the last two decades and more. As a result, he had the loyalty of some of the army's most competent men.

He would need all of that and more if the insurrection he was planning against the traitorous Archmage Heramiir, and his accomplices was to have any chance of success.

Hassan's thoughts strayed back to his family, to his wife Sumi and their son Luthor. Heramiir still held them against his cooperation in the archmage's schemes, and they were far from alone. Most of his men and their families were in the same predicament.

He had to find some way to free them from the archmage's grasp.

His men had been loyal once, loyal to the rightful king of Jeranon. All that had changed last year when Heramiir had seized Miralthrall for his own, then set out to conquer as much of the country as his forces could take.

How Archmage Nereth, the general who had planned the strike, had shifted so much of the guard's loyalty before the coup, Hassan still hadn't been able to unearth. To the best of his understanding, a mage couldn't affect another person's mind. After many years of campaigning beside various battle trained magi, he'd thought he had a good sense for the limits of what they could do. Then he'd seen Nereth use a level of power at Stonekeep that according to everything he knew to be true, no mage should be capable of. Maybe Nereth had found a way to influence the minds of others.

Whatever the truth, the takeover had been swift and utterly decisive, leaving Hassan and a few thousand others isolated or in small groups and on the wrong side of a hopeless battle. When it was over, Heramiir had demanded that he join the new order, using the prisoners of the coup and their families as leverage. With so many lives in the balance, Hassan had been forced to turn his back on his king and his own oath of service to gain his men, and the civilians, their reprieve.

So now he was out here in one of the most remote corners

of the country with only a dozen trusted men at his back, obeying the orders of a traitor. They had been tasked with finding an end to where the slew of missing villages which had been discovered in the wake of the battle at Stonekeep lay.

Nereth had given the orders which sent him and his men all the way out here directly, normally enough reason to resist or disobey. Hassan had to grudgingly admit that on this one occasion, he was in complete agreement with the traitorous general.

What they had found at Derrack's hometown and the site of the other villages along the border had been disturbing enough. That the disappearances hinted at larger consequences being just around the corner was worse. So far, at least Clearbrook and Hillcrest, which they knew of, had been erased. Nothing had remained but undisturbed grass, and the King's Road leading away in either direction from where the village should have been. There had been no sign of destruction or foul play at either location, save a faint residue of Augrahl magic if the magi were to be believed. Every building, every animal, every person, was simply no longer there.

Both he and Nereth had assumed at the time that the western nations beyond the Dark Iron Mountains were to blame. In response, it had forced him to split his unit into scouting parties in order to cover more ground and locate an end to the path of destruction. As he had travelled with his own squad towards Greentree Lake, he had become less certain.

Normally, if a western raiding party snuck past the border patrols, they would burn or blast everything they could find until they were hunted down or attempted to return to their own lands. Brute force was almost always the chosen method for the few enemy troops who made it all the way through Jeranon's defences. This elaborate game of making the villages seem to have disappeared just didn't fit that pattern at all.

Apart from the jagged peaks above, the surrounding scenery was monotonous. Grass as high as a man on horseback dominated their field of vision until the wind brought it low for a moment, allowing a view of the grass behind. Much of the Sammorand plains was covered in the stuff, making it feel as though you were riding through a moving, swaying trench all day. There were stories of it having driven men mad.

It wasn't until hours later that Hassan led his squad around a sharp corner in the rough path. What lay beyond had been obscured until they rounded the bend, but caused him to order his men to a halt.

He reached over his shoulder and drew the broadsword from the harness on his back, listening for any sign of unnatural movement in the grass.

Ahead of them he was profoundly relieved to see the village of Greentree Lake now visible in the distance. However, to either side of the dirt path which led to its main gate were two rows of sharpened, fire hardened stakes, the impaled head of a Nostahl adorning each one. It was that gruesome sight which had caused him to draw his weapon.

The loathsome little creatures were a sub-race of the Augrahl Imperium which were used as either scouts or fodder for the military by their far larger brethren. In life they stood barely three feet tall and shared the grey, leathery skin of the Augrahl race. Unlike their more intimidating cousins, the stunted black horns of the Nostahl barely poked out from their skulls. They were cowardly on their own, but in groups they could prove devious opponents capable of shocking acts of violence. Worse, they enjoyed doing so, almost as a form of sport.

As Hassan inspected the nearest severed heads, he noted that the lack of decay meant they had been recent kills. Perhaps part of the band that had destroyed Clearbrook? Others further along the lines had clearly been there for quite some time. Once he realised his men were in no immediate danger, he put his sword away. The ones who had done this would be on his side. Not the king's side perhaps, but the human side at least.

Beside him, Jarl shifted in his saddle even as Derrack rode up beside them, shaking his head in disgust at the grizzly sight.

"Trophies?" the young mage asked as Hassan got the men moving again.

"More like a warning I would imagine," Hassan replied as they walked the horses cautiously towards the village.

"Halt where you are!" a commanding voice called from a concealed vantage point. Hassan held up a hand to order his men to comply.

"We mean you no harm," Hassan called back in his least intimidating manner.

There was a long moment of silence, as though the sentry were considering whether to believe him.

A boy, no more than fifteen years of age, stepped out of the grasses almost abreast with Hassan's men, startling some of the horses.

The boy was wearing clothes of a light brown weave that blended almost perfectly with the grass, and in his hand was a foot-and-a-half long machete which he held as though comfortable in its use.

The boy examined Hassan's men before motioning them onward towards the village, where the faint sound of singing was now audible in the distance.

"You may pass," he grudgingly permitted, as if alone he could have stopped them.

"If you hurry, you might still be in time for the feast."

"What are your people celebrating?" Derrack asked as Jarl led the rest of the men on at Hassan's nod.

"Victory," the boy told him with an enigmatic smile, before disappearing back into the grass without another word.

Hassan motioned Derrack to continue, and a minute later they were entering a cleared area which surrounded the well-constructed wooden palisade which protected the village.

Someone opened the gate as they approached, revealing another pair of men standing guard inside. Each was wearing a leather gambeson and armed with a heavy crossbow. Both men also sported a short sword strapped to their waste in an easily accessible scabbard.

The guards watched them suspiciously as they entered the village, but otherwise made no move to stop them. A decidedly odd feeling was growing on Hassan about this place, despite the contrasting scene of utter normality which confronted them once they were inside the palisade wall.

"Look Lena, we have guests!" a portly man announced as he looked up at the sound of their approaching horses.

As the cheerful man stood and walked towards them, most of the villagers started singing a raucous ballad that was apparently a favourite around these parts. Hassan looked past the approaching man, down the main street at the four bonfires which were blazing in the town square. It seemed the entire village had turned out for this celebration, whatever it might be. The smell of roasted meat wafted to them on a slight breeze from the last of the spits, making Hassan suddenly ravenous after phases on the road. The sound of several men taking large breaths behind him let him know his men felt the same way.

A pair of young men on the far side of the small but packed town square delivered the slab of roasted meat to a nearby counter where a dozen villagers were crowding around a long table. They'd already been butchering the animals from the other fires and were eager to finish the task so that the feast could begin.

The two men slid the last stake out from the cooked animal and propped it up against a nearby wall alongside seven others, which had no doubt been used as well given the pair of stands overlooking each fire. Hassan couldn't help but wonder what type of victory was so great that this tiny village would slaughter so many animals for a single day of feasting.

"Welcome to Greentree Lake. I'm the Mayor of this village, and you've arrived just in time," the portly man announced as he met them just short of the square. Hassan had difficulty hearing him over the sound of the singing, which was now reaching a crescendo. There must be close to two hundred villagers belting out the obviously well-known song, though Hassan had never heard it before. It impressed him that they did it in something approaching unison.

"It's been a quite a while since we had soldiers from our own nation come to our fair town gentleman. Please, won't you join us for the feast?"

Hassan looked around for a moment at the rows of neatly

tended houses which surrounded the town square. There was nothing out of place. If anything, the small community appeared a little *too* prosperous, though that was hardly a crime. Apart from the palisade, every indication suggested these people had enjoyed several decades of unremitting peace, which was not the case.

"That would be welcome," Hassan replied, motioning his men to dismount.

After several weeks of hard riding, they were all too eager to comply.

"Indulge my curiosity, Mayor, but your scout mentioned that a victory was the cause for this celebration. What did he mean?"

"Ah yes. A small band of Nostahl tried to raid the village last night, but not more than a half dozen or so thankfully. Due to the excellent work of our sentries, we were able to rout them without losing any of our own this time. That is cause enough for celebration this close to the border, wouldn't you say?"

Hassan nodded in silent agreement before turning to Jarl.

"Take two men and put a watch on the wall."

Jarl nodded his acknowledgement and chose Masik and Clide, who handed off their reins to other soldiers and followed him to a set of stairs leading to the balcony of the palisade. From up there they would be able to see for many miles over the long grass of the plains.

"Come, come," the mayor encouraged the rest of them as he turned back towards the town square and began to walk at a comfortable pace.

Hassan shrugged to himself and followed in silence until a few buildings later, the mayor stopped outside a small corral on the left side of the street, opening the gate.

"You may leave your mounts in here for now," he offered, and Hassan motioned for his men to do so after eyeing the small but clean enclosure.

"Larran," the mayor called to a nearby youth who was hurrying towards the festivities in the square.

"Larran, see these horses get some water from the well, and when you're done, you can have a double helping from the feast."

"Yes, Mayor," the boy replied with a sideways glance at Hassan before changing directions to carry out the task. The mayor once again motioned them onward.

Something is just not right about this place, Hassan thought again as he waited for his men to exit the stall and latch the gate behind them. After all the rumours which had surfaced on the way here, he had been expecting a half wild town full of lawless, destitute peasants. Nothing he had seen so far would justify those stories. These folks appeared well disciplined, not to mention being more welcoming towards his men than a lot of the rural towns he had visited over his career as a soldier.

Soon enough, the mayor led them past the outer edge of the square and over to a large carpet. An ascetically thin woman sat on a canvas chair near to the closest of the fires.

"Lena, will you see that these fine men get a share of the feast, please my dear?"

"Certainly, husband," she replied with the slightest of smirks.

As the woman turned away, she gave Hassan a flat look, one which he was sure he hadn't been meant to catch as she headed towards the table where the freshly roasted meat was still being carved.

"So, tell me, Colonel," the mayor said flatly. "What brings

your squad, accompanied by a mage no less, this close to the foothills? Most travellers tend to avoid our humble village unless they have urgent business."

Hassan stared at the mayor for a second. It took him a moment to realise that he'd been unconsciously contemplating the man's wife as she had gone to fulfil the errand her husband had requested.

Hassan looked around for a moment, but apart from Derrack, no one else was close enough to overhear what was better told to the mayor in private.

"There have been several attacks against border villages in the last phase," he began, brushing over the minor incident and prompting a nod from the mayor as if the awkward moment were nothing out of the ordinary.

"To date we know that both Clearbrook and Hillcrest have been destroyed, or more accurately, removed."

"Removed?" the mayor mused with a frown. "I'm not sure I understand."

"Neither do we," Hassan confided. "When we arrived at each of the villages, nothing remained."

Derrack interrupted. "Every piece of construction and every person and animal had been removed, as if they had never been there at all. All that remained was the King's Road leading away on either side of where the village should have been."

Hassan put a steadying hand on the young man's shoulder. The disappearance of his family at Clearbrook still weighed on Derrack's mind, as was to be expected, and they were still no closer to finding out what the fate of those villagers had been.

Dead or alive, they couldn't even consider mounting a rescue until they found out where the villagers had been taken.

Hassan nodded to the young mage, and he continued in a more objective tone.

"The grass where the villages should have been was undisturbed as though the sites had always been that way. The only clue we have was the faint trace of Augrahl magic lingering at Clearbrook."

"Our mission," Hassan took over, "As well as several other squads, which are on the way to other villages right now, is to see how far this destruction goes. Are you sure that there are no more Nostahl lurking nearby? It's possible the ones you encountered last night could have been an advance scout for a much larger force."

The mayor considered the idea for a moment before shaking his head.

"No, the party we dispatched last night was alone, and had no support from a shaman. I believe this incident to be independent from your destroyed villages. I thank you for the warning nonetheless."

He's taking this news very calmly, Hassan thought, and couldn't help but remember the rumours of collusion with the dark nations.

"Would it be possible to see the bodies of the Nostahl you killed last night? They might provide some insight into what clan is operating on this side of the mountains at present," Hassan asked.

All rumours aside, there was something a little too perfect about this place. It set off the hairs at the back of his neck, making him very uncomfortable indeed.

"I'm afraid that will not be possible Colonel. We burnt the bodies already, but we kept their gear if you would like to see it? You're lucky. This far from civilisation resources are at a premium, so whenever they attack us and fall in battle, we strip their gear before we burn them. I'll say one thing about the Nostahl, their swords make excellent machetes when wielded by a human hand, perfect for operating in the deep grasses. Come with me, I'll show you where we keep them."

Hassan nodded his consent, and the mayor began walking towards a street on the other side of the square. Before following, Hassan motioned his men to remain behind, although Derrack followed him as always. The three of them turned a corner, and then entered a side alley where an unobtrusive door sat a few dozen feet down the lane.

The solid blue glow of a Gift-wrought shield encircled the three of them as Derrack's face turned ashen.

"There's Oo'vi magic coming from inside this building!" He hissed.

The mayor recoiled and tried to run, even as Hassan whipped his broadsword free from its harness.

"High shaper!?" Hassan demanded. The overweight Mayor recoiled off the interior of the shield, and fell to the ground.

"No," Derrack replied. "No, it's not that powerful. But it's more than strong enough to sense that I'm here."

"You have two seconds to explain…" Hassan hissed to the mayor when no assault materialised.

The mayor backed up, panic in his eyes as Hassan slightly raised his blade. Then his shoulders slumped.

"It's not what you think. Come inside and I'll show you."

"You want us to just stroll into a building where your village is sheltering one of the most dangerous creatures alive?"

The mayor stood, brushing his clothes nervously as he looked Hassan in the eye, taking his measure. "It's not an Oo'vi," He eventually said. "It's something they left behind. Something that keeps us safe."

Hassan's eyes narrowed and Derrack's head snapped around. "It's gone!" he exclaimed, letting the shield drop.

"What's happening?" Hassan demanded as he looked around at the sudden lack of protection.

"He's telling the truth," Derrack responded, shooting the mayor a withering look. "The magic I sensed just stopped. If it were being maintained by a living shaper powerful enough to cast that spell, I'd be able to feel their aura at this range. Now there's no magic and no aura. The spell was being cast by arcana of some description."

"You're sure?" Hassan replied.

Derrack nodded. It seemed they would survive this day after all.

"Show me," Hassan demanded of the mayor.

The man grimaced, but soon enough the three of them were standing outside the door of the fired brick building down the lane. A moment passed while the mayor fumbled with a key chain, hidden on his belt until now.

Finding the one he was searching for at last, the mayor inserted the iron key into the lock. There was a click as it unlatched, and he pushed the door open and preceded the others inside to show them it was not a trap. As Hassan followed the portly man into the unlit room, the sheer number of swords, shields, bows and sets of armour which lay stacked in neat piles around the edges of the chamber immediately took him aback.

On the opposite wall a dim blue light shone through from underneath, betraying a carefully concealed door. Hassan frowned at the Gift-wrought glow as Derrack nodded at him in confirmation. He arched an eyebrow at the mayor to exact an explanation.

The mayor raised an eyebrow back and pointed towards

a nearby stack of armour, larger and more numerous than the others.

"This is what you wanted to see. Gear from Nostahl we have killed over the last twenty years. The eight sets at the top are from our most recent victory. Please help yourself."

Hassan's other eyebrow raised at the mayor's change of subject. Surely the man didn't think he would be put off investigating a source of enemy magic that easily. Hassan glanced again at the coruscating blue light coming from underneath the doorway. Before the mayor could react, he took three quick steps and kicked the inner door as hard as he could, sending it flying into the concealed room beyond.

An old man yelled in shock and deactivated the object he was working on. It was too late though, Hassan and Derrack had both seen the image floating in mid-air of what looked to be several square miles of the surrounding grasslands, as he was sure it would appear from above. Greentree Lake marked blatantly at the picture's centre.

A quick look at the device showed it was covered in Oo'vi glyphs, and Hassan drew his sword. It was a defensive move, though the two villagers took it as anything but.

"Wait!" the mayor commanded in a completely different tone than Hassan had heard him use so far.

"This is not what you think," he repeated as he shoved himself between Hassan and the old man.

"And what might that be?" Hassan returned. "That you're colluding with the western nations?"

"Don't be ridiculous!" The mayor yelled back, you saw the entrance to our village, did that look like collusion to you?"

Hassan's instincts had been screaming at him that something was not right since they had seen that grotesque procession of severed heads lining the entrance to the palisade. The contrasting, squeaky-clean interior of the village had only reinforced the feeling.

As Hassan took a moment to glance around the room, he saw only a desk and a single shelf adorning each wall, where a collection of arcane objects was stored. On the shelf at the far end of the room were two more objects containing Oo'vi glyphs, which he couldn't read, but only recognise the language. To his left, the shelf held several items, all of which bore the sharp angles of Augrahl writing. The various materials on that shelf carried a similar aspect to each other, as if they had all originated from the same source. The shelf to his right contained a half dozen carvings made of bone. From long experience he knew these were the chosen form for arcane objects fashioned by the northern plainsmen across the mountains, and suddenly he understood.

These items were not the product of collusion with the western nations, they were spoils of past battles, just as the armour and swords in the other room had been.

"This man is your real sentry, isn't he?" Derrack asked as Hassan slid his sword back into its sheathe.

The mayor sighed in annoyance; all pretence of the affable peasant now gone from his demeanour.

"Him and a few others who take turns using the device," the mayor grudgingly returned.

"This is how you actually keep your village safe from the western nations? By using a stolen Oo'vi scrying device?" Hassan couldn't help but laugh.

The mayor and the old man shared a meaningful look which was not lost on Hassan, and he looked around again at the gathered items.

"Don't worry, I have no intention of taking it from you,

nor of informing the magi that you are in illegal possession of arcane items."

"What?" Derrack interjected. "You can't be serious Hassan, we need to confiscate everything here for study and cataloguing back at the college. We will try these men for trafficking in arcana and collusion. You know the law as well as I."

Now it was Hassan's turn to raise an eyebrow at Derrack.

"The law? Are you joking? What law would that be, Derrack? The king's? Jeranon's? The moment you joined Heramiir's rebellion you declared yourself no longer part of that system of government. Unless you're saying you still wish to be part of the king's regime?"

Derrack frowned.

"Of course not. But even if I accept that argument, these items are far too dangerous to be left with the ungifted."

The mayor snorted.

"Son, we've had this device in our possession for over sixteen years… If it was dangerous to us, we would have found out long ago."

"Why are you even fighting me on this?" Derrack asked suspiciously, fingers twitching as if ready to pounce if Hassan gave the wrong answer.

For a moment Hassan thought about his response, knowing he needed to not only convince the young mage with his answer, but convert him.

"Two reasons," Hassan told him, opting for the simple truth. A portion of it anyway.

"First, I would no more take something so vital to these people's defence than I would knock down their palisade, especially with at least two missing villages within a week's ride. Second, your superiors hold my family, and those of my men hostage against our continued services. I have no explicit orders to bring these items back, and so I see no reason to give Heramiir more power than he already possesses."

"That's obeying the letter of the law by gutting its spirit," Derrack retorted.

"Alright," Hassan countered. "If you won't accept that reason then consider this. Your body bears the scars of a fire from your youth, does it not?"

"You know it does."

"A fire started by western troops?"

"Yes," Derrack confirmed. He knew where this was going.

"From an attack that never should have happened. That's what you told me after we left Seal Cove."

"It's not the same," Derrack began.

"It is. Imagine if Clearbrook had access to a device such as this. That attack might never have reached the town. Now tell me you can just take away such a vital defence to this village because it violates a system of law which you fully admit you no longer uphold."

Derrack opened his mouth, but then closed it again, reconsidering whatever argument he'd been about to make before looking the mayor straight in the eye.

"Given the current situation along the border, I will allow these devices to remain here for now, and I will not submit criminal charges to the college. In return, once this situation is resolved, I will come back. At that time, I expect your full cooperation and access to the device for as long as I see fit in order to replicate its design. If I determine anything here is dangerous to the user, or cannot be controlled by the Giftless, I will take it with me when I leave. These are my conditions."

"And no criminal charges for anyone?" The mayor repeated.

"So long as every device is still here upon my return, and you adhere to every condition I just set out, no."

For a long moment the mayor was silent, then looked at his hand, in which a small stone glowing with a greenish light had appeared from somewhere. He nodded in surprise.

"It seems you are telling the truth," he said at length as he motioned the old man behind him to relax.

"Very well. Your warning has been delivered, and as you can see, our village is exactly where it should be. I think perhaps it is time for you to leave now, yes?"

Hassan looked the mayor in the eye and saw no question about the issue written there. Without doubt his kicking in of the door had just overstayed their welcome in Greentree Lake. With a concurring nod, he turned his attention to the pile of gear neatly stacked and inventoried, yet still approaching his own head for height.

"We still have one more piece of business to attend to," Hassan said as he looked the pile over.

There must be over five hundred sets of armour here, he thought as he appraised the stack. As he removed the pieces he was interested in and lay them aside, the old man returned to his desk and the mayor stood watching him impatiently.

Ignoring the others, he examined the items for anything that might shed some light on what was happening with the missing villages, or even this small raiding band. It was possible they were part of a larger assault force and had become separated from their command. He supposed Greentree Lake's sentries might have intercepted them on their way back across the mountains. But if that were the case, it begged the question, why they would come so close to the village with an obviously inadequate force? The Nostahl's only real advantage in battle lay in their numbers.

After several minutes of study, the only thing he had learned from the armour was that it was devoid of the usual clan markings representing which Augrahl tribe owned the Nostahl slaves.

That was unusual. A thorough search of the weapons they'd been carrying also failed to turn out any additional information. He returned the gear to the respective piles.

"You have quite a collection," Hassan told the mayor, who had waited to the side while he conducted his inspection, but was now once again ready to usher them out of the dim room.

"We waste as little as possible," the mayor repeated, motioning towards the outer door.

Hassan still couldn't shake the feeling something else was wrong, but without knowing what, he had little choice but to follow the mayor's lead.

It was true. Their mission here was complete, and there was too little left to be gained by staying longer just to assuage his strange concern.

Besides, there was no telling what other arcana these people may have collected over the years. Whatever the other objects were in the back room, they could clearly help them defend their tiny village.

His men were highly trained, but if things got out of hand and the villagers closed the only entrance to the palisade, they would be trapped. Even with Derrack by their side, that could get very ugly with the arcane support which these people commanded.

As they all returned to the town square, it was to find his men finishing up their portions from the feast, which some thoughtful villager had also carried up to his men on the wall.

Hassan gave a short but sharp whistle. As his sentries looked down, Hassan motioned them back from their stations. They soon joined the others as those in the square put down their plates and came over from where they were eating.

"I'm satisfied with what we've seen," Hassan told them once Jarl and the others had re-joined their ranks. "If the attack here is related to our investigation, it is only by unfortunate coincidence. Let's move out."

"Round up the horses," Jarl ordered two of the men, and they saluted and left to retrieve their mounts from the small stockade.

"You should be safe enough with the precautions you have in place, but if you see any sizable force heading for you…"

"We will deal with them," the mayor returned, once again the affable peasant now that Hassan's men were watching, "We are a lot… stronger, as a community, than you might suspect."

Hassan nodded, wondering what other surprises these people might have stored away for their enemies if it came to that. Then decided he was better off not knowing.

Soon enough the men returned with the horses, and a minute later they all mounted up at Hassan's command as Lena hurried towards the group. Two well-muscled young men followed behind her, each of them carrying a pair of the stakes they had used for roasting the feast in each hand.

"Here," she said with a smile, "For your journey," and passed both he and Derrack a small joint of the roasted meat wrapped in some kind of large leaf.

"Thank you," Hassan said, taking a bite of the strongly flavoured meal when she just watched him expectantly.

With a nod of farewell and a somewhat strained smile, Hassan turned his black charger, Stormcloud, toward the gate and led his men through and away from Greentree Lake. The final predatory smile Lena had given him when he'd tasted the meat disturbed him no little amount.

They had not gone more than a dozen steps outside the gate when the creaking of wood sounded behind them, and the only entrance into the town slowly closed, barring them from re-entry.

Hassan stopped for a moment in puzzlement, and as he realised he was sitting between two rows of severed and decaying heads, he lost his appetite.

Why did they close the gate so soon after we left? And why had Lena, who had seemed so cold at first, suddenly brought him food for the road, and then appeared so delighted when he'd eaten it?

With a sudden suspicion he brought the meat up to his face and took a deep whiff, attempting to determine if it had been poisoned or drugged. He was no expert, but as far as he could tell the food seemed unaltered, although it gave off a slight odour he was unfamiliar with.

"Do any of you feel ill in any way?" Hassan asked as he motioned them onwards, eager to be away from the smell of rotting flesh. This close to the palisade the kills were older, and mostly bone. As they continued to ride, it was clear now that he knew what to look for, just how many enemy troops these people had slain over the last year or so. The number of Nostahl killed in each more recent battle was marked by the level of decay in the heads.

As they continued, the men all told him they felt fine, one of them even remarking that the meat had been delicious, and wondering what animal it had come from.

The idle remark stopped Hassan dead in his tracks. He thought back on the four pairs of roasting spits that Lena's bearers had been carrying when she'd brought him the food, and the eight sets of armour the mayor had shown him from their last encounter with the Nostahl. With a horrified glance, his eyes were drawn to the end of the lines where eight new heads lay mounted on stakes near the corner of the path that would lead them away from Greentree Lake.

Almost pitching over the side of his saddle, Hassan violently emptied his stomach as he realised just where the meat for their feast had come from. He hurled the remaining portion into the grass as if it were a live adder in his hand. Behind him he could hear some of his other men, hard bitten veterans all, gagging as they caught on to what had distressed their stoic colonel.

Once he had remastered himself, Hassan stared back at the closed gate of Greentree Lake. He had no hope of re-entering right now without a far larger force, or having Derrack blast them apart. He considered it.

The Nostahl were not human. They were also vicious beyond belief, but they were still intelligent creatures, and eating them was the next best thing to cannibalism, if not exactly the same thing.

As he watched the gate, Lena popped her head up over the balcony and laughed when she saw their distress.

"Enjoy your meal!" she called after them with a mocking wave before disappearing from sight.

Hassan stared daggers at where the evil woman had been and promised himself he would return here one day and burn this place to the ground, king's city or not.

With a too hard kick to Stormcloud's ribs, he got the horses moving beyond sight of the cursed village.

It wasn't until several days later that his stomach stopped trying to make him retch every time he thought on the unspeakable act which the residents of Greentree Lake had forced him and his men to unknowingly commit.

Every journey begins with a single step, and yet at their fulfilment, things are never so certain.
Ancient Jeranonian Proverb.

CHAPTER I

A TIME TO KILL

With a slight pulse of the Gift, Archmage Tolmarak opened one of the huge carved doors that led to King Erian's main audience chamber, and stepped across the threshold. He rarely called on the Gift for such trivial matters, but the message had read 'urgent'. For King Erian, that meant a private meeting with only his pair of personal guards in attendance. Those men would be by his side as always, not here in the corridor to open the overly large doors for a tired old mage.

Proceeding further into the throne room, Tolmarak spotted an exhausted older man in fine robes stooped over a table off to the left of the chamber.

Almost as old as I am, the archmage thought with a wry grin as he traversed the short distance. Crossing between the huge row of columns which marched from one end of the throne room to the other, he soon arrived at the king's table.

The Monarch was dressed in the red and white of the royal house of Jeranon, and to either side of him stood a guard in deceptively heavy armour. The royal guards' plate was lacquered in the king's colours, though with the white predominant rather than the red of house Savani.

Every part of them was covered in enamelled steel, except for their faces, over which a guard could be pulled down from their helmets at a moment's notice. Both men had a heavy bow strapped over their flowing red cloaks. The royal bodyguards also carried a curved scimitar, counterweighted with a quiver of Gift enhanced arrows on their belt. In the left hand of each rested a scutum, a giant metal shield almost as tall and wider than the man holding it. The royal guards stood still as stone, their shields resting at precise angles as they faced away from the king, alert for threats even here.

To any outsider they would look a formidable threat. But only Tolmarak, the king, and the men themselves knew just how deadly those weapons they carried really were. Tolmarak himself only had that information because he had been the one to design and create the arcana which made up the majority of their equipment. There were some lethal surprises waiting in that armour for anyone traitorous enough to attack the king.

"You summoned me, Majesty?" Tolmarak said, his tone a question as he studied the worn-out man he approached.

"Join me," the Monarch replied as he waved his old friend and adviser over to where he was standing.

Tolmarak did as instructed, but found himself disturbed to see a look of deep resignation etched into the Monarch's features as he studied the map before him.

In the barest of predawn light filtering through the stained-glass windows high above, the two men stood silently for a moment before the rightful ruler of Jeranon finally spoke.

"It begins today," was all he said.

A few minutes passed in silence as the two men each

contemplated what those words would mean for Jeranon, until the king continued.

"I have ordered the army ready to march by week's end. They will take this route," he said tiredly as he traced his finger around the northern reaches of the Wraith Woods. He traced a line up past the cities of Caruel and Jephstat until he stopped at a dot representing the city of Midway. The city had been called something else originally, but had been renamed when the Sammorand Plains had finally been cleared at the end of the wars of founding.

"Several shiploads of infantry will also embark from Aramar and act as an advance force. After sailing for Half Moon River, they will land and march to Midway ahead of our main force. Upon arrival, they will reinforce the garrison and secure the city until the rest of our men arrive. A final contingent of infantry will march to Aiden's Inlet. Once our navy has delivered the first load of troops and returned to Aramar for supplies, they can pick up these reserves on the way back west. By the time they make landfall and arrive at Midway with the extra supplies, the main army should be in place. From Midway they will merge into one command under General Messand and divide into two expeditions. The first will assault Cordova and draw off some of Heramiir's troops. The second, larger force will head south, crossing the Mirallyn River below Lake Pristine and securing the towns there as quickly as possible. They will then move up to assault Danarel, which will force Heramiir to pull his men back upriver from Cordova or risk having them cut off by our attack."

"The plan looks solid," Tolmarak said, "Though you and I both know that campaigns of this nature rarely go according to the wishes of those who initiate them. The only real problem I see is that Heramiir could avoid the trap by either not defending Cordova, or by sending his full force against it. If he were to abandon Danarel at the correct moment, he could rout our smaller expedition."

"That is true," Erian replied. "But that would require foreknowledge of our plans. If he withdraws from Cordova all the better, since he can't burn a city that big without enraging the entire populace of western Jeranon. It would turn too many of them back to our cause. If he sends enough of his force to defeat our expedition, our main army can take Danarel with little resistance. They can then attack from his rear, cutting off Heramiir's force from their supply lines. That outcome would quickly neutralise those forces, making Miralthrall a great deal easier to take when the time comes."

"What do you wish me to do?" Tolmarak asked. The king's deployment was a good one so long as Heramiir did not attack Midway in force between the time the advance infantry units and the main army reached the city. Although that seemed unlikely, as Midway was nearly a hundred and fifty leagues from Heramiir's nearest point of control.

"You will send enough magi with the advanced forces on the first shiploads of troops to cover their retreat should the need arise. The main force of your power however should stay with the overland column. I want Midway secured until the army can merge, but I'm not willing to separate the full strength of the college from the main army to achieve it. Once all elements have safely arrived, they will merge with Messand's command."

"Yes sire," Tolmarak answered before asking, "And where would you have me?"

For a moment the king frowned in thought, as if only now coming to a decision too long delayed.

"You will remain in the capital with enough magi and archmagi to effectively defend Aramar should the worst occur. As will two dozen battle trained magi of your choosing on top of that number until this other matter is resolved," the king ordered.

"But Erian," Tolmarak protested. "You know my presence on the battlefield will be more valuable than a dozen of the younger magi…"

"You are needed here for that same reason," the king told him with finality.

"Besides, what good does it do us if my army wins the day and yet we still lose control of Aramar itself? No, this infiltrator that you have been tracking must be dealt with before I can allow you to leave, my old friend."

"Yes, sire," Tolmarak acceded as he became suddenly sure the king's mind would not be changed by any amount of argument.

Erian was right, Aramar had to be protected. In his heart though, he also knew the assassin, and that was how he now thought of the killer whom he had been hunting for the last several weeks, had been sent for exactly this reason. With the king's order now given, the infiltrator, who almost certainly had to be one of Heramiir's men, had achieved his goal. He or she had created enough chaos, fear, and death that the king had ordered two dozen magi to remain behind. Magi who by all rights should march with the army to confront Heramiir's forces, but would now sit in the capital doing nothing but trying to hunt him down.

"Then with your leave I will keep Jayden and the rest of the more powerful apprentices with me here to attend to that task."

For a moment the king frowned.

"You have grown attached to that boy, old friend. Is he truly so powerful as you describe?"

Tolmarak thought for a long moment about the troubled young man he had found on the Anchorhead Promontory last year. Jayden still had more power within him than sense at this point. His display in the throne room just a few weeks past was proof enough of that. Yet in the days since that near disastrous episode, the young man also seemed to have taken hold on the grief that had wracked him since the night his local noble had been responsible for the death of the woman he loved. Tolmarak had cursed himself a hundred times since for not arriving just a single hour earlier, but what was done was done. All he could do now was painstakingly guide the most powerful mage the College of the Arts had known in a very long time onto a course that would benefit both the boy, and Jeranon as a whole.

"If he can be properly moulded into what we want him to be, it is likely he will one day take my place as leader of the college," Tolmarak answered after a protracted moment.

For a long time, the king was still as he considered the archmage's words.

"That's quite a recommendation," the ageing Monarch responded. "But for now, can he be trusted?"

"I believe so," Tolmarak replied, "So long as he sees that his eventual path to revenge, or justice, on Count Dael lies through my goodwill. Provided he is not provoked further on the matter, I think he will do as we wish."

"You think?" the king returned with a raised eyebrow.

"It is a near certainty, so long as the status quo remains unchanged."

"Can you, or can you not control this young man?" Erian

asked as he turned to face his longest serving advisor.

Tolmarak said nothing as he pretended to study the battle map laid out before them to give himself a moment to think. He had hoped to avoid this conversation until much later, but he would not lie to his king.

"No," he finally answered. "But I have known that since the day he woke from his injuries back in Grandell. His spirit and his Gift are too strong. Fortunately for us, however, we need not control him. What we need to do, and what I believe can be achieved, is to convert him to our cause. To Jeranon's cause, so that he serves willingly, as we do."

After a long time, the king sighed.

"Very well, old friend. I will trust your judgement in this matter, for now. But if he becomes a threat to this kingdom, you will follow the law and act accordingly. Am I clear?"

"Yes, sire," Tolmarak replied, unhappy with the king's order. It was one he fervently hoped he never had to carry out. If he were forced to, it would mean that Jayden had already been declared renegade and expelled from the college. The boy would then be hunted by any mage he came across, and despite his enormous strength in the Gift, would eventually make a mistake and fall in battle. Perhaps even to one of the other students he now called friends.

Perhaps even to me, Tolmarak mused, for surely none but these few had even a slight chance of defeating Jayden in his wrath.

"Very well, if there is nothing else, I will return to the college and begin making preparations for the magi to march," Tolmarak said after a moment.

With a slight nod from the king, Tolmarak turned to leave the vast audience chamber and begin the trip back towards the college grounds. He barely noticed the trip as his mind raced through everything that needed to be done, now that war was upon them.

*   *   *

"Listen up!" Lieutenant Bickerall shouted.

Within moments, the hubbub of conversation died to nothing. All eyes were diverted to the front of the practice yard where a small, raised platform had been set up for the captain to address them.

With the entire mageguard ordered to attend, the square was full with the almost fifteen hundred men that made up the elite force of the king's army. Every eye was on its ranking officer as he attached a small object to the top button of his coat and began to speak.

It was not the shout that Bickerall had used a moment before, but a steady, measured tone being projected by the small object, or so it seemed to Wyll.

A few phases ago, he would have been in awe at that trivial piece of arcana. Since then, he'd grown more familiar with the young magi of Jayden's class during their sixth-day meetings at the Man at Arms. He'd also been promoted to sergeant, and his squad transferred to the mageguard. Now that had been an eye opener. As a result, such things as the lapel clip, while still interesting, no longer drew his attention as they used to.

"There is much to be done today, so I will be brief," Captain Tarrent Ravenburg, head of the mageguard, notified them in an even tone.

"The King has given the order to march. Already the infantry, cavalry, and navy have begun preparations for the journey west. Some of you will attend your magi on the march, others will do so by sea, forming the spearhead of our advance. Still more will remain in Aramar to see to the city's defence in the event the campaign does not go as planned. I know each of you will hold yourselves to the highest standards of honour and valour in the coming phases, regardless of your assignments. Defend your charges, fight with honour, protect the weak. Honour and valour!" Ravenburg finished as he thumped his chest with his right hand.

"Honour and valour!" the square full of veteran warriors shouted, repeating the captain's gesture. At least, all of those not new to the guard did. Wyll raised an eyebrow, and he wasn't alone in his confusion. Many of the new mageguard recruits had been chosen from those conscripted by the king the previous year. In that exact moment, many of them realised just how much more they still had to learn before being fully accepted by the veterans of this elite group.

Without another word, Ravenburg stepped back, removing the pin from his coat, and allowing Bickerall to return to the front of the dais.

"All right," the well-muscled lieutenant shouted at them once again, "Disperse to your normal duties. I'll be sending runners to the squad leaders throughout the morning with your orders. Those of you with the advanced scouts will leave at first light tomorrow and may take the rest of the day to prepare and say your farewells. Mageguard, dismissed!" Bickerall pivoted on his heel and left the dais, even as the men in the square began moving away to begin whatever tasks the day held for them.

"All right," Wyll told his men after a long moment, "Let's get our weapons and armour. It looks like this morning is going to be drills again," he said without relish.

He tried to keep the frustration out of his voice, but wasn't sure he succeeded from the subtle look Seth sent him at the comment. It wasn't as though he resented the constant drilling, or the sometimes-bizarre scenarios the magi came up with to test them. They were more interesting than the heavy labour and mindless repetitive tasks they had endured at camp five while the men built up their strength and endurance. But the waiting was beginning to grate on them all. Besides, it had been common knowledge that they would leave for war in the next few days, even before the announcement. The first snowdrifts were already melting.

They'd all been hoping the assembly would relieve the tension of not knowing what was happening, but now Wyll felt even more tightly wound than he had before the gathering. At least they should get a definitive answer by this afternoon. Wyll wasn't sure whether he felt more excitement or dread at the prospect. The coming march would be a journey, and an adventure, something he had always enjoyed. On the other hand, while he was no coward, the cold hard fact was that at the end of that journey lay many battles. Not a man in the yard expected they would all come back with their lives. Not to mention that of all the soldiers here, his unit was one of those with the least training, and that didn't bode well for their chances.

Without another word, Wyll began the walk towards their rooms, while the others followed suit behind him. Within twenty minutes, they had gathered and donned their gear and were back in the courtyard for advanced sword techniques. It was a class Wyll liked and did better at than some of the others in the squad. Though according to the instructor, a grizzled old veteran called Callen, he still had a long way to go. Marad's constant arrogance had slowed the enormous man down a bit, not to mention getting a sound thrashing the day before from both Seth and their trainer. Though his pride had been wounded, it was counted as no shame by the others to lose to Seth. In fact, all of them had done so on every occasion so far. The only exception had been about a week ago when Cale had managed a draw. It hadn't been by fighting him to a standstill though, but rather by committing to a move where in actual battle he would have been mortally wounded to gain position for the killing thrust. Even Seth had agreed that they both would have been killed, but that was the only time he had not soundly thrashed his opponents. Even Cale, who Seth now traded blows with even more fluidly than the others, could not keep up. It was almost as if the top-knotted man had realised Cale's newfound skill and stopped holding back. If that were indeed true, then Wyll knew he would be very glad to have the man by his side in the coming conflict.

The lesson seemed an indeterminable length as they fought each other and the instructor in mock combat. Next, they practised drills against multiple opponents, in which again only Seth prevailed. Not even Cale could win this one today, and to everyone's surprise, Charran disarmed the mute veteran while Tauman got in a lucky thrust with the practice blade, almost breaking skin as he ended the match.

In all, it was a dissatisfying performance, and the instructor was little pleased with the results. The man gave them a stiff dressing down once they were done, centring around the unpredictable nature of combat, and learning to control their emotions.

It was a valid point, Wyll thought objectively. Though not one especially appreciated right at this moment as the instructor banished them from the practice yard.

Wyll found himself in a dark humour as the squad headed back towards the barracks and stowed their gear before making their way to the noonday meal.

"Sir, your orders," a soldier announced as he came to stand in front of Wyll, holding out a packet which Wyll took and opened, dismissing the runner as he did.

He read the orders, and then again to make sure there was no mistake before turning to face the others, a frown etched upon his brow.

"Listen up, men!" he told them a bit more sharply than he'd intended.

"There's been a change of plans."

*   *   *

"Be seated," Tolmarak told his five strongest students. As he strode into the room, he took his place at the front of the semi-circle of plush chairs.

He remembered when they had first convened here early in the previous autumn. At that time, Jayden had barely been able to speak for his grief. Now, although he was not yet near healed from the horrors he had experienced at the hands of Count Dael, the boy moved as swiftly to his seat as any of them did. The sight made Tolmarak smile slightly in approval.

"All right," he said as they finished settling in. "As I am sure you are all aware by now, the advanced elements of the army are making final preparations to march at first light tomorrow. The rest will leave by week's end. They will be joined by a good portion of the magi in Aramar's college, and of course a large contingent of the mageguard as well."

Tolmarak took a breath before continuing, and then gave them their orders.

"None of you will go with the expedition."

"But," Nadeara interrupted, "If we are not to fight, then why all the accelerated training? Archmage…" she trailed off in consternation.

"I said you would not be going with the expedition. Sadly for us all, that does not mean you won't be required to fight," the archmage wearily returned.

"Officially, you will remain in Aramar to continue your training, and, if necessary, to defend this city. A few dozen magi will also remain, in the unlikely case that our forces are turned back this spring."

"And unofficially?" Lady Clarion Firerose asked as soon as he was finished, her long red hair cascading over her shoulder as she tilted her head.

Tolmarak returned her questioning look before sighing in resignation.

"We have a problem," Tolmarak told them.

"What I am about to divulge to you is never to leave this room, no matter how justified you may think that telling anyone else may be. Before we continue, I will have each of your word's on this. If not, I will have to ask you to remove yourself from these proceedings," he finished firmly, leaving no room for argument.

Billy agreed immediately, then Jayden and Nadeara, and then a bit more slowly Firerose nodded her assent until only the now fifteen-year-old apprentice Missy was left.

"How can we promise not to tell anyone when we don't know how important the information is?"

Tolmarak just looked at her for a second before realising the brown-haired girl from the isolated community of

Angara in Jeranon's extreme north was being completely serious.

"A fair question," the archmage allowed, "But in this matter you will have to trust my judgement, or excuse yourself from further discussion."

For a long moment she thought seriously about it, but then twisted her mouth as if tasting something unpleasant, and agreed.

"Very well," Tolmarak said as he stood, unconsciously pacing back and forward in front of them as he was sometimes want to do.

"Late last summer, before most of you arrived at the college, we began to see signs that accidents involving those capable of manipulating the Gift were increasing in frequency. We thought nothing of it at first, but after several incidents of this nature, a young mage by the name of Heroth was killed in one. He was on the roof of the college building, and as far as we could determine, slipped. An examination concluded that he had hit his head, rendering himself unconscious and unable to use a levitation spell to break his fall as he slid from the peak, regrettably falling to his death."

For a moment the old man was silent as he let the information sink in.

"After a few weeks, a mage in the city simply fell over dead. Her heart had given out, Archmage Trellis determined, though the unfortunate Miranda was a strong and vital woman just over half my age. Still, these things have happened from time to time, though it is rare. Next was the very day you arrived," he said, nodding towards Jayden.

"I assume you remember me rushing out of your room immediately after settling you in?"

"Yes," Jayden replied.

"I had felt the aura of one of the magi wink out, which by now you all know can only mean one thing. Poor Melven had been crushed by a stone fallen from the roof of the gallery. Again, all signs pointed to a tragic, yet freakish accident. This time I became suspicious though as the surrounding mortar was in good repair, not crumbled like you would expect if it had given way due to the stone's weight. And yet there was still no solid evidence that foul play had been a factor. No sign the Gift had been used to pry the block from the ceiling, or do anything else involved, for that matter. However, the fourth mage was a very different story."

"With Orwin's demise the pattern became apparent. Every thirty-five days, no more, no less, a mage was dying under almost unbelievable circumstances. At this point, I, and a few trusted archmagi began to rigorously investigate what we now saw as murders despite the lack of evidence, either physical or Gift related. Since we started readying the supplies and assigning men to active units for the coming campaign, the murders have become more frequent. Once a week to be exact, although the times and places always differ. The assassin, for that is what we are sure this must be, is now acting openly, and killing at will by direct use of the Gift. Yet as the time for the army to leave draws near, along with the majority of Aramar's magi, we are no closer to catching this menace than we were back when poor Heroth was killed."

Tolmarak subsided and sat back in his chair as he assessed the impact of his words on each of them. His students' expressions ranged from horror to anger, and something cold in Jayden that made his eyes burn a little too brightly.

"Given the timing and increasing frequency of the attacks, it is our working theory that this murderer is most likely an assassin sent by Archmage Heramiir. His purpose appears to be to make as many of our battle trained magi remain in Aramar as possible, hunting him down," Tolmarak continued with a sigh. "Something which King Erian has now ordered."

"But why would he do that?" Billy asked with a frown. "Why would an assassin want to be hunted?"

Sometimes Tolmarak forgot how young Billy was due to his strength in the Gift. Then he made a comment like that.

"Because for every mage he kills, and every one who remains behind, our expeditionary forces will be that much weaker when they confront Heramiir's army. If Heramiir can defeat them without the western nations taking a hand, all of Jeranon might well fall before him in time."

"And you expect us to help hunt down this assassin?" Firerose exclaimed, "After everything you've just told us?"

"I expect you to continue your training," Tolmarak flatly returned to his nobly born student.

"I also expect you to be on your guard. Once the army and the magi march, you five will be among the most powerful Gift users in Aramar, and therefore prime targets for this assassin. It is my belief that at least one more attack will occur after the army leaves. That way the assassin can be sure we won't think he has gone with them and follow with another group of magi to support the campaign. You are to take all necessary actions to defend yourself from these assaults."

"Are we authorised to kill this assassin?" Jayden asked bluntly, sending all heads turning towards him as he leaned slightly forward on his chair. The outward picture of calm.

"Only in defence of yourself or another at this point. It would be infinitely preferable to take him alive. There is much we still need to know about what Heramiir plans for the coming conflict," Tolmarak replied.

"Also, one last thing. Logic tells us that the assassin is strong in the Gift, but I have detected no auras but the ones belonging to those magi who are in and around the college grounds. Unfortunately, this leaves us with the disturbing, yet distinct possibility that the killer is one of our own, and not an outsider at all. That is why you must tell no one what you know or suspect, except myself or each other. Even then, only speak once you have set a ward against eavesdropping. Which brings us to today's lesson," Tolmarak announced as the students listened intently, each realising that their lives might depend on how well they could learn this new spell.

Otherwise, a Gifted assassin could eavesdrop on their every conversation, determining when and where they would be alone.

Then take advantage of it.

CHAPTER 2

THE FIRST BLOW

"Left behind! I can't believe we've been left behind," Marad growled into the dark mug of ale in front of him, which was still considerably lighter than his own ebony skin.

"Believe it," Nadeara replied, annoyed at the hulking man sitting across the table from her, "And what's more, be thankful for it."

"She's right, Marad, give over already," The musically inclined Kienan agreed. "There's not a one of us that couldn't use a fair bit more training before we have to put it to the test, and you know it."

"Ahhh… you're all just a bunch of craven, yellow-bellied, muck-crawling layabouts that wouldn't know a good fight if it came up and hit you in the face," Marad spat back, including the rest of the group in his statement, and gathering several less than patient stares in response.

"You know," Bosric said, leaning over to the mouse-haired Tauman, yet speaking loud enough for everyone at the table to hear. "If he ever actually insults us, without sounding like more of a fool than he makes us out to be, I think I'll have to kill him."

Tauman snorted and took another bite of his dinner.

Whatever the college kitchens had served them tonight, he was on a life-or-death mission to make sure none of it went to waste.

Marad gave Bosric an evil stare, which the short red-headed man threw right back with mock intensity before laughing as if someone had made a fine joke. He shrugged when no response was forthcoming, and returned to his meal, habitual smile showing through, even as he chewed his food.

Word had come down this afternoon that the army would begin the long march towards the west tomorrow, though rumour had at least some of the men travelling by sea. That news they had all expected. What had shocked them to the core was that not only Tolmarak's advanced Gift class, but also Wyll's entire squad, were being left behind in Aramar to continue their training.

Wyll had been relieved when he had first heard the news. Not that he was a coward, but as Kienan had already pointed out, several of his men were not yet as ready as they could be. Both Tauman and Kienan were still weak at their weapons, though Tauman was pulling ahead of Kienan in that regard. The brothers, Sarran and Charran, were excellent at following orders, but as far as initiative went, they were no better than the day they had all arrived at camp five. Both were dependable and good in a fight though, which counted for a lot. Marad was just the opposite. More talk than anything else, he was stubborn to a fault. Even if he had accepted Wyll's promotion over him now for the most part, he still disagreed with almost every order given on general and varied principal. Of all of them, only Bosric, Cale and Seth seemed ready to fight and follow orders in a tight spot. There was no surprise there though, they were also the only three in the squad with previous battle experience.

No, what had shocked Wyll was that the five magi they had been spending their downtime on sixth day afternoon's these last phases had also been left behind. Supposedly for the same reason.

From what he had gathered over the last few weeks since squad four twenty-two had been promoted to the mageguard, an average battle mage was worth about a hundred disciplined warriors on the field. More, even, depending on how advanced the mage's training was. But when they worked in concert, two or three of them could disperse five hundred times their number without other aid. An experienced and hardened archmage was another story entirely.

The purpose of the mageguard was more to guard individual magi on their way to and from assignments, not to mention while they slept, than it was to play a pivotal role on the field. Even so, he was assured by other mageguard officers that it was sometimes required, usually when the spell casters were being pushed especially hard by their opponents.

"What do you make of it, Jayden?" Seth asked in his calmly flat voice.

The rest of the table went quiet. Seth hardly ever spoke.

Jayden looked up from his absent study of whatever was in his cup, surprised at being addressed by the often-silent warrior with his raven black top knot of hair.

"Reserves," was all he said as he locked eyes with Seth for a moment.

Seth nodded as though this were his notion as well. He then returned to his plate, while the rest of them looked around at each other in puzzlement.

"But aren't we supposed to be the best? I mean, isn't that

why we're here in the first place?" Billy, the youngest member of their combined group at only eleven years of age, asked with a confused frown.

"No, Billy," Nadeara said to the young orphan boy, "We are among the strongest, but we are not yet the best."

'They will keep us safe until we can do it for ourselves,' Cale wrote on his pad before sliding it into the middle of the table.

"They don't want us to die too quickly," Marad snorted while Nadeara gave him a significant glance, and then one towards the two youngsters sitting at the table.

"Don't look at me like that, woman," Marad growled before turning towards Missy and Billy, the two of whom always sat together now.

"When we get to fighting, there will be blood, and fire, and death, and it won't all be on the other side," he said vehemently to the youngsters before anyone could stop him.

"And if anybody tells you differently, they are just lying to make you feel better!"

"You are a first-class fool, Marad," Nadeara snapped as soon as he had finished.

"Really?" the enormous man replied. "They can learn all they like out of a book, but if you keep coddling them, the first time they see what goes on, and comes off, on a field of battle, they will freeze up and cost good people their lives."

"Oh come on, Marad, ease up a bit will you. They're barely more than children for crying out loud," Kienan snapped back at him.

"*That's* where you're wrong music man," the huge soldier shot back as the rest of the table grew uncomfortably silent. "They *were* children. Now they are apprentice magi, and in the king's service. They go where he points, fight when he says, and they die should he choose. Just like the rest of us. And if any of you think a single thing I just said is a lie, you need to have a good hard think about it."

For a long moment, the silence at the table continued as some of them glared at Marad while others considered his words. Of them all, only Cale and Seth seemed unaffected by the tirade.

Missy and Billy were staring around the large table at the others, trying to gauge their response before Seth once again spoke up.

"Enough of this. Marad, only a fool would seek to instil fear in his own allies."

Turning to the two youngsters, Seth continued, "And yet there is some truth in his words. If you are called to a field of battle, you *will* see many terrible things. But know this, your lives will be in the hands of your escort, and theirs in yours. You will move as one, and no matter what happens, whether in victory or defeat, you will not be alone."

Billy nodded, taking the veteran swordsman at his word while the slightly older Missy locked eyes with Marad.

"That's good to know, because if my escort abandoned me in the middle of a fight, they wouldn't get very far at all I imagine."

"Missy!" Nadeara admonished the girl.

For an instant the girl's eyes flashed yellow as though she were a cat on the prowl, before settling back to their normal green. It was only an instant, but enough to make Marad flinch and break his stare.

Missy smiled the tiniest smile as she sat back in her seat, satisfied that she had stared the dark-skinned giant down.

Jayden wasn't sure that anyone else had noticed, but he'd felt the merest flicker of the Gift as her eyes changed colour.

He wondered idly where she had learned that trick. It hadn't been part of any lesson he'd been to, and he'd been to them all.

For another long moment there was silence until Bosric piped up.

"The great and mighty Marad, silenced by a girl of fifteen summers," he announced with a huge grin. "Could this day get any better I ask you?"

He laughed out loud as he spoke, and several of the others joined in, though none quite so heartily.

"That's it!" Marad roared as he stood, sending his chair sliding into the next table, not impressing the soldier it collided with.

"I have put up with your insolence for long enough, you pint-sized maniac!"

Bosric laughed even harder as Marad made a grab at him across the table, which the acrobatic little man avoided with ease. After two more lunges, Marad gave it up and stalked him around the circular table, chasing the much smaller man as Bosric skipped merrily ahead of his furious squad mate, who was now out to hurt him.

Jayden felt Missy use the Gift, and noticed a slight hand gesture under the table. He winced as Marad tripped on the solid spell of air that manifested just in front of the man's feet.

Before the enormous soldier had even crashed to the floor, the spell dissolved and she returned to eating from her plate, only Jayden, and perhaps Firerose, the wiser.

Bosric took another two skips around the table and without hesitation gave the large man a reasonably hard kick in the backside before returning to the other side of the obstacle. The soldiers at the next table which Marad's chair had impacted laughed uproariously at the big man's ill fortune.

"Enough. Bosric, Marad, return to your seats," Wyll ordered as the big man rose. He wasn't hurt, but he was furious to the point he had lost all perspective on the situation. From the look in his eyes, Marad might actually try to kill the smaller man if he somehow got a hold of him.

With a glance at Wyll, Bosric saw his sergeant was serious and returned to his seat with a shrug and a grin.

"It was fun while it lasted."

"Don't make me tell you again," Wyll said as Marad stayed where he was, fists clenched in rage as he stared death across the table at Bosric. The far shorter man popped a piece of food in his mouth in reply, chewing quickly before displaying the wreckage to the barely restrained man whom he dearly loved taunting.

With an audible growl, Marad took a step towards Bosric. A deep voice called, "Sit down!"

The soldiers and magi all turned toward the next table where the soldier who had been hit by Marad's sliding chair had surged to his feet.

"Sit down right now," the man repeated. His rank insignia proclaimed him an ordinary member of the mageguard, not an officer as Wyll had first expected from the authoritative tone.

"Who in blazes do you think you are?!" Marad shouted at the man, whose companions had come to stand behind him.

"I'm the one who is going to beat some respect into you if you don't give it to your commanding officer, as it is due. You were given an order, soldier. Obey it."

"Thank you, gentleman, but I can handle this on my own," Wyll told the standing men in no uncertain terms. Though giving them a friendly nod whilst saying it so they wouldn't feel slighted.

"Aye, sir," the soldier acknowledged before he and his comrades returned to their places, though keeping an unfriendly eye on Marad all the same.

Wyll stared at Marad for a long time, neither man blinking, nor talking, until after what seemed like ages, Marad returned to his seat with a sulky glower.

Wyll breathed silently in relief. Repeating his order might have undermined his authority with the others, and half the college kitchen's occupants were now watching the exchange. Wyll returned to his food. After a few minutes, once conversation had returned to the room and its denizens' attention was no longer focused on his squad, Wyll stood calmly and moved behind Marad's chair, squatting down to talk with the man privately.

"I've had enough, Marad," was all he got out before the enormous man began interrupting.

"Close your mouth, soldier," he ordered before Marad could get going.

"You have had your last warning. The next time you question my authority or my orders, either in public or in private, you will be out of this squad. You will find yourself dishonourably discharged from the mageguard so quickly that you'll think one of the magi has used the Gift on you."

Without hurrying, but also without waiting for a reply, Wyll stood and returned to his own chair. Soaking up the last of the thick gravy with a piece of bread, he finished the fine meal of some unknown roast meat with vegetables as conversation returned to their own table.

"Can you teach me how to use a sword?" Billy asked Seth abruptly, halting the talk once again as all eyes turned towards the top-knotted warrior.

For a moment the man was still as he looked across the

table and into the boy's eyes, as if there were more to see there than flesh alone.

"I can teach you to use the most powerful weapon you possess, but first you must tell me what it is," he responded.

For a long time, Billy looked confused until Missy spoke out.

"It's the Gift, silly."

"No," Seth told her. "It is not."

Of them all around the table, only Cale seemed certain of knowing the same answer Seth was after, and after a minute Billy shrugged.

"I'm sorry, I don't know."

"Tell him," Seth said, inclining his head towards Cale.

The mute soldier with the straw-coloured hair took his pen in his left hand and wrote two words on his ever-present Gift-wrought pad before sliding it across the table to the young boy.

"My mind?" he asked as he read it before sliding the pad back to its owner.

"Yes, strength is all very well, but it avails little against a foe with actual intelligence."

"I think I understand," Billy replied after a moment, though still unhappy.

"Good. When you have learned *when* to hold a sword, then I will teach you how. Not before. Do you understand that?"

After a moment of consideration, the boy nodded with something of an excited light in his eyes.

"Yes sir, I think I do."

Wyll saw Nadeara blink in surprise at that, and realised Seth might have just gone up a rung in her esteem.

After that the conversation died down for a while as the

kitchen master called out that dessert was ready. The men and women lining up according to their table numbers, which the cook read out in random order. Just as he did every night to avoid complaints.

By the time Wyll had returned to his seat with a bowl full of spiced apple pie with fresh cream, the talk had moved on to when the magi would leave for the front.

"If he has been ordered not to talk about it, just let it drop, Marad," Kienan was saying in no uncertain terms as Wyll took his seat.

"Don't talk down to me, music man," Marad growled, still in an ill humour from being put in his place.

"I'll talk to you in whatever tone I need to, to get the point across."

"You'll show a bit more respect if you know what's good for you."

"I will. When you earn it," the far smaller man replied, returning to his food.

Marad stared daggers across the table at their resident musician, and Wyll sighed. He was coming to the conclusion that Marad would have to be transferred out of his command if there was to be any real unity within the squad. As their sergeant, he should be able to handle the problem himself. But to his understanding, the friction Marad habitually caused within the unit was well above the norm. The unresolved issue continued to make him painfully aware of how new he still was to having men under his command. He decided to seek out Captain Ravenburg and ask his advice on the matter. How the head of the mageguard would react was anybody's guess, but as the old saying went, *'Better to risk looking foolish today than ruin tomorrow through ignorance.'*

Wyll finished his food as he was musing over how he would broach the subject to his superior when the kitchen bell rang to signal the end of the meal. The staff began removing plates so they could clean and set up for the second shift of soldiers who were already queuing at the door. Any slow eaters swallowed down their last few bites of food before the soldiers and magi were shuffled out of the room by the long-practised kitchen hands.

Once outside the bustling kitchen and corridor beyond, most of the soldiers, and those magi who were present, drifted off to find their own entertainments. They only had a few spare hours until they were expected to be in their bunks. For most of those men and women, peaceful rest would be scarce tonight. Tomorrow would comprise taking ship, or beginning the long overland march. Either way, their destination was war.

Eventually the rest of their group dispersed, and only Jayden and Firerose remained nearby in the brisk night air. Both were staring off into the clear, winter's dusk sky, though for different reasons Wyll suspected as he walked over to join them. If it had been any other young man and woman, he would have left well enough alone. He knew full well, however, that Jayden had no romantic interest in the young noblewoman who reminded him so much, at least physically, of his murdered love.

Jayden had come a long way in the last few phases, Wyll thought as he approached the bench they were seated on. Although he still held himself apart from the others somewhat, he had at least opened up enough to begin making rudimentary friendships with many of the men in Wyll's squad. Certainly he had achieved more than that with those in his advanced Gift class. The only problem was that Wyll knew him well enough now to recognise that his almost insatiable thirst for revenge had not been dulled, only put on hold. As a friend, Wyll had to admit it concerned him, because it meant Jayden's grief was only covered over, not healed. He had heard others say this kind of deep hatred had a way of festering, just as any other wound left untended might. Unlike any normal wound, however, it was not your flesh that became rotted, but your soul.

Perhaps I'm being overly dramatic? He would hate to see something undo all the painstaking progress Jayden had made since leaving Grandell though.

"What has you so deep in thought?" Wyll asked as he approached their bench.

Jayden seemed surprised for a moment, as Wyll had expected he would. Although the young mage had been staring up at the stars, he had clearly been looking more inward than out. It was an expression Wyll had grown used to on his friend's face. It was often a sign he was sliding back into depression brought on by the dark memories that refused to leave him in peace.

Wyll was happy to interrupt.

Lady Firerose sat with her hands tucked into the sleeves of her robe against the chill of the evening and gave Wyll a grateful smile. He assumed it meant she had noticed Jayden's mood, but didn't yet feel comfortable enough with their friendship to try interrupting it.

She called up a Gift-wrought chair for him from the pavement with a flick of her wrist and Wyll sat down cautiously, testing his weight before committing to the seat. Firerose raised an amused eyebrow.

A small rueful grin played across Jayden's mouth and

then ceased as he looked first at Firerose at then at Wyll.

With a long sigh, Jayden seemed to deflate.

"I did something really stupid a few weeks ago," he eventually admitted, without meeting either of their eyes.

"In a bad way, or a funny one?" Wyll asked.

"I was nearly executed for treason," Jayden told them, then gave a rueful grin at the shocked expressions that bloomed on both their faces.

Firerose's head had snapped towards him at his comment, and for once not playing the role of the noble lady she exclaimed, "But, I mean… what did you do?!"

"Dael?" Wyll asked.

Jayden nodded in return.

"He was at the promotion ceremony, and he had the gall to taunt me to my face," he told them, voice wound tight with strain.

"Oh, Jayden, you didn't kill him in the king's own throne room, did you?" Firerose exclaimed in consternation.

For a long time, Jayden was silent as he stared at the ground.

"I tried to," he admitted.

"How is it that the royal guards didn't cut you down where you stood?" Firerose blurted out.

"They would have, if the archmage hadn't used the Gift to restrain them."

"Tolmarak used the Gift to attack the King's royal guards?!" Wyll broke in, not quite believing what his friend was saying.

"Not quite, but he stopped them from attacking me," Jayden confirmed miserably.

"He could have been executed right alongside me for doing it, and yet he didn't hesitate. I have no idea how to pay him back for doing that."

There was an even longer silence after that statement, until Firerose asked, "So Dael still lives?"

"Yes… Sparing his life was the price for my pardon, though even now I am not completely sure why I chose as I did."

"You made the right choice, Jayden. If you'd killed him in front to the King…" Wyll trailed off.

"I know. But at least Rhianna's murder would have been avenged."

"It will be," Wyll replied.

Jayden nodded in mute acceptance.

"Anyway, I'm on a kind of probation now, I guess. If I don't obey the laws of Jeranon to the letter, the King has ordered Tolmarak to pronounce me renegade and take the appropriate action."

Again, there was a long pause as the others soaked in the full meaning of his words.

For a mage, to be declared renegade was the worst kind of rebuke, and was reserved for only the most heinous of Gift-sensitive offenders. The stigma carried with it a standing royal order for the subject to be hunted down and executed by any magi who came across them.

"Perhaps it's for the best," Firerose offered after a time. "At least now that you know taking revenge on the Count is out of the question, it might be what you need to put all this behind you."

It was exactly the wrong thing to say, and Wyll winced at the inevitable explosion that was sure to come. But his friend just went still.

"Dael will die by my hand," Jayden said as he stared off into the distance. Across the vast yard between the mageguard's building and the college itself, a lonely goat bleated.

After that remark the conversation died off for a moment until Firerose stood from the seat they had been sharing and turned on him.

"Jayden Torell, you are a fool!"

"Look around you! All this is yours. I may have been stripped of my title when I was taken by the magi, but I come from a wealthy and powerful family, and I know the paths power takes. You are the youngest Mage in college history, and powerful enough that only a handful of archmagi can even attempt to teach you. None of the others are powerful enough to know how. There is every chance you will end up becoming Tolmarak's protégé once he has time to teach you separately. Even you must be aware that would put you in prime position to become his successor, if not directly, then in time. How can you fail to see that your future here is taking you towards becoming leader of the college in Aramar, and *all* the magi in Jeranon? A station linked with that of king's advisor. You could affect the fate of millions, and all you have to do to take hold of all of it is to let the past remain in the past, and not kill a man who is less than nothing in the sight of both man and Maker."

She stared daggers at him, waiting for a response.

Jayden looked up at her for a long moment, his expressionless face studying the young noblewoman as if he had never seen her before.

"Dael will die by my hand," he repeated implacably, then gave a yelp of pain as she kicked him hard in the shin.

Wyll blinked in surprise and almost laughed as Jayden asked in annoyance, "What was that for?!"

"Because as childish as it was, what you are doing is even more so," she said, now every inch the noble lady. She met his eyes a moment longer and then turned and walked away as Jayden sat, rubbing his leg.

"What was that all about?" Jayden asked once Firerose was out of sight.

Wyll looked after her for a minute instead of answering, but finally turned to regard his friend.

"I understand your need for revenge," he said. "I knew Rhianna too, though not as well as you, I admit. And yet…" he trailed off.

"You think I should just forget about Dael's crimes?! Is that it?"

"Of course not."

"But she has a point. Your future at the college, assuming you don't get branded renegade," he said with just a hint of a grin. "It *is* a bright one. Losing it all just to get at Dael sooner will not bring her back, no matter how much we both wish it might."

Jayden opened his mouth to say something, then thought better of whatever angry words he'd been about to commit to and closed it again. The young mage gritted his teeth and settled on a short, "I'm going to bed, I'll see you on the morrow."

*   *   *

"On the morrow then," Jayden heard Wyll repeat from behind him as he turned and walked away into the brisk night air.

It was a few minutes' walk back to the college building, and Jayden's mind was on other things as he climbed the now familiar spiral staircase in the antechamber. He took the exit to the floor where his new accommodations had been assigned. Another minute took him to nearly the end of the corridor and the door of his room, which he pushed open with a wisp of an air spell and entered.

He was no more than a foot inside the door when he felt it. A presence like the aura of another mage, but twisted somehow beyond his knowledge. In the corner of the room, a figure stood, hooded and cloaked beyond any chance of recognition, hand half raised in preparation for unleashing a spell of frightening power.

Jayden raised his hands in an instinctually defensive move, forming the strongest shield spell he could between himself and the other mage. It was a flat, artless thing. It was also strong, and the reflexive action saved his life as the enemy mage unleashed what looked to be a full-strength bolt of lightning from his outstretched hand. The blazing light was followed an instant later by a thunderous roar that knocked both of them off their feet. The bolt of power careened off Jayden's shield and rebounded into the wall on the far side of the room, shattering the masonry and exploding a ten-foot hole in the outer layer of the college building. Debris cascaded into the courtyard below.

The light and noise from the blast were enough to stun him. With a start, Jayden realised he was now laying sprawled on the floor, hoping the blast had disoriented his assailant as much as it had him. If it hadn't, the next blow would surely end him.

A moment later his vision cleared, and Jayden realised his shield was still in place. The assassin, for that was who this must be, had already regained his feet. The two men just stared at each other for an instant, then the assassin turned and ran at the hole in the college wall which his attack had created.

He didn't expect me to still be alive.

Jayden hurled a small ball of fire at the escaping figure. It was all his stunned mind could come up with on the instant. Most of it missed, only singeing the assassin's cloak, and setting a small fire in the wreckage of his own bed.

Without looking back, the assassin dived out the gaping hole and into the starlit night. He must have known they were at least a hundred feet above the ground, yet didn't hesitate. Without a word, his attacker was gone, leaving Jayden alone in his ruined room, his heart pounding, but otherwise unharmed.

'Aside from the Gift, we are like them in every way. They cannot tell us apart. As with so many other things, that privilege is ours alone.'
Excerpt from 'The Gift'

CHAPTER 3

ASSASSIN

Picking himself up from the floor, Jayden stumbled to the ragged hole in his bedroom wall. He reached the precipice of the hundred foot drop just in time to see his assailant employ an unfamiliar spell of air, and land roughly, but not dangerously, on the stones of the courtyard below. There was a muffled shout of challenge from somewhere on the ground, and an answering ball of fire lit up the night before a distant scream sounded, and was abruptly cut off.

Without looking to check on his handiwork, the hooded assassin turned and sprinted towards the gate that would take him back into Aramar. If he made it that far, he would lose himself in the city before the other magi could respond.

Jayden took a deep breath. He was the only one who knew what was happening and could give chase in time, but the spell the assassin had used to escape was new to him. Still, it was a spell of only middling complexity, and composed entirely of air. He was confident he could duplicate it without trouble.

Saying a brief prayer to the Maker under his breath, he took a step back from the edge of the gaping hole, then flung himself out into the freezing night air. For a moment he felt weightless, and his heart began trying to beat its way out of his chest. It was a familiar sensation. Much like the many times he'd jumped off cliffs into the ocean when he and Rhianna, and Dael of course, had been children. He pushed that part of the memory away.

After the briefest of moments, Jayden called up the Gift and copied the assassin's spell, creating a cushion of air on the ground below. Heart racing, he hit the spell hard, but not hard enough to injure himself as he bounced wildly, careening past its edge. With the ground rushing up to meet him once more, he desperately formed the spell below him again to diminish the impact. This time he hit the cushion softly enough that he only found himself rolling off its edge instead of bouncing. Somehow he ended the right way up, and landed on his feet. Trying not to think about what he'd just done, Jayden ran after the hooded figure as fast as his unsteady legs and pumping heart would take him.

As he crossed the huge, stone yard, Jayden thought back on the assassin's warped aura. The man had been strong in the Gift, and he should have sensed him lurking in the room well before he'd entered. He'd been blind to the twisted sense of his attacker until he was well within the assassin's striking range. Tolmarak needed to know that. It explained why the archmage hadn't been able to pinpoint any intruders, or extra auras, while the other attacks were taking place. Even the ones inside the college walls themselves.

It made the assassin a hundred times more dangerous. How could they find someone who wanted to kill them, and could do it at range while they themselves had to be at arm's length before they knew he was there?

With no suitable answers coming to mind, Jayden pushed himself to breathe evenly, and run faster. If he lost the assassin now, his attacker would have no trouble blending back into the population without a trace.

As he passed the city gates, feeling the exertion, another thought surfaced. With the assassin's aura altered in some manner, how strong in the Gift was he really?

Powerful, that much was certain.

He's not stronger than I am though. Otherwise he would have stayed to finish me off.

The thought gave Jayden hope as he ran towards the first corner, where he had seen the hooded figure disappear just moments before.

He knows more about the Gift than I do, but I'm stronger. I should be able to at least hold him long enough for the others to arrive, even if I can't take him down by himself.

Behind him, Jayden could now hear a deep bell ringing, and knew the alarm had been raised at the college. Someone must have discovered the dead guard.

Jayden stopped just shy of the corner. Looking up at the sky, he reached out with the Gift and set the night ablaze with the simplest of spells. A fiery arrow pointing down towards the intersection he was about to cross.

It only lasted a few seconds before he felt the spell unravel under a sudden assault. It was enough. Someone at the newly awakened college would have seen it.

Jayden ventured a quick look around the corner. A couple of rats scurrying across a cart on the far side of the square were the only movement he could discern in the dimly lit area.

Another tense moment of scrutiny produced no further results, so he cautiously headed out into the intersection.

As he took his second step, Jayden knew he'd made a serious mistake.

Without warning, a translucent green cloud enveloped him, burning his skin as though it were fire.

Using his entire strength in the Gift, he pushed the choking miasma away from himself with a shield. It seemed to take forever to repel the green gas from his skin, which was already turning a deep red where his clothes had not at least partially protected him.

Falling to his knees, Jayden realised to his horror that his vision was blurring, his eyes throbbing even worse than the rest of his exposed skin. He could make out that the stone squares of the intersection around him were pocking deeply, melting under the enemy mage's assault. If he didn't get himself out of this soon, that could be his fate as well. He could feel the assassin maintaining the attack, and knew he must still be close by. His damaged eyes made it impossible to see where, and the scathing pain of his now blistering skin was distracting enough that only raw animal instinct was keeping his shield intact. He thought he could make out a slight movement around the corner to his right.

With what little concentration he could muster, Jayden worked a base earth spell, causing the corner of the building to explode outward in a shower of debris. A blurry figure tumbled out into the square to sprawl on the cobblestones of the intersection. Jayden knew he'd hit his mark as the spell assaulting him weakened, though the enemy mage wasn't quite distracted enough to lose control of his spell.

"Jayden!" a woman's voice cried out from somewhere behind him.

A bar of flame lanced out, passing him in an instant. It careened off into the sky as it hit an invisible shield the assassin had called up in the merest of instants.

Again, the spell imprisoning Jayden weakened, and

despite the pain of his burns he pushed at it with the Gift as hard as he could. His survival depended on it.

While he was focused on the gaseous assault, the enemy mage used the moment to fashion a brutal spell of fire and earth. With an ear shattering rumble, he tore down the three-storey building behind the woman. From the relative strength of the aura, some dim portion of his mind informed him the mage must have been Nadeara.

In an instant she was gone, enveloped by rubble as a great cloud of debris came flying out into the square, hammering at the shields the two magi continued to maintain, along with everything else.

Watching helplessly as Nadeara disappeared under the rubble gave Jayden a sudden burst of cold strength. He put the agony of his burns aside, and focused only on forcing the green cloud away from himself, just as the rush of wind from the collapsing building hit.

Thrown forward by the force of the blast, Jayden's skin exploded in agony as he slid across the ground, stunned and further injured by a piece of flying debris which struck him below the shoulder. The chunk of brick had penetrated his shield, piercing the barrier while still maintaining enough force to break his arm. Jayden grunted in pain as he tried unsuccessfully to move the limb. The assassin was still out there somewhere. Examining the jagged bulge under his sleeve, he was forced to concede the painful injury was far beyond his ability with the Gift to fix right now.

Sensing movement, Jayden looked over to see the assassin stumble to his feet across the way. The cloaked figure had been half buried under a large piece of debris, and taken some moments to free himself, though he appeared otherwise unharmed.

A shout echoed from somewhere nearby, and the sound of hooves clattered on cobblestones in the distance. The assassin looked up, and Jayden took the chance to launch a ball of flame that even he knew was weak. Yet it was all he could concentrate enough to form, with every exposed inch of his skin still feeling like it was on fire. How his shield remained so steady, he wasn't certain.

The assassin batted away his spell. Then scowled in the direction of the soldiers approaching their position. Without fanfare he turned away, and in less than a dozen unhurried steps melded with the darkness on the far side of the square.

Concentrating for all he was worth, Jayden used the Gift to light the area from one end to the other. But the mage had already dissolved into the shadows beyond the square.

A moment later, a few dozen mounted men in the uniforms of the mageguard, along with a contingent of battle-hardened magi, galloped into the square at a dead run.

"Jayden!" Tolmarak shouted as he leapt from the horse before his war trained mount could even come to a halt. The archmage ran the last few steps and knelt beside him to begin inspecting his wounds.

"Form a perimeter and scout the nearby streets." He called loudly. "Sarah, I need you!"

"What happened?" Tolmarak demanded in horror as he took in the young man's raw and blistered wounds.

"Nadeara," Jayden coughed, sending red specks flying from his mouth. He must have breathed some of the green cloud into his lungs before he could use the Gift to push it away.

"Nadeara did this?"

"No. Under, there," Jayden gasped, pointing with his

unbroken arm, the cloth of his sleeve falling away, decayed and burnt as he pointed towards the immense pile of rubble. It was all that remained of the building she had been standing in front of.

"Still alive… can feel her," he choked out.

Now that the adrenaline was wearing off, the extent of his injuries were making themselves forcibly known. Jayden found he couldn't stop shivering as he began coughing more violently. The world dimmed around him.

*   *   *

"Do not let him die, Sarah," Tolmarak told the elderly woman who had arrived to kneel beside him. The light around the intersection faded as Jayden lost consciousness, and he stood to give the college's most talented healer room to work her magic.

Turning towards where he could feel Nadeara's aura under the collapsed building, he saw two of the other archmagi already attempting to clear the rubble.

He needed to question Jayden about the identity of his attacker. From the amount of blood now leaking from the young man's mouth though, those answers would have to wait until Sarah had finished her work.

"Jane, Kelta. Do you require assistance?"

"Not at this point, Archmage," Kelta replied.

"That may change, however, dependent upon how complex the debris is underneath," Jane added.

Tolmarak nodded, and the two archmagi continued their efforts while he went over to talk to a returning officer.

"I'm sorry Archmage, there is no sign which direction the attacker took after he fled."

"What makes you think it's a he?"

The officer began to speak, but then stopped and shook his head, indicating he had assumed it.

"Very well. I want a double layered perimeter around this square while Sarah tends the wounded."

There was no malice in the command, but the officer saluted crisply, as if receiving a formal reprimand. Tolmarak gave the issue no more thought as he went back to assist the two archmagi in moving the dense pile of rubble.

"How can I help?" he asked again.

"We can handle the removal," Kelta replied. "What we need is for the rest of the pile to be stabilised as much as possible while we work."

Tolmarak nodded. Manipulating that many heavy objects at once would be no simple task, even for him.

"I'll do what I can. You two peel the pieces away from the top with upward pressure."

The pair of archmagi again nodded their agreement, and Tolmarak closed his eyes, sending a wave of spirit magic mixed with air into the jumble of debris. He struggled to maintain focus as he manipulated each of the thousands of pieces of remaining rubble. It was like trying to hold a completed jigsaw with only your hands to hold it up. Pieces began to slip. The pile ranged in size from fragments of single bricks to whole beams of wood which had once held up the structure's roof. He couldn't do this for long without the whole thing falling in on itself.

Sensing the strain he was under, Jane and Kelta worked as quickly as they could. Even so, it was many minutes later when the two archmagi lifted a crucial piece of debris off the pile. Shoving it to the side with a spell of air, a tiny portion of the pale blue glow of a Gift-wrought shield appeared.

Most of it was still obscured underneath a large section of masonry.

"There," Kelta pointed.

Tolmarak released the majority of the pile, which slumped back to the ground with the grinding of broken masonry. In moments they cleared the surrounding area of rock and wood, and Jane pushed a final heavy section of wall leaning on Nadeara's shield away and to the side.

As soon as the last segment of rubble was safely removed, the blue glow winked out. Nadeara began coughing as the dust which had remained on top of the barrier collapsed in on her.

Tolmarak let his own spell fade as Kelta rushed over to help the beleaguered mage to her feet.

"Are you hurt?" Kelta asked as he looked her over to check for any hidden injuries.

"Exhausted, but fine," Nadeara replied. "Is Jayden ok?"

"Thanks to you he's still alive, though with several injuries. Archmage Trellis is doing everything she can," Tolmarak assured her as the pair came towards him.

"By the way, you did extremely well with that shield," Tolmarak complimented her to take her mind off Jayden's injuries, which he'd purposely understated.

"Not much of a choice," Nadeara replied.

"Nevertheless, you performed well under pressure. I have seen good magi fall in battle from lesser attacks than that, simply because a surprise caused them to hesitate."

"Sit," he said, fashioning a chair out of earth and air for the apprentice magi to rest in, then called up another one facing her for himself.

"Tell me what happened. Start at the beginning and leave nothing out."

For a long moment Nadeara collected her thoughts as the brisk winter night washed over them. She rubbed her arms against the cold, and after a few more lung clearing coughs, began to speak.

"I was in the second-floor supply room when I heard a scream and saw a flash from outside. I reached a window just in time to see Jayden dive to the ground from somewhere above. He used some kind of air spell to break his fall, and started sprinting towards the city gate. I looked ahead of him and saw a cloaked figure just about to reach the entrance, and realised he was following the attacker. From the blast a moment before, it was clear they had access to the Gift, whether via talent or arcana. I made my way out of the college as quickly as I could, but by the time I reached the door, the alarm had already been raised."

She stopped for a moment to consider, and coughed again.

"About halfway across the courtyard I saw Jayden's signal in the sky, and knew he was in trouble. When I reached the intersection, I found him under attack by a mage in a brown or grey hooded cloak. It wasn't a magi cloak. I couldn't see any more detail in this dim light," she told him.

"Jayden was obviously struggling with defending himself, so I launched a blast of flame at his attacker, more as a distraction than anything else. If Jayden couldn't defeat him, I knew I would be no match, but I also knew that help wouldn't be far behind. It seemed to work for a moment as Jayden began to overpower the spell he was fighting off. Then the world exploded around me. The explosion threw me off my feet and I saw the building, the entire building, collapsing towards me," she recounted, hands shaking ever so slightly.

"I barely got my shield up in time before the wall of debris buried me," she finished quietly, wrapping her arms around herself and drawing her knees up to her chest.

"That's all right," Tolmarak assured her as he used a flicker of the Gift to heat the air around Nadeara's seat to make her more comfortable.

"You did very well. If you hadn't arrived here right when you did, Jayden may well not have survived until our arrival."

She nodded slightly in acceptance of the archmage's praise and Tolmarak stood, letting his chair dissolve back into the cobblestones and atmosphere.

"Archmage Kelta, please escort Nadeara back to the college infirmary. Archmage Trellis will check you over in a less dangerous setting as soon as she is able."

As Tolmarak left the pair, he motioned to the young archmage Jane, young for an archmage anyway, to join him. They returned to where Sarah was just standing from beside Jayden's unconscious form, and she turned to address the college's leader.

"He'll live," she said without pre-amble, "But if we had been *any* later…"

Tolmarak let out a breath he hadn't realised he'd been holding, and nodded.

"What have you learned?"

"It was a brutal spell the attacker used this time," Archmage Trellis answered.

"It was in a gaseous form, but something akin to acid would be my guess. Jayden has severe burns on all areas of his exposed skin, including his lungs and eyes. The lungs only suffered minor damage thankfully. I was able to repair them, and he will recover in time. His sight may be a different matter."

"He's blind?" Tolmarak exclaimed, trying not to let the edge of fear creep into his voice.

"We won't know that until he wakes." She sighed. "I've repaired the flesh, but the nerves and veins are so delicate in that part of the body. I'm sorry, I just don't know if it was enough."

"I see," Tolmarak replied without enthusiasm. It would be a tragedy for the boy if this attack permanently blinded him. Perhaps more importantly, it would be an incalculable loss to their war efforts if Jeranon's strongest mage were incapacitated before the fighting had even begun.

"Also," Sarah continued, "All other parts of his body are burned to varying degrees, though his boots protected his feet somewhat. I was able to repair these lesser burns completely, but most of his exposed skin has suffered mild scarring which should be treatable once his body has recovered its strength."

Tolmarak nodded in acceptance. If Sarah couldn't heal the boy's wounds, there was nothing more he could contribute.

"Very well, let's get him back to the college then, if it is safe for him to be moved?"

The grey-haired old healer nodded her permission, and Tolmarak ordered some of the mageguard to assist. When they were ready, he levitated the young mage's form onto a litter composed of air and spirit, which Sarah called up. It was a spell she had long since perfected in her role as instructor for the college's healers. It was also one of the few new uses for the Gift which Erian had approved during his decades long reign.

"I'll escort him back myself," Sarah offered.

"Go with her," Tolmarak ordered a squad of mageguard

along with a nearby mage. Both had finished their sweep of the surrounding area, returning empty-handed.

The sergeant gave a quick salute, and motioned his men to take up protective positions on either side of the litter. They took their job seriously, keeping a sharp eye on the surrounding buildings as they began the slow march back to the college grounds.

"Come on, let's see if we can find anything ourselves," Tolmarak said to Jane as the pair of them walked across to the other side of the square.

*   *   *

"Unnngh," Jayden groaned as he woke. The dim light of his new room stabbed at his eyes as he regained consciousness. He squeezed them shut against the sudden pain.

"How did I get here?"

"You're awake. And you can see," a satisfied voice came from somewhere out of view.

Again, Jayden tried to open his eyes despite the pain, attempting to determine who the unfamiliar female voice belonged to.

"Who are you?" he asked as the hazy form came over to sit on the edge of his bed. "Is Nadeara alive?"

"She is fine," the voice assured him.

"She is resting, as you need to. Before you do, though, I will tell you a few things to ease your mind. First, my name is Archmage Trellis. While in my care you may call me Sarah. The second is that your friend was able to protect herself from the falling debris and suffered less serious wounds from the fight than you did. No need to concern yourself there. Third, Archmage Tolmarak himself has set wards around your room, both inside and out. If anyone uses the Gift within their proximity, they will activate, and a dozen magi will come running, including the pair standing guard outside your door. Fourth," she said, ticking the points off on her fingers. "You will need to keep your eyes away from even dim light for the next few days, *at the least,* so they continue to heal properly. To that end, before I leave here, I will seal your windows shut the rest of the way with an earth spell so that no light at all enters. If you ever want to regain your full sight, do not break the seal, or leave this room. My staff will see to all your needs while you are confined here. In the meantime, there is wash water and a towel on the drawers, and a chamber pot under the bed. Everything is in the same places as your old room, though I expect you to rest and sleep as much as possible for the next few days. Also, I will return at least twice a day to check on you and send someone up with your meals, which I expect you to eat promptly and wholly. The level of healing I had to use on your damaged flesh takes great reserves from the body. You will need as much energy as you can gather from the food so that it recovers in good order. Finally, when you hear a knock at the door, make sure your eyes are closed when it opens. Although this room may be dark the outside corridor is not, and the sudden burst of light could permanently damage your eyes in their current weakened state."

The old archmage paused for a moment before speaking again. "I know this is a lot to take in, but do you understand all that I just told you?"

"No light or permanent damage. Eat everything," Jayden responded weakly.

"Well, not necessarily everything," the healer replied with an amused grin. "Just what I send up to you." She leant over and conspiratorially whispered, "The furniture just isn't that tasty."

Jayden gave a vague smile and fell back into a deep sleep before Sarah could even rise from his bedside and leave the young mage to his recovery. She would return later once he had slept some more and eaten his fill, and perhaps tomorrow she could better assess the extent of the damage. He wasn't blind, and she was now hopeful that barring any unforeseen complications, given time, and her not inconsiderable talents, the powerful young mage should make a full recovery.

*　　*　　*

It had only been two days, but Jayden felt as though he were going out of his mind. His body was depleted to the point where he could hardly get out of bed to relieve himself, but his mind was as active as ever. Coupled with not being able to see, and therefore read or do any other practical activity, the confinement was beginning to take its toll. Despite the lethargy that consumed him, he felt much improved than he had upon first waking with the old healer beside him. The pain in his skin and lungs was almost completely gone now, but she was taking no chances with his eyes, and that special treatment made him wary enough to heed the archmage's words. She had allowed him a visit from his classmates this morning, but except for that brief interlude, the silence reigned supreme. With his body on the mend, that absence of anything meaningful to occupy his mind was beginning to tire him as much as the damage the assassin's wounds had caused.

A knock sounded on the door and Jayden closed his eyes, surprised by another visitor, but glad of any break from the monotony.

Turning his head away from where he knew the door to be, he called, "Come in."

Even through his eyelids, the light seemed bright as the door opened and then closed. Footsteps entered his room.

"Hello Jayden," a voice said as the halting footfalls met the chair that Sarah had placed in the room the night before. There was a sound of wood impacting wood, and a soft curse as the visitor sat on the chair he had bumped into, before placing something on the floor.

"Is that you, Kienan?" Jayden asked, unsure of whether he had correctly identified the bodiless voice.

"Oh, yes, sorry," the musician turned soldier replied.

"Firerose was telling us you were going stir crazy in here without being able to see or do anything, so I thought this might cheer you up. Here."

So saying, he passed something cool, light, and wooden over to where he imagined Jayden to be. After a fumbling moment, the young mage took it awkwardly, causing the object to clang as he jostled it.

"What is it?" Jayden asked as he examined the design with his hands. It was an instrument of some strange design, he realised as his fingers brushed across the strings, causing a discordant sound.

"Something of my own making, based on an Avsanian design," Kienan replied.

"There are six strings on it instead of the usual four, giving the player a much broader variety of notes and chords than is offered by a standard lute."

To prove his point, he took up a second instrument and played a short little ditty that made Jayden grin in appreciation at the shorter man's skill.

"Archmage Trellis said you could have it so long as you didn't tire yourself out, and Firerose and Nadeara used the Gift to help me fashion one for you this morning."

"Thank you," Jayden said after a long moment, "But I can't play this. I don't know how."

He could hear the grin in Kienan's voice as the musician answered. "No one does when they begin. Besides, this way you'll have something to do which refines your other senses while your sight recovers."

"Thank you," Jayden said once again, this time meaning it as he plucked a string experimentally.

"Basically, like any string instrument, you put pressure on the strings to change the tension and create distinct notes. Unlike a lute, this instrument is specifically designed to play combinations of notes, called chords, across some or all of the strings."

He demonstrated, and Jayden thought he knew what Kienan had done to create the sound which issued from the device.

"Anyway, the archmage said I only had a few minutes. I'll play something to show you what can be done with this instrument and then leave you to figure out the rest. No simple task, I admit, but it will give you something to do," he finished with a grin. "If you take to it, I'll give you some proper pointers once you can see again."

"Okay," Kienan breathed before launching into a frenzied playing of a vaguely recognisable tune which Jayden had always considered to be dull. His opinion rapidly changed as Kienan worked his own special brand of magic on the music.

All too soon the merry song was over, although Jayden could still hear the last notes echoing in his mind as the conscripted musician stood.

"I'd better go before I get thrown out," he said with a laugh even as another knock sounded on the door.

"I wish you a speedy recovery, Jayden, as do we all," Kienan told him.

Jayden closed his eyes yet again and called out, "Enter."

"Kienan, thank you," Jayden said as he heard the man's footsteps retreat whilst another, now familiar set, entered the room.

"You're welcome," he called back as his steps receded down the corridor and Sarah closed the door behind him.

"Lunch time," she said cheerfully, closing the door before lighting the faintest of glows with the Gift behind her back so Jayden could not even see its source. She then placed a steaming tray full of roast meat, gravy, bread, vegetables, and sweet pastries on the side of his bed.

For half a second, Jayden tossed up whether to try the instrument for himself first, or dig into the lavish spread. The choice was taken from him as the first smell of roast beef reached his nose, and his body cried out for the meal. He set the instrument down beside him and began devouring the food like a man who hadn't eaten for days. Archmage Trellis watched the entire time, making sure that every scrap was attended to.

She needn't have bothered.

SPRING

CHAPTER 4

MISDIRECTION AND ATTRITION

Another fine spring day, Master Andrew Dannish thought as he opened his bedroom window. The city seemed so much less crowded now that most of the soldiers had gone from Aramar. Although he had information that some of the training camps in the Emerald Sea were still being manned.

It had been weeks now since the last of the snows had melted, and the first deliveries from his coffee plantations in central Jeranon should arrive in another phase. Winter had been heavy but quick this year, and with any luck the rebellion in the western provinces would not spread to the territory around Rolling Hills. His holdings were located well to the south of the Mirallyn River, where the soils surrounding the small city were lush and fertile. It was an area with little to no strategic importance to either side, so with a little help from the Maker, his concerns there would be unaffected.

This would be a good year for him, maybe the best one yet. He dressed and called for his coachman to make the carriage ready. His principal competition for raw coffee beans came from the lands around Danarel, which his contacts told him was now under the heel of Heramiir's forces. Normally that would have been a significant concern for him, but with the only larger producer of the precious beans out of the marketplace, he was anticipating a record windfall from this season's crop.

By the time Master Dannish exited his three-storey mansion overlooking the Camar River, he found his carriage waiting out front. The coachman stood ready to open the door at his approach.

"Take me to the office," he told the man as he climbed in and sat on the cushioned seat. The carriage rocked slightly as the driver clambered back on board to take up the reins. Soon enough, the team of horses were moving down the driveway, and into the heart of the city. It was a longer journey than he liked, but the views of the river in this part of the merchants' quarter were worth the inconvenience of the extra travel.

Eventually the carriage pulled up at the immense bluestone building known as Mercantile Square, home to the administrative offices of some of Jeranon's largest trading concerns. Dannish Fine Goods was one of the smaller companies in the palatial structure. Nevertheless, that his offices were in there at all meant something to a man who had built his company up from nothing. He'd inherited a few hectares of land from a rich uncle when he was little more than a boy, and discovered early in life that he had an aptitude not only for growing things, but also selling them to the right people. They were traits which had seen him in good stead over the years, raising him from common peasant, to near the top end of the kingdom's merchant class. While his wealth would only ever rival that of the most minor noble, it was far more than a simple man like him needed to be happy.

Once the coachman had opened the door for him, Andrew stepped down onto the polished redwood platform and walked the short distance into the building. He crossed the main lobby with barely a glance at the ornate tapestries and sculptures, all hand-produced by actual artists. Nothing Gift-wrought made its way through those doors. The enormous statues existed for only one reason, to awe the wealthy clientele which visited the companies who held their headquarters here.

He wound his way through the corridors to the place that was like a second home to him. As he entered through an expensive glass doorway, he found his assistant Lionel waiting for him with the steaming hot cup of coffee. It was his morning custom to partake, and had been for years. The beans from which the exquisite drink was made were grown on his very own plantations.

"What news?" he asked the pimply youth as the teenage apprentice followed him through the rooms where his employees worked, and back into his private office. Dannish sat in his leather-upholstered chair before taking a careful sip of the steaming black coffee.

"Not much," the boy replied.

"Mort thinks he may have lined up a new buyer. Even if the contract goes through though, it's only a minor amount, and not likely to make much impact on either supply or demand."

He fell silent after that, and Andrew looked at him.

"Very well," he replied at length. "All right, go about your duties if there's nothing else."

"Yes, sir," the boy replied, then left.

For a long time, Andrew just sat, watching as the people who worked for him arrived and began their day. He always liked to be the first one into the office, except for Lionel of course, whose job it was to have everything ready for his arrival. It was not so much to check up on his employees, though doubtless there were some who thought that the case, but rather to set a good example. He had always found they worked harder when content, and got sloppy or lazy when not. Valuing efficiency, he did his best to give them no reason to complain.

An hour trickled by as he looked over the books, signing orders and receipts until a quick knock sounded on the door. He glanced up from the latest ledger and motioned for Lionel to enter. The boy hurried over to place something on his desk.

"Message from the rookery, sir," he announced as Andrew took up the thin roll of parchment and read.

The rookery was an extensive building across the way from Mercantile Square, housing thousands upon thousands of messenger pigeons. Every company here relied on it for the fast delivery of news and tidings to and from their many holdings around the kingdom.

The parchment was small of course, having to fit in a pigeon's leg harness, and as Andrew carefully unrolled it, his heart sank at the contents. The note was brief, as all carrier messages were, but it was enough to throw his entire world into chaos.

"Sir, are you all right? You're as white as a sheet?" Lionel enquired.

Andrew looked around, stunned, but recovered enough to tell the boy what the message contained.

"But, I mean, I've heard nothing of this," Lionel stammered.

"I know, I don't think anyone has," Andrew stated, suddenly far more concerned than he had been even at receiving the news.

By the time he finished speaking, he realised the boy now looked much as he himself must have done a moment ago.

"What… what can we do?"

Andrew just shook in head from side to side.

"There is but one man in Jeranon who has the power to deal with this, and we must see him immediately. Bring the coach around to the front and tell no one of this. He probably knows already, but if not, the King must be informed."

*   *   *

"What do we know for sure?" Tolmarak asked in profound frustration.

"Nothing solid Archmage, just that he was seen coming into his room last night. When the servants came up to bring him his breakfast… they found, this."

"I don't understand. How is it that no one felt his aura wink out?" Tolmarak demanded. He'd just returned to the college this morning after running an errand for the king. It was unlikely the timing had been coincidence.

There were blank stares and shaking, defeated heads all around.

"All right, take it all away," he said, rubbing his eyes in weariness and grief.

The body they had discovered this morning lay amongst the shattered ruins of Archmage Kelta's quarters. The assassin had left the corpse in such a state that they weren't even positive whose it was. Kelta couldn't be found though, and Tolmarak feared the worst.

It had been several weeks since the attack on Jayden, and yet the boy was still the only mage to have survived the ordeal. Less than a week later the assassin had struck again, killing an apprentice, and now it looked as though Archmage Kelta had been his latest victim.

"We have got to find out who is doing this!" Archmage Jane Winters hissed as the two serving men placed a sheet over the ruined form before them.

"I agree," Tolmarak returned, "But there is little more that we can do. Wards have been set; they don't get tripped. Guards have been posted, they see and hear nothing of these attacks."

"It is time to take more direct action," Winters told him. "Half of the younger magi and apprentices are jumping at every odd sound, and even some who know better are scared out of their wits. Just yesterday, an apprentice almost lashed out at a servant. She could have given the boy serious burns when she found him in her room performing his assigned duties. Thankfully she realised her mistake right at the last moment, and possessed enough control to stop the spell," she finished with a sniffle.

Winters and Kelta had been close friends since childhood. They'd even been brought to the college on the same week, Tolmarak recalled with a pang of sympathy. She would be feeling his loss keenly, perhaps the more so since they couldn't identify the body positively without further study.

"What do you suggest then?" Tolmarak asked, his sympathy for her situation warring with deep frustration. He was willing to listen to almost any idea at this point.

"Order the mageguard to perform a non-optional escort for every archmage, mage and apprentice until this is resolved. At this point none of us should be alone," she argued intently. "I know it's extreme, and that it seriously curtails our personal freedoms, but right now we are fighting a losing battle. If we don't take action now, we may not have a chance to fix this later on."

Tolmarak sighed, feeling every one of his seventy-nine years.

Despite all their efforts, the assassin continued to elude them, striking at will in any location he or she chose. It was almost as though they could use spells the Aramarian magi had never heard of and had no way to counter. At this point, the few dozen remaining magi who hadn't left for the front were close to open rebellion. A feeling of inevitability had settled over the college. The more so as no one, not even they themselves, could seem to make any headway in exposing the assassin's identity, or in slowing down the killings.

"All right," Tolmarak eventually agreed to Jane's surprise.

"But I won't make it an order. Any mage who wishes to do so may draw up to four of the mageguard for their personal security. That should at least calm some nerves. Make it known they are not to draw from the pool of new enlistees or the officer's training them, understood?"

"Yes Archmage," the younger woman replied before leaving to see to the college leader's orders.

He had already examined the devastated room, and there was little else to be gained by staying. After a last look around at the scorched walls and debris, Tolmarak sighed and left the chamber to seek out Jayden once more.

The boy had told them everything he remembered about his attacker, but after last night's death, he felt compelled to ask again.

When he entered the boy's room, Tolmarak was pleased to see that Sarah was there, already checking on the young mage. From the long-suffering look on Jayden's face, she had worked her healing arts well.

"There has been another attack," Tolmarak said as he tiredly took a seat in a comfortable chair across the room from the other two. The quarters for any mage were a far cry from the closets which the apprentices were made to live in. They had to be, as many Gift users never made it beyond that rank, no matter how many years they lived.

"Are my services required this time?" the grey haired archmage asked without looking up.

"I wish they were, Sarah," Tolmarak replied.

"I see," she responded, continuing to examine Jayden's eyes.

"We think it was Kelta."

That was enough to make the other archmage straighten from her examination and look at Tolmarak directly.

"But he was one of the five strongest magi left in the college."

"I know."

Tolmarak rubbed his eyes and shook his head, "And three of the four still alive are sitting in this room. Jayden, is there anything else at all you recall about the assassin that you haven't told us, or might not have thought important at the time? Anything would be a help," Tolmarak tried again.

Jayden shook his head, "I'm sorry, Archmage. I've told you everything I know. You know I wouldn't hold back about this," he added after a moment.

"I know you wouldn't," Tolmarak assured him. "But is there anything you sensed about the attacker, other than his aura being masked somehow, that might help us?"

For a long moment Jayden rolled his memories of that night over in his mind as Archmage Trellis went back to examining his eyes. A thought occurred to him.

"It appeared once his initial attack failed, the assassin's only goal was to escape, as though he was only after me by happenstance. The more I think about it in fact, the more I realise that self-preservation motivated his subsequent actions more than making sure I was dead. Even when he attacked me in the city, it was because I was the only one tracking him at that point, stopping him from getting away. As soon as he sensed you coming, he fled."

"If that were true though, why would he take such pains to make you suffer with that acid spell rather than neutralising you quickly. As he did with Nadeara?" Tolmarak countered with renewed vigour. The line of reasoning wasn't much, but at least it was fresh.

"It could be because you survived. It would be his first failure after all," Trellis interjected with furrowed brows.

"That's possible," Tolmarak conceded. "The very spell he chose suggests a cruel and capricious nature."

"You mean because I made him fail by surviving his attack, he wanted to make me suffer?" Jayden asked.

Uninvited, his mind returned to another man with similar traits.

"It's not Dael," Tolmarak said gently, seeing the look on Jayden's face.

"I thought you couldn't read my mind, Tolmarak," Jayden rebuked him.

"With that expression, Jayden, I had no need."

After a long moment of sullen silence, Jayden took a deep breath.

"I'm sorry Archmage. I try so hard to move past it, but everything brings me back to that moment on the cliff. The way this assassin attacks, and then disappears, as if nothing we can ever do can touch him. It enrages me. I don't have a way of identifying him, and without that, I can't stop him, and that just makes me want vengeance on Dael even more. I know who and where he is. I want to move on with my life, but I don't know how to move forward when everything I am tells me to leave this place and finish with that task before I can stand away from the past. To try to pick up what's left of my life here at the college. Only I know that if I do what I need too, to find peace, I won't be *able* to come back here again because King Erian will have me declared renegade."

Jayden couldn't help but laugh at the stunned silence his outburst created. The sound was as thin and humourless as he now felt.

"I am the most powerful mage in Jeranon, and helpless to do the one thing I know I must."

"In time, it will ease," Tolmarak told him as convincingly as he could, but Jayden just looked at him.

"I used to believe you when you said that. But if it were true, it would have begun by now."

Tolmarak was lost for words. He knew all the conventional wisdom, and some not so. But truthfully, he already feared the words Jayden had just uttered. It had been most of a year since that night on the cliff top. Surely there should have been some lessening of the guilt by now, some relief from the grief and fury which clouded the young man's mind.

"I want you to think," Tolmarak began, trying to distract Jayden from plunging into one of his darker moods. "If you were back in your room where you were attacked again, what would have helped you survive?"

"I don't know," Jayden replied, "Some form of warning

certainly. Only we already know that the assassin can disable our wards without detection. Other than that…" He shook his head. "It all happened so fast. I only remember acting on instinct and adrenaline. It wasn't until I was running across the courtyard that it even hit me what I was doing."

"What about the physical description?" Tolmarak probed, "Can you tell me anything more about that?"

"I don't even know if it was a man or a woman. In the dark, in that cloak… All I can say for sure is that they were about my height and quick on their feet. Other than that, they used spells like nothing I've seen before. Although I'm sure there are lots of those," he added after a reflective moment.

Tolmarak nodded his agreement.

"I'm going to assign an escort of the mageguard to you until we get this matter resolved," he told the young man. "I don't think they will be effective against this assassin, but so far you are the only one to have survived an attack. Being the strongest mage in Aramar, you will be crucial to helping stop this murderer once we finally glean his identity."

"If they can't stop him, why assign the escort at all? It only puts them in danger as well," Jayden replied, a little confused.

"Because," Tolmarak answered with a tired sigh, "They might provide you with the small warning you just mentioned if the assassin makes another attempt on your life."

"But how would they do that if they can't sense the Gift…" Jayden stopped, realising what the old archmage was suggesting.

"You think that in sensing my aura the assassin would

expect me, but encounter my guards first, don't you?!" He accused the old man. "I won't have it. He'll kill them without a thought. No one else is going to die because I can't protect them," he growled at his mentor in no uncertain terms.

Again, Tolmarak sighed.

"Jayden Torell, you know full well what these men call themselves. The protectors. And they are anything but helpless. It is the entire purpose of the mageguard to place themselves between their mage and harm. Every man among them has dedicated their lives to this end, because they understand two things. First, the magi's importance to defending our realm against the western nations, and second, how scarce our numbers truly are. I am sorry, Jayden, but the escort stands. We cannot afford to lose you."

*　　*　　*

After a long moment, Jayden calmed himself enough to speak, and looked over at the imposing archmage.

"You should leave,"

Surprisingly, Tolmarak stood.

"I know the situation is anything but ideal, but if we do not stop these attacks, even more people will die," he said before opening the door.

"If you wish to save anyone else from that fate, think hard on a way to either locate or identify the assassin before they strike again. I've already told the others to do the same. As of now this is our number one priority."

"Even more so than the war?" Jayden asked acerbically.

"What good is it to win a war if you have no home to return to?" Tolmarak returned, then walked out the door, leaving Jayden and Archmage Trellis, who had remained, silently examining Jayden's few remaining injuries, alone in the room.

"He's right you know," Archmage Trellis said when Jayden's anger refused to leave with Tolmarak.

"I'm well aware," Jayden replied. "Which makes it worse."

"I can see how it would," the healer replied.

"You are right to think that those mageguard men's lives are every bit as important as your own. So think long and hard on what the archmage said, because one way or another you will meet this assassin again. Either when he attacks you, or Maker willing, we find out who it is. Should that occur, you will no doubt be called upon to help neutralise him, since no one else has survived an encounter with this murderer."

"When he shows himself, I'll be ready," Jayden promised.

But despite all those he has murdered, the thought occurred in the safe privacy of his own mind. *He is not the man I most want to kill.*

*An unknown enemy can cause more damage with smiles and
lies than a known enemy with blade unsheathed.*
Terraliv Proverb.

CHAPTER 5

INVESTIGATIONS OF DARKNESS

"Call them in," Captain Ravenburg ordered without
preamble. He clasped his hands behind his back and waited
for Wyll to comply.

"Sir," Wyll acknowledged before bellowing at the other
men, who were still taking part in the day's drills, to halt
their tasks and attend the captain.

It had been more than a phase since the army had
marched, and Wyll hoped the captain would give them
some solid news at last. Some of the more vicious rumours
which had been circulating needed putting to bed once and
for all.

"I'll keep this brief," the leader of the mageguard said as
soon as the last of the sweating soldiers formed up before
him.

"You are not finished your training, yet matters have
come to light which require I put you, and several other
squads, on the active-duty list."

He let that sink in for a second and then continued.

"For now, continue to train hard and learn all you can. I
hope it will not be necessary to deploy you. However, you
deserve to know that from this moment, there is a strong
possibility you will have your training cut even shorter than

originally planned. For that I am sorry. There is little I despise more than sending good men into the field under-prepared. Nevertheless, we are now in a state of war, and there may soon be no other option."

After a brief look at each man standing in line before him, Ravenburg nodded in approval at what he saw, then ordered them to carry on.

"What do you think's happened?" Kienan asked of nobody in particular as the captain moved out of earshot.

"Must have been a battle," Marad put in.

"I heard Heramiir's got twice as many men as we do," Charran said right after.

"Doesn't matter," Wyll announced over the top, stopping the gossip in its tracks.

"You heard what the captain said. From this moment on, we could be assigned our first mission. The reason doesn't make any difference, nor will how ready we think we are if they are desperate enough to call up trainees. All that is in our control right now is to train as effectively as possible so that when that order comes, we're not all killed in our first engagement. So, back to your drills, and keep in mind that while your partners today won't try to kill you, that safety won't last much longer. Seth, you'll drill with me. The rest will pair off, Cale and Bosric, Marad and Sarran, Charran and Kienan. Tauman, you'll be free to jump into any combat and choose your foe. From now on there will be no yielding," Wyll decided. "You will press your opponent until one of you is at sword's point. I don't want any broken bones today, but I expect bruises. The victors will face off against each other. Questions?"

There weren't any, but that was to be expected. They had run this drill each morning since coming to the college. The new 'no quarter' rule was different, but it was a measure of the men's mood that none of them so much as made a joke about it.

The morning's drilling went slowly after that. Wyll did his best, but it was less than a minute before Seth had him on the ground with the pointy end of one of his curved practice Drakheras pointed at his throat.

Wyll conceded the match, annoyed that he had let himself become distracted enough that the admittedly superior swordsman had made such light work of him today. In recent weeks he had pushed the top-knotted warrior until only Cale could give the man more of a challenge. But not today. Without a word, Seth tucked one of the curved blades under his other arm and offered his hand, helping Wyll to his feet. After that it was Seth and Marad's turn, then Cale and Charran, who had overcome Kienan and Tauman together. Both of those men looked worse for wear after going up against the expert staffman in the first round. Seth made quick work of Marad, as was expected. Charran's improvement with proper training and his new quarterstaff was now becoming obvious. He'd attached blunted paddles where the blade hooked in at either end, and the modification saw him in good stead. With a lightning quick spin, he took the smaller man's legs out from under him with the blunt part of the staff. Then finished the duel with a pulled blow to Cale's head.

The mute soldier shook his head to clear it, then nodded to Charran as he felt his scalp to make sure he wasn't bleeding, before getting to his feet. Wyll ordered the final round between Seth and Charran. They all expected it to be a quick match, but as Seth performed a hard downward slice intended to cut the staff man's weapon in half, Charran took the blow squarely on its shaft. The bigger man laughed as Seth was forced to momentarily retreat in indecision, his weapon recoiling without leaving so much as a scratch in its wake.

"I asked Nadeara to put a spell on the wood," the younger of the squad's brothers told him in good humour. "Not even a battle axe could split this staff now."

"That was good thinking, Charran," Seth said as he brought his second blade to bear and closed again, this time a good deal more wary than he had been before. In an instant they clashed, Charran's doubled-bladed staff somehow keeping up with Seth's fluid movements. The others watched, engrossed in the sight of what was possibly the finest martial display they had yet seen from one of their own squad mates. It was Charran's best performance to date, Wyll thought as the two men sliced and spun, dodging and blocking each other's strokes, sometimes with only inches to spare.

After more than two minutes of this, Captain Ravenburg came back over to observe. The combatants continued trading blows, the pace now fast enough that the ends of their weapons only became unblurred in the instants when they connected.

The others called out encouragement to either Seth or Charran, depending on how the mood took them. Wyll watched silently, waiting for Seth to end the fight as he was sure the strange man could have done at any time. As Charran began to tire, Seth brought one of his blades down on the shaft of Charran's weapon and slid it sideways. He turned the blade again, just in time to avoid breaking his squad mate's fingers.

Charran gave a yelp as he lost his grip, and in an instant Seth's second blade was at his throat.

All was silent for a long moment, until the large man nodded, annoyed with himself for having done so well, and still not winning the match.

"Your next improvement?" Seth asked as he lowered and re-sheathed both his blades in a single smooth motion.

"Hand guards," Charran responded ruefully as he massaged an already swelling knuckle.

Seth nodded with a small grin.

"You did very well today. I have never met my match on the field, but just now, for a moment, you pressed me into defence."

The warrior inclined his head to Charran, who looked pleased at the gesture of respect. Ravenburg glanced over at Wyll, giving the new sergeant an approving nod before leaving again to see to his other duties.

"All right, well done Charran and Seth. Tauman, Kienan you both need to improve quickly, and to listen carefully to the answer to my next question. Seth, Cale, you both have battle experience. In your expert opinion, how long would two men with their current skills last in a full assault situation?"

Tauman went a little pale at the question. Kienan looked from one to the other as though the two men were about to impose a death sentence upon them.

"I would not send them in the first place," Seth admitted.

"Agreed, in an ideal world," Wyll replied. "Assume they are there anyway."

Seth looked over at Cale, who shrugged slightly before raising three fingers on his right hand. Seth gave a slight nod in agreement.

Wyll winced, sure that he was correct about their timeframe.

"Three minutes gentlemen. That is your life expectancy in a full battle situation at your current skill level."

The two men nodded unenthusiastically, but Wyll ignored them. There was little more he could say to encourage their efforts than leave them with that thought.

"Next drill is monster training. Today I'm told we have Imbic," Wyll told the men as he led them off in the direction in which that drill was always held.

"I hate monster training," Kienan grumbled. "Why can't we ever have 'sit around the tavern and play to crowds of beautiful women training?'"

Wyll chose to let it go on this one occasion.

"Or maybe we could change the location out to Market Square so the citizens can watch," Marad suggested.

Wyll groaned, and Bosric of course laughed at the giant man's idea.

"You want us to fight monsters in Market Square? Do you have a brain in that oversized head of yours?" the short man laughed out loud.

"Enough," Wyll said before things could once again get out of hand between the biggest and smallest members of his squad.

"Marad, don't you think that would get a little, chaotic?" Wyll asked.

"Of course we would have to let them know first," Marad responded flatly. He stared venomously at Bosric, who pretended not to notice.

"Perhaps," Wyll allowed. "But don't forget that while we are used to seeing the constructs the magi design for us to train on, the citizens of Aramar are not. Most of them probably wouldn't know the difference between a construct and the real thing either. In Market Square that could end up in a riot."

"Fair enough," Marad allowed after a long moment, although it was obvious the dark-skinned man still wanted to show off his supposed prowess to the citizenry at large.

Monster training went slowly that morning. By the time they were done, there was not a one of them, even Seth, who wasn't covered in bruises and welts. That was not unusual for monster training, but it was a measure of their distraction that Sarran's arm had been broken by a vicious blow from one of the constructs. The instructing mage had been forced to use the Gift to heal him before the large staffman could awkwardly continue. The injury would have been far worse had the situation not been a drill.

When that exercise was over, and they had eaten a quick lunch, Wyll took the men over to the stables to find their mounts. The next few hours were a blur of mounted drills with sword, lance, and bow, until finally, as dusk fell, the day's instructor dismissed them. The horses were taken to be re-stabled by grooms and the squad went to clean up before reporting to the dining hall for dinner.

Thankfully, tonight's meal was far less eventful than some of the other dinners they had shared. Wyll could only put it down to them all being lost in their own thoughts on the captain's announcement. Soon enough the dessert course was served and devoured, and the men shuffled out so the second shift could eat. By the time they left the dining hall, the sun was disappearing below the horizon. The various men dispersed to find whatever entertainment they could in the few hours left to them before they had to sleep.

Of all the things Wyll liked about the military life, curfew was not one of them, even if he understood the reason for it.

"Marad, don't forget it's your turn on guard duty tonight," he called to the big man as they went their separate ways.

Marad waved an acknowledgment without turning back, and Wyll left it at that. He didn't like the hulking man, but at least this time it seemed he would follow his orders without an argument.

Guard duty was something that all members of the mageguard were required to take turns at, from the lowest recruit up to the rank of lieutenant. Even the dour infantryman Bandell and his cavalry counterpart, Lieutenant Bickerall took their shifts without complaint. Only the captain who led the mageguard itself, whoever that was at the time, was excused from the duty. Or at least that was the mageguard tradition as it had been explained to Wyll shortly after they'd arrived.

Wyll was feeling tired tonight though, and instead of seeking the usual entertainments that were to be found on the college grounds, he decided to return to the squad's barracks rooms and unwind for a bit before sleeping. By the time Charran announced he was going in search of a carpenter to organise the hand guards for his staff, most of the others had already dispersed. Wyll found himself alone, and started walking towards his destination. It was an interesting weapon, he had to admit, and most enemies would not be used to dealing with an opponent wielding a six-foot, iron bound staff with a pair of short sword blades attached at either end. Apart from sheer reach, the momentary hesitation that would cause would give Charran a slight advantage at the outset of most combat situations.

On the way back to his room, Wyll stopped to watch a veteran squad running through a lancing drill at the lists. He couldn't help but admire the easy confidence the men exuded as they went about their business, each hitting their intended targets with pinpoint accuracy.

After a few minutes he got bored though, and continued wandering toward the barracks, enjoying the brisk dawn of spring air on the way to his destination. Bosric and Cale had beaten him back, and the two men were already engaged in a complicated game that involved recreating battles with squads of miniature figures Bosric claimed to have carved himself. Though Wyll had no idea when he might have found the time. There were also several dice rolls that somehow affected the outcome, and Wyll supposed it made sense if you understood it. To him, it was nothing more than a jumble of playing pieces that often took his men hours to untangle.

Wyll acknowledged the soldiers with a nod, and passed through the communal living area into his tiny room, which led off the narrow corridor behind. Heading to his locker, he retrieved the book on military tactics that the captain had given him to study. Book in hand, he kicked off his boots and lay back in his bunk to read a few more chapters before he could let himself sleep. After what must have been at least an hour of intense study, he got up and put the text back on his shelf. He left the room to perform his ablutions, and on returning, removed his uniform, stowing it before returning to the bunk in just his small-clothes. Privacy wasn't something the military was big on, though these cramped rooms were a welcome step up from the communal bunks they had shared at Camp Five. The captain had told him a few days ago that once they'd been on their first official mission and were no longer considered to be 'in training', their accommodations would become substantially better. For now though, with all the new recruits conscripted over the last phases, the college was hard pressed for space. Until the new wing was finished on the mageguard barracks, these rooms would have to do. None of the men had complained when shown the small unadorned rooms they had been assigned though. Just the opposite. They all knew they were part of the biggest influx of soldiers into the mageguard in nearly five hundred years, and by this point his men were glad for even this much time alone.

Wyll let his thoughts drift as Bosric laughed at a lucky throw of the dice, while Cale groaned. The man could still make noises, but without a tongue he couldn't form legible words. Still, the frustration was evident in his tone, which was unusual, as he won their games more often than he lost. Tonight seemed to be the exception.

As he drifted off to sleep, Wyll hoped Marad was going to obey whoever's orders were being given at the guard post tonight without argument. The fatigue muted rattling of dice was the last thing he heard for the night.

*   *   *

'Guard duty is always so boring,' Marad thought as he stood at the outer gate to the grounds. He was one of eight mageguard soldiers assigned here tonight, all from different squads, along with a sergeant to oversee them. This was his second time at the gate since coming to the college, and he had little or no interest in standing around in the bitingly cold wind.

Even if we are needed tonight, it is going to be back at the college building where the assassin might strike. It's not like we'll need to stop the ravening citizens of Aramar from overrunning the grounds and killing the helpless magi inside, he thought with a mocking grin.

The two remaining hours of his shift took an interminable time to pass. The only highlight of the night was when a stray bat flew overhead and did its business on one of the other soldiers. The incident provided almost a full minute of amusement for the rest of the men, but then it was over.

He was having a great deal of difficulty staying awake. Still, falling asleep would have meant falling over, so he focused on the coldness of the wind, and somehow got through it.

Finally, somewhere past midnight, the next shift came over from the barracks. The sergeant dismissed the current watchmen to their quarters for the rest of the evening.

It was a long walk back to the mageguard's huge barracks, and the men spread out along the way. By the time Marad entered the actual structure he was on his own, the others heading to entrances nearer their own rooms.

He sighed in relief once inside. It was much warmer in here, and without the constant wind tugging at him, he found himself suddenly sleepy. He turned a corner as he trudged along the carpeted hallway, and then rounded another before the soft sound of footsteps registered behind him. That was not so unusual. After all, there were many men stationed here in the barracks, and some of them kept odd hours.

He stopped to pick a small stone out of the tread of his boot, which had wedged itself in there on the way back from the guard station. It wasn't until a few steps further on that he noticed the soft footsteps resume. That meant the person following him had stopped at the same time he had.

It was unusual enough to give him pause. The magi in the college hadn't yet been able to locate their assassin.

He kept walking until he rounded another corner, and then

stopped, drawing his blade as he waited for his pursuer to come around the bend. It didn't take long until the soft footsteps were loud enough to hear distinctly. They were also hurrying as they approached, until Marad thought their owner must be just beyond the corner. And then they stopped.

For a long moment nothing happened. He took a chance, walking up and down on the spot for a moment, his sword ready, each step slightly lighter and quieter than the last. To the person around the corner, it should sound as though he were walking away from the intersection.

As soon as he stopped stepping, the other footsteps continued, and a moment later a figure came sneaking around the corner, surprised at being caught out.

"You?" Marad said with an exasperated sigh, lowering his sword. "For a moment there I thought you might have been the assassin."

The figure smiled.

*   *   *

"Wyll, you need to come with me," Lieutenant Bandell's voice said as a firm hand on his shoulder shook him awake.

For a moment Wyll looked around groggily until his mind registered the lieutenant standing over him. Whatever was happening must be important for Bandell to be sent to fetch him. He wiped his face once with his hands to help wake himself up, and then swung out of his bunk to quickly don his uniform.

"What's wrong, sir?" he asked the veteran cavalryman as the man waited impatiently for him to be done.

"Not here," the lieutenant replied, motioning to the sleeping men in the other tiny, thin-walled rooms next to his as Wyll tugged on his boots. A moment more and he was done, and they left the room while Wyll tried using his fingers to bring some semblance of order to his sleep-matted hair.

They didn't have far to go before Wyll found out what the commotion was. As they rounded a turn in the corridor, he missed a step and fought the sudden urge to retch at the sight which confronted him. In the middle of the corridor, Marad lay prone, his eyes glassy and unseeing. The hilt of Marad's sword was still jutting out from where it had been thrust through his heart in a blow that would have killed the big man instantly.

"What happened?" Wyll asked in disbelief, not only because the man had been fine just last night, but also that this had taken place inside the mageguard building itself.

"We're not sure yet," Captain Ravenburg answered as Wyll noticed for the first time not only his commanding officer, but also Archmage Tolmarak beyond the body as well.

"I do not believe that this is the work of the assassin we have been chasing," Tolmarak said with a furrowed brow.

"But what of Kamala? She was killed only three doors down within an hour of this attack, and that clearly *was* the work of the assassin," Bandell put in.

"Someone else was killed here last night?"

Tolmarak sighed.

"Yes, a visiting mage was attacked last night, but as the lieutenant says, that was the work of the assassin we have been tracking. This, however, is not. In fact, I can sense nothing of the Gift having been used on him."

"But how did Marad's killer get his sword?" Wyll asked in confusion. "He wasn't the smartest guy, but he was as strong as a bull. If there had been a struggle, someone would have heard it."

"I agree," Ravenburg returned after a moment. "Which leads us to the unfortunate conclusion that Marad probably knew his killer, and trusted them enough to hand over his weapon voluntarily."

Wyll looked down at the big man's corpse in confusion, wondering how anyone could have persuaded the argumentative man to lower his guard that far.

"Is there anything you can tell us about him, Wyll? Did he have any enemies you know of?" Tolmarak asked with a raised eyebrow.

"None that I know of, not serious ones at any rate. Though he had a penchant for rubbing people the wrong way," Wyll added as his mind spun at what seemed an inhuman pace.

"He hated Bosric, but to be honest, I don't think it went both ways, and Marad never would have given him his sword. Apart from that, he had very few strong connections here. As far as I know, he didn't know enough people well enough to have made any real enemies."

"I see," the archmage replied, frustration clear in his tone.

"Captain. Deal with this. We have enough troubles right now without having to worry about a second murderer running loose on college grounds."

Ravenburg tossed the archmage a crisp salute as the old man turned and stalked away, now in as foul a mood as Wyll had ever seen him.

"Is there anything else you can tell me?" Ravenburg asked once Tolmarak had disappeared from view.

"Anything about his past, his family? Friends? What he's been up to over the last few weeks?"

"Not much, sir, he had no family. He kept to himself when not on duty. While a lot of people didn't like him very much, I doubt he'd offended any of them enough to provoke them to… this." He motioned at the still form blocking half the corridor.

"I'm sorry, Captain, but the last I saw of him was last night after dinner, first shift. I reminded him about guard duty, and he walked away, then this."

"Where was he heading?"

"Towards the exercise yard, I think, but I returned to the barracks just after he left. He could have gone anywhere after that. As for his personal life, I don't think any of my squad knew him that well. He was not the kind to make friends easily, and I doubt that anyone here would know him well enough yet to have reason to want him dead."

Wyll realised he was repeating himself now and stopped, at a loss for anything more to say that would help the captain in his investigation.

"So you have no useful information about this at all?"

"No, sir, I don't think I do."

Ravenburg sighed. "Very well. You may return to your room. Oh, and Wyll, as squad leader, it is your duty to inform your men of this loss. See to it they hear it from you, and not over the morning gossip."

"Yes, sir," Wyll answered with false bravado.

He turned on his heel and headed back towards the dorm room where the rest of his remaining men would shortly wake for the day's activities. Although the walk was short, by the time he reached the door to their common room, he was dreading telling them that yet another of their number had fallen.

That was two now, from the ten who had begun training

with squad four twenty-two, and they were still yet to see combat.

CHAPTER 6

DESPERATE MEASURES

The throne room is becoming a familiar place these days, Tolmarak reflected as he passed through the huge double doors that gave access to and from the rest of the royal palace.

The map table had been permanently shifted further back into the room now, beyond the throne, and off to the left in a restricted section forbidden to all without the king's express approval. Crossing through the line of columns, he continued to his destination to find King Erian and General Hurcarl leaning over the table.

The two men were already deep in discussion, but looked up as he passed between the royal guards. Erian nodded a greeting, and beckoned Tolmarak to join them.

"We have a problem," the king announced.

"Our Arborii and Terraliv allies have gathered their

strength and are moving to reinforce the western border. It is their intention to hold it against the nations beyond should it become necessary, rather than become involved in our own internal conflict. Both Terall and Droik reasoned it would only deplete our overall effectiveness further if they came to our aid. In truth, no matter how much it irks me, I understand their reasoning. The western nations must be held in check. However, that is where the good news, if it can be called that, ends. In the last week I have received several reliable reports from both military and civilian sources that indicate Heramiir's primary force is not where we had first thought."

Tolmarak raised a surprised eyebrow at that, and picked up a small scroll full of impeccable writing which lay near him on the table.

"That one was the first," Erian said as he began reading. "It was brought to me by a concerned coffee merchant earlier in the week, whose livelihood is being threatened. If these reports are accurate, Heramiir's entire army is advancing through the Laketown Peninsula."

"The Laketown Peninsula?" Tolmarak repeated, stunned at the news.

"But all our previous reports indicated his army is still situated outside Cordova, north of the Mirallyn River."

"Correct," Hurcarl responded as he studied the table map.

As the king's top military advisor, the stocky general with his ever-increasing bald spot had remained in Aramar to oversee the capital's defences, but now looked perplexed.

"And to make matters worse," Hurcarl continued. "Our best information still holds that his main force has not moved from its base outside Cordova since the initial siege was completed last summer."

"That can't be," Tolmarak answered with sudden certainty, "Our best estimates put almost eighty thousand men in that camp. There is no way that Heramiir could field a second army that size."

For a long moment, the three heads of Jeranon's power structure thought on the subject.

"He could… if he emptied the cities and villages he was conquering of able-bodied men, and pressed them into service," Hurcarl mused as he stroked his chin in thought.

"Perhaps…" Tolmarak allowed. "But while Heramiir may be many things, stupid or incautious would be the very last of them. He would know full well that if he did what you suggested, there would be widespread shortages of food over the winter due to an incomplete harvest. If the war drags on more than another season, he will lose a good portion of next year's crop as well. That would turn shortages into famine, and in all likelihood, full blown rebellion of the lands he has already conquered."

"I agree," the king interjected. "But until we can get more information, we must assume that he has in fact fielded this many men, and act accordingly."

The two advisors reluctantly agreed, and the general moved the discussion forward.

"All right, assuming these armies are as large as the reports suggest, we could fight either with a decisive advantage in numbers, but not both. Now while I would loathe giving up the Laketown Peninsula, I think we can all agree that the army holding Cordova is a far more immediate threat. In addition, our army is already well on the way to meeting that force now. Any expedition of consequence we could spare from the defensive position at Midway to meet this new southern force would likely be defeated if these numbers are correct. A defeat at that position would allow Heramiir to press on across the Mirallyn Fjords and take and hold Midway. From there his forces would have unlimited access to central Jeranon, and our main army would be trapped behind his lines if we decide to continue towards Cordova. This is something we cannot allow."

The general stopped for a moment and studied the map again, measuring out some distances with his hands before continuing.

"The biggest problem, if these numbers are true, is that even if we fielded every officer, conscript, and mage with their retinues, we could only match this new number of troops. Not better it," Hurcarl sighed. "We must act for now as if both these forces are real, I agree. Yet my gut also tells me you are correct, Tolmarak, there is more at play here than meets the eye. I cannot believe that Heramiir has enough genuine support to control this many men, not as well as subduing Miralthrall and the entire Sammorand Plains at the same time."

"I concur," Tolmarak added after a moment of thought.

"Our best guess is still that the assassin we have been tracking here in Aramar is one of Heramiir's men sent to disrupt our efforts in defence. He has already forced us to hold back valuable magi from the campaign. His secondary aim is likely to be weakening the capital for an incursion. By now, to my great distress, we have seen enough of this assassin's talents to know that they are aware of spells that no one in Aramar is familiar with."

"How does that relate to the matter at hand?" the general asked without taking his eyes from the map.

For a moment Tolmarak winced, knowing the king would not like what he had to say.

"I think we should at least examine another possibility. That Heramiir, or one of his inner circle, has learned to produce some kind of mass illusion that is bolstering what we believe to be the true extent of his forces."

"What?" was all the startled response that the monarch made for a long moment. "Are you saying that Heramiir might have a real advantage over us in the Gift, as well as in the size of his army?"

"Actually, Sire," Tolmarak was quick to answer. "We have known for some time, from the manner of the assassin's attacks, that they have been experimenting with unauthorised uses of the Gift. To my everlasting chagrin, you know well that I taught both Heramiir and Nereth during their apprenticeships. Either of those men is clever enough to come up with a ruse such as this. What they may have lacked until now was the means to execute it. What we must determine is whether they have developed their capacity for illusion beyond what we had thought possible. Or whether Heramiir's army is truly as formidable as he wishes us to believe."

"Have you made any progress on that front?" Hurcarl inquired.

Tolmarak clenched a gnarled fist. "No. Just yesterday we found the remains of what we think was Archmage Kelta."

"I see," Hurcarl replied, straightening to look the old archmage in the eye. "Well, I'm not sure how much help the military can be if your magi can't stop him, but let me know if there is any way at all that we can assist."

"Thank you, I appreciate that," Tolmarak answered, consciously having to relax his clenched fist.

The talk at the table faltered for a long moment as they

studied the map again for some time before an idea occurred to Tolmarak.

"We could use the Chalice of Ajerio."

"Excuse me?" Hurcarl asked.

"The Chalice of Ajerio," Tolmarak repeated.

"It is a relic that came over with our forbearers from Jeranah on the desolate fleet. Even then its origins were unknown, but it has the effect of cancelling out all spells which remain active within a certain range, such as wards, arcana, or other relics. Basically anything that is not being constantly maintained by a living mage."

"Interesting. But how do we know that this illusion, if that is even what this is, is not being maintained by a living mage as you say?" the king asked.

"That part is simple," Tolmarak replied as he clasped his hands behind his back and subconsciously fell into his teaching posture.

"For the illusion to be convincing, it must be constant. That army near Cordova has been there for phases now. If it had faltered at all, someone would have seen it by now, and since there is no effective way for magi to share spells of that complexity between ourselves…"

"The illusion would be disrupted every time the mage went to sleep," Hurcarl finished with a grin.

"Exactly," Tolmarak replied with a slight smile of his own.

"So, there is actually a chance this will work?" the king asked.

"I don't think we can afford not to try," Tolmarak answered. "If one of Heramiir's armies is a farce, we need to re-plan our entire campaign. If they are both real, the same applies, only more so."

"The real question is, how are we going to get someone there in time to make any difference?" Hurcarl wondered out loud.

The three men went back to studying the map again for a moment before all reaching the same conclusion.

"They will never get there in time," Erian noted.

"Even by ship they can't make the march from the nearest coast to the army before it leaves Midway. By that time, they will not be able to turn and face the force on the peninsula before it crosses the fjords below Lake Pristine. I have no doubt that is the location that army will head if it turns out to be real," Hurcarl added.

Tolmarak sighed and made a hard decision.

"There may be another way, though the chances are exceedingly slim of anyone we send making it through to the army alive."

The others looked at him for a moment in confusion until finally Erian's eyebrows climbed as he realised what the archmage was suggesting.

"You want to try sending someone through the Wraith Woods?" he asked in surprise.

"You can't be serious?" Hurcarl added an instant later. "No one has survived that journey for near on nine hundred years."

"I don't see that we have much of a choice," Tolmarak replied. "There is no other way to warn the army in time. Besides, I think I may know of someone who has a chance of successfully making the journey."

"You do?" Erian stated, clearly becoming annoyed at the constant barrage of surprises this meeting was serving up.

"Perhaps," Tolmarak mused.

"There is a young man named Wyll, a friend to the Mage Jayden of Grandell. I trust you remember him?"

That gained a stern stare from the king, and Tolmarak ploughed forward.

"The first time he came to the college the oracle made certain… predictions about his future, none of which have yet come to pass. But in all my years I have never known her readings to be wrong."

"So you think this, Wyll, will survive the Wraith Woods because he has, what, a destiny?" Hurcarl asked incredulously.

"A crude way of putting it, but essentially correct. This coupled with the Chalice of Ajerio might just give him enough of an advantage to survive the ordeal," Tolmarak mused after a moment.

"In the event my reading of the oracle's words is flawed, I suggest sending a backup messenger around the woods accompanied by a mage, just in case. It won't give us time to reposition the army, but at least they might be able to determine what our forces are about to engage before the fighting commences."

"I don't like sending men on hopeless missions old friend, so be honest with me now. Do you truly believe this idea of yours has a viable chance of succeeding?" the king asked quietly. He coughed deeply once, then ambled tiredly away from the map table and crossed the spacious room to sit wearily on his throne.

"I think we have to try," Tolmarak responded once the ageing monarch was seated, the royal guards shadowing the old man to his new position.

Tolmarak found himself growing concerned by the king's sudden bouts of fatigue. They had been coming on for almost two years now, but since first news of the rebellion had reached them, they had grown considerably more frequent. Sadly, Tolmarak suspected that his old monarch's health was finally beginning to falter. The timing couldn't be worse.

The king had only one son, but had long since appointed him successor to the throne. At least if the unthinkable occurred, the wrangling for power amongst the nobles would be minimal. Added to that, Prince Jaric was not only intelligent, but capable and highly schooled as well. It was a great pity the young man was on foreign soil at present, attempting to repair relations with the island continent of Avsan. Erian had revealed this to Tolmarak just weeks ago, and he hadn't been happy.

Of course, everyone knew the prince had not been in residence in Aramar for over a year now. As to the details of why, the king had kept those to himself for phases, other than to state publicly that Jaric was on royal business, and would return at a future date.

Tolmarak hated not knowing where the crown prince was in case some disaster visited his father before he returned. Thankfully Prince Jaric was an intelligent, well-tempered young man, and Tolmarak had few concerns about his ability to govern once his father met the Black Lady. All concerns of the kingdom aside though, Tolmarak would miss his old friend once he was gone.

Then again, I don't have a vast number of years left myself, he dryly reflected.

"Very well," The king spoke, breaking him free of the unproductive thoughts. "In the absence of other options, proceed with your plan."

"Yes, Sire," Tolmarak assented.

"The only question left then is, where do we send these men?" Hurcarl mused.

"To Cordova," Tolmarak answered without hesitation, his mind now firmly back on the job. "For the simple reason that it is closer to the position the army will be at when the messengers arrive. Scouting that force will give our army the maximum time possible to re-plan their attack or change direction should the need arise. From various reports, we know that at least a portion of the force on the peninsula must be real, since they have taken towns in that district. Our goal must be to determine if the same is true of the army occupying Cordova. It has not moved since the initial siege, and would be a far easier illusion to maintain than a moving army. It is possible that if we are correct in this assumption, his forces at Cordova may be minimal."

"I still can't believe that Heramiir would intentionally strand his real army at Laketown," Hurcarl returned. "It just doesn't make sense."

"None that we can see right now," Tolmarak agreed. "But at least some of his forces there are real, so either Heramiir wants us to believe he wants that promontory, or he actually does for some unknown reason."

"But there's nothing there," Hurcarl rebuffed. "Why would Heramiir go to all the trouble of creating a fake army only to march his actual force onto the Laketown Peninsula? A piece of land that holds no real strategic value, and only has one route west that could reasonably accommodate his force. What advantage does it give him to risk being trapped there between Cordova's defences if we retake the city, and our army marching from the east?"

"Only one that I can see," Tolmarak replied after a moment, frowning again at the map.

"And that is?"

"That he gets to choose the ground the battle will be

fought on. Even going through the Wraith Woods, we cannot hope to send a messenger to warn the army and then reach the fjords below Lake Pristine before he does."

That made the general scowl.

"I do not want to fight this man on his own terms," Hurcarl responded. "Not with Nereth as his General."

"Nor I," Tolmarak replied, "But his major force, whichever location it is at, must be dealt with before we can move into western Jeranon in strength. Our only other option is to cede half the Kingdom to Heramiir, for we cannot hope to attack Miralthrall with his army at our backs. Nor can we afford to wait him out, as each phase we delay tightens his grip on the countryside surrounding Miralthrall and the Sammorand Plains above. Not to mention the Laketown Peninsula, which he now appears to be concentrating on."

"All right," Hurcarl consented after he had taken a long moment to digest the archmage's reasoning, "We'll do it your way. I just hope that you're right about that destination," he added with a slight frown.

"As do I General, but this at least gives us the most options if I am not."

To that, Hurcarl could only nod his agreement.

Being sent to my death by you is of little consequence compared to knowing that my life's purpose will not be brought to fruition. It must be freed.
Excerpt from the trial of Eldrik the Black - last statement before execution.

CHAPTER 7

A MISSION OF IMPORTANCE

"Come in," Tolmarak called at the brisk knock on his office door.

A moment later the heavy wooden panel opened, and Wyll, whom the archmage had been expecting, entered.

"Reporting as ordered Archmage," the young man said, standing correctly at attention despite the lateness of the hour.

"Relax boy," Tolmarak told him with a sigh. "Just looking at you standing like that makes my back ache."

"Yes Archmage," Wyll returned with a more familiar grin.

Tolmarak motioned the young man to join him at the table, on which a map to rival the one in the throne room lay. He waited until Wyll joined him before speaking further.

"I've called you here today for several reasons," he began. "The first of which is that over the last week we have been receiving reports of a hostile force moving in great numbers onto the Laketown Peninsula. We believe that once they secure the area, they will head west over the fjords in the

Mirallyn River northwest of Rolling Hills. Our best information puts this force at just under a hundred thousand men." He gave Wyll a moment to digest that fact, then continued. "This force will cause us substantial difficulties if not kept in check. However, the real problem is that we also have reliable intelligence stating that Heramiir's main force is still camped at Cordova with close to ninety thousand men."

Wyll felt his mouth open and close as he stared at the archmage in shock.

"But, even counting the enlisted squads, that's almost as many men as we can field without stripping our defences," the younger man eventually replied.

Tolmarak nodded his agreement. "I see you have been paying attention," he said with approval. "Which brings us to why you are here. Neither I, nor King Erian, nor General Hurcarl for that matter, believe that Heramiir could have this many men at his disposal. Combine this with the fact that the assassin knows spells which no one in Aramar is familiar with… In short, we believe there is a good chance that one force or the other is in part, or in total, an illusion."

Wyll furrowed his brows in thought.

"I know little about the Gift, other than what I've learned in the short time my squad has been assigned here, Archmage," Wyll countered. "But I didn't think something like that could be done on this kind of scale?"

Tolmarak nodded.

"Ordinarily, you would be right, but Heramiir and his men seem to have found some source of knowledge that we here in the capital are not yet privy to."

"I see," Wyll replied, momentarily becoming lost in his own thoughts.

"Yes, that was much my reaction as well. Before the army can march on from Midway though, we need to find out which of Heramiir's forces are real, or whether his troops are spread evenly across both fronts. However, we have two problems facing us. First, due to the unknown nature of the spells involved, we have only one genuine option for reliably nullifying them. A powerful artefact in our possession known as The Chalice of Ajerio. This relic has the unique ability to negate all aspects of the Gift within a radius of just over one mile, so long as they are not being actively maintained by a mage. Your squad's task will be to take the chalice within range of Heramiir's forces and make it back to General Messand alive to report what you have seen."

For a moment Wyll looked at the archmage to see whether the old man was serious, but quickly decided he'd meant exactly what he said.

"The problem with this mission is that by the time you complete it, it will be too late. The army will be too far west to intercept Heramiir at the Mirallyn Fjords if the position at Cordova turns out to be a diversion. Therefore, you must first inform General Messand to halt with special orders signed by the King. Unfortunately, even then you will only have enough time to check on one of these forces before returning to the army and setting them on the appropriate course. I cannot overstate how critically important this mission is, Wyll. If we continue to march on Cordova and it is a diversion, Heramiir will consolidate his hold on the Laketown Peninsula and cut behind our lines. From there he could move however many troops he has across the fjords, unopposed in any meaningful way. If this occurs, three things will happen. First, they will cut our supply lines upriver to Midway, preventing the entire second ship-borne element of the army from linking up with our main force. Second, elements of Heramiir's force will be in a prime position to lay siege to our staging area at Midway. This would bog our forces down at that position instead of them moving west where they are needed. Third, the remainder of his army moves east into central Jeranon, shifting the entire momentum of the war into Heramiir's favour."

Wyll took a deep breath as he studied the map. While he was no expert tactician, he could see what the archmage was saying was true, and why it must be avoided.

"Which force are we to spy on?" he managed to get out more confidently than he felt.

"The army at Cordova will be your target," Tolmarak told him without hesitation. "Not only is that force more threatening, but it is also a far more important strategic point for us to hold should Heramiir be using it as a bluff."

Tolmarak paused for a moment to let his words sink into the young man's mind before pressing on to give him the truly disturbing part of the mission.

"As you have no doubt seen on the map, the Wraith Woods run directly across your path, and yet we have no time for you to go around them. Therefore, your mission is as follows. Take the King's orders through the Wraith Woods, and deliver them to General Messand, who leads our army. These orders state that he is to halt and wait for your report. Your squad will then ride hard for Cordova and ascertain whether the force there is real, and if not, then what percentage of it is illusion. Upon returning with this intelligence, General Messand will march the army to intercept the true main force of Heramiir's troops. The first ship-borne element of reinforcements will continue onto

Midway as planned, or else merge with our main army at the Mirallyn Fjords, as the situation requires."

For a much longer time now there was silence in Tolmarak's office, until Wyll found the courage to break it. "Are you sure about this Archmage? I'm not questioning your orders, but... the Wraith Woods? I mean people go in, and some who haven't ventured too far come back out. But to the best of my knowledge, no one has crossed it successfully in nine hundred years. The last man who did, took a whole battalion of troops with him, most of whom were killed by what the survivors later described as 'demons of fang and claw'. Not that the history is too clear on what that actually means."

Once again, Tolmarak sighed.

I'm doing that too much these days.

"No Wyll, to be brutally honest, I'm not sure about this at all," the archmage confided at last. "But we have no choice. None of our other options is viable, and even this will not work unless you can reach the army faster than would normally be possible. Therefore, the King has ordered this mission to be carried out immediately, which brings us to the other reason I called you here today. I could send a more experienced squad on this mission, and possibly should, but as you said, the Wraith Woods are an almost impenetrable barrier for any normal traveller. For many, many years we considered them to be anathema until Jairus won through at horrific cost. On the other hand, we both know that you are no normal traveller. Consider what Tammy told you the first time you entered the college building. That you would recognise the signs when you came to them. Tell me now if you have seen anything that could be interpreted even vaguely as the gem, or the King of the Dead, or especially the Well of Tears."

After a moment of consideration, Wyll shook his head, and Tolmarak nodded, satisfied at the response.

"In all my life I have never known Tammy to be wrong, about anything. If she says you will be there to recognise those signs, then I must believe that is true."

"That's why you think I can cross the Wraith Woods while all others would be lost?"

"Yes," Tolmarak replied. "I know you may not believe her words as I do. But this is the best chance that we have to warn the army in time and still meet Heramiir with our full force of arms intact. If this mission fails, and Heramiir wins through into eastern Jeranon, at best it will extend the war by years. At worst, Heramiir wins, but at a cost of weakening Jeranon to the point where we may be incapable of repelling the next attack by the western nations. Regardless of who is victorious in the current conflict, that would doom us all."

"I won't let you down Archmage," Wyll told the old man, trying to sound a lot more confident than he felt.

"When do we leave?"

"Immediately," The archmage replied without further banter, handing him a rolled-up scroll on which the king's orders for General Messand were scribed.

"Gather your men, say your goodbyes, and stow your gear. Extra pack horses and provisions will be waiting in the courtyard. I want you on the western road in an hour. Archmage Volnar will meet you at the five-mile marker stones from Aramar to give you the chalice. From there your squad will proceed alone. Good luck Wyll," Tolmarak told him as he stretched out a hand which Wyll immediately shook.

"Thank you, Archmage," Wyll replied as he released his

grip. He saluted the old man crisply before turning and leaving Tolmarak's office, both of them very much hoping it would not be for the last time.

* * *

"Jayden, over here," Wyll called as he finished stowing his gear behind Socks' saddle.

The time Tolmarak had allowed was almost up. Wyll would have preferred to wait until morning, but the archmage had been adamant. It was close to midnight now, and besides his squad, the western courtyard of the college grounds was deserted. The randomly halted constructs used during the day's training shone dimly. The reflected moonlight lending their curved and gleaming surfaces an otherworldly aspect.

The only sound other than his own voice was coming from a few horses over where Kienan was still arranging his gear. Tauman was busy checking the state of their three packhorses before they set out on the long overland journey. Somewhere in the distance a goat brayed.

"I was hoping you would get my message," Wyll said as he turned to face the two magi who had come to see them off. Jayden was still being flanked by the four mageguard officers the archmage had assigned him, and he looked none too happy about it.

"We heard you had orders," Jayden said. Both he and Firerose stopping in front of the squad of men they had both come to be friends with over the better part of the last year.

"Indeed. We ride out in a few moments," Wyll responded, checking the straps on Socks' saddle and tack one last time before turning his full attention to his friends.

"We're to determine which of Heramiir's major forces are real and which are illusions," he said in answer to the inquisitive look on the young mage's face.

"That sounds a little dangerous," Firerose responded with concern.

"You have no idea," Wyll muttered.

"We are to ride through the Wraith Woods so that we can accomplish the mission in time."

Firerose's jaw dropped, and even Jayden seemed taken aback at the statement, but of the two of them, Firerose recovered quicker.

"You can't be serious! That's suicide!" she managed to get out before Wyll could stop her.

The other men in the squad heard her and looked around, but none of them flinched. Wyll was grateful to see that their resolve, at least at this point, remained unbroken. The first thing he'd done upon returning from the archmage's office was to brief them on the mission's details, so it wasn't new information she'd blurted out. Nonetheless, the spur-of-the-moment comment from the young noblewoman was not good for morale.

"Tolmarak believes you can cross the Wraith Woods?" Jayden asked once he could bring himself to speak.

"I hope so," Wyll replied. "Because that's where he's sending us."

For a moment there was a pause as the two young magi digested that.

"What happens when you complete your mission?" Jayden asked, abruptly changing the topic.

"I assume we'll join the campaign after the mission is complete," Wyll answered with a shrug. "But in the end it will be up to the highest-ranking mage with the army.

"Then this is goodbye," Firerose said with what sounded to be genuine regret.

"Only for now. I have a hunch we'll see each other again," Wyll told her more confidently than he felt.

"I hope you're right," she said, stepping up and giving the young sergeant a hug. Wyll almost laughed out loud at the surprised expression on Jayden's face, but managed not to embarrass himself as he returned the gesture. As Firerose stepped back again, he smiled.

"Farewell, milady," he said with a mock bow and a smile.

Growing serious again, Wyll stepped up to Jayden, and the two men shook hands.

"Be well, my friend," Wyll said. "And remember, only you control your future. Do not allow your memories of the past to override your will in this thing."

Jayden nodded, and then said with the slightest hint of a grin. "And you, don't forget it's the pointy end that you stick in your enemies."

Wyll couldn't help but laugh at the absurdity of the advice as the two men released each other's hands.

"In all seriousness, Jayden, stay your path. When I return you will have my aid, should you still require it."

Jayden nodded, and without further delay Wyll mounted Socks' saddle and ordered his men to do likewise.

"We have to go now. Time is of the essence I'm told," he said as he looked down at the two magi standing before them.

"Go save the world then," Jayden replied, and Wyll couldn't rightly tell whether he was joking.

"If Tammy's right," the young mageguard officer returned instead. "You'll get your turn soon enough."

The two men shared a knowing look, and after a moment

Wyll dug his knees into Socks' sides with a shouted order to ride. Just like that, the squad was off, quickly moving to a gallop. They rode across the open ground of the college towards the western gate, and disappeared into the forest, leaving Aramar and its people behind.

*   *   *

As the sound of clanging hooves faded, Jayden and Firerose stood silently, watching Wyll and the rest of his squad ride away on their first mission. A mission given to them because Tolmarak didn't believe even his veteran squads could accomplish it on their own.

Jayden said a quick prayer to the Maker that they would all return safely. Wyll's squad was already down on men after losing some of their number to both accident and foul play.

As they crossed the threshold of the college grounds and were lost to sight, a sudden strange sensation crawled over Jayden's spine. It was strong enough that he compulsively had to look back over his shoulder.

It wasn't the Gift, more like the feeling that you get when someone is watching you unawares. It saved his life, nonetheless.

Diving frantically out of the way, he tackled Firerose to the ground. Before they'd even hit the unyielding stone of the courtyard, a double handed broadsword being wielded by the Imbic construct behind them sailed overhead. Two of his mageguard escort had not been so lucky, one brutally cleaved in half, dead before his parts hit the stonework. The other was left screaming in pain and shock as his arm was severed above the elbow.

With its swing unsuccessful, the construct roared into motion, taking a step forward with murderous intent. Jayden dragged Firerose away from the thing's next strike. She was reacting more slowly than she should.

"Move!" Jayden shouted in panic, forcing himself to rise. The enormous sword hit the courtyard just behind them, and Jayden spun Firerose out of its range once more. As they landed in a tangle, all the wind was knocked out of him. He couldn't afford to stop. Taking hold of Clarion, he scrambled up and away despite the lack of air, trying desperately to get some distance between them and the flailing construct as it continued to advance.

The two remaining mageguard who had been out of range of its initial strike had reacted instantly, drawing their weapons, and attempting to gain the construct's attention.

Well before Jayden regained his feet, they were ineffectually attempting to delay the huge metal monster. It seemed intent on ignoring them, and continued coming after the two magi.

There was blood on Clarion's forehead, he finally had time to notice. She must have hit her head in the initial fall. Jayden continued dragging the concussed woman out of the way as the construct took yet another swipe at them, this time with the oversized flail held in its other hand. The thing was strong enough that it could wield each of the deadly weapons with no more difficulty than Jayden would have had using his own light Oo'vi blade.

The spiked ball of the flail missed by a foot as it swung towards them on its chain, shattering its way several inches into the paved ground. For a moment the weapon stuck in the cracked stonework, allowing Jayden to put a few spans between the two of them and the construct.

"Can you run?!" he shouted at Firerose as he blessedly succeeded in wrenching in a breath.

For a long moment she only held her head in her hands, blinking rapidly as he continued putting as much distance between them and the rogue construct as she could manage.

"I think so," she replied at last, but it was clear she could barely stand on her own. Once again he pulled her further away as the creature freed its weapon from the pavement, once more advancing on them.

"You two!" Jayden yelled at the remaining guards. "Get the wounded out of here. I can deal with this myself!"

Leaving no room for argument, he never took his eyes off the thing in front of him as the guards backed away. One of them darted around the construct to get to his fallen comrade. Slinging the dismembered soldier onto his shoulder, he stopped momentarily to hand the man his own severed arm to hold on to so that a mage could hopefully reattach it, and ran towards the college building. Meanwhile, the guard closer to Jayden withdrew from his defensive stance and sheathed his weapon. Wrapping Firerose's arm around his shoulder to support her weight, he half escorted, half carried the still disoriented noblewoman away from the fight.

Somewhere in the distance, the goat bleated while Firerose groggily complied with the guard, then gripped her head in her free hand as dizziness once again took hold. Even so, she stumbled onwards, and with his help stayed on her feet as they hobbled back towards the main college building as fast as she could go.

Jayden wanted to watch, to see she was safely away, but the construct was free. Lumbering forward again, it began swinging both of its weapons in a rapid succession of blows, any of which would have killed him had they connected.

Using an air spell he had recently learned, Jayden used his momentum to spring away from the rampaging machine. Once clear, he took a long moment to issue the hand movements necessary to activate the commands which would render the construct still, cancelling its orders.

Jayden frowned as the thing kept coming. He knew he had cast the spell correctly. It just hadn't worked. The construct lumbered forward again and once more Jayden sprung away to give himself time. Out of the corner of his eye, he saw Clarion had made it most of the way back to the safety of the building. Satisfied that she was no longer in any danger, he turned his attention to the matter at hand.

He threw the first thing he thought of at the construct, a fireball that would have left a good-sized house in ruins. Apart from making a large patch on the thing's metal chest glow red with the heat, it had no effect at all. He knew something of the blacksmith's trade from his family's business concerns, and it gave him an idea. With a deft motion, he pulled the water out of the surrounding air and turned it into ice, packing it as solidly as he could around the super-heated metal. There was a loud hissing for several moments, and the construct began to slow. Jayden took it for encouragement as he summoned a bolt of raw power to follow up. After taking a moment to erect a shield around himself, he flung the bolt of raw power at the creature's chest.

I should have thought of that as soon as the monster attacked, he chided himself. With a deafening crack, the weakened metal exploded, one of the construct's arms flying away across the courtyard as metal slivers tinkled down onto the stone ground around them.

Somehow Jayden found himself little more than bruised as he picked himself up from where the force of the violent explosion had flung him. His shield had been disrupted as he hit the ground.

He looked around and could only stare as the remnants of the thing that was supposed to be a training tool moved erratically towards him. The arm which had held the broadsword was gone, as well as most of its head and chest. The huge flail remained attached to its chain, and was ready to be used.

Jayden scowled. There was no longer any doubt in his mind that someone was controlling the construct. The things were designed to stop by default and lie down when they sustained a 'mortal' wound. The construct stumbled forward, and the thin strip of twisted metal which was all that remained of its torso sagged under the weight of the enormous weapon it carried. Jayden backed away, and within a dozen steps what was left of the construct's body snapped, sending its other arm clanking to the ground while the thing's legs wobbled onward.

Jayden abruptly remembered Tolmarak's tactic in the throne room. Using a simple spell of earth, he pulled the stones up from the surrounding brickwork to halt its already sketchy movements until help could arrive.

In the meantime, Jayden had more pressing concerns.

Looking around the dimly lit grounds of the college courtyard, Jayden searched for the target he almost knew had to be somewhere nearby. After only a few seconds of searching, he found his suspicion confirmed.

Half hidden around the corner of the stables was a figure he would not soon forget. Almost of a height with himself and cloaked and hooded beyond all further description, the assassin leant casually against the wall of the building.

The figure nodded respectfully, and Jayden could almost see the person beneath the hood grinning. Then with an unhurried gait, the assassin was gone, slinking around the corner as if he or she had never been there at all.

The casual indifference to having just tried to kill not only himself, but Firerose as well, made Jayden's blood boil as the attack itself had not. Before he fully knew what was happening, Jayden found himself running at full speed towards where the assassin had disappeared around the corner.

He didn't think he had ever been so mad in his life. *Well, apart from that one night.*

He rounded the corner, a protective shield already up in front of him this time. He had learned his harsh lesson about the assassin's tactics during their last encounter, and would not fall victim to that kind of surprise attack again.

Nothing happened as he cleared the building, and Jayden stopped, examining the area for his foe. Breathing hard more from fury than exertion, for a long moment all else was quiet. Then a dull flash from the direction of the guard post which led into the city. With a vague sense of déjà vu, Jayden once again used the levitation spell and sprung off after his target, covering twenty or thirty spans at a step. It was a useful little spell, this one, he thought as he rapidly covered the distance. To his dismay, he arrived too late. As he reached the guard post, shield still firmly in place, it was to discover the mageguard soldiers assigned there tonight had been slaughtered to a man.

A movement caught Jayden's eye, and without hesitation he sprung after the assassin, who had now entered the city proper and was still no closer than before.

The assassin glanced back and saw Jayden in pursuit. With startling ease, the figure jumped straight up onto the roof of a familiar three-storey building. It lay across the very same square where the destroyed structure from their last fight was still being rebuilt. The assassin once more turned, causing Jayden to smile. From this angle, the moon shone just brightly enough on the assassin to reveal that he was indeed a man. A man sneering down at the younger mage. There was not enough light to identify him further. Still, it was more than they'd known before tonight, and cut out half the population as suspects.

Realising his mistake, the assassin's smile dropped from his face, and he fled. With a tight smile of his own, Jayden ran towards the building. With as much force as he could muster, he used the levitation spell to propel himself up onto the roof. He overshot by a few feet and landed hard, barely keeping his balance on the tilted tile footing. Ahead of him, Jayden could see the assassin clearly. With a shout of rage used a hand motion to help focus his will into the strongest ball of flame he could. What came out shocked even him as he summoned up something more akin to a rope of flame than a ball. The mass of flame shot out from his hand, striking the assassin squarely in the back. It should have burned the man to a cinder, but he had his own shield in place. Instead, it knocked him sprawling, rolling wildly down the far side of the building until he was thrown out into mid-air, and disappeared over the edge. Jayden scrambled after him across the intervening buildings, but when he reached the ledge himself, the assassin was nowhere to be seen. Cursing himself for a fool, Jayden examined the street below for any avenue of escape or concealment which the laneway might offer. The low fence across the alley was the only place the assassin could have made it to in the short time he had been out of visual contact. Taking a few steps back, Jayden made a running leap and propelled himself onto the roof across the alleyway. A loose tile skittered down the slope of the building as he landed. Jayden kept his footing. He looked carefully over the peak of the structure he was now on, and down at the fence where he thought the assassin must be. A quick glance told him he was wrong, and Jayden bolstered his shield as he scanned the area, trying to locate the enemy mage. There was a thunderous crash as something blindingly bright hammered at his shield. It knocked him forward over the spine of the building, sending him tumbling head over heels towards the far edge. Before he could even get that far, another bolt of blue lightning appeared, punching upwards through the roof and only missing by a few feet.

Jayden let himself tumble from the rooftop to get away from his attacker. He used a spell of air to cushion his fall before climbing stiffly to his feet, then ducked around the edge of the structure.

"What's going on down there?" a demanding call came from one of the adjacent buildings.

Jayden ignored the woman's voice and darted around the corner of the structure to find the assassin once again had stayed a step ahead of him.

"Where are you?" he shouted as he scanned the surrounding area.

With a flash of insight, Jayden darted away from where he was standing and propelled himself into a nearby tree. From there he leapt to the rooftop of a building diagonally across from where he'd just been attacked. He couldn't see his previous location from here, but he could watch the only place that could. A moment later he realised his mistake. Just because he could not feel the assassin's aura, the same was not true in reverse. Jayden found himself stuck in a tree as the assassin appeared around the corner of an unexpected building.

Cursing himself for a fool, Jayden gathered his focus and hurled a bolt of raw power at the assassin as the man spotted his hiding place. The assassin tried to leap out of the way, but Jayden's reflexes had been faster, and his spell blew half the wall off the building. The assassin hurtled through the air to collide with the building behind, once again falling out of view. Without hesitation, Jayden propelled himself out of the tree with the Gift and over to the next building. From there he sprung to the next one, where he would be able to see his target on the street.

As he cleared the last obstacle, Jayden couldn't help but let out a growl of pure frustration as he discovered the assassin had once again eluded him.

"Where are you!" he shouted, starting a dog howling somewhere in the distance.

There was no response.

"Spread out and be careful. The assassin must be around here someplace," Tolmarak's distant voice reached Jayden's ears.

With a minor spell of flame, Jayden recreated the arrow signal from his last encounter with the assassin, and called back to the archmage. In moments the old man came into sight, flanked by half a dozen other magi, and at least a hundred of the mageguard. Some of them had not even had time to don armour by the looks of things.

"He was here less than a minute ago," Jayden called down, and the others spread out in groups no smaller than a dozen.

Without waiting for a reply, Jayden took off, leaping from one roof to another as he sought his quarry. As the minutes of fruitless searching went on, Jayden was forced to admit the assassin had once again escaped.

Clenching his fists in rage, he looked around one last time. There was nothing more he could do.

The acrid scent of smoke reached his nostrils like a splash of cold water.

Coming back to himself, Jayden looked around at the destruction their short duel had wrought on the residential area, and instantly felt guilty. Most of these buildings were houses, and the one the assassin had shot lightning through had begun to smoke. He put the small blaze out with a thought, and then jumped down into the most damaged part of the structure to make sure no one had been hurt. After a quick inspection he saw that although the damage to the roof was severe, its high sloped sides meant that only the attic had suffered major damage. Thankfully, no one appeared to be home. He jumped out again, propelling himself over to the building where he had last seen the assassin, and repeated his check. Again, no one seemed to be hurt. A grey cat didn't take too kindly to his intrusion, attempting to scratch him as he tried to coax it away from the rubble.

Leaving the creature be, he jumped out the hole in the roof. landing in the street below, this time he managed to keep his footing before setting off to find Tolmarak and report to the college's leader.

"It doesn't look like any civilians were hurt," he said without preamble once he located Tolmarak on the street.

"But we should check the damaged buildings more thoroughly."

The archmage raised an eyebrow, but nodded to a mage Jayden didn't know to carry out the task.

"So once again you survive," Tolmarak observed. "And this time you appear to have fared far better than the last."

"Yes, Archmage," Jayden answered, a little pleased with himself.

"You fool boy!" Tolmarak yelled at him. "That construct could never have overcome a mage of your power!"

Jayden recoiled in confusion at his mentor's harsh tone.

"There was only one reason for the assassin to strike at you that way. To get you mad enough to follow him into the city where he could attack you without interference from the rest of us!"

Tolmarak's shoulders slumped as he shook his head, "You played into his hands exactly as he had planned."

Jayden felt his jaw working, trying to get something out in return, but with a sinking feeling realised the old archmage was right. His shoulders slumped as Tolmarak's had a moment before, and the archmage relented.

"Jayden, you have to realise that as the most powerful mage in Aramar, maybe in Jeranon itself, you are a target for all of our enemies. Whether or not you will it, they will see you as our greatest asset, and therefore their biggest threat. You must not allow them the victory of… neutralising you. Do you understand?"

"Yes, Archmage," Jayden replied dejectedly, feeling even more out of control of his own destiny than ever.

"At least I learned something about the assassin this time," he added, looking Tolmarak in the eye once more.

"You did?" the old archmage returned, sudden hope and curiosity lighting his weathered features.

"For a moment as I was pursuing him, he was standing at

just the right angle that left his face partially exposed to the moonlight. It wasn't enough to make out any of his features sufficiently to identify him," Jayden spoke quickly, holding his hands up defensively at the sudden excitement in Tolmarak's eyes.

"But the person we have been chasing is definitely a man."

"I see," Tolmarak returned, losing a good deal of his excitement. "Well, at least that cuts out half the population as suspects."

"That was my thought as well," Jayden replied. "I'm sorry I couldn't get more. I take it Clarion is all right?"

"Yes, Archmage Trellis and I both happened to be in the main foyer when the group came in. The construct did little damage to her aside from a nasty lump and mid-range concussion, but Sarah was able to fix those without difficulty. The mageguard soldier was another matter, but Archmage Trellis is the best we have, and is currently reattaching the limb. What is more, because the cut was so clean, Sarah thinks he will most likely regain either full use of his arm, or something very close to it."

"Good," Jayden responded. "But this is exactly why I told you I didn't want an escort. There is a dead man out in the courtyard now for no reason at all except that he happened to be standing near me."

Tolmarak stared at Jayden for a long second once the younger man had finished, then spoke in very certain terms.

"That man died fulfilling his duty, Jayden. He understood the reasons behind it, and believed he was doing the right thing by keeping you as safe as he possibly could. He did it so that Jeranon itself would be the stronger for your continued presence. Make no mistake, young Clarion was in no form to fight, or even retreat by herself. She is only alive because one of those mageguard soldiers you so readily dismiss was able to guide her safely away from the fight. Did you think the word 'mageguard' was a ceremonial title? You dishonour the man who died by saying he was there for no reason! You dishonour the men who survived by not acknowledging they did their duty well. Even in obeying your orders to retreat, they preserved Firerose's life by removing her from danger when she could no longer defend herself!"

For a long time Jayden just stared Tolmarak in the eye, unwilling to back down. The old anger seethed through him even without related cause, but privately, as the awkward seconds went on, he was once again forced to grudgingly accept the old man's wisdom. This was indeed what the men of the mageguard willingly signed on for. What they trained and fought for. Even knowing they might die doing so.

"All that aside, you kept two of your men from harm under difficult circumstances. Another will recover, and Firerose was only slightly hurt. For an ambush such as the one the surviving men described, that is about as good a result as anyone has a right to expect."

Jayden grudgingly accepted the assessment, knowing there was little else he could have done to prevent the injuries his companions had sustained in the heat of the moment. He felt bad about being the direct cause of Firerose's injury however, slight though it was.

"Actually, it was my fault that she was hurt," he owned up after a moment.

Tolmarak harrumphed at that. "Hardly. From what she told us, your quick action was the only thing that kept both of your heads on your shoulders. And she holds no grudge about it. Quite the opposite in fact."

"Good," Jayden replied, feeling vastly more relieved than the situation warranted. He turned the sudden rush of emotion over in his head for a long moment before it hit him.

She is not *Rhianna,* he told himself sternly within the confines of his own mind.

"Are you all right?" Tolmarak asked, frowning at his silent change of expression.

"Yes, Archmage," he answered mechanically, retreating to formality as he struggled to clear his mind of the sudden rush of images that cascaded unbidden into his thoughts.

Although Clarion was almost Rhianna's perfect double physically, personality wise, they were two very different young women. Knowing that fact did absolutely nothing to stop Jayden feeling uncomfortably aware, every single time he looked at her, of what he could never get back.

He was trying to put it all behind him, as Tolmarak wanted him to do. But this constant reminder he had to live with every day was enough to drive any man to breaking point. He had tried to get to know her, even to become friends with her over the past few phases. To show himself once and for all. To draw a distinct line in his mind that she was not Rhianna, no matter how alike they looked. But if his reaction just now had proved anything beyond a doubt, it was that he had failed miserably in that endeavour.

"If you'll excuse me Archmage, I think I need to rest."

"Of course," Tolmarak allowed after a moment of consideration.

The archmage had been about to say something else. Apparently it could wait though, because he ordered two of the other magi and fifty of the mageguard to accompany

Jayden back to his rooms. It was overkill, he thought, since he had been the only one to survive the assassin's attacks, not once now, but twice.

All he wanted right now was to be alone with his thoughts, which had once more turned darkly towards Dael.

As he set out towards the college with clenched fists and the mageguard compliment guarding him in formation, Jayden wondered how much longer he could make himself stay here in Aramar. Every day he felt his resolve wearing thinner, becoming more stretched out. Every time he was forced to violence it was harder, and taking him longer to regain his composure, and he had long since given up on stemming the nightmares. He wanted nothing more than to walk away, to go now, this very night, to end the man who had abused and killed his love. Yet the people here had been good to him. Even in his fury, Jayden acknowledged that without the friendship of Wyll, Tolmarak, and the others, he never would have made it this far. He couldn't just leave them to the assassin's ministrations.

It was a long walk back to the college building in the cool night breeze. By the time they approached the grounds and passed through the hastily re-manned gate, a mage now added to the watch, Jayden nodded silently, making himself a promise. He would find the assassin, somehow, and as Tolmarak had said, neutralise him. Then, on the instant his friends and mentor were safe, he would leave, whether he had the old archmage's blessing or not. And return to Grandell, for Dael.

CHAPTER 8

THE WRAITH WOODS

It had taken almost two weeks of hard riding to reach this point. Wyll slowed Socks to a canter as they rounded a large rock pile, then halted as his squad came within view of their target.

The first week out of Aramar had been slow going, constantly bogged down by the snow and slush which covered the ground around this part of Jeranon at winter's dusk each year. Once the road had dried out, they had made much better progress.

"There it is," Kienan announced, the last to leave the outcropping of rock behind. Before them, the Wraith Woods stood, revealed in all their twisted grandeur.

Less than half a mile ahead, the wall of misshapen trunks waited, brooding as they watched the small group of men approach. The first in many, many years.

"This is not a good place," Sarran declared, breaking the oppressive silence which had fallen over the men.

"Come on," Wyll told them as he moved Socks out ahead of the others.

When they were about halfway between the rock outcropping and the tree line, a sudden squall of wind picked up without warning. The horses whickered in fear as the giant trees at the outer edge of the woods bent low towards them, seeming to reach out further than could be explained by mere air movement alone. An eerie keening began to issue from the forest.

It took almost half a minute for the unnatural cry to fall quiet, the haunting wind dying as suddenly as it had come. Without the wind behind them, the trees returned to their normal positions, though the men's hearts refused to comply so easily.

"What was that?!" Sarran demanded once he had his horse under control, giving voice to the strangeness they all felt as they stood exposed in the open field. The unbroken wall of trees before them stretched high above a barren, rocky strip of ground surrounding the woods as far as the eye could see. If he didn't know better, Wyll would have sworn that even the surrounding plant life were afraid to venture too close.

But I do know better, Wyll reminded himself sternly.

"Calm yourselves," Seth told the other men without taking his eyes from the scene in front of them. "If there *is* something in there, a clear mind and a sharp sword will serve you better than fear and panic."

Sarran swallowed, but nodded at the warrior's words as he unlimbered his blade in its scabbard, not to mention checking the staff which was slung across his back.

Wyll looked around at his men, then west towards a sun sinking behind the tree line in the far distance, before coming to a decision.

"We'll return to the shelter of the rock wall and make

camp for the night. I see no advantage in attempting this in the dark," he told them as steadily as he could.

It took some effort, but Wyll turned Socks and managed to calmly walk him back to the nearby outcropping. Having his back exposed to the strange forest felt like someone was about to strike him from behind. Nevertheless, the others followed his example, and made it around the corner and into the shelter of the rock pile without incident. Once they were away from the strange wind and out of sight of the forest, the feeling ceased almost immediately. That was a cause for concern in itself.

"See to the camp, and Sarran, make sure to pile the fire high tonight," Wyll ordered, more to give the man something to do than for any practical reason. At least that's what he told himself as he dismounted and passed Socks' reins to Cale, whose turn it was to care for the animals.

Gathering his resolve, Wyll walked back around the corner of the outcropping, and was instantly drawn into the sight of the trees swaying in the unsteady breeze. The keening was just audible from here whenever the wind picked up, and Wyll found himself straining to hear the almost hypnotic sound.

With a start, he realised Seth was standing beside him, and had been for some time. The man was staring into the forest the same absent way Wyll had found himself just a moment before. It made him wonder how long he'd been standing there like that, transfixed by the sight, before Seth had joined him.

"I care not for this place," Seth said, quiet enough that none of the others could hear from their sheltered position behind the rock wall.

They were only six small words, but they sent a chill down Wyll's spine more acutely than the keening or the groping tree limbs had done.

"Nor I," he responded in just as hushed a tone.

"There seems… a malice about this place, as though the very trees themselves wish us harm."

"Nonetheless, at daybreak we will attempt to cross them, whether they will it or not," Wyll responded, determined to keep everyone's morale as high as he could, including his own. Judging from tonight's performance, he already knew that as soon as they entered the looming trees, the men were going to get skittish. He just wished he could shake the nagging feeling of unseen eyes watching his back, which had returned almost instantly once he left the shelter of the outcropping. The men behind the rock wall seemed unaffected as they continued setting up the camp.

He had shared none of Tolmarak's talk about fate and prophecies with his men. His men. That still sounded strange to Wyll, even though he had been in command for a few phases now. They were finally starting to trust him as a leader, and he had no intention of undermining that faith with any information other than that the archmage believed they could win through.

Wyll stared across the barren stretch, the wind whipped trees dancing in the last rays of sunlight. He couldn't shake the feeling that something was very wrong with what he was seeing. It was almost as if the world didn't work right here. All the sun and light in the sky made no impact past the first row of towering boles lined up in perfect unison. It was almost as if the forest had been designed, rather than grown.

Again the wind howled, and all along the front row of the woods, trees bent down at what Wyll now saw from this distance was an impossible angle, every limb and branch straining towards where Wyll and Seth stood. In all the ghastly sight though, the thing that made the hair on the back of his neck stand straight up was the fact that the trees to the south were not pointing in the same direction as those to the north. Rather, each and every one of those appalling shapes was stretching directly out to where the two men now stood perfectly still. Their basest instincts forcing them to act like nothing more than small animals hiding from a predator, desperately hoping not to be noticed.

A moment later the wind died down, the trees returning to normal as though nothing had ever been amiss.

Wyll looked at Seth, whose eyes were wide, his hands clenched in fists.

"Tell no one about this," Wyll told him. "That's an order."

Seth tore his eyes away from the woods and then, after a long moment, gave a brisk nod.

Wyll let out a relieved breath. At least it would have been relieved if he hadn't just seen what he had. At any rate, Seth would keep his mouth shut. The man was smart enough to realise the effect that news of what they'd just witnessed would do to the others' already dented morale.

It was hard not to hurry back into the false shelter of the outcropping, but the two men kept their apprehension well hidden, their eyes locked on the camp.

Once again, the sensation of malice disappeared almost completely as soon as they were behind the rock wall. With a last significant glance, Wyll and Seth separated to see to their own duties. By the time Wyll had his tent set up, Sarran had a roaring blaze going. Charran had gone to gather the water from a nearby creek, and Kienan was cutting up dried vegetables and adding them to the pot for tonight's soup. Cale had brought down a Coney with his bow earlier in the day, so they would have at least a little fresh meat in the soup, which was always welcome on the road.

When they had first left Aramar, there had been almost no game. With the snows all but melted now, they were sighting birds and animals more frequently each day. Wyll estimated that in another fortnight they would be able to hunt enough that rations would no longer be an issue.

It was almost another hour until Kienan declared that dinner was ready. That meant only that the dried vegetables had softened enough to be edible, but the men fell to with an appetite. For a long time, the only sounds in the camp were the slurping of soup, and the horses. The animals were picketed further back along the rock wall, and were busy munching oats while the men finished their food. Wyll had to admit the meal was pretty good, all things considered, but then it was gone.

There was little talk that night. All of them knew what awaited the squad once the sun rose, and none of them felt easy about it. No one had suggested not going through with it yet, which was about as much as he could hope for, given the circumstances. After all, while they might be in the mageguard, only a few of the men had any genuine experience as soldiers. Add to that it had been almost nine hundred years since anyone had successfully accomplished what they were about to attempt, and Wyll would count himself happy if he woke in the morning to find no one had snuck off during the night.

For some reason that made him think about Marad, and

what the large man might have done if he'd lived long enough to be part of this mission.

Probably sit around whining about all the reasons we shouldn't be doing it, Wyll thought with regret. That in turn made him consider what Brendan might have done under these same circumstances. The tall, tattooed man had always had an answer, or known how to find it. Still, all Wyll could think of to do was obey his orders and hope to the Maker that Tolmarak knew what he was talking about with all that fate stuff.

Otherwise, come first light, I will lead every one of these men into their graves.

He stood and moved over to the water bucket to wash his bowl.

"All right," he said to get the men's attention. "Let's keep watch by pairs at all times tonight. We all know what's out there, and I won't have us being ambushed before we've even entered those woods. So Kienan, Charran, you're first, then Seth and Sarran, finally Bosric and Tauman. Three-hour shifts and we leave at dawn. I want to be as far through that forest as possible before night falls."

There was a chorus of 'yes sir's' and nods, and Wyll moved towards his tent.

"Tauman, wake Cale and I an hour before dawn so we can see to the camp. Everyone else get some sleep. I have a feeling we're going to need it tomorrow."

Again the nods came as his words sank in, and the men began drifting off towards their tents even as Wyll entered his own. He removed his boots, but couldn't bring himself to divest his body of the thick leather armour he was now used to. He lay on the thin sleeping mat for some time before drifting into an uneasy sleep filled with dreams of inhuman figures, and trees that moved without the aid of the wind.

*   *   *

"Sir?" was the first thing Wyll heard as he awoke in his tent.

"It's time, Sir," Tauman repeated as Wyll returned to consciousness and waved the man at his tent flap away.

He sat up, purposefully donned his boots, and began stowing what little gear he had back into his pack. Once done, he met Cale outside, and the two men began feeding and saddling the horses. After that, they doused the fire, dismantled their own tents, and stowed their gear in the packhorses' bags.

The first glimmer of pre-dawn stained the eastern sky.

It was time to get on with this. Wyll ordered that the others be woken, and the rest of the men dressed and began stowing their gear. After a quick breakfast, they dismantled the camp, and within a quarter hour the men were waiting by their horses, ready to leave.

Wyll found himself more thankful than he probably should be that all of them were still present. If any of their number had deserted, it would have destroyed the squad's morale completely, and was the reason he had set the sentries in pairs. No one had tried though, and Wyll now trusted these men far more than he had the previous day, or any other since Karthael had placed him in command.

"Did anyone see anything unusual during their watch?" Wyll asked as he mounted up, the others following suit.

No one replied except to shake their head in the negative, and Wyll was relieved.

"All right then, you all know what is at stake on this mission. The outcome of the entire spring campaign may well depend on us pushing through the Wraith Woods and delivering vital information to General Messand. The archmage believes we can succeed in this task. He would not have entrusted such a valuable relic as the Chalice of Ajerio to us if he did not."

There were nods all around, some determined, others unsure.

"I don't know what's in there, but keep your eyes peeled and your swords ready. Whatever the rumours and stories claim, somewhere within these woods lies a real and substantial cause as to why no one has crossed this forest in nearly nine hundred years. We *must* not fall prey to it. Archmage Volnar's best estimate was that crossing the woods at this point will take us three days. I want to be through it in two. Think on it gentlemen, nine hundred years. Today we set the count back to zero."

This time there were determined nods all round. That was good, because he had run out of things to say.

"Are there any questions?" he asked, not expecting Bosric to raise his hand.

"Yes," he allowed, motioning at the short red headed man.

"Can I have my statue made of stone? I don't think I'd look very dashing in bronze."

For a moment Wyll looked at the short man, nonplussed.

"If you make it to the other side, I'll see what I can do," Wyll told him with a smile. He turned Socks to face the end of the outcropping, and took a deep breath.

"Let's go," he said, setting Socks to a canter with his knees.

A few minutes' ride was all it took to bring them back to the very edge of the forest. Wyll slowed Socks to a walk as he surveyed the now normal looking trees for the easiest path through.

After a few moments of searching, Wyll realised there would be no straightforward path through such an undisturbed forest. Taking a deep breath, he decided that this was as good a place as any. With a flick of the reins, he moved Socks under the first row of gnarled trees while the others followed behind.

Wyll looked around at the silent spectacle. Aside from his men, nothing moved under the canopy of the ancient forest. With a small shiver, he realised that not even the birds made their home in this place.

With his hand on his sword hilt, Wyll guided Socks forward, every sense alert as he left the sunlight, entering the sudden dimness of the woods. As he passed through the first row of giant trees, a sudden gust of wind picked up, swirling leaves and branches all around them.

It was a natural wind this time, causing the trees to move only as they should.

Once Wyll had his heartbeat under control again, he extracted his hand from the hilt of his blade and looked back at the others.

"Move out!" he called a little too harshly as he kneed Socks back to a canter.

While the Wraith Woods were wild land in the truest sense, there appeared to be almost no undergrowth beneath the canopy. Further beneath the trees, even the contours in the land seemed somehow suppressed.

So long as we don't make contact with whatever creature haunts this place, we should, for now at least, make good time.

There was no way to tell for certain as the thick forest canopy obscured the sun, but at what Wyll assumed to be around midday, he called for a brief halt when they chanced across a shallow stream.

"Water and feed the horses, and get your own provisions from your packs. We'll eat in the saddle today," he ordered as he peered into the silent gloom around them.

There had been little conversation that morning, but that was all to the good since it meant the men were paying more attention to their surroundings.

A lark called from somewhere off in the distance, making most of the men jump after the total silence which had encompassed them all morning. There was some nervous laughter at each other over that, but when the bird call cut off a moment later, so did the men's laughter. The compulsive silence of the place shifting to oppressive in the blink of an eye.

On the other side of the stream, about twenty spans from where they were stopped, there was a sudden movement in the bushes.

Within a heartbeat, every member of the squad had their weapons ready in hand as they spun to see what was happening.

For a long time there was no further movement as the men peered into the dark gloom of the forest, ready for anything to appear in the shadows beyond the river.

"Tauman, Kienan, light torches and pass them out," Wyll ordered without taking his eyes off the spot where the undergrowth had moved.

In less than a minute the men had taken the brands from one of the packhorses and struck sparks to light them. Wyll took the first and motioned Cale and Seth to follow as he dismounted and began making his way across the ankle-deep stream on foot. The torchlight shimmered on the slowly moving surface as he made his way closer to where they had seen the movement. By the time he was a dozen steps away, Cale and Seth were flanking him while the others had mounted, ready to back them up should the need arise.

There had still been no further movement in the bush, so using the silent hand signals Cale had been teaching them, Wyll motioned for his men on foot to surround the large plant. The signals were another way for the tongueless man to communicate even though he couldn't speak, but Wyll also found them very useful to coordinate troop movements without making noise.

When the others were in place, Wyll stepped forward, keeping his balance steady as Karthael had shown him a swordsman should, and trying to control his breathing. Another step, then another, and still no movement. Wyll extended his sword arm and slowly pushed back the top layer of foliage with the tip of his blade. As the leaves parted before him, Wyll was both relieved and dismayed by what he found. With a quick look around the dim forest, Wyll knelt to examine his grisly discovery a little more thoroughly.

It was the lark which had been calling a moment before. It had fallen, or from the look of it, been thrown down from high above once something had finished with it. Bringing the torchlight in closer, Wyll used the end of his sword to flip the dead bird over. A shiver ran unchecked down his spine as he stood and backed away, looking high into the trees as he moved. The bird looked to have been ripped from one end to the other by brute force. Its internal organs removed in what must have been the mere moments between when its call cut off and when they had heard it hitting the bushes. Wyll turned in a circle, looking up as he did. But once more there was only silence in the Wraith Woods. Not even the breeze stirred here.

"Back to the horses," Wyll ordered, and in moments the squad was riding as fast as Wyll could lead them in the increasingly dim light.

Eventually they had to slow, and Wyll ordered the men to dismount and walk the horses for a while. He could neither see nor hear anything threatening, and hadn't since the stream. Something had killed that bird though, and the feeling they were being watched had returned shortly after, refusing to go away again no matter how much he willed it.

Another hour passed, and they rode and walked the horses until a time when what little light remained to them drifted away. Full nightfall had come to the outside world. Wyll's training told him to call a halt for the sake of the horses, but he couldn't bring himself to just wait here. He ordered the men to dismount and lead the animals, and they walked for another five or six miles until even Wyll's nervous energy was spent. He called an end to the march when they found another of the small streams which crisscrossed the woods at almost regular intervals.

"Sarran, Bosric, Cale, gather wood for a fire and make sure it burns high all night. Tauman, Kienan, see to the horses. Everyone else stand guard. No one strays more than fifty feet from the fire for any reason tonight."

There were no vocal responses to his order, but the men moved off and set about their tasks with a hushed determination that bespoke their apprehension.

Once the horses were seen to, Wyll ordered Tauman and

Kienan to prepare the squad's meal before rifling through his saddlebags to find the map which Archmage Tolmarak had added to their packhorses' panniers before they left. There was little information to be gained from it except the marked route and the total distance from one edge to the other, which some enterprising cartographer had made centuries ago by traversing the outside of the woods, and marking out its boundaries. Wyll could only guess at how far they'd come. From the speed and time they had travelled, he calculated they must be somewhere between a third and halfway through the designated route.

Wyll sighed. He had not wanted to spend a second night in these woods, but they had made the best time possible today, and not quite made it halfway. The thought of spending another night in here made Wyll's skin crawl. There was something that just wasn't right about this place, and he still couldn't shake the feeling they were being watched, which was why he had ordered the fire. Whatever was out there in the darkness, it already knew where they were. Of that much he was certain.

Soon the men had a roaring blaze going. Unlike in the Emerald Sea, they had no compunction about ripping the nearby plants apart to get the wood and kindling to start the smoky blaze. Less than an hour later they were eating the habitual reconstituted soup and bread they were all used to by now. The shallow stream provided more than enough fresh water for them to drink and wash up in. No one was in a mood for small talk, and Wyll wanted to get as early a start as possible. He still had some small hope they could reach the edge of the forest without spending another night under the silent watchfulness of these woods, and whatever lurked within.

"We'll take watch in threes tonight. Sarran, Charran and Cale. Bosric, Kienan and myself, then Seth, Tauman and I'll pull the double shift. I intend to push us hard tomorrow, so get what rest you can."

"No Sir," Kienan answered as all eyes turned towards him.

"What I mean is, I'll take the double shift, Sir. With all due respect, we need you to be focused and alert tomorrow since you'll be the one making the decisions. It just makes more sense if I do it, Sir."

For a long moment Wyll didn't know what to say. He had to maintain his authority, but how to tell someone off when they were doing you a favour?

For an instant his eyes caught Seth's and the tall, shaven headed warrior nodded almost imperceptibly in approval.

"All right," Wyll conceded after a moment, "Thank you Kienan. Seth, a word if you please. Everyone else not on duty, turn in," he told them and then left the circle of firelight behind while the other man joined him.

"Why should I let Kienan take the shift when I had just given other orders?" he asked once they were out of earshot of the others.

Although Seth was one of his men, he was also by far the most veteran warrior among the squad, and Wyll valued the man's opinion and advice.

"You've done well in your new rank until now," Seth returned without preamble. "But shouldering the burden, and the responsibility, is enough weight to crush any man. You must learn to give your men trust if you are to gain theirs as well. Also, never allow yourself to forget that while you started out as these men's friend, you are now their commanding officer. You must never become so close that you cannot order them to perform a duty, risk their lives, or even send them to their death should the worst outcome occur."

"I am already not sure if I could," Wyll confided.

"That only shows that you are a good man, Wyll of Grandell. But should the situation ever arrive, you must think on what is to be gained by such a sacrifice, not only on what is being lost."

Wyll nodded, accepting the man's advice, even while hoping he would never need it.

His eyes sketched over the surrounding trees again, and he couldn't help but frown into the now oppressive darkness. He was glad the men had the fire going so soon. Visibility was down to less than a hundred feet now that night had fallen. The bonfire cast a multitude of flickering shadows on the sides of the trees facing it, creating flickers of movement which grabbed at the mind. Even that was better than the oppressive darkness beyond. Above them, the canopy of branches was invisible except where burning cinders reached up towards it. With no stars or a moon capable of shining down through the thick, layered foliage, it appeared as though they had descended into a vast, living cave.

So far their journey had been easy though, and Wyll allowed himself to think that just maybe they could get through the woods unscathed. That maybe Tolmarak *had* recognised the right of it with all that destiny talk.

And then he saw the eye.

Placing a silent hand on Seth's arm, he nodded in the direction where he had seen the creature. Its attention was focused not on them for the moment, but on the men still building up a fine woodpile that would soon become a second roaring blaze.

Seth nodded back and unsheathed his sword. Wyll circled around the creature, trying hard not to draw attention as he led Seth in a wide arc, attempting to come out behind whatever it was they had seen.

A few minutes later the second fire was kindled. As the bonfire roared to life, the two men could see the outline of a grotesque creature now that it was between the fire and themselves. Whatever it was, the insectile thing had four chitin covered legs on which it stood upright. Or would have had it not been crouching behind a bush, watching with clear agitation as the fire gained momentum. Its spiked tail looked something like a scorpion's, and its thorax was thin and hard with a shiny, armoured covering. In its left fore-claw Wyll could see what looked to be a well-made trident held steady, and with full notion of what the weapon was about.

The thing reared back, raising the trident in preparation to throw the triple pronged spear at Kienan, who happened to be the nearest target. Wyll shouted to distract it even as he charged.

The thing spun, startled, reflexively throwing the trident at him instead. The creature was off balance as it threw, and Wyll was able to deflect the weapon enough with his sword that it missed entirely.

Once it saw its error, the thing growled at them with a mouth full of inch long teeth. A pair of red eyes were the only other feature visible on its emaciated face as the firelight silhouetted it. Without further challenge, it turned and darted off into the brush, and within a few steps it was moving as fast as a good horse could run.

By the time the two men had pursued it as far as the edge of the firelight, it had already well outdistanced them, vanishing into the darkness.

"What, exactly, was that?" Wyll asked Seth as the two of them stood at the edge of the circle of light. The rest of the men had taken up a defensive position around the fires as soon as Wyll had shouted. Wyll and Seth both stood, straining their eyes and ears for any sign of the creature's passage or intent. After a long minute it became clear that it wasn't coming back, and Seth finally spoke.

"I have never seen or heard of its like. We should examine its weapon."

Wyll nodded his agreement, and after backing away several paces the two men turned. Having their backs to the darkness, and whatever else it held, was by no means a comfortable experience for either of them. A few moments of searching led them to where the trident lay embedded in a nearby tree, and a sharp yank allowed Wyll to dislodge it. As Seth joined him, he noticed with an increasing level of agitation that the weapon was expertly made. The metal was well forged, and the wooden shaft carved and smoothed with a quality of work that would have impressed most of the tradesmen in Aramar.

"Careful of the tips," Seth warned, and as Wyll examined them, he noticed the slight discolouration of the metal.

"Poison?" he asked the veteran warrior beside him.

"It looks that way, though from the colour I am unfamiliar with the particular one. Perhaps something native to this forest?"

"Let's get back to the others," Wyll decided, and without further conversation the two men headed back into the firelight, which offered warmth at least, if not comfort this night.

"Stay on your guard," he told them as he approached. "Whatever that thing was, it was attempting to attack you with this when we intercepted it."

He hefted the trident as he spoke, and the quality of the workmanship was not lost on the men.

"It knew how to use its weapon, and the prongs appear to be coated in poison, so despite its alien appearance, it was most definitely not an animal. Now, I don't want to stay here anymore than you do, but we cannot move forward in this darkness. So the watches stand. Sleep in your armour, sound the alarm at the first sign of movement, and stay alert. If there are more of those things out there, they could well be the danger that haunts this place. try to get what sleep you can. We will leave the instant it's light enough to lead the horses on foot."

He nodded to the rest of the squad before moving off towards the kettle, intent on cleaning it of the nightly meal. He did a poor job as his attention remained focused on the forest beyond the campsite. After a few tense minutes, the others broke up. The three guards continued their vigil while the others went about the business of setting up their sleeping rolls, casting nervous looks towards the forest all the while. By silent agreement, no one seemed to want to be confined to a tent this night. There was little more talk from that point on, and Wyll was glad for the silence. It would make it easier to hear if anything tried to sneak up and surprise them again during the long hours before dawn.

*   *   *

It was hours later when a hand shook Wyll awake.

The darkness beyond their fire was complete now, and after half a groggy second, Wyll reflexively reached for the blade stowed beneath his small pillow.

"It's ok," Charran's voice reached him as he woke. "It's

just your watch, Sir. So far there's been nothing to report."

Wyll grunted as he shook his head to clear away the sleepiness, thanking the man with a nod. Charran returned the gesture before moving off to get a drink and head to his own sleeping roll to grab a few hours' sleep. Wyll rose, and taking his own cup, dipped it into the water bucket which someone had filled from the stream. He took a long drink of the liquid before returning the cup to his pack. Wyll rubbed the last vestiges of sleep from his eyes. Moving into position, he nodded to Kienan and Bosric as he took his place on the other side of the fire, and began his watch.

For the first hour, Wyll strained both his eyes and ears towards the all-enclosing darkness which surrounded them. From this close to the fires there was nothing to find, not even the sound of the trees swishing. Only the dull crackling of the bonfires behind him broke the absolute silence that pressed in all around.

"Hold your positions," he told the other sentries. "I'm going to do a sweep."

Taking a deep breath, Wyll started forward into the darkness. When he was a little under fifty feet from the fire, he stopped and peered out into the blackness, trying to adjust his eyes while searching for any sign of movement. When that failed, he closed them with a shiver and strained to hear any hint of the foliage being disturbed. There was nothing, and yet something wasn't right. This deep in the Wraith Woods, no wind stirred the ancient trees, no bird sang out in greeting. Even the very air itself seemed still, somehow staler than forest air had any right to be.

After a long minute of motionless observance, Wyll began to circle the fire to his right, making his way around the very edge of its light. All the while he peered into the blackness beyond, attempting to get a better view of their surrounds than could be seen from near the light of the twin fires.

It took him half an hour to complete his cautious circuit. By the time he returned to where he had begun, Wyll had the unmistakable feeling that he was being watched by something unfriendly.

Once again, he peered into the darkness, his inspection failing to turn up any solid proof to back up the hairs now standing at attention on the nape of his neck. He had little choice but to return to the fire.

Wyll eased his sword in its scabbard and returned to his post, every sense alert as he stood the rest of his watch. There was something out there in the blackness. He was sure of it now, even if his mutinous eyes and ears told him otherwise. But the horses couldn't continue in this darkness, so all he could do was stare and listen. And hope the reason the creature had been watching them from beyond the frail circle of firelight, was not that it had been waiting for its friends.

CHAPTER 9

THE FOREST TEMPLE

So far, so good, Wyll thought as the squad readied themselves to leave the dying campfires behind.

They had made it through till morning without further incident, despite the sensation of unfriendly glares growing more persistent as the night wore on.

There was now the vaguest hint of light from above. Just enough to lead the horses by, and no more. Wyll ordered the men to prepare.

All of them were eager to be off, and in less than a minute the fires were hissing and spluttering, and the last remnants of the camp were stowed. Wyll took a moment to speak to his squad.

"Be on your guard. Something is out there, and it is at least as aware of us as we are of it. I don't mean to spend another night in here, so let's move."

He took Socks by the reins and led the mostly white rahiri mount on foot across the shallow stream, and deeper into the woods. There were soft splashing sounds as the others crossed. Wyll ignored them, his eyes scanned the forest as they passed the spot where the insectile creature had been hiding last night. There was no sign of it now, nor of anything like it. The vanishingly small amount of light making its way through the canopy above didn't help. He was less than certain he could have spotted one of the creatures' dark, chitinous exoskeletons from more than a dozen spans away.

It was not a pleasant thought, and Wyll beat it down as he continued to scan the forest for anything unusual. The feeling of being watched suddenly intensified. He was not the only one who felt it, and had to take the reins more firmly as Socks took a few sideways steps, uttering a nervous wicker.

Nothing came bursting out of the underbrush, and for the next hour they continued moving forward as quickly as they could. Apart from the occasional equine snort, the silence was absolute as dawn broke in the outside world. The canopy here near the heart of the Wraith Woods was impermeable. Dark and solid above them, it resisted the sun's influence well enough that only the dim glow of a quarter-moon night broke through, creating more shadow than useful light along their path.

Again, Wyll ordered torches be handed out. Once the men had the burning brands lit, he ordered them to mount up, though in retrospect it would have been easier to do it the other way around. He would remember that for next time, but for now the men were ready, so he gave the order to ride.

In a few moments, the squad was travelling at a good canter. Their combined torchlight created a moving pool around them as they headed east into the thickest part of the forest. Another hour passed, and they pushed the horses as hard as was safe in the dim light. Wyll found himself grateful that the sparse undergrowth near the border of the woods had continued underneath the thick canopy.

He judged it about midday when he called a halt.

"Ten-minute break to feed and water the horses. Grab your own rations. We'll eat in the saddle," he told the others quietly. This was not a place one shouted.

He was just about to follow his order and dismount when he saw them. Right in front of him and not ten paces away, a blazing pair of red eyes had opened. Or perhaps they were reflecting the light of the burning torches, his mind supplied as the initial shock wore off.

"Remount!" he shouted as a second pair of eyes appeared off to his right. Wyll drew his sword, which jolted the others into action, and they followed suit as quickly as possible.

Not fast enough, Wyll thought grimly as at least a hundred pairs of eyes started opening all around. Their red gazes turned balefully towards the intruders.

Charran jumped back into his saddle, the last to do so, and drew his staff, wielding the bladed weapon as though it were a lance.

"Take point!" Wyll shouted at the brown-haired wrestler.

Without hesitation, the big man nodded and kicked his brown stallion into a straight gallop while the rest of the squad fell in behind. Wyll took up position as rear guard, and nearly took a flying trident in the side for his trouble. He ducked low and booted Socks into a gallop after the others. For long moments they ran the horses between the dimly lit boles, their sudden flight further into the woods seeming to catch the creatures off guard. As Wyll returned his gaze to what was in front of him, he saw a dark blur swinging down from a long vine and shouted a warning.

It was too late. The creature tackled Kienan to the ground before he even saw it coming. Without direction, the packhorses the man had been leading scattered, and were gone in an instant. Ahead of him, Tauman pulled on his reins, turning his mount towards where Kienan was about to be set upon by more of the creatures. Wyll saw it as well and turned Socks to help.

The men ahead had their own problems, and the sound of trees being disturbed was now coming from every side. Wyll knew they had only moments to get away before being overrun by whatever these insectile assailants were.

Tauman rode past the creature, swinging his sword as he passed in a blow that would have split an unarmoured man in two. Unfortunately, the creatures' skin proved to be every bit as hard as it had looked the previous night. There was a dull thud as Tauman's sword cracked the carapace for about a foot along its back. The injury caused the creature to drop its hold on Kienan as it screamed shrilly.

It's more angry than hurt, Wyll noted as he charged it on his own pass. These things were tough, and definitely not stupid. When it saw him bearing down, the creature launched itself at Socks' legs, avoiding his blade altogether.

Tangling itself there, it knocked the horse off balance and sent Wyll flying over Socks' head as they both crashed ingloriously to the ground. He fell hard and lost his breath, though somehow kept a grip on his sword. As he scrambled to his feet, he saw Socks break free of the tangle and rise. The horse deftly kicked the insectile creature in the head with his hind legs, putting it down hard. When it skidded to a halt a few feet away, it remained there, either prone or dead.

"Come on!" Tauman yelled as he swung at another creature which had scuttled up towards him. He knocked it out of the way, but failed to see the one approaching from the other side.

"Behind you!" Wyll shouted.

Tauman instinctively brought his weapon up, the result of phases of hard training saving his life as a trident became snagged by the soldier's blade. It was more of a reflex than a block, but the man was alive to tell the story.

Thankfully Socks seemed uninjured by the fall, and Wyll and Kienan scrambled back to their own mounts before any more of the creatures could attack.

From the direction they had first come, Wyll could hear the scuttling noises become louder. If they didn't leave here right now, they never would. He vaulted onto Socks' back, and the moment Kienan and Tauman were ready, he led them on what he hoped was the correct course to meet up with the others. It was tricky to tell which way they'd been headed. Every tree here looked the same. After a few seconds, Wyll heard the sounds of steel ringing, and guided them a little left to head in the right direction. He pushed Socks harder. The sounds of battle more urgent than any call for help. Within moments he rode into a small clearing where his men had formed a tight circle, and were desperately fending off a dozen of the creatures, for now. Wyll charged. Socks ploughed into the closest creatures from behind, kicking as hard as he could. Kienan and Tauman followed the example to either side. Together, it was enough to break a temporary hole in the ring of flailing creatures.

"Ride!" Wyll shouted as soon as the way was clear. His men needed no encouragement as they swarmed through the gap, fending off the nearest of the massive insects as the rest followed in close pursuit.

We have to get away from these things!

There were far too many to fight, and the edge of the woods was still at least a day's ride from here, maybe more.

At the pace these things could run, it was possible they could outdistance the horses over the long run. Yet there was little choice but to try, and hope their attackers' endurance was not as great as their speed. Wyll pushed Socks mercilessly, wishing he could let the horse rest, but knowing that if they stopped now, none of them would leave these woods alive.

With dismay, he saw his men were falling behind after only minutes. Their mounts just didn't have the speed or stamina of Socks' rahiri blood. Wyll was forced to slow a little from Socks' dead run until the others caught up, the mass of creatures hot on their tails.

They weren't going to make it. Behind them, Wyll could already hear the scuttling of the creatures. His men's horses were trying with all their might to outdistance their pursuers, but were nearly spent. At the dead run they were trying to hold, they would give out in minutes. He had to make a choice. Continue this futile run until the horses' exhaustion claimed them one by one, or stand and try to fight off the horde of monsters that were even now gaining ground.

It wasn't hard to see that dying one by one as the creatures overtook their mounts was utterly pointless. He held out little hope of surviving a fight against these things, but at least together they might have some slim chance at resisting. A chance that only held if they made a stand now, before they were too exhausted to fight.

Off to his right he saw a tree larger than anything he had ever encountered, its base dwarfing even those of the giants in the Emerald Sea. Its sixty-foot diameter was the best cover they were likely to get.

"With me!" he shouted and turned Socks towards his

goal. The men followed his lead and in less than a minute Wyll was pulling Socks up between two of the ten-foot-high roots.

"We can't outrun them," he said to his men over the panting of the horses. As he spoke, the first of the creatures came scuttling out from between distant trees, followed by many, many more.

"You need to go," Seth said as all eyes turned from the hundreds of approaching creatures towards him.

"You have the chalice and the best mount here. Wyll, the army must still be warned."

"I'm not about to abandon you all!"

Wyll dismissed the idea at once as he turned his attention to the creatures, the first of whom would be on them in mere moments.

"He's right Wyll," Bosric added, though for once his usual manic grin was nowhere to be seen. "But I still want that statue."

"Go Wyll," Tauman added his voice, "Socks is the only one of our horses that can outrun these things. Dying with us here serves no purpose."

A bowstring hummed and Cale shot the nearest of the creatures through the eye, dropping it in its tracks, though none of the other creatures seemed fazed by the loss. He nodded to Wyll his agreement with the others.

Wyll didn't see it though. He was too busy looking at the black figure that had sprung into being the moment Cale's arrow had struck home.

She was tall and slim, and every bit as beautiful as he remembered from their last encounter. She looked up from touching the thing. Sending it on its way to the next world, he thought with a shudder, and their eyes met. He knew his were worried, but hers were horrified, and then she was gone.

"Go now," Seth said. Oblivious to his vision, the man drew his second curved blade from the scabbard at his back and edged his mount forward so that he had sufficient room to fight. Charran moved up to flank him, attaching the second blade to his staff. Together they waited for the creatures to reach them as the horses continued trying to recover from the sprint. It wouldn't be long.

Wyll was torn. They were right. The message had to be delivered, and the chalice as well. He was loath to leave his men to fight these things without him, and the consequences that decision would entail. He found himself rooted to the spot as another of the creatures fell to Cale's bow, though strangely enough, this time Sa'rayna did not appear to claim it.

"I did not expect the advice I gave you last night to be needed so soon," Seth told him calmly.

Without waiting for an acknowledgement, he dug his heals into his shining black stallion and charged into the mass of oncoming creatures, ploughing them out of his way. He felled those on either side of him in a heartbeat, his twin blades swinging impossibly fast. Others skittered towards him, taking their place without hesitation. With a roar, Charran charged as well. Then all the men were moving, save Cale, who continued to pick creatures off with his bow from the shadow of the tree. The main mass of insects had reached them, and chitinous bodies swarmed around his men as Wyll watched in horror at what was taking place. A hand clamped down on his shoulder, and he spun to find Cale staring at him. The man just nodded, the look in his eyes speaking for him as he told Wyll to go, to not let their deaths be in vain. To save more lives than would be lost here and help the king's forces achieve victory with the mission he had been tasked to carry out. And for the first time, Wyll understood. Seth had been right. It was his obligation to focus on what was to be gained, not what was to be lost. Otherwise, he would never leave this place, and all of them would have gone through this for nothing.

Wyll sorrowfully returned Cale's nod in farewell, and then once more booted Socks into a gallop, heading west, away from his doomed men and into an uncertain future.

Before he had even rounded the giant tree, he heard Cale's bow take up its humming song again as he rode. Wyll tried desperately not to think about what he was doing. He had to carry out the mission. He had to.

It was no more than a minute later as the sounds of the battle receded that something blurry passed in front of his eyes, colliding with his forehead at great speed. Wyll fell from his saddle, sliding towards unconsciousness. As his head impacted again on a forest floor rushing up to meet him, Wyll's last thought was a grim one. On the subject of an old man, and his ideas about fate.

*　　*　　*

First, there was motion. Wyll's body swayed side to side in the unmistakable motion of sitting astride a walking horse. He groggily tried to open his eyes, but to his alarm found they refused to obey his command. Without thinking, he reached up to feel for what was keeping them closed, but after only inches his hands came to a swift and slightly painful halt. He was restrained. His hands tied to... something.

Probably the saddle, and each other as well.

With a growing sense of dismay he bent over forwards, just enough to reach his head. With a sinking sensation he found the obstruction, discovering it was sticky, and slightly wet.

Blood. He must have been injured, and the blood had run down his face and dried there while he lay on the forest floor. But that couldn't happen quickly. How long had he been unconscious before he'd been found? And why were his hands tied if his men had gotten him out of there alive? He needed to see what was happening, now. Bending over again he tried to prise some of the caked material from his face, and succeeded only in granting himself an agonising amount of pain. It had been a dull ache in the background, but roared to life as soon as he disturbed the scab.

"Leeeeave it," an alien voice hissed right beside him.

Wyll recoiled in surprise, almost losing his seat as he realised what had just spoken.

"Who are you?" he asked, trying to sound more confident than he felt. Something that was not too hard to achieve right at this moment.

"Unimporrrrtant," the hissing thing replied after a long silence.

"Where are my men?" he tried, not sure he wanted to hear the answer to that particular question.

"They are neeeear. You have been suuuummoned. It isss, a greeeat honour."

"Sound off!" Wyll called as loudly as he could manage, and to his vast relief Seth answered almost immediately.

"We're all here," the veteran warrior replied, sounding tired, or maybe hurt to Wyll's unfocused mind.

"Every man is injured, and Kienan and Cale are still unconscious, but we're all here."

"Thank the Maker," Wyll muttered under his breath, glad beyond relief that the creatures hadn't decided to slaughter his men out of spite, even if they were now in enemy hands.

It was a long minute later when Wyll had rallied his strength, and what senses he could muster, to speak to the thing again, but he had to know.

"What, are you? I've never heard of anything like your people before this."

The thing next to his horse, at least he thought it was Socks from the animal's gait, gave a high-pitched trilling that could have meant anything. Wyll tried not to cringe. Without his sight, it could strike him down any time it pleased.

"We are proteccccctors of this place, and servants of the great missssstress," it answered in a civil enough fashion.

Wyll tried to focus his thoughts, but the pounding in his head wasn't helping. If these things were in fact insectile in nature as well as appearance, their great mistress was likely some form of hive queen.

"Is that where you are taking us, to your queen?" he tried, unsure of why this thing beside him could even speak his language. They must have had at least *some* contact with humans he supposed, probably the odd traveller who was stupid enough to stray too far into the woods. Much as they had done.

"Yesss, to our queen you will go. You haaaave been summoned."

"Are people summoned often?" Wyll asked, trying to get as much information out of the thing as he could.

"Is first suuuummons in over nine hunndred yearrrrs. Is greeeat honour."

"How long have you lived?" Wyll asked, the creature's

words setting off a strange chain of thought at the back of his still fuzzy mind. One he couldn't quite grasp hold of.

"We do nottt die as you do, we are alllways."

"But I saw Sa'rayna take one of you back there," Wyll said in confusion.

"Thaaaat name must never be saaaid!" the thing hissed in his ear, making him jump at the proximity.

"Why not?" Wyll asked, turning his blinded eyes to face where the thing's head must now be.

"She will heeeeear," was the hushed reply.

The odd conversation lapsed into silence for a long time, and Wyll had the uncomfortable feeling that they were being led back into the heart of the woods. For a short time he was able to stay alert. Eventually though, the lack of vision and constant headache from his wound caught up with him, and he slouched back into unconsciousness.

The next thing he knew he was being handed down from his saddle. Human hands, not insectile claws, guiding him to the ground, and then to a sitting position against a cold, mossy rock.

"They're stopping here for the night," Charran told him.

"There's a small stream nearby. Wait here while I get some water so Bosric can clean off this wound."

Wyll nodded, then wished he hadn't as he heard the big man's footsteps get quieter as he walked away. It was only then he realised his hands were untied. The first thing he did was to gently probe the wound on his head. The amount of blood that had pooled and dried around his face horrified him. Head wounds always bled a lot though, and even a cut as small as an inch could look like a fatal wound to the untrained eye.

He could hear the stream himself now that he thought

about it, and also Charran rummaging around in the packs for a bowl to put the water in. That was good. It meant their captors were allowing them some freedom. If the insectile things were not paying close enough attention, they might yet have the chance for at least one of them to escape and complete their mission.

Charran returned with the water, giving Wyll some to drink before placing the bowl on a nearby rock.

"Can you tell me where the actual wound is?" Bosric asked as the short man knelt beside the two of them, taking Charran's place as the big man left. "I need to clean it off, but I don't want to disturb the scab over the actual cut."

Wyll thought he could, so he pointed to a spot on his forehead about two inches above his right eye. Lightly as he could, he traced the line of pain which he presumed was the wound, all the way up past his hairline.

"That's good," Bosric sighed. "Your eyes might be all right then. From the amount of bleeding you did, we couldn't tell."

Even without his eyes, Wyll could tell the red headed man was grinning.

The sound of a knife being drawn made Wyll uncomfortable.

"Are you sure you know what you're doing?"

"Sort of," Bosric replied with sincerity. "Now hold still. You must have fallen face down and the blood pooled and dried while you laid there. It's too thick to wipe away. I need to cut through the scab so that it doesn't disturb the rest of the wound when I peel off the excess. Also, this is a very sharp knife, so if I accidentally cut you, try not to flinch. Just tell me to stop."

"Wyll was about to do just that when he felt the blade

touch the scab and begin cutting into it, causing a sharp pain where the actual wound was. Bosric must have seen him grimace, because he stopped.

"All right, we'll try this another way," the short man said. Before Wyll could react, Bosric guided his head back to rest on the rock behind him while he took Wyll's jaw in his left hand to hold him steady. Once again the knife came down, though this time instead of a cutting motion, he pressed it further into the caked blood and then withdrew it.

"How was that?"

"Much better actually," Wyll responded, tired again, and a little surprised.

"Okay then," Bosric replied cheerfully. He continued scoring the scab through, somehow avoiding cutting the skin below. When he finished cutting a line in the dried blood from one side to the other, he let go of Wyll's head and put the knife down.

"Are your eyes completely closed?"

"I'm not sure," Wyll responded after a moment. "I think so, but I can't tell."

"I'll try to be careful then." He took the lower side of the scab he'd just separated, and began pulling it away from the unharmed portion of Wyll's face.

It was disgusting work, but the short, redheaded man never complained as he went about his business. He finally reached Wyll's eyes, which he was happy to discover were indeed closed.

There was some momentary discomfort as the main scab came away from Wyll's eyelids. Bosric threw the excess away into the bush.

"I still can't open my eyes," Wyll said, trying not to let panic overtake him.

"It's ok," Bosric assured. "That was just the crusted layer, now we can wash the rest off with a cloth. You should be able to see after that."

Wyll sighed in relief. He must have been pretty bad if all that Bosric had done so far had only removed an outer layer. He heard the man squeezing a cloth into the bowl of water Charran had left, and without warning felt the cold liquid on his eyes, running down his face.

"You should probably lean forward for this," Bosric said before helping him into position so the bloodied water would not run down all over his uniform.

Not that it isn't already stained beyond repair, he thought.

For the next few minutes, Bosric continued to wash away the dried blood, telling him to keep his eyes closed while he worked. Eventually he squeezed the cloth dry a final time, and mopped away the water that was left on Wyll's face.

"All right, open your eyes slowly," he instructed, and Wyll complied. He knew the light would be exceedingly dim this far under the canopy of the Wraith Woods. Even so, it felt as though he were being blinded when he tried.

It took several minutes for his eyes to adjust, but he could see again, his eyes seemingly unharmed despite his throbbing head wound.

He thanked Bosric sincerely for his efforts, and the man grinned before leaving to see to the others. As glad as he was to have his sight back again, what Wyll saw around him filled him with chagrin.

As Seth had reported earlier, all his men were injured to some extent. Cale had a broken arm, and both Seth and Charran had large gashes on their upper bodies. Though neither man's wounds seemed to be life threatening, they would no doubt leave scars to add to both the men's collections.

Looking further, Wyll saw Sarran had an enormous bruise over half his face, and seemed to be concussed, while both Tauman and Kienan appeared to have sustained broken ribs. Of them all, Bosric had fared the best, only walking with a slight limp as he saw to the others' wounds as best he could.

Around them, Wyll took in their captors properly for the first time. They were some form of giant insect, ranging in size from that of a large dog to about the size of a small horse. They had bodies covered in natural armour and a keen look in their eyes that spoke of intelligence. An intelligence which despite their alien physiology, might well at least match that of Wyll and his men. Worst of all though, there were at least two hundred of them guarding his squad. Now that he thought about it, Wyll realised he could hear many more of the creatures. There was no telling how many more waited beyond the immense trees which blocked all view beyond a hundred spans in any direction.

Not all the creatures carried the wicked looking tridents, but even those who didn't still had claws capable of stabbing a man with little difficulty.

They couldn't escape this. Their only hope was to be brought before these creatures' queen and try to somehow talk their way free. With his squad in this bad a condition, there was no chance at all they were fighting their way out.

Wyll tried to stand. His head immediately began spinning though, and the unpleasant sensation forced him to reach out and lean against the rock until the nausea passed.

When he had remastered himself, he stepped away from

the boulder and looked around again. The sight only confirmed what he'd seen earlier though. If anything he thought he may have underestimated the number of creatures which were now going about whatever strange tasks they performed around their camp.

Wyll made his way over to where Socks and the other horses were hobbled, and was pleased to find them all unharmed. For whatever reason, the insectile creatures had even rounded up the packhorses which had bolted early in the fight, bringing them here with the rest. Most of their supplies were with those horses, though the chalice itself Wyll had stowed in his own saddle bag. Finding it right where he'd left it was a great relief. The creatures either hadn't recognised its value, or didn't care about loot.

"Bosric!" Wyll called, making his head spin again. He leaned on Socks to support himself, causing the horse to snort in disapproval. Thankfully he didn't sidestep away.

Bosric hurried over, assuming he needed help, but that was not why Wyll had called him.

"Find out which one of these creatures is in charge, and see if you can persuade it to let us have a small fire to cook with."

The short man's habitual grin slipped for a moment, but returned at the thought of the hot meal he would eat if he managed to successfully carry out the order.

"Sure, no problem at all, sir," Bosric said too solemnly to be serious.

He looked around for a moment before shrugging, then headed towards the nearest of the insectile things. Wyll moved away from Socks and down the line towards the packhorses. He couldn't do much in his current state. Just walking in a straight line was taking most of his concentration. Nonetheless, he needed to set a good example for his men. While he was recovering, Bosric and Charran had bound up the men's wounds with bandages from the packhorses' panniers. Several of them were still in pain, and Cale's arm looked as bad as ever. He would have to set it himself. None of the others seemed to know how, or surely that injury would have been their priority.

Wyll took some more bandages from their supplies, and some salve that would ward off infection. The other jar had already been emptied and returned to the packs he noticed. He thought for a moment and took the sewing gear as well. On his way over, he called Charran and sent the man to get more water from the stream so he could wash out Cale's wound. He could see the bone poking out from the skin even from here, and winced. It was a nasty break that would fester and leave Cale incapacitated if not taken care of promptly. Wyll hoped his basic knowledge of bone setting was up to the task.

In his weakened state, he only reached the mute soldier at the same time Charran returned with the water. He would need the big man's help for this. It would have been better if Cale were still unconscious, but that couldn't be helped now. This had to be done soon.

He sat down beside the agonised man, waited till his head stopped spinning, then inspected the wound. He breathed in relief at what he saw. Although quite bad, it seemed to be a clean break. The bone had not splintered as he'd feared, and although the sharp edge of it had broken through Cale's skin, Wyll thought he was up to the task of setting it back in place. It would no doubt cause the tongueless soldier an excruciating amount of pain, but he would keep the arm.

Instructing Charran to clean off the wound, he waited

until the big man was done before checking it again. With most of the blood gone, he could see what he was doing now, and found that his opinion hadn't changed. Setting about the business of putting the bone back in place, Charran held Cale still as he cried out in wordless anguish. After what seemed like ages, the mute soldier lapsed into unconsciousness. Without his pained resistance to Wyll's admittedly none too gentle ministrations, he was able to complete the process without causing the man further agony. Once finished, he judged it a good job since the bone once again felt whole beneath Cale's skin. He had Charran wash the wound off again, and with the supplies he had brought over, began sewing up the long gash in Cale's arm. Once the wound was closed, he ordered Charran apply the salve liberally and dress the wound with a bandage before leaving the man to rest.

By the time they were finished, and had washed their hands and stowed what gear they still had back in the packs, Bosric had managed to start a small fire. Somehow the short man must have attained their captors' permission.

Wyll looked around, making his head spin anew, but since none of the other outstanding tasks seemed urgent, he went to sit near the fire. He rested his head in his hands while Bosric took care of the meal without being asked. After checking on the others, Charran had gone to sit by Cale, waiting for the man to regain consciousness. The others slowly drifted over to share the fire's warmth while Bosric continued his task.

It was quite a while later when the clicking of insectile claws on the ground made Wyll look up, his head no longer spinning as badly as before. One small thing to be grateful for.

"Put theeeese in your fooood. Will ressstore your

strennngth," one of the creatures said as it dropped a large animal-skin pouch full of berries on the ground next to him. Wyll tried not to cringe as the huge bug, which stood well over him now that he was sitting, addressed him in heavily accented Jeranonian.

With nothing further to add, the creature turned and scuttled away. Wyll watched it go, and after a few moments picked up one of the berries, contemplating it as intently as his foggy mind would allow. It was of a type he had never seen, small and purple with a pungent odour that was strange, but not unpleasant.

He popped the skin of it with a fingernail and licked the tiniest amount of the juice. When after a minute he still felt okay, he stuck the whole thing in his mouth.

"Is that such a good idea, Sir?" Kienan asked, his hand still protecting his broken ribs.

"We'll see soon enough," Wyll told him. "But if they want us dead or harmed more than we already are, they simply don't need to go to the length of poisoning us."

"I suppose so, Sir."

After another few minutes had expired, Wyll looked around. He didn't feel any different, but as he stood to survey the area once again, he realised his head had stopped spinning.

He'd taken knocks on the head before. From experience he knew that it should have been at least another few hours, or even overnight before he'd recovered past that point.

Turning to contemplate the strange berries once again, he made his decision.

"Add them," he told Bosric, and the man shrugged as if to say, *'I hope you know what you're doing,'* but followed the order without a word.

Seeing Cale awake, Wyll made his way over to the two men and helped him to his feet. Charran gathered up the last of the gear while Wyll helped Cale over to the warmth of the fire where the food was just about ready.

When the meal was cooked, Bosric served it into the bowls and handed them round to the men too injured to get up. It was a far more substantial soup than was usual. Given the state of their health though, he was not about to rebuke the red headed man for using a little more of their carefully rationed supplies than was set for a single meal.

Bosric had also used up the last of the flatbread with it, and again Wyll couldn't fault him. The men would need all the strength they could gather for whatever was to come when they met these strange creatures' queen.

They ate the meal in silence for the most part, their captors leaving them alone for the moment. They seemed not to have any interest in eating meals of their own. Once the men were all finished, there was a little of the soup, or more of a stew tonight, left over. Wyll ordered that it go to the more seriously injured men on the premise that if the berries did in fact have any real medicinal properties, they would be the ones to most benefit from the extra serve.

None of the men who missed out on seconds so much as batted an eyelid at the food not being shared out equally. They had become a close-knit group over the last seven phases since arriving in Aramar, and Wyll was pleased.

Looking back now, he could not have imagined his life being like this even one year ago, but one strange event had happened after another, all leading him here. First, the situation with Dael and Rhianna, then his friendship with Jayden as they travelled to the capital where he had met the men who now served under his command. Most importantly, or perhaps disturbingly, he had encountered Sa'rayna, the fabled 'Black Lady' who moved your soul on from this world to the next when you died. A woman he had seen in his dreams since he was old enough to remember having them.

Once he finished the last of his own stew and bread, Wyll got up and made his way to the small stream where he washed off his bowl and spoon. He rubbed his eyes against a sudden tiredness now that his belly was full. As he turned back to the others a sinking feeling squirmed into his gut as he saw that Cale and Sarran had already fallen into sleep. By the look of it, both Tauman and Kienan were right behind them. In fact all the men who'd eaten a second helping were now on the border of sleep, or past it already. As Wyll reached for a sword that was no longer there, he staggered back towards the others, dropping the implements as he realised what was happening.

From the corner of his eye, he saw two of the creatures coming towards him. As he fell to his knees, overcome by whatever was in those berries they had eaten, the last thing he thought as one of them lifted him up onto its bony back was, *'Why?'*

*   *   *

Once again Wyll woke in the saddle. This time though, his eyes were working as they should, and his mind seemed clearer. He registered his new surroundings, and realised that his head no longer throbbed as it had before the creatures had drugged them. He reached up a hand, which curiously was not restrained, and gingerly felt around the wound. For a moment it confounded him as the expected pain never occurred, and he had to press a little harder to confirm what he'd found.

The wound was gone, as was the huge patch of dried blood which had been covering it.

Looking around to find the others, he noticed that his head was no longer spinning. In fact, he hadn't felt this refreshed in phases. Certainly not since they had left the college with its hot meals and warm beds every night at the very least.

It wasn't just his own wound that had disappeared, he noticed with a sudden grin. The enormous bruise which had covered half of Sarran's head was gone. He was sitting alert in his saddle, looking thoughtfully about himself as he studied the rows of creatures which still flanked their party to either side. The gashes on both Charran and Seth's arms had faded to dull scars. Even more astonishingly, Cale's arm seemed to have healed, except for, as with the others, a dull scar where the broken bone had punctured through the skin. The mute soldier was flexing it slowly, studying the arm as though he couldn't quite believe it himself.

Bosric rode up to him once the short man saw he was awake, and Wyll shook his head in disbelief.

"How long?" he asked the grinning man.

"All night and it's about midday now I think, though it's hard to tell time under all... this," he whispered. He motioned upwards at the almost unbroken forest canopy through which only the slightest of the sun's rays now penetrated. None of his men had torches out despite the dimness. It made it hard for them to see, but Wyll could understand their captors not wanting naked flames travelling through their home forest, lush and damp though the vegetation here was.

The trees they had seen at the border of the woods had been gnarled things, twisted and menacing. The ones nearer the heart of the forest however were more reminiscent of the giant boles in the Emerald Sea, their bright colours visible even in this dim light.

Ahead of him, the lines of insectile creatures stopped in unison. Wyll ordered his men to follow suit as the creature at the head of the column turned and scuttled back towards them.

"Goood, you arrrre awaaake," the thing hissed at him in its strange mangling of the common tongue.

"Thank you for healing our wounds," Wyll returned when the creature failed to say anything further.

"It waaaaas herrr wiiish," it sybilised, though Wyll could not have guessed the thing's mood if his life depended on it.

"You muuust leave your horrrrse here," it hissed before turning away, and Wyll jumped down from Socks' back without even considering his recent injury. It was as if his body had never been in better shape, and he followed before the creature could outpace him.

"Where are we going?"

He no longer felt as if they were in imminent danger since the creatures had taken the effort to heal both his and his men's wounds. He expected that would remain the case at least until he met their queen, and found out why they had been summoned.

The creature's bony lips pulled back in something that could have been a smile or a snarl as it looked at him directly.

"In the glaaaade beyond those treeees, She waaaaits for you."

Wyll looked to the front of the column where several

huge old trees blocked out the view beyond, not to mention the sun above. Anything could be in there.

"Are you not coming with me?" he asked hesitantly, not sure which answer he was hoping for more.

The thing in front of him blinked its vertically slitted eyelids and lifted both forelegs off the ground. The gesture clearly meant something to it, though nothing at all to Wyll.

"Thhhhe suuuumonnns issss only forrr you," it told him, and this time the irritation was clear in its voice.

That was understandable enough Wyll supposed. If it had been truthful before about the last summons from its queen being over nine hundred years in the past, the creature would be keen to communicate with her itself.

"Through there?" Wyll asked, nervously pointing at the trees before them.

"Yessss. Do noooot keep her waaaiting."

Wyll took a deep breath, looking back at his men as he did so.

"Seth, you're in charge until I return," he announced, trying to sound more in control than he felt. After all, who knew what was waiting behind those trees. The creature didn't seem to be in any mood to return his weapons.

Not that I would give one of these things its trident if it were going into King Erian's throne room either.

He started walking in the direction the creature had motioned a moment before. He should be more worried he thought, but he just couldn't bring himself to shake his good mood at having found his men healed. He wondered if this near euphoria was a side effect of the strange healing berries the creatures had given them.

It took some doing to get to the gap in the trees. There were several large plants in the way, not to mention a huge half rotted log which he had to scramble over. With a bit of effort he eventually made it.

Beyond the narrow gap, all he could see were more trees, and Wyll looked back at the creature which had spoken to him for confirmation. It waved a bony forelimb at him, and Wyll realised that was all he was going to get. Turning back towards his goal, he continued.

All around him the trees grew huge and bright, the colours on them now more visible as the light got a little better. The creature had said that its queen was in a glade, which would explain the increasing light. Any disruption in the trees would also mean a break in the overwhelming canopy above.

Looking around, Wyll saw a tiny beam of sunlight breaking through the trees at the edge of his vision, and headed towards it. The light was better here, and as he rounded a final ancient tree, harsh, unobstructed sunlight blinded his eyes, pouring into what must have been a full clearing high above.

Blinking back tears from his watering eyes, he let them adjust to the blinding glare. When they stopped hurting somewhat, he slowly opened them the rest of the way.

What he found before him staggered Wyll to the core.

He recognised every detail of the scene before him, almost as though he had been here many times. For the memory to be this accurate, in some strange way, he must have.

In my dream I see a stone building, overgrown with vines and cracked deeply with age. It's some kind of temple I think, but not like anything any human ever constructed.

He had spoken those words to Jayden long phases ago. They had been just approaching Aramar at the head of the recruiting column at the time.

Ahead of him lay a clearing filled with all manner of flowering vines, each one growing wild as they crept over boulders and clung to the thin trunks of blossoming fruit trees. Bordering each of these was a series of crystal clear, interconnected pools which meandered throughout the glade. Some form of small, colourful fish filled the waterways, launching themselves into the air at frequent intervals to catch insects flitting tantalisingly above the surface.

Connecting the pools and streams to each other were a myriad of paths which ran throughout the lush forest garden, each laid with a deep black soil and bordered with mossy log halves.

After a stunned moment of staring, Wyll realised with admiration that none of this was in any way wild. Someone had painstakingly tended the entire glade to give the illusion of natural growth. Around the clearing, tiny insects, and even a few butterflies flitted from one pool of crystalline water to the next, avoiding the fish and enjoying the bright sunshine streaming down from above. How any of them had made it this far through the Wraith Woods was anybody's guess, but they appeared to be thriving.

The only unnatural feature of the glade was a stone building at its very core. Its four turrets leant inward to meet at a hollow pinnacle, from which hung a giant bell cast from what looked at this distance to be solid silver. Across every wall of the structure, vines and moss grew in random patterns, lending the place an ancient, neglected aspect.

There were no windows in the strangely aspected building, only a carved double door facing him that Wyll could see.

He would have known those doors were there even if they'd been on the other side of the structure. Wyll found himself almost unable to think as he waited silently, just as he did in his slumber.

He had seen this clearing in his dreams all his life, never changing, and always present at the back of his mind. He had always thought the dream must have some meaning, persistent as it was. The realisation that this was an actual place, not one borne of his own imagination made him shudder, for he knew what must happen next.

I walk out into a clearing of some kind and the doors open. They're huge and carved with a rune that looks like an uprooted tree laying on its side without any leaves, and don't ask me how I know it's a rune, I just know that it is.

Looking at the carving on the door, Wyll now knew he was right. It… meant something to him. What, he didn't know, but whilst examining the rune he felt a strange tugging at the back of his mind, as though it were something he should recognise.

Wyll took a deep, relieved breath. He was in no danger here, he now knew who these creatures' queen was. He had met her before.

Slowly he stepped out into the clearing, walking quietly into the centre until he felt he was standing in the proper place.

At exactly the moment he expected, the double doors of the temple swung slowly open with the low creaking sound of wooden hinges unused in a very long time. It took a long few seconds to happen, but when the creaking ceased, there was complete silence in the forest. Even the crickets halted their incessant song.

There's a pause then, once the doors have fully opened. In my dream at least it seems as though the whole forest is holding its breath, waiting for, something.

And so it was, at least until the sound of footsteps from inside the pitch-black interior of the temple reached his ears. A moment later she came into view. Tall, slim, and utterly beautiful. Her midnight black hair hung loose and reached almost to her ankles. Her eyes were an emerald green to rival the surrounding forest, and her lips were a startlingly red contrast to the paleness of her skin.

As with the last time he had seen her, her dress was as black as her hair, and just a little longer. It swayed past her ankles to reveal only the tips of her bare feet, which somehow seemed only right for her in this place.

Wyll didn't know what to do. Everything was happening exactly the way he had always seen it in his mind. For a moment he had the strangest feeling, wondering whether this was even real, and not a dream induced by the creatures' drugged berries. He dismissed that thought though. Now was not the time to be second guessing himself.

He couldn't help but smile as she walked towards him, amazement written plainly on both their features.

"Hello Sa'rayna," he said in little more than a whisper.

CHAPTER 10

THE CULMINATION OF A DREAM

When Sa'rayna was little more than a foot away, she stopped, and Wyll had a hard time not taking a step backwards. For several long phases he'd thought of little else but the training, this mission, and how he felt for the strange apparition he'd first met in the Emerald Sea. The prospect of facing her in this place was daunting.

Sa'rayna was the Black Lady. In combination with what he knew her touch could do, he could no longer doubt it after seeing her exit the temple from his dreams. She had taken Brendan with that touch. She could take his soul just as easily, even if she claimed she could control the ability. It didn't mean she would.

"Wyll," she breathed.

"I would have come sooner, but your house is hard to find," he returned with a slight grin, immediately cursing himself for a fool. What kind of stupidity had made him say that of all things to the Black Lady, to death herself?

Before he could jump back, or even blink, she had wrapped her arms around him and was kissing him deeply.

After a shocked and somewhat terrified moment, Wyll realised he wasn't dead.

Far from it, he thought as he recovered his wits enough to return the passionate embrace.

He did not know how long they remained there like that, but when Sa'rayna finally released him and stepped back, she took in his expression and laughed.

"My touch will do nothing to you while I am here in this plane," she confided with a smile that contained all the warmth of the world. "And I would not take you anyway. In thirty thousand years you are the first person, the very first, who has been able to see me in the realm I exist in. At least without me having to first come through the portal, which is too dangerous to risk more than once or twice a century."

Wyll frowned.

"Thirty, thousand years? You've been alone all that time?" he asked, barely able to grasp the enormity of that concept.

For a moment Sa'rayna looked out around the clearing and took a deep breath of the rich earthy air which permeated the glade.

"It is necessary," she said with a sad smile, which turned joyful again once she looked back towards him.

"You should come back with me," she said, certain he would agree.

"Didn't you say that it was dangerous to go through the portal?" he asked, trying to buy some time to think. He was more than curious at the offer, though in the back of his mind a small voice told him he should be more worried. Somehow he just couldn't seem to manage it while she was right there in front of him.

Again the smile lit up her features.

"Not to us Wyll. You have so much to learn and plenty of time to do so. For now, suffice it to say that it is dangerous to the world for us to be out here where we can be harmed."

Wyll found himself grinning at Sa'rayna's obvious joy at him being there. He needed to control himself better, despite the utter sense of contentment which had descended upon him the first time she had smiled.

He was aware he was acting strangely, but for some reason that knowledge gave him no discomfort.

"Why is that?" Wyll asked, curiosity getting the better of him.

With a smile Sa'rayna took a step towards him, claiming his arm before starting them down a path that led through the sparkling pools of the glade.

"Imagine if no one ever died," she answered, her contented manner at odds with their topic of conversation.

"That would be wonderful," Wyll returned, thinking of both Brendan and Marad as he did so.

"No, it wouldn't," Sa'rayna corrected as she guided them to a spotlessly clean wooden bench.

"I told you before, I don't cause death, I simply move the spirit on when that person's time comes. Try to understand, while what I am about to tell you would take tens of thousands of years, the process would begin the moment I was no longer able to carry out my task."

Wyll nodded with a slightly furrowed brow.

"People's bodies are flesh," she continued once she had his full attention. "They only last so long. If I were not there to pass on their spirits, those souls would be stuck in their decaying bodies. The rotting flesh and skeletal husks would quickly become useless to them, yet the inhabitants would be tied to them until even the dust of their remains had decayed. Their spirits would then be freed from that long imprisonment. But freed to do what? Eventually, over many, many years, they would learn enough of their ethereal state to affect things in the real world. Even to the point where they could eventually possess the bodies of others against their will. Imagine even further, after several generations of people had passed into this state. An ever-increasing number of these spirits would emerge, twisted beyond recognition by centuries or millennia of isolation. The number of possessions would rise in an exponential number until eventually the spirits would begin fighting with each other for the use of a shrinking supply of bodies. The hosts would have no way of fighting them off, and by necessity the spirits would take victims younger and younger as competition for the use of physical forms increased. Even newborn babes would eventually become displaced by vengeful spirits clamouring for control of their flesh. Society would collapse long before that point, and humankind would end in madness and chaos. At the end, you would become worse than animals, until some other race was forced to hunt you down as you yourselves do with dangerous or rabid animals."

Wyll sat there for a long moment once she had finished, trying to think.

"I see," he replied after a while, unsure what else to say in response to the horrors she had just revealed.

An uncomfortable silence descended, and Sa'rayna cleared her throat gently, determined to break it before it could take hold.

"There is plenty of time for matters of such import later though. For now, tell me how you came to find me here?"

Wyll looked across at Sa'rayna again, relieved to see her intent borne out of genuine interest, rather than in response to some perceived intrusion of her well-guarded home. He couldn't help but smile back.

He thought about the question for a long time before answering. Sa'rayna seemed content to wait for him to gather his thoughts.

"I'm not sure," he admitted, "I thought I was simply following my orders to deliver a message from King Erian to the army. Everything was going along from day to day much as can be expected, until your creatures attacking us in the woods. Except, the moment I walked out into this clearing I recognised it from a dream I've had all my life. I can't believe for a second that the sheer level of detail is coincidence. Nor that we have run into each other again, especially in this place," he told her. "But the only alternative I can see is that my actions have somehow been guided my whole life to bring me here. I claim no expertise on things magical, but if it wasn't you, who would have the power or the inclination to arrange such a thing?"

Sa'rayna frowned at the question as she took his hand in hers.

"There are only two beings of which I know who have the power to affect *my* fate. One of them is the Maker, whom I serve. The other is the Destroyer, who remains chained far below Miralthrall's streets in a prison built by others of his race."

"The Destroyer?" Wyll asked, surprised. There was obviously a great deal about the world he had yet to understand. Just sitting here with Sa'rayna was proof enough of that.

"A matter for another time," she replied.

"Suffice it to say, that of the two of them, only the Maker would be so benevolent. I guess that really does make it fate then," she grinned. "I'm sorry that I was so cold to you when last we met, Wyll, but I had a job to do, and my conversation skills are… somewhat out of practice."

Wyll sighed. He had been hoping to avoid this conversation since the moment she had told him she would see him again at their last encounter. The subject had been broached though, and he needed to speak his mind, to clear the air between them. He needed to be honest with her, even if it would be uncomfortable in the short term.

"I think I hated you for taking Brendan back then," he said without preamble, and then went on after seeing the stricken look on Sa'rayna's beautiful features.

"But in the weeks afterward, I thought a lot about what you told me that day. Eventually I came to see that you were right. Everyone must die, otherwise the world would simply fill up with people. Once I accepted that fact, I realised I didn't hate you, but rather my inability to save my friend. It took some time, but I understand now that his rightful time should have been back in the Emerald Sea. I wanted you to understand that I don't hold taking Brendan against you anymore."

After a long moment Sa'rayna nodded slightly, her meaning indistinct.

"I'm glad you recognise that, Wyll. What I must do is never easy on those left behind, but I would not want that to come between us."

"Nor would I," he answered, only then truly realising that he meant it.

"Then you will join me, beyond the veil?" she asked, hope shining in her eyes.

"You would live forever Wyll, once beyond this plane we are not subject to time, such as others are."

With a sinking feeling Wyll let her hand go and stood, though not quite remembering when he had taken it in the first place. He walked a few steps away to look out over the lush glade and the strange temple which resided at its heart.

I could go with her right now and leave the coming war behind, the responsibility, the mission. I could hand it over to Seth, he would be at least as good a leader as I am, probably better. It was all he had wanted since he had first had the dream in his youth. He realised now that somewhere in the back of his mind he had always known it would come to this.

But to do so now would mean leaving everything behind, his family, his duty, the men whose safety he had been entrusted with. He looked back at Sa'rayna; at the woman he had dreamed of all his life. She was now standing as well, stunningly beautiful and smiling at him, as regal and sure of herself as any queen. She was waiting for his decision. For a long, long moment he considered going with her anyway. But that was not who he was.

In a sudden moment of clarity, he knew beyond all shadow of a doubt that this was his path. He would go with her through that doorway.

With an entire war hanging on what he and his men did next though, to abandon his mission now would leave a stain on his conscience that would sour over time.

"I can't, Sa'rayna. At least not yet," he told her with a discontented frown.

"Don't mistake my meaning, I want nothing more than to be with you. There are too many lives depending upon the completion of my current mission though, not to mention the fate of this entire country. I cannot in good conscience abandon either of those responsibilities."

Sa'rayna's shoulders slumped slightly, but then she smiled.

"It is good that you take your obligations seriously. But when they are done?" she asked hesitantly, even as a butterfly alighted unnoticed upon her shoulder.

"When they are done, there is nothing in the world that could stop me," Wyll told her before his mind had even properly processed the words.

He was not sure what he had just agreed to. Only that as he thought about the promise, he realised that no decision in his life had ever felt so completely correct.

Sa'rayna came over and took his hands in hers, kissing him again before stepping back.

"Wait here Wyll, I have something to give you."

Without another word she backed away, then turned and seemingly swayed more than walked back through the open doors of the temple, her form lost abruptly to the portal's unbounded blackness.

Wyll found himself standing alone in the clearing at the heart of the Wraith Woods. A bird called out somewhere. What strange force had brought him here, and why were his feelings so strong about this woman he had only just met in person for the very first time. As the minutes wore on, he conceded that however it had happened, he had been prepared for this moment for most of his life. Even if he hadn't consciously realised it before now.

It was almost like being under a spell. He'd received some training since being at the college in recognising when the Gift was being used, and he didn't think that was it. Still, there were other kinds of magic, and it was possible she had access to one of those.

He didn't think that was the case either though. It just didn't feel right.

Is this what love feels like?

The rogue thought popped into his mind of its own accord, and Wyll stopped breathing. For a moment, he wasn't sure whether to feel frightened or elated at the prospect, especially given who and what Sa'rayna was.

His thoughts were interrupted as she swayed back through the temple's open doorway, her long black hair lifting in the breeze as she crossed the threshold.

Wyll went to meet her halfway, and raised an eyebrow when he saw what she was carrying. They stopped a foot apart, and she held up the scabbarded sword between them.

"This is the Sword of Ages. The Maker gave it to me himself," she said as the forest around them once again grew silent in her presence. "When I was first given this blade many, many years ago, I was told that one day, far in the future, I would know who to give it to. And that man would help to change the world. Not to save it himself, but to help those who would."

She looked up at him intently, though they were almost of a height, and when she seemed satisfied with whatever she was searching for in his face, she continued.

"This sword will summon me to wherever you are. You need only scratch an enemy's flesh with it, and I will come and move their spirit on. Here."

Wyll took the sword gingerly, its polished ivory scabbard was without adornments save two rings at either end where it could be tied to a belt or back harness. In addition, the hilt and pommel were fashioned from some kind of incredibly well-made steel. When he began sliding the sword from its sheathe, it surprised him to find the blade itself completely black. At first he thought an enamel had been applied to the surface. As he looked closer, he realised the sword was made from a black metal which he had never encountered. As he removed the rest of the three-foot blade from the scabbard, Wyll was once again surprised. Three runes were etched along its surface, each glowing as though on fire. They were centred towards the pommel half of the blade, spaced about six inches apart, and Wyll had the strangest feeling he should know what they were. The first of them was the same as the rune on the temple door, which looked to be a tree uprooted and on its side. The second was of a vaulted arch with an inverse chevron through its middle. The last rune was similar to a letter c, with a bigger backwards c around it and a third c enveloping them both.

"What do they mean?" he asked Sa'rayna as he studied the strange runes.

Her face fell when he spoke though, and she pursed her lips.

"After five thousand years of keeping that blade safe, I had hoped *you* would know."

"Even so, I am certain it was for you I have been holding it all these years. Now tell me, what is it you must do that is so important you would rather complete that task than be with me?" she asked as she took back the sword. She slid the blade smoothly back into its scabbard and leant it on a nearby rock.

"The King has sent us on a mission to warn his army of impending danger. If we don't get to them in time, the whole war effort could unravel," Wyll answered. The urge to step forward and take her in his arms again was almost overwhelming.

"Of course… there is always war, sooner or later. Tell me,

what is the source of this one?" she asked with a sad little smile.

Wyll grimaced. "An archmage named Heramiir has conducted a coup in Miralthrall, and his army now threatens central Jeranon."

"Yes… there has been much death lately," she mused.

"Tell me, is this, Heramiir… powerful?"

"I'm told he is one of the strongest archmagi in Jeranon's history."

"That could present dangers of which you are not yet aware, Wyll. You must be careful. This blade will only help you up to a point. I can only move souls on. I have no power to heal the body, so be vigilant. When you come back to me I expect you not to be missing any limbs, because however you enter that portal is how you will remain for the rest of eternity, save that you should return to the natural world and come to harm. I have no desire to spend another eternity by myself," she told him as she motioned to the temple door.

"I'll be careful, Sa'rayna," he assured her with a smile.

"And I will return as quickly as I can."

"That would be best," she said with a mischievous smile, taking a step closer and brushing her hand lightly across his cheek.

Wyll bowed his head and kissed her again. Sa'rayna returned the embrace with vigour, until finally, with a low growl in his throat, Wyll forced himself to stop and take a half step back.

"I have to go. It is imperative that we reach the army as soon as possible," he told her unhappily.

She nodded in resignation, seeing he had made his decision, then gave him another of those beautiful smiles.

"Then go. I will be here whenever you choose to return,

but remember, do not wait too many years Wyll, for however you enter the portal is how you will stay."

"I don't intend to wait years," he told her, retrieving the Sword of Ages from its resting place at their feet.

"My protectors will allow you, and any men you directly lead, free access to the woods from now on. The sanctuary itself will remain open only to you," she added, tilting her head to indicate the clearing around them.

"I appreciate that," he told her with a roguish grin which she infectiously returned in kind. "It will make things a great deal easier when I do come back."

Stepping up close again she reached up and gave him one last chaste kiss on the forehead before moving away.

"Don't be gone long Wyll," she entreated him, suddenly more intent.

Wyll nodded to himself, consciously making the choice as he smiled back at her.

"I won't, Sa'rayna," he assured her. With a last long look, he turned and for now at least, walked away from the woman he had been dreaming of since he had been old enough to walk.

As he left the lush glade, and the woman he now knew beyond any shadow of a doubt that he loved, Wyll found himself dwelling on their unexpected, and all too brief encounter.

As he crossed out of the sunlight and returned to the all-encompassing canopy of the Wraith Woods, he realised he had to get his mind back on track. As the glade receded behind him, he clambered over fallen logs and other obstructions to reach the place he'd left his squad. As he walked, he thought seriously on the coming mission in a futile attempt to appear composed and in command before returning to his men. But no matter how hard he tried, even once he arrived to find only a single remaining insectile protector watching over them, he still couldn't get that stupid grin off his face.

CHAPTER II

THE DESTROYER'S GIFT

He had been in these catacombs for phases.

After the coup, and his initial meeting with the creature which called itself the master, Heramiir had returned to the surface of Miralthrall for a time. His intention had been to rule there for some phases whilst the city became used to his new regime. Soon after leaving the catacombs though, he had felt the familiar tug of what he now knew was the master's influence. At first he had resisted, but as the weeks went by, the mental tugging had refused to leave him in peace. It gnawed at him in a way that an attempt to overwhelm him with its will never could have.

The unremitting buzzing in the back of his brain had been too much to ignore. Leaving Deshara in charge of the city, he'd packed what he needed for an extended stay, and returned to the catacombs beneath the city. He had a campaign to execute, and this infernal pressure the master was placing on his will needed to stop.

Once the wounded from the coup had been attended to,

and those malcontents who refused to see reason ejected from the city, Miralthrall had been almost quiet. At first the streets had been deserted; the citizens too scared to come out of their homes. His men had kept an iron control over Miralthrall's less affluent areas at first, supporting the martial law edict he had passed down. It hadn't taken long for the organised criminal element which had been plaguing the city for as long as anyone could remember to be all but dispersed. As the weeks went by, the peasants had come to wonder why it hadn't been done years ago, and slowly returned to their places of work, and normal routines.

Another boon of the coup was that he now had the authority to inaugurate Gift users to oversee the justice system. Several times over the last decade he'd tried to convince the duke to implement this change, to no avail. The duke had reasoned that since magi couldn't read minds, there was no advantage to installing them in positions which might lead to political power. Yet now that they were in place, it seemed most of Miralthrall's citizens were less inclined to lie to a mage than they had been to the previous administration.

Weak minded fools that they are.

Every first week student knew a mage couldn't read minds. Except for Deshara's unique talent, of course. While the duke was aware of this, it seemed the citizenry at large was far less educated. For once the schism which had been growing between the magi and the general populace over the last decades had worked in his favour. Besides, it had turned out to be a most effective method of getting people used to the magi having the ultimate authority in the city.

Dragging his mind back to the present, Heramiir surveyed the glowing shaft of light in which the master was imprisoned, and walked towards it. He was sure the creature within would not like what he had to say. He had learned much from it over the last few phases. However, he was still no closer to getting the master free than he had been the first time he'd come down here.

Taking a deep breath and steeling himself, Heramiir crossed between two of the massive slanted red crystals which surrounded the master's prison, and strode towards the shimmering column of light.

The runes on his cloak flared as he crossed some invisible boundary, as they always did now. He suspected the first time he'd crossed the threshold, he had simply been too preoccupied to notice the small oddity as the spectacle of the master's prison unfolded before him.

As he approached the prison itself, the indistinct form inside seemed to stand and regard him in its usual distant manner.

"I must go," Heramiir told it without preamble, hoping very much that it didn't take offence. This close to the prison, the master could reach out and affect his very mind.

"I am not yet free," the creature in front of him replied in icy tones. "It would not be… good, for you, if you left now."

Heramiir didn't know whether he felt more nervous or angered by the master's thinly veiled threat. He had to press on, regardless.

"I must leave," he repeated in a more moderate tone.

"Nereth is in position, and if all goes according to plan, the King's army will be routed and no longer a significant threat to us. This will allow me to return here for as long as is necessary to free you."

"There are more important things than your petty wars," the master said as it moved to the very edge of the prison nearest where Heramiir was standing. Its outline became somewhat more defined, though the details of its features were still blurred by the shimmering curtain of light.

"Perhaps you are right," Heramiir allowed. "But our primary advantage over Erian is that right now he does not know where to commit his forces, giving us ample time to prepare. If we lose this battle because I am not there to oversee it, the King's army will eventually make its way here. Who knows, they might even win. And if they do, then who will you have to release you from your bonds, since they will certainly execute me for treason?"

The master cackled at Heramiir's words, as it was sometimes inclined to do. He was well used to the creature's erratic behaviour by now, and chose to ignore it.

"Very well," the creature before him giggled. "Play your little games, Heramiir. Just do not pretend that you want the King's army defeated so you can spend more time with me."

"Regardless," Heramiir pressed on. "We both want something from each other, something we can *only* get from each other. When the King's army is no longer a threat I *will* return, and we will both achieve our goals."

He said it with confidence, but after phases of trying, Heramiir was no longer sure he had the ability to do what the master was asking. He kept that thought tightly guarded. If the master ever found out the truth, its use for him would come to an abrupt and likely blood-stained end.

"You would do well to remember that, little one. I have shared less than a tenth of my knowledge with you, and none of my power. But if you must play soldier, I will make sure you return. Your death would not serve either of us."

Heramiir fell to the floor as a vision of terrifying power overcame him. Vast armies on a distant world with two suns ran towards each other while he watched from a distant hill. His thousand bodyguards surrounded him in a living shield while he worked his magic over the course of the field. For hours the massacre lasted until finally, just before dusk, the only troops left alive on the field were his own. His dominion was complete. This world was now his. The last defenders trodden underfoot. There was a terrible pain, and he looked down to see the jagged tip of a long knife sticking forward through his ribs. He fell, dead before he hit the ground. As Heramiir came back to himself, the imagined pain in his chest blossomed anew in his head. Instinctively he knew the master had done something more than show him a vision of a new type of spell being worked this time.

"Wh… what have you, done to me?" Heramiir gasped once he could roll back to his knees, a few moments later struggling to his feet.

The master chuckled. "Only what you have wanted, my dear friend. Only what you have desired. I have given you the knowledge you need and a taste of the power you will one day wield. It will only work once though, so do not use your Gift until you need it, and choose your time carefully. I do not give second chances."

When the creature's meaning reached Heramiir's agonised mind, he didn't know whether to thank the master or scream at it. If it was telling the truth, then he now had an even better chance of destroying the king's army, which marched ever eastward while he loitered down here. On the other hand, it meant that he could not use the Gift even to open a door ahead of himself until they were destroyed. That would be phases from now.

The master cackled, sensing his thoughts.

"Consider it a small bit of revenge for making me wait,"

it cackled again, adding to Heramiir's fury. Still, there was little to be done about it now. He'd been honest about one thing. They did still need each other.

"I will return when I can."

He turned his back on the glowing prison and walked away. It wasn't until he was nearing the door and the few supplies he had left that the master called out from behind him.

"Yes, you will. And before you leave again, I will be free."

It was arrogantly sure of that. Heramiir knew it was stupid, but couldn't resist the urge to needle it in petty revenge for denying him the Gift until the key battle with Erian's forces had taken place.

"And what if I can't free you?" he shouted back, trying to make the words offensive, and not to be taken as a serious question.

He should have known that the master would not understand the nuance.

"Then you will not leave."

*   *   *

The next thing Heramiir knew, he was walking up the stairs which led into the underside of Miralthrall's basements, and he stopped, bewildered. He turned and saw the dead end to the room in which the circular passage to the catacombs lay. It was the same room where he had slain Archmage Rellarin on his first trip down here all those years ago, and he shuddered. Had the creature transported him here through some arcane art, or had it once again manipulated his mind into forgetting the intervening journey? He thought for a moment, and as he climbed the stairs in earnest, he realised his legs were stiff. He also felt as though he hadn't slept in days, and took that as his answer. The other question which sprang to mind was how much time had passed since he had been standing in the master's chamber? Had he come straight here, a journey of a few days, or had the master forced him to take a side trip, doing the Maker knew what in the meantime?

For hours he trod up dank stone steps that seemed to go on forever. Exhausted, he emerged into the deepest shadowed recess of the college building. From there he made his way up to his own rooms, which took another quarter hour to reach. When he arrived, he assigned a servant to stand by his door and make sure no one disturbed him. Finally alone, he lay down on his large, neatly made bed and slept. After a time, he awoke and had a bath and water sent for so he could clean the grime of the caverns off himself. Normally he would have used a spell of water and fire to clean up, but thanks to the master's 'gift', that was no longer an option at present. Once he was clean, and the tub removed from his quarters, he finished dressing and left the spacious rooms for his office on the highest tower of the college building. He had taken it for himself after the changeover of power, and why not?

The huge room took up the entire turret, save the staircase and door. As he entered, he found a servant cleaning his desk and sent her running to fetch Deshara.

"And bring me Davoor and Mendacai as well," he called after her, referring to two of the other archmagi who had been so instrumental in his sudden rise to power last year.

While he waited for them to arrive, Heramiir sat behind his desk and began to review the literally hundreds of reports which had been left for him during his absence.

Some by other archmagi, others by upper-level servants and clerks, all of which he now needed to wade through.

Most of it was trivia, things others had already seen to, but thought important enough to let him know about. Some of them were right, others would have to be told not to bother him with these pointless reports. That the crop had not been good this year and magi would have to be sent out to help it along was important. On the other hand, he had no interest in the fact that the Smith's Guild was petitioning for a new hall after it had been burnt to the ground during the coup. There were others to see to that kind of thing. At first he couldn't understand why so many projects that should have begun phases ago had been left to wait for his signature. At least until he noticed that each of them had been noted at the bottom, *'Waiting for your approval to commence work, Archmage Poller.'* Or some variation of the same message.

The wrinkled old man was trying to create irritation with the new order amongst the general populace by holding up public works. He had no doubt also seeded plenty of rumours that the magi couldn't run the city as efficiently as the old duke's men had.

It was a smart move Heramiir allowed, and might have gone unnoticed for a time except for the sheer number of documents which Heramiir now had to wade through. They made the pattern stand out like a sore thumb.

He would have to do something about Poller soon. The old man's continued attempts at undermining his regime were becoming more than a simple irritation. The question was what? Poller was among the most knowledgeable archmagi in Miralthrall, and Heramiir was loath to lose that store of wisdom by executing him as a traitor. He couldn't leave an archmage of Poller's prominence free to challenge his authority though. If the old man hadn't seen the light by the time he returned from the coming campaign, he would have no choice but to act. Fortunately, most of the other magi, even those who had opposed the coup itself as treason against their rightful king, seemed to have come around to his way of thinking. No doubt due in large part to the fact they'd now had a taste of what life could be like without the Giftless watching over their every move. There had already been several advances in the Gift's use. Most of which Heramiir suspected were spells that the 'discovering' magi had already known, but not been able to publicly reveal because of the longstanding ban on unauthorised experimentation. Added to the removal of the ban, he had granted any mage who requested them, funds and permission to either buy or build their own residences outside the college walls. It hadn't taken long for most of the western college to see the benefits of working with the new regime as opposed to the old.

He smiled.

Even the strongest supporters of the monarchy were losing credibility now that crime in the city had been so drastically reduced by his order for martial law. That edict would be an unnecessary precaution once the king's army was routed, and he intended to rescind it when he returned. It had served its purpose already, and if he wasn't leaving Miralthrall for the front, he would do so sooner. With not only himself, but Nereth, Deshara, Korvith, and Davoor all out of the city for the next two phases or more, it was necessary to leave it in force until they returned.

He continued sorting through the pile of reports that lined his desk, separating those he needed to attend to before he left for the front, from those which were of no relevance other than to keep him apprised. Whenever he came across one with Poller's name on it, he put it into a third pile to be dealt with immediately. He was about halfway through the stack when there was a sharp knock on the door. Sensing the approach of two powerful auras, he called for the two archmagi outside to enter.

Deshara led, a she-wolf strolling her domain, utterly confident without crossing into arrogance. The woman always carried an intense air about her. The only thing he'd ever been able to compare it to was a lioness crouching in the long grass, waiting for the right moment to spring into action and begin the chase. Although her physical features would never be called more than simply pretty, she was one of the most attractive women Heramiir had ever known.

Behind her entered Davoor, another of his inner circle. The man was tall, bald, and had the blackest skin Heramiir had ever seen, making his broad grin a shockingly white contrast on the rare occasions he showed it.

"You two took your time," Heramiir chided once they had seated themselves across the desk.

Davoor looked uncomfortable, as well he should. It had been an hour since Heramiir had sent off the servant who was cleaning his room. Deshara simply looked him in the eye.

"What do you want us to do?" she asked, making no apology for her tardiness, and expecting no forgiveness in return, simply getting on with whatever business was at hand.

Heramiir couldn't help but feel a small smile tug at the corner of his mouth. Of all his lieutenants, he liked her best, and trusted her least. Not that he thought she would intentionally betray him. But trusting Deshara was like trusting a half-tamed animal. It might do what you wished, or it might turn and bite you for no reason at all.

"We will join Nereth for the duration of the campaign against the King's main force. Gather what you need and see to your affairs. We leave at first light."

Deshara nodded and stood.

Davoor took a moment longer. The man no doubt expected more information after Heramiir's phases long absence, but then stood as well.

As they left the room Heramiir called out behind them.

"Find Arana and Mendacai, and send them to me."

Neither of them answered, but they had heard, and would not dare disobey.

He had finished sorting the stacks of reports by the time Arana arrived. Of them all, only one troubled him deeply. In the fourteen weeks since Nereth had discovered the spate of missing villages along the western border, no one had yet come up with a definitive answer as to what had happened. He'd only just received word of those events before leaving for the catacombs, and left Nereth to seek out the truth. There had been no large-scale incursion from the west though, and the ranger battalions had fought no major actions while he'd been away. News of that would take days to reach them here though, even by pigeon.

The short, grey-haired woman, who was well into her sixties, sat in the chair which Deshara had vacated. He passed one of the piles of reports across to her.

"You have done a good job administrating the city in my absence," Heramiir commended her. "But in future I trust you to take care of these things on your own."

Archmage Arana scanned through the first few pages to

get a feel for the kinds of documents she'd been presented with before nodding.

"As you wish."

"These others I have either approved or not. You will follow this pattern while I leave again for a time to help Nereth confront the King's army."

He passed the second pile of parchments across that were of greater concern than the others.

Again, the severe old woman rifled through the pages and then placed them crossways over the first pile.

"This pile," he continued, "Are works that Archmage Poller has been holding up, no doubt on purpose. I want all of them seen to within the week, or at least started where that is not possible. Any documents he sends for approval, I am giving you direct authority to action, or not. I leave it to your discretion, but I don't want the old prune stirring up the citizens with a lack of apparent action on our part to their legitimate concerns."

"Understood," she replied as crisply as any soldier. "Your city will be in good hands while you are gone, Archmage."

"Of that I am confident, Arana," he told her, and then more seriously. "With more than half of my circle of lieutenants out of Miralthrall, you should remain cautious. Others such as Poller and his friends may think to seize the city back from us while they see our numbers diminished. I will not be able to help you if that occurs. Keep your eyes and ears open. I don't think I need to remind you that all we have achieved so far will be for nothing if we lose Miralthrall now. If you sense some plot in the works, stir up the magi who have been swayed to our cause. It will be infinitely harder for Poller to take on the majority of the college than to remove a few key magi in an attempt to reassert the King's rule."

When Heramiir lapsed into silence, Arana waited a moment before asking. "Is that all Archmage?"

"Except for one thing," he replied after a thoughtful moment.

"I take it you've been told about the missing villages along the western border?"

She nodded in confirmation, but otherwise remained silent.

"Our initial attempts to ascertain their fate have as yet been unfruitful, but given the location of those villages, there can be little doubt who is responsible. I am therefore sending Mendacai out with a few supporting magi and a strong contingent of the mageguard to investigate further. If the western nations are trying something serious, we need to know. It could also be nothing more than a battalion of Nostahl with a few shamans supporting them. Some of them may have been able to sneak across the mountains because of our reduced patrols. Either way, Mendacai will investigate and report back for reinforcements if he cannot deal with the incursion himself."

"I see," Arana replied, unperturbed. "So it will only be Carmilla and I left in Miralthrall then?"

"For now. Larola should be back within a few days, and while I know you think little of her personally, she will obey your orders while I am away."

He stood, pacing a few steps to stretch his legs after the long sort through the pile of reports.

A small smile crept its way onto Arana's face at that bit of information, and Heramiir scowled.

"Use her as you see fit. But Arana, don't use her up. She is, after all, my loyal subject. As are you."

"As you say, Heramiir," the older woman replied, eyes turning hard.

He didn't know what it was between those two, but there had been bad blood there for as long as he could remember. From what little he knew, the ongoing feud between the two women had started before he was born. It was likely to go on until one of them was dead.

"See to your work," Heramiir dismissed her, irritated at the old archmage's attitude.

As if we don't have enough challenges facing us right now without them squabbling amongst themselves.

The oldest member of his circle stood and walked to the door without a word. Her posture remained stiff as she turned her back on him.

"And find Mendacai!" he called as the door began to swing shut behind her.

It was only a minute later that the last member of his inner circle in the city pushed the door open with a slight spell of air, and entered the spacious room. He moved to stand in front of the desk, not taking a seat since Heramiir himself was still standing.

That was always the way with Mendacai, polite and respectful in civilised company. Put the man on the field of battle though, and he came into his own. He was fully capable of cutting a swathe through an enemy, and preferred to fight in the thick of the action, even if he had to cross half the field to get there. Once he had, there were few opponents that the soldiers of the western nations feared more. Perhaps the man's most distinguishing feature, if it could be called that, was his physical plainness. Mendacai was of average height, with short brown hair and blue eyes, a frame that was neither slim nor stocky, and a build neither fat nor muscular. In fact, if Heramiir couldn't feel the strength of the Gift aura around him, he would have been forgiven for thinking the man was a well-to-do merchant. Perhaps even a most minor member of the old nobility.

"Have a seat," Heramiir told him, suppressing the childish urge to yell at the man for taking so long to answer his original summons. He would wait at least until he had a better idea what had held up the usually punctual archmage.

"Thank you, Heramiir," Mendacai replied as he sat in the proffered chair, but not until Heramiir had taken his own seat.

They had been friends for a long time, even before he had begun his long march to power all those years ago. Mendacai had been second only to Nereth in joining his quest to change Jeranon's power structure, and done so for no reason other than he believed the cause to be just.

"What took you so long?" Heramiir asked, hoping for Mendacai's sake that he had a good enough reason for his tardiness.

"I was conducting an experiment," the powerful archmage answered. "It took me some time to get back within the city walls."

"I see, and did this experiment bear fruit?"

After the coup, he'd issued an edict that any new discoveries were to be made public. There was to be no more hoarding of knowledge. He'd expected the younger magi to be excited, but to his surprise, the change had received overwhelming support from every layer of the college. Indeed, many of the instructors seemed to enjoy it for no reason other than increasing the knowledge and skill of the college as a whole. That was what Larola was doing out of the city, confirming the new spells in a safe area, and coordinating the flow of information between the magi.

All that was for the good, but the real reason he'd given them such freedom was so that the magi would begin to experiment with battle magic as well. They would need every edge if the coming dawn of summer campaign against the king's army did not go well. He didn't enjoy making his magi fight, but the number of Giftless troops Jeranon could call upon would be drastically reduced after the coming battle, no matter which way it went. Despite everything else, keeping Jeranon secure from the western nations was one of his few goals which had not changed after meeting the master that first time. After all, what good was it for him to depose Erian if he himself was swept away by the next inevitable invasion? And there was always a next invasion.

That was something he would look to once the rest of Jeranon was secured. This pointless, never-ending warfare which the western nations subjected them to served nothing but to hold Jeranon back. It was a constant distraction, dividing and diminishing resources and men who could use their lives in so many better ways than to be the arm which swung a sword. None of that, however, compared to the utter waste it was when a mage died in battle. When every piece of knowledge they'd accrued, every secret they'd garnered about the foundations of the world was lost. And for no better reason than some Augrahl shaman or Imbic mutation had been taught from birth to want a piece of land back which neither they, nor those teaching them, had ever actually laid their eyes upon.

"So to speak," Mendacai answered, breaking his train of thought and bringing him back to the present.

"I've been trying to increase the crop yield to offset the planting that didn't get done this season. While my original efforts to speed its growth cycle were unsuccessful, I seem to have found the key to enlarging what is already there."

"Really?" Heramiir inquired. There were several applications for that spell he could foresee if it were true, so he waited for the man to continue.

"Yes, it's surprisingly easy. Nearly all our magi should be able to do it. The problem is that each piece of fruit or grain must be enlarged individually. Therefore, while it should solve any food shortage we may experience next season, it will also tie many magi up to do so."

Heramiir thought for a moment of how to get around that, and then came up with a potential solution.

"What would happen if you enlarged the plants themselves, perhaps seedlings, rather than the fruit?"

Mendacai thought about it for a long moment, turning the idea over in his mind and looking for flaws.

"It might work well for trees with hanging fruit and berry shrubs, but ground crops like wheat and carrots would still need the room to grow. Although they would be bigger, you would get far fewer of them in a field. I'm not sure that the food to space yield would be any higher. Not to mention the difficulty of pulling up a thirty-pound carrot."

"Still, it's worth investigating," Heramiir told him. "Now show me the spell, on this paperweight if you please." He picked up a rounded stone from his desk and tossed it onto the floor near the corner of the room.

Mendacai concentrated for a long moment, and then with an annoyed wave of his hand, focused the spell of earth, water, and fire into the small stone until it grew into a rock. It continued growing until it became a small, smooth boulder which now adorned the corner of his office. Heramiir smiled one of his rare smiles in appreciation of the spell's simplicity, and then frowned. He very much wanted to try the spell for himself, but for the sake of his troops he could not use the Gift again until the fight with the king's army was joined.

"Is something wrong?" Mendacai asked, puzzled by Heramiir's scowl.

"No. Not anymore," He replied. "But to think that something this simply done, and this beneficial to not only ourselves, but all of Jeranon has been kept from us for over five hundred years because some king decided to blame us for something that couldn't be proven. To institute that ridiculous ban on experimentation. It just proves that everything we have done to remove the old regime has been right and worthwhile."

"I agree," Mendacai responded. "I would not be here if I did not. But while the ban should have been lifted within a dozen years of being implemented, there remains a crater over one hundred miles in diameter where the city of Harverness used to stand. That… error, bears witness to why the ban was put in place, and even now, all these years later, reminds us why we still need to be careful."

"It was never proven that experimentation with the Gift caused that," Heramiir reminded him, and Mendacai grinned.

"When a hundred miles of rock, and everything on it simply disappears, what evidence can there be?"

It was a conversation they had held many times over the years, as far back as when Mendacai, along with Archmage Tolmarak, had been some of his first teachers. Mendacai was one of the few who had provided Heramiir with the mental stimulation to test his already considerable abilities.

"Be that as it may," Heramiir said, forestalling the inevitable debate which would no doubt follow. "We have a mystery far more pressing on our hands, and I am sending you to investigate."

"I always have loved a good mystery," Mendacai returned with a cautious smile.

"Of that I am well aware, my old friend," Heramiir replied, returning his grin.

"How much do you know about the missing villages near the western border?"

"Not much more than that," Mendacai answered with a frown. "There are rumours going around in the city that they were not destroyed, but had simply vanished. Most people are putting it down to the western nations becoming more active again. It's been a decade since they attacked in force. The feeling on the streets now is that it's only a matter of time before the warning bells at Stonekeep are rung out once more."

Heramiir nodded in agreement.

"What we know for certain is this. Several villages along the western border have been swept off the face of Jeranon. People, buildings, even the animals are gone. In each case, all that is left is a field of grass at the end of a road. In one town, the faint residue of Augrahl magic from at least three shamans remained. What I need from you is, first and foremost, to find out why they are attacking strategically meaningless targets along the border. Second, why the theatre with making the villages seem to disappear when they could have blasted them with any number of destructive spells, as is their habit. Third, I need you to locate this force and destroy it, if possible. At the very least you are to send for reinforcements while you do what you can to slow its advance. Finally, try to establish communication with the bands of Terraliv and Arborii who are flooding up into the mountains. Find out whatever you can about how the attackers have been able to cross the border undetected. That could be disastrous if allowed to continue."

"Very well," Mendacai said, standing as soon as Heramiir was finished. "Is there anything else I should know before I leave?"

"Only that you should be careful. Until the campaign against the King's army is won, I will have precious few troops to support you with for anything short of a full-blown offensive."

"I understand," Mendacai returned. "How many troops do you want me to take?"

Heramiir thought for a minute about what he could do without, and then answered.

"Take five of the more experienced magi with you, battle trained but not yet archmagi themselves. One hundred of the mageguard for an escort, and a thousand of the regular army. Under your command that should be enough to deal with anything short of an invasion."

"Yes, that should do it," Mendacai agreed, a tiny grin pulling at his mouth.

Likely the man thought he could handle the three shaman and whatever else the raiders had all by himself. He might not be wrong either. Besides himself and Nereth, and definitely Archmage Tolmarak from Aramar, no one in Jeranon was more implacable on the battlefield than the unassuming man before him.

"See to whatever you need, and leave at first light," Heramiir told him as he stood, clasping forearms with his old teacher by way of respect. "Be safe, but be swift. We must know if the western nations are simply probing, or if this is the beginning of a major new offensive."

"I won't let you down, Heramiir. Just make sure that you deal with the King's army decisively. If you're right about the western nations, we can't afford to be fighting on both fronts. Since the dark nations will be a threat which can't be ignored, Erian's army will retake the lands which we have conquered so far with ease."

"Of this I am painfully aware," Heramiir returned, dropping the man's arm and sitting once more.

"Go see to your travel arrangements, and choose the magi you want as your escort. I will see you again when we both return victorious," he said, putting a slight emphasis on the last word.

Mendacai was his friend, and the closest thing to a mentor he'd ever had. And yet there could never, not for one second, be any doubt who was in charge here in Miralthrall, and the Maker willing, soon all of Jeranon.

Mendacai nodded and left, and Heramiir found himself at peace. What had to be done, had been. His lieutenants were in the field or had their orders, and there was little left for him to do. His next step was to catch up to Nereth and the army to prepare for their battle with old King Erian's men. If he was decisive enough in victory, his men could be inside Aramar's gates within a year. The power the Destroyer had given him would help greatly with that vital task. If all went as planned, Jeranon would know an age of prosperity like it had not since before the time Eldrik had blackened the reputation of magi the world around. Since before Harverness had disappeared in a fashion that caused the earth to quake across half the country, and precipitate the five-hundred-year ban on experimentation with the Gift. He would see Jeranon built up in knowledge and power until it rivalled even the ancient stories of the ancestral lands of Jeranah.

Whatever the cataclysm truly had been, such had been the scope of the disaster that the last remaining survivors of a nation had been forced to flee an entire continent. They had abandoned almost everything, setting sail for a desperately uncertain future, failing even to properly document its cause. The desolate fleet, as history knew it, had sailed beyond every known map of the day, languishing for phases at sea before discovering a new continent. A landmass that after the Wars of Founding had been named Jeranon, in tribute to the now devastated homeland to which the survivors could never return.

All that stood in the way of his plans was the king's army, and for the western nations to leave them alone for just one more year. Once he consolidated his hold on the country, he could return to the master and finish learning all he could from the powerful being. He would glean every scrap from its ancient knowledge, take every bit of power it offered, and then he could begin his true life's work. He would lead the full forces of Jeranon beyond the Dark Iron Mountains, and deal with the western nations once and for all.

All he needed was a little more time.

It is the nature of a child to forgive. It is the nature of an adult to require it.
Common Jeranonian saying.

CHAPTER 12

NIGHTMARES AND INNOCENCE

The sun was burning bright as Jayden levered himself up onto the cliff top plateau overlooking the Sea of Dreams. The wind was fresh today, carrying the tang of salt all this way up here while sea birds wheeled below, searching the waves for fish swimming too close to the surface. Ahead of him, Rhianna sat right on the precipice, long legs dangling out into the air as she contemplated the pristine scene before them.

Without speaking, Jayden somehow knew she was already aware of his presence, so he crossed the rock outcropping and sat beside her.

"Have you ever wondered what it would be like to fly?" she asked before pushing off from her perch to fall silently away.

Jayden made a desperate grab at her and missed.

"No!"

He watched the woman he loved plummet to her death a thousand paces below, until there was a vague splash in the ocean, and then nothing. Jayden examined the waves in anguish, desperate to find any sign she might have resurfaced, but of course there were none.

"What are you staring at?" Rhianna asked from beside

him. She was sitting perched on the edge of the cliff again, as she had been a moment before. Her long red hair swirling in the fresh breeze while she looked at him, a confused expression on her face.

Jayden looked at her, and then down at the water again, and back at Rhianna, who was now inexplicably soaked through. Her hair was plastered to her face and her clothes saturated. The smell of brine radiated off her in waves.

"You should have saved me," she said, giving him an unforgiving stare.

Jayden scrambled to his feet, backing away as quickly as he could.

"This isn't real," he said as she stood and began walking towards him.

"Of course it's not," Rhianna returned. "How could it be? I'm dead. You let me die, Jayden. You abandoned me to that monster Dael, and you let me die!" she hissed as the surrounding wind picked up and the skies turned dark with clouds.

A hundred reasons he had done what he had popped into Jayden's mind, and a hundred excuses followed. He offered none of them though, because in the end, she was right. It was his fault she was dead. Had he not allowed his father to talk him into leaving Grandell, she would never have needed saving in the first place.

"You might as well have killed me yourself."

Jayden felt himself backed up against the edge of the cliff.

Somehow he must have gotten turned around. A bash of thunder out of a clear blue sky announced his doom. Rhianna stepped up close to him, and everything fell quiet. Once again she was dry, her long hair motionless now that the sudden wind had fled. The sweet smell of her perfume caught in his nostrils as she looked up at him.

There was no love in that gaze though, her expression more like a judge about to dispense a sentence.

"For abandoning me to Dael and allowing me to die, and for not avenging my death, you will now share in it."

With a quick blow, Rhianna shoved him hard in the chest, causing Jayden to topple backwards. He tried to secure his footing, to regain his balance, but there was nothing there to brace against. As he fell, plummeting over the edge, he saw Rhianna smile for the first time since she had drowned in the muddy river what seemed like a lifetime ago. For long, long moments Jayden spun through the air, terrified as each time he turned the ocean was vastly closer. With a sickening thud, he hit the water.

Jayden jolted upright in his bed in the college building, gasping for air. His hands grasped at his throat, and he swore he could still taste the saltwater burning his lungs.

He groaned as he continued trying to catch his breath.

Every time he thought he was getting past the nightmares, a new one would start, each different and more potent than the one before. He had seen her die a hundred times by her own hand, or by Dael's, but never had she blamed him so directly. It left him shaken to the core as he rested his head in his hands and tried not to weep.

After what seemed like a very long time, he calmed enough to think straight, and vowed once again to destroy Dael the moment the assassin was dealt with. There would be no mistakes this time, no second chances. The next time he saw the assassin, one of them would die. There could be no other way.

Without warning the door to the adjoining bathroom opened and Rhianna slipped through it wearing nothing but a sheer nightgown. She climbed into bed with him, rearranging the pillows more to her liking as Jayden stared dumbly, mouth hanging open.

"Why are you staring at me like that, Jay?" she asked. "We've been married for almost a year now. You know perfectly well what I look like," she told him playfully as she pulled the covers back over herself.

"But.... but you're, you're dead," Jayden whispered in absolute shock, sure he must have been as pale as the sheets which lined their bed.

"Ah... no. Pretty sure I'm right here. Thanks to you," she told him with a small, sleepy smile.

"You do remember convincing Archmage Tolmarak to intercede on our behalf, don't you?" she asked him.

"And you had better remember we got married right afterwards," she told him as she gave him a meaningful poke in the ribs.

Jayden shied away, noticing for the first time the small circle of gold that now adorned his finger as Rhianna frowned.

"Are you all right?" she asked as he came to his senses and jumped out of the bed, crossing the room to be as far away from this impostor as he could.

"What's going on?" he said, more to himself than to the all too familiar woman in his bed.

For an instant he toyed with the idea that this was some sick joke on Firerose's part, but dismissed the idea almost immediately. Whoever this was, it was clearly not his classmate.

Rhianna stood, or at least the person pretending to be her did, and crossed to the door leading out of his rooms, and opened it.

"I have to go now. You should have protected me Jay, then all this would have been real."

With a sad smile, she left, closing the door behind her.

After a bewildered second, Jayden regained his composure enough to chase after the woman, flinging open the door and stepping out into the corridor. Looking around wildly, he could find no trace of her in either direction. It made no sense. There had been nowhere near enough time for her to have rounded the nearest corner and disappear. With a start he realised the wedding band on his finger had disappeared at the same time she had, almost as though by the Gift.

Not the Gift, and not real.

As his sleep deprived mind finally realised what was happening, Jayden slumped down next to the wall and wept.

He awoke in his bed in the college building feeling utterly drained, both physically and emotionally. He couldn't help but take several deep breaths, though of course there was no trace of the lingering perfume. When he arose sometime later, he found his room returned to the state he had left it in before going to bed the previous night.

Opening the heavy curtain which covered his large window, Jayden looked out onto the city beyond the college grounds. To his surprise, the moon was still high.

Dawn must be hours off yet.

He thought about trying to go back to sleep, but the idea of revisiting this new nightmare wakened him far beyond any desire to renew his slumber.

For a long time Jayden stood, looking out into the darkness while he tried to come to terms with this new dream. Instead, all he achieved was to send his thoughts chasing each other in circles, again and again until he felt like screaming.

He felt the sudden need to be away from his rooms. They seemed empty and stifling now, despite being a significant improvement on the small apartment he had lived in as an apprentice. Roughly pulling on a pair of pants and a top, he headed out to the central stairway. It was welcomely deserted for once, and he began heading up to the very peak of the building's spire.

It was a long hike up the spiral staircase. Round and round the perimeter of the entrance hall he travelled, passing doorways and corridors at each landing which led to various parts of the immense building. Eventually, he came to the top of the winding way, and without paying much attention walked through the unadorned opening. He climbed the switchback flights of stairs that would take him up to the roof. The stairs were not wide, but were kept in good order for the few magi who did their work up here. Most of those magi had left with the army, and he was hoping the rooftop landing would be as empty as the rest of the college seemed now.

It was several minutes of climbing until Jayden reached the top of the stairs. As he stepped through the inner door, it closed with a loud noise, causing a flock of pigeons that must have been roosting in the rafters to take sudden, terrified flight. Jayden couldn't help but yell in sudden fright as he was assaulted by the shrieking birds. The entire flock mindlessly flapped and flew every which way as they attempted to escape the confined area in their pointless avian panic.

Being buffeted by dozens of fluffy wings did nothing to improve Jayden's mood. But once he realised he was not under some sort of attack, his heart rate returned to something approaching normal. With some difficulty, he pushed through the mass of birds and shoved the outer door open with the Gift, giving the flock somewhere else to go. The instant they had another option, the birds were off, diving for the freedom of the cool night air as they continued their raucous clamour.

Taking a moment to compose himself after the unexpected encounter, Jayden stepped out onto the roof as he plucked a few stray feathers from his clothes. The unwelcome sound of a laugh greeted him.

"You should learn how to tame them," Missy told him good-naturedly as she turned her head towards where he was standing.

Jayden's heart sank a notch. He'd really wanted some quiet out here with only the stars as company, but apparently that was not to be.

"You know how to do that?" he asked her, his mind abruptly registering what the younger girl had said.

With a crooked smile, she laughed again.

"I have my ways."

Jayden weakly returned the smile. Of all the things they had learned over the last year, persuasion of the Giftless was one of the stranger subjects. Not that the magi used the Gift to do it, or even knew how to. Nevertheless, classes were offered on how to make non-Gift users accept your authority without resorting to force. A task apparently made easier if they never knew what skills an individual mage possessed. Of course, manipulating people in that way could only ever work if your bluff remained intact, hence the classes. Classes that Missy seemed to have taken in stride.

"What brings you up here tonight?" she asked as she

leaned back against the curved wall, resuming her gaze up into the cloudless night.

"I couldn't sleep."

They had been in the same class for the better part of a year now. He had never really connected with Missy as he had with some of the others. Because of the age difference, he supposed. It was nothing personal. That, and the younger girl preferred the company of Firerose and Nadeara to his own. It was understandable given the state he'd been in when they'd first arrived, and still somewhat was. Tonight's new nightmare had proven that in explicit detail.

"Obviously," she replied, but not mockingly. "But very few people come up here in the middle of the night unless they're working or have something weighing on their mind. You don't look like you're here to work."

He didn't know what to say to that, or whether he even wished to share his experiences with the younger girl. Perhaps he should return to his bed and try to sleep away the grief and weariness that was shrouding his thoughts this night. And would no doubt do so for several yet to come.

"Come, sit," she offered, motioning to a spot beside her.

"I know we are not the best of friends Jayden, but I hold no grudge against you."

With an ironic smile, Jayden sighed and went over to sit next to Missy before taking a long moment to look up at the twinkling stars himself. From up here the lights of Aramar were invisible behind them on the other side of the college building, blocked from view and creating little more than a distant glow.

With a slight easing of his mind, Jayden realised he hadn't seen a sky so clear since leaving Grandell's small township behind at Dael's behest. He missed it, he realised as a shooting star scorched its way through a portion of the sky before burning out, as they always did. The many lights of the city blotted out all but the brightest stars from ground level, or even where his own rooms were. While Aramar held many wondrous things, the simple ability to look up and see the starry night sky was not one of them.

"So why do you come up here?" Jayden asked as he continued to stare up into the grand celestial display.

For a long minute Missy was quiet, until finally, when Jayden had long since thought she would not answer, she looked at him.

"You see that group of stars up there, the archer's bow?"

Jayden nodded.

"They look the same from my home village of Angara. It's north of the Ice Ranges on the coast of the Great North Ocean. The Fox too, and the Satyr's horns," she pointed out the constellations.

"They sit lower in the sky there, but they are the same stars. No matter how far away from home and family I am, I can always look up and know that half a world away, my parents and sisters are looking up at those same stars each night. Maybe even right at this very moment."

"You miss your family."

Missy just looked at him, "Don't you?"

Jayden looked away, then back up at the stars.

"I miss my sister, and I suppose my parents as well. But for every good memory I have of home and hearth, there are a dozen more which are better suited to a nightmare than the life of a merchant's son."

Missy nodded to herself almost imperceptibly before deciding to speak her mind, as was her habit.

"I don't know much about that, but from the little I've

heard I'm surprised you have done as well at your studies as you have," she told him. A sudden squall of wind picked up a strand of her hair, which she brushed back into place behind her ear.

"What do you think you'll do once the war is over?" Jayden asked, changing the subject.

Missy looked at him sideways, but accepted that he didn't want to talk about his past this night, and let the subject drop.

"I don't know yet," she replied. "I guess it depends on which side wins."

Now it was Jayden's turn to shoot a glance at the young girl beside him.

"I mean, I want us to win, of course. But the rumours that Heramiir has made life better not only for the magi, but for everyone under his control are just too prevalent to continue being ignored. No matter how much the King's men try to squash them on the streets."

"Have you forgotten the assassin Heramiir sent? The one that has killed more than a dozen of us now, who has even tried to kill me not once, but twice?"

No," Missy replied. "Of course not. But for one thing, no one has actually proved any sort of connection between him and Heramiir yet, and even if Heramiir did send him... it makes sense. This is a war that is being fought on several fronts."

"What do you mean?" Jayden asked, not sure he enjoyed being lectured by a fifteen-year-old.

"Don't you ever listen to Tolmarak in military command class? Heramiir is trying to take over the country, but to do that he needs the support of the magi and enough of the military to achieve that goal. If you ask me, all these freedoms he has given Gift users since his coup are for the sole reason of solidifying their support. With that in place he can use fear of retaliation from those already converted to enlist a high enough portion of the common people to his cause that most other citizens won't want to declare for the King. They'll be too afraid that one of those who is loyal to the magi will overhear, and pass the information along."

Jayden just looked at her and she grinned.

"Are you still with me?"

He gave a rueful nod, and she continued, looking back up at the stars.

"Once he had the local populace and western magi under his control, he could begin expanding his geographical territory and claim even more lands, people, resources, and crops. All of which he can use to further his aims until he is opposed by a superior numerical force. Or one that has some other tactical advantage which can stop his expansion."

For a moment Jayden had the sudden urge to pinch himself, just to make sure he wasn't still dreaming. Missy gave him another slightly cheeky grin.

"You should try to learn from the archmage's classes Jayden, not just listen to them. Otherwise all your strength will count for nothing when you come up against a mage who knows how to work around or nullify your spells."

For a second, Missy fell silent, then with a guilty grimace pulled a small stone out of a pocket in the white lining of her apprentice mage's cloak. With a flick she sent it spinning off until it came to a sudden halt near the far edge of the roof.

"Can I trust you?" she asked him.

Jayden looked at the younger girl for a minute, saw she was serious, and nodded that she could.

"Good, I thought so. Watch the stone," she said, then began concentrating on it herself.

Jayden looked from Missy to the stone and then waited, wondering what was supposed to happen. It took two full minutes, but eventually the small rock shimmered and disappeared, and Missy smiled in satisfaction.

"Could you stop that?" she asked.

Jayden shifted in his seat and looked back at his companion in consternation.

"Tolmarak was very clear that you can't experiment without the king's permission. It's dangerous, not to mention illegal," he told her. He wondered if anyone below had felt the large surge of Gift energy she had caused when she made the tiny rock vanish.

"Forget that for a moment," she told him. "Could you stop it if you wanted to?"

"I don't even know what you did!" Jayden whispered, even though there was no one up here to hear them.

"Exactly," Missy returned with a raised eyebrow.

"All your power would have gone for nothing had I turned that spell on you."

Jayden sat back against the wall for a second, feeling as though he'd been slapped. Ever since the night of his failed attempt to claim vengeance on Dael, he had known that he was strong in the Gift. Since then it had been confirmed in a multitude of ways. Not the least of which was the archmage's blunt assertion that he was one of the two most powerful magi in Jeranon. Possibly the better of the two, though apparently it was a close thing.

Even as the assassin fled his room, he'd been confident that if he could just catch up with the murderer he could bring an end to the man's reign of terror. Now all that seemed in error. As his perspective shifted, he realised it was not his own strength, either physical or in the Gift, but luck that had saved him the first time he had been attacked. Nadeara had come after him, distracting the assassin long enough for him to escape the acidic spell. She had almost sacrificed herself in the process. If not for that selfless act of bravery, things might have turned out very differently indeed.

The second time he had fought the assassin, he'd only heard the construct at the very last instant, allowing him to dive to the ground. Thankfully he'd been close enough to tackle Clarion out of harm's way as well. It had been a close enough thing though that one of his escorts had been killed, another maimed, not to mention Firerose being concussed. Again, nothing to do with his strength in the Gift. Instead, it had been his hearing on that occasion which had given him the crucial warning in time.

"What are you thinking?" Missy asked after a long moment had gone by, breaking him out of his reverie.

"That you should be teaching that class," Jayden replied, only half joking. "I think I just learned more in the last ten minutes than I have in the past two phases."

Missy smiled, pleased at the compliment.

"Thank you, Jayden, but what about you?"

"What will I do after the war you mean?" he finally replied after searching his memory for what she was asking, before looking back up at the stars.

Missy nodded.

Jayden thought for a long time about how much to tell the young girl. He thought it likely he could trust her since she had already shown him the trick with the rock disappearing. It could have been enough to put her in prison if he pushed the issue and could prove it. Not that he would do that to her of course.

The truth was, like most powerful magi he disagreed with the ban on experimentation. Some days he wanted nothing more than to test the limits of his power and see what new spells he could dream up. Of course, that could be dangerous, and the more powerful the spell, the more likely it was to go wrong while the mage was attempting to perfect it. Sometimes even with disastrous consequences, hence the original reason for the ban. Still, the thought of experimentation was always in the back of his mind, as it was for most of the others. There had even been some small talk among the magi that perhaps Heramiir had the right of that when he'd abolished the age-old law. Rumour was that he'd given his people free rein so long as they took the proper precautions.

Tolmarak had squashed that talk, lest it be allowed to ferment too much in the Aramarian magi's own minds.

The archmage had been looking into where all the information about what Heramiir was doing was coming from. It seemed to be leaking in from the city itself. Aramar was full of these little titbits about how Heramiir had abolished crime in Miralthrall, and how things were better under the leadership of the magi.

Tolmarak had told the class he suspected the assassin was involved. The man's job in Aramar seemed to be twofold now that the army had marched. First, wearing down the city's defences by eliminating as many Gift users as he could, and second, sowing dissent within the general populace.

It was having some effect from what Jayden had been told, since most of Aramar's citizens had a connection to someone in the west. Many even knew someone who had marched or ridden out with the king's army, possibly never to return home again. The problem was not that these men had gone to war, but that the constant rumours were causing the citizenry to see Heramiir's regime in a much more ambivalent light than the king would have liked. If the rumours were true, if Heramiir's new order provided a superior system to the way the nobility ran things now, it cast doubt on the entire validity of the campaign.

"If the war doesn't go as planned, they want me to kill Heramiir for them," Jayden told her at last. "And I think you just showed me I can't."

For the first time Jayden truly comprehended what it was Tolmarak had been alluding to over the last year. A great wall of hopelessness washed over him as he leant back and looked up once more at the starry night. If he couldn't even deal with this assassin, how was he supposed to defeat the man's master?

He couldn't stay here. If he did, eventually he would be sent after Heramiir, and he now knew that there was every likelihood he would fail. The prospect of his own death held no fear for him. On the contrary, he would welcome it when the time came, but before that happened there was still something he had to do. Something that couldn't wait on the chance of his returning alive from that mission.

He had promised himself to wait until the assassin was stopped, and he dearly wanted to hold on to that. His classmates were not family, not even really good friends, but they were all he had. He would take his last breath before letting the assassin have his way with them. Even so, the prospect of missing the opportunity to repay Dael for his crimes was enough to make him seriously reconsider. He could not, *would* not, let that sorry excuse of a man go unpunished for Rhianna's death. Not even if it meant abandoning his friends, and what little honour he had left, to achieve it.

"Are you all right?" Missy asked, concern clear in her tone.

Jayden looked at her and then realised how he must look. He wrenched the snarl from his own features before looking away, gaze hard as flint. He had already decided he could trust her, and now, for the first time since coming to the college he told Missy the whole tale of the events leading up to and including that night on the cliff. He didn't shy away from his mistakes, or the guard he had killed, or trying to take vengeance after it was all done. He even found himself revealing the extent of the nightmares that had driven him up here tonight.

"That is why I have to go back, even though the King has ordered that I be declared renegade if I do."

There was a long, shocked moment of silence, and Missy's jaw was even hung slightly open as he told her the last part.

"But Jayden, you can't. If you're declared renegade, every mage in the kingdom will try to execute you on sight. And you know who they will send first."

"Yes, Tolmarak," he replied flatly. "And he would do it too."

"Not by his own choosing," Missy returned, becoming a little angry at his fatalistic attitude.

"No," Jayden agreed. "But he would do it all the same, even though he knows that I'm right."

Missy frowned.

"Even if you could kill the archmage, and that is what it

would take, you know that. The King would just send others, and more again if you defeat them. You can't kill us all, Jayden."

"Actually, I probably could," he told her. "So long as you didn't all come at once."

"You would try to kill me?" Missy stated, her eyes turning to agate.

"Because that is what you're talking about Jayden. Me and every other mage you've met here and everywhere else. What about Billy, or Nadeara, or Clarion? Would you kill them too?"

Missy stood now, coming around to stand in front of him, forcing him to look up at her, or away. He looked away, and even as he did so she slapped him as hard as she could.

The surprise of it knocked him off balance, and he had to put a hand on the ground to stay upright.

"Look at me!" she commanded; voice cold as winter's heart. Jayden complied, though he was sure his eyes matched her tone for frost.

"Two deaths do not make a life, and nothing you can do will ever bring her back. But if you start killing magi for trying to uphold the law, I will come for you myself. And if Rhianna could see you now, I very much doubt that love would be the emotion you would be sensing from her."

With a final hard look she stalked off towards the door that led back into the tower.

Once again Jayden felt as though he'd been slapped, not because of her anger, but, much as he was loath to admit it, because she was right. Impulsively he used the Gift to put up a spell of air across the doorway, barring Missy's path and causing her to turn on him furiously.

"Decided to start early have you!" she yelled at him,

making a futile attempt to dissipate his spell.

Jayden flinched at the accusation, which only reinforced the fact that she'd been right a moment before, and he stopped, trying to think of something to say. Something that would undo the probably fatal damage he had just caused their new friendship.

After a long minute Missy shook her head, and sighed in exasperation.

"So you *can* still listen," she said almost to herself.

"You're just stubborn as a mule, and more than half blinded by your own hatred."

That was far too close to home for Jayden's liking, but a wrong word right now would end what little trust they still had for each other permanently.

"You have got to let this go Jayden. Kill Dael if you must, but you must find a way to let this go before it destroys every good thing about you. Even if I knew nothing else about her, I know Rhianna would not have wanted that. I mean, I don't even know you Jayden, and even I can see you have changed since you came here, and not for the better. At first it was just grief like anyone would go through at losing a loved one, but lately you have been more and more distant, harder somehow. It's as though you are storing all the anger you want to take out on Dael inside yourself in preparation for that moment. Only you don't realise that in the meantime it is harming you far more than it is him."

Jayden sat back down where he had been, though he couldn't quite recall having stood now that he reflected on it, and rested his forehead on his hands.

"I can't," he told her eventually. "I have tried… everything."

"Then go," Missy said as she made her way back to where he was sitting.

"Leave tonight, don't look back. Finish this so you can move on. I can't believe I am giving you this advice, but we need you Jayden. And the way you're going, in a very short amount of time you will be just as lost to us as if Dael had killed you too."

He leaned back against the wall, and Missy resumed her seat beside him. For a long time afterward there was silence.

"I want to. But I can't leave yet. Not until I know you are safe. You and the others," he amended.

"We will be all right. By the time you return, our army will have defeated Heramiir's, and the assassin will have been caught. And then, once you have grieved, you will finally be able to move on."

She gave him an encouraging smile.

Jayden just looked at her in return.

"I made the mistake of listening to that advice once before," he told her. "I will leave when you are safe, not before."

"And not a moment after," he added under his breath, though she could still hear.

"Have you had any thoughts on that front?" she asked, changing the subject.

Jayden just shook his head though. "What about you?"

"Short of quarantining all of Aramar and having the magi search the entire population one by one? No, nothing useful I'm afraid," Missy replied with a vague shrug.

"There must be something we haven't tried yet. From what I could tell during our last encounter, the assassin is a fair bit less powerful than I am. If I could ever get my hands on him, I should be able to deal with him once and for all.

We just have to come up with a way of locating him without tracking his aura. Or without getting close enough ourselves that he can pick us off before we even know he's there."

"Agreed," Missy added. "And we had better do it soon, because at the rate the assassin is going, in a few more phases we won't have enough battle trained magi left to effectively defend Aramar. Not to mention the rest of Jeranon. If Heramiir's forces win the battle out west, there will be precious little between here and there to stop him marching straight up to the city gates and demanding our surrender."

"I know that," Jayden replied. "But until we come up with a viable plan, there is nothing more we can do except be on constant guard. Our only hope is that one of us will avoid or survive an ambush and be able to stop him. Or at least hold out long enough for the rest of us to help."

"Then I hope he comes for you again," Missy said, then noticed Jayden's sideways look before realising how that had sounded.

"I mean, not because I want you harmed. But so far you're the only one who has beaten him. All the rest of us seem to be able to do when he appears is to die. If even Archmage Kelta couldn't defend himself, then we apprentices have little to no chance. You may well be our only hope Jayden. I know that's a horrible responsibility to put on you, especially on top of everything else you have to deal with. But there it is. We need you. If you can't pull yourself together, I doubt very much that any of us will live to see another year before this assassin finishes his work."

Jayden looked at the earnest expression on the young girl beside him before turning away, ashamed. Had he really fallen so far as to consider leaving to pursue his own agenda while what few friends he still had were being hunted through the streets?

Nothing is simple anymore, he thought as the first glow of predawn stained the horizon and the stars began to fade. A new day was coming, and as a final shooting star drew a small white line across the heavens, it appeared he had a great deal of work to do.

"I won't let you down Missy," he said, feeling calmer than he had in a very long time. Not serene though, more the calm of an arrow that has been fitted to a knocked bow, waiting to be loosed as it stares down its target from afar.

As he stood, Missy gave him a concerned look, but rose as well.

"I had best get down to the library if I'm going to figure this thing out. Tell Tolmarak that I won't be in classes today, probably not for the rest of the week."

"I don't think he's going to like that Jayden," Missy prompted as she followed behind the older mage, who was already heading for the doorway.

"Then tell him to come and help me! It's past time that this ended. Once and for all."

*   *   *

Missy watched him go as Jayden unbound the forgotten air spell blocking the doorway without so much as a hand motion, leaving her behind on the rooftop. She didn't know whether to smile or not. She had gotten through to him it seemed, even focusing his rage on a course other than revenge for once. But something in his manner had changed just before he left.

It was true, she had talked him around to doing

everything she wanted, what they all wanted truth to tell. But watching him walk away with his too straight back and hard, faraway glare, she couldn't shake the feeling that she had just made a terrible mistake. That she had loosed something dreadful inside him. Something that once free to pursue its own path he might never again be able to rein in.

What she also couldn't help guiltily wondering, was what else Jayden might do once he had accomplished his mission, and what the eventual cost of her manipulating him here tonight might be. For all of them.

CHAPTER 13

JARL

"I'll say this for Nereth, at least he keeps us well fed," Jarl remarked with studied nonchalance as he reclined, head resting on his well-worn saddle.

The campfire was blazing, and the sky was clear. If it was a little cold outside the circle of light and warmth, at least there would be no rain tonight. The meal they had just eaten would never be called a feast, but was still a good deal better than the trail rations they were used to while on campaign. It was a combination that had put most of the men in a decent mood.

Of course, that 'most' didn't include their colonel. Hassan was sitting across the fire from Jarl, scowling into the flames at something only he could see, while the rest of the men talked and ate.

Jarl had been marching east with the others for over two phases now. His squad, with Hassan still attached, had joined up with Heramiir's main force after their investigation into the disappearance of the villages along the border. There had been nine such losses in the region as it turned out, all to the south of Stonekeep. The young Mage,

Derrack, had left with Hassan to make that report, and not returned after being reassigned.

The thought of their visit to Greentree Lake still played on Jarl's mind every time he ate a piece of roast meat. For once, he was thankful there had been little occasion for that to be an issue since leaving Miralthrall behind.

As far as he knew, even after all the reports had come in, the magi still could not find out what had become of the villages. The border patrols had reported no incursions, and Stonekeep stood guard on the eastern pass as it had for many, many years without allowing an enemy to break through. They had of course altered that longstanding record themselves when they'd taken the castle last autumn's dusk, he reflected as he stretched out in front of the fire's warmth.

Overhead, a shooting star tracked its orange glow across the sky, and Jarl watched its progress until it faded into nothing off in the north.

Some of the men had nodded in agreement at his previous comment, and he smiled inwardly. Every day, whether they knew it or not, they were becoming more and more Heramiir's army. Hassan did what he could to discourage it, but now that Heramiir had allowed their families to return to Miralthrall, the colonel was fighting a losing battle. The civilians were still being used as leverage, but as the phases had rolled by, nothing more had come of those threats. Life after the coup had continued with few other changes, leaving most of the men who had initially opposed Heramiir's seizing of power wondering why they had done so. Other than the sheer surprise of being faced with a hostile armed force inside the city of course.

Heramiir and Nereth had worked hard to make that

change of attitude happen in a variety of ways. First, more magi travelled with the army than was usual, and they were being uncharacteristically free with the Gift. Part of the instructions Nereth had given Jarl were to convince the men that the king's strictures against experimentation were no longer relevant. In addition, the army was better equipped and provisioned than he could ever remember. Most of the officers had been allocated at least one item of Gift-wrought armour, or Gift-wrought weapon, and that was just the start supposedly. Nereth had instituted a daily mail run in the form of carts which ran between the army and Miralthrall, so the men could keep in touch with their families. It was this measure more than any other which had won the most men over Jarl believed. Until now, a year after the initial coup, only a few hundred hardcore supporters of the monarchy remained loyal to Hassan, and the resistance he was trying to form.

Jarl was undermining that effort at every opportunity. It was a mark of his old companion's trust in him that he hadn't caught on yet, and Jarl felt a small pang of regret.

It wasn't that he hated Hassan, quite the opposite. They had campaigned together on and off for over twenty years, and owed each other their lives more than once. Nereth was the best tactician they had though, and the man knew full well that any rebellion against the new order would almost certainly begin with Hassan. In return for blunting that future problem, the archmage had promised Jarl a title. Not to mention governorship over what amounted to almost a third of the Sammorand Plains once the campaign against the king's forces was over. He would still be subject to the magi of course, but the deal Nereth had offered him would make him an important and extremely wealthy man. Maybe when that happened, Aria would see sense and come back to him. It had been a year since she'd left, right before all this had begun. He hadn't seen her in some time, though to the best of his knowledge she hadn't taken up with anyone else. Yet. Maybe some time apart had helped, after all, they hadn't started having problems till he'd been stationed permanently in Miralthrall. At any rate, it was irrelevant until they concluded the current campaign.

He hoped Hassan would survive his ill-informed attempt at rebellion. Jarl was doing what he could to discourage the man's direct involvement in its day-to-day affairs. Not a simple task when the colonel was its leader, but he owed him that much.

"That was a good meal," a lanky young soldier whose name Jarl didn't recall mentioned in passing as he finished with his food.

"Only if you enjoy the taste of a bribe," the colonel returned without looking away from the flames. The young soldier cleared his throat nervously and stood.

"If you say so, sir."

Once out of Hassan's line of sight though, he gave a shrug to one of his companions.

Jarl's smile grew a fraction more. When a man was on campaign, and still warm and well fed, he counted himself lucky. In most cases lucky enough not to question the why of it. Nereth was no back room general, and knew this well, which was no doubt why the army was now so well catered for. Soon these men would be asked to fight the king's army, possibly even against people they knew and maybe liked. Before that happened, they needed to be prepared mentally for it, and the only way to do that was through fear or loyalty. Nereth had opted to gain the men's allegiance by making their lives better than they had been before. To give them a reason to fight beyond mere force, or threat of such. It was a risky tactic, but Jarl had to admit that over the last year, the men's attitudes towards the new order had changed for the better. And of course there were those, like himself, who had willingly taken part in the coup for reasons of their own. In all, he estimated that perhaps two thirds of the men now supported Heramiir's new regime directly, or didn't care who was that far up the social tree to be interested enough in opposing them in any real way. The remaining third was made up of those who had fought the initial coup and survived, or not been in the city at the time. Those last had been folded into Heramiir's army later on. Of the men who truly opposed the magi's seizing of power, only a tiny fraction were part of the actual resistance. Everybody else went along with Heramiir's plans because they had no other viable option.

When Nereth had first approached him, Jarl had been hesitant to aid in the plot even though the archmage had once saved his life. It had been more than a decade since that battle, but Jarl still felt he owed Nereth. When the archmage had shown him what was on the table in exchange for his cooperation... Well, it had been far more than a simple soldier like him could hope to earn in ten lifetimes, maybe even a hundred depending on how he could develop his new lands. It was an offer he hadn't been able to refuse, especially not when the coup would have gone ahead, regardless. Not to mention that he still suspected if he'd turned the archmage down, there was every chance he might not have left the room alive.

"Think I'll go look for a game of dice before I hit the sack," he announced to whoever wanted to listen. He rose from his camp roll and wandered off after checking the small coin purse was still attached to his belt.

Hassan watched as he stood, but said nothing. Jarl left the fire without another word, wandering off in a random direction and trying his best to look like he had no particular destination in mind. For a few minutes he wandered through the lines of campfires and tents, bedrolls, and supply wagons. Once he was out of sight of his own regiment though, he headed more purposefully in a different direction.

It took him longer than expected to reach the small tent on the far side of the camp which was his true destination. On one of its guy ropes a small blue ribbon was tied near the ground on a steel peg, identifying this particular tent among the masses. As he approached, Jarl looked around, trying to appear casual as he did so.

Only once sure he hadn't been followed did Jarl push back the entry flap and enter.

The room comprised a bare dirt floor with a table and two chairs. A lamp was lit in the centre of the folding camp table. The canvas of the tent must be thicker than normal as he hadn't seen the light from outside.

On one chair Archmage Nereth sat, his hands folded in his lap, the picture of composure. The other seat was for him, and empty. Nereth motioned towards it, his Gift-wrought plate armour, as always, remaining silent as he moved.

Jarl sat. Nereth was not a man you wanted to anger, not even had he been without the Gift at his command.

"Report," the archmage said, showing no signs of impatience at Jarl's slightly late arrival.

For a moment Jarl considered where to start, then once his thoughts were in order, began.

"The men are becoming more and more amenable to the new order by the day. The measures you introduced for gaining their loyalty are becoming effective, and given time I think most of the men would be swayed by them. However, given what they will soon be asked to do, they need something more to ensure their loyalties do not suffer a fatal lapse of conscience. For now they are happy and well fed. Once the blood of our countryman is shed however, I think many of those still sitting on, or near the fence, may revert to their old values."

"I see," Nereth replied, "And how would you counter this?" he asked. Jarl understood it was a test, so he considered for a moment before answering.

"The problem right now, at least as I see it, is that most of the men now see the new order as a good thing. Very few however consider it a necessary thing. Nor one that will justify the incredible lengths they are about to take against the same army that until last year, most of them belonged to. If you wish to keep them as yours, they need a victory that is very costly for the enemy, and very light in casualties on our side. Also, they need something to cement their belief that fighting this battle is in both their own interests and those of the kingdom as well. They need some goal, some plan that extends beyond this battle, or even this war. If you can make this just the first step to that place, you may have a chance at keeping their allegiance. If not..."

For a long moment Nereth did not move, and Jarl could almost see him dissecting his words. It made him feel as though he were a child again, handing in an assignment for his school masters to grade. He prayed he would pass.

"That was more insightful than I expected from you," the

archmage eventually told him.

"As long as you continue to use your talents for our benefit, you will be well rewarded. Now tell me of Hassan. Has he laid his plans for disrupting our battle with the King's army yet?"

Jarl felt his jaw drop. Hassan had only told him that there *was* a plan this very afternoon, also mentioning that he was the first one to know.

Nereth smiled slightly. "It would be the best time," he said in response to the puzzled look on Jarl's face.

Jarl sighed, his old friend was an exceptional warrior, but he had no chance against an opponent that knew what he was planning almost before he himself did. Jarl was once again glad he had thrown in his lot with the new order, but not so glad at what he had to tell Nereth next.

"I'm afraid I have not been able to determine that yet. We were interrupted before he could give me the details, and another opportunity has not yet presented itself to gather that information."

"Very well," Nereth told him without hesitation. "I will send Hassan on a scouting mission tomorrow with a squad of his own hand-picked men. Make sure you are one of them. That should give you plenty of opportunity to get him alone, or with other men he trusts to be part of his schemes."

"Excuse me, Archmage, but if you allow him too much rein, he will know that you are up to something."

He hesitated as he said it, not because he was uncertain of his assessment, but because he was smart enough to acknowledge that Nereth was by far his intellectual superior, and didn't want to annoy him.

"I agree, so I will send a mage with you. One you have both worked with before I think. Derrack should suffice since

Hassan knows I have assigned the man to watch him before."

"But if a mage accompanies us for the sole purpose of spying on Hassan, how will I talk with him about his plans, Archmage?" Jarl asked in slight confusion.

"Try a privy stop," Nereth responded flatly.

Jarl blinked for a moment, digesting the idea.

"Yes, that might work," he mused, "If he thinks he is being clever in avoiding your spy, that should allay any suspicions he might have away from me."

Nereth nodded in confirmation, and Jarl awkwardly realised that this had been the archmage's intention all along.

"As you wish Archmage," Jarl responded, sensing that this meeting was coming to its conclusion.

"Do you have any other orders?"

Nereth thought for a moment then shook his head.

"No. I am satisfied with your work so far. Continue to be subtle though, it would not do for Hassan to realise you are an informer. You will report back to me here the night following your return from this patrol, two hours after full dark."

"Yes Archmage," Jarl stood, saluting the man and then leaving. He checked again as he exited, but no one had noticed his departure from the small tent on the outskirts of the camp.

*   *   *

The sun was warm on his back the following day. Nereth's orders had come in that morning and Jarl had been the first of the men Hassan had chosen to accompany him on the mission. There were twenty of them, all men who were loyal to the king and part of the rebellion, and of course Derrack was there as well. The young mage had accompanied them on their mission to convert Seal Cove, Railain, and Nestarn after the coup, then on to Stonekeep and the missing villages. Clearbrook had been his home, and Derrack still chafed over not finding the answer to the mystery of what had become of its citizens, chief among them his family.

The day was not as hot as the last few had been, and Jarl was glad. Riding in armour even on a hot spring day was a taxing duty, and while ostensibly on a scouting mission, the men were all weary from the tension of being constantly alert. Throughout the day they rode, miles to the left flank of the army, where they could spot an approaching enemy and give the main force time to prepare. No enemy appeared however, and they kept riding until the sun began to sink below low hills laden with the massive coffee plantations which covered this part of the country. Hassan ordered the men to make camp near a copse of trees that marked the boundary line between two neighbouring properties.

A campfire was built, and one of the men was preparing their meal while the others began erecting the small travel tents each man carried as part of his pack.

Derrack made himself useful by starting the fire with a wave of his hand, saving the men on duty considerable effort. The wood they had gathered was still quite wet from the brief and unexpected showers which had moved in just before dawn this morning.

"I'm going to check the perimeter," Jarl announced to no one in particular, and since his other duties had already been performed, Hassan nodded.

He left the encampment and walked for a minute until he reached the edge of the stand of trees, then began a circle of the small copse. The woods were almost thick enough to hide the camp from outside view but some of the firelight shone out from between the branches. There was little enough cover around, but when he was halfway through his circuit, Jarl was interested to see a huge termite mound sticking out of the grass. The seven-foot hillock intersected the farmers' fence as though it had begun life as an infestation in one of the wooden posts. Time and neglect had allowed it to become a fully-fledged colony of the little white pests. As he circled around the curiosity, he was pleased to see Hassan waiting for him out of sight of the rest of the men.

"We need to talk," the captain said softly, taking no chances they would be overheard.

"We only have a minute, Derrack thinks I am on a privy break. I like the boy, but the last time he accompanied us, Nereth set him up as a spy. We can't afford that now."

"Are you sure he can't overhear us?" Jarl replied, feigning concern.

"He could if he were listening, but he thinks I'm on a privy break. Unless he's some kind of deviant, he has no reason to as long as I don't take too long."

Jarl nodded as if accepting his reasoning, and Hassan continued.

"I am being watched closely, so I need you to organise the men still loyal to the monarchy. We will soon come against the king's army, and when that happens, we must be ready to turn the tide of battle at just the right moment. You must tell them to act as though they are still a part of Heramiir's army until I give the signal. Once that occurs, they are to follow my orders to the letter. I can't make a more detailed plan yet because we don't even know where the battle will be fought. Once we have that information, I will have a better idea of what needs to be done. Until then, just organise a signal, and tell them to make ready."

"Yes sir. I'll take care of it," Jarl replied. "It will be good not to have to sneak around anymore," he added, though of course not for the reasons Hassan assumed.

"Finish your rounds," Hassan told him and then left the shelter of the termite mound to head back to the camp. Jarl waited a moment until the other man was out of sight before taking a privy break of his own, then did as Hassan had bid. The rest of the circuit was uneventful, the highlight being when he had to jump the small fence on the other side of the copse. A few minutes later he returned to the camp to find Hassan and Derrack engaged in conversation, so he went and sat across the fire from the pair.

"Nothing to report," he told Hassan in a bored tone as he warmed his hands. "Some game trails, and a few head of cattle in the distance, not much else."

"Very well, we'll keep a standard watch tonight since there have been no reports of loyalist movements in this part of the peninsula. See to it Jarl."

"Yes sir," he responded, picking himself up again from where he had just unbuckled the first clip on his armour. As he left, the conversation between the two men resumed, and Jarl realised he'd been dismissed so that Hassan and the young mage could discuss some matter in private. That wasn't of any great concern, but in the current climate it would be prudent to try to find out what that conversation had been about.

"Markov, Shultz, Resler. You men pick a buddy and take watch in that order."

He gave the orders to a group of soldiers idling away a few free moments until dinner was ready. There were some sighs and rolled eyes, but no one complained so Jarl left it at that and went to check on the food. Not that he was hungry, but the cook pot was close enough that he might overhear some of the conversation between Hassan and Derrack if he was careful.

Wandering over, he was disappointed to see Derrack rise and stalk off through the trees while Hassan sat, watching him go with a thoughtful expression.

Jarl went over and sat, leaning up against the same fallen log where Hassan had planted himself, and again began unbuckling his armour.

"What's he so upset about?" he asked, pretending to pay more attention to the buckle than his carefully chosen words.

Hassan looked at him for a moment as if deciding what to say. "I don't believe our friend enjoys being used as a spy."

That was interesting, Jarl thought, though he had his head turned towards the buckle so that his face could give nothing away no matter what Hassan's answer had been.

"What makes you say that?" he probed, this time allowing himself to show a little more interest in the subject.

"Just an impression," Hassan replied, though there was obviously more to it from the slight hesitation before he'd answered.

"Can you help me with this?" Jarl asked, turning his back to Hassan so that he could undo the latched buckle which was stuck. Coincidental, yet useful.

"Do you think we can make use of him?" Jarl whispered once Hassan was close enough.

"I'm not sure yet. Perhaps," Hassan muttered back.

"There you go," he announced, getting the buckle free and leaving the rest to Jarl as he returned to his seat near the flames.

"Thanks," Jarl responded, undoing the rest of the clips with practised ease. Once he had the leather armour off, he brought it over to the fire so he could examine the bent clip more closely.

"Hmmph. How did that happen?" he grunted as he stood, going to retrieve some tools from the packhorses.

By the time he'd used a pair of pliers and a small hammer to bend the metal clip back into shape, their dinner was ready. He exchanged the tools for his eating implements, and went back over to take his share. The food was not quite so good here as it was back in the main camp. However the thick soup still had more vegetables in it than he was used to getting on patrol. There were even a few scraps of meat from a large rabbit one of the men had brought down with his bow earlier in the day. Things were proceeding apace, and while he hadn't gleaned a firm plan from Hassan, at least he could give the archmage some new information when they returned. Jarl sipped the hot soup as he leant back against the log, warming his feet by the fire as he looked up at the night sky.

'Baron Jarl' had just about the right ring to it. All he had to do was blunt the inevitable rebellion which Hassan had just asked him to help plan.

He brought the steaming bowl to his lips and when he had tipped it high enough to hide his mouth, Jarl finally allowed himself to smile. Hassan would never know what hit him.

CHAPTER 14

GRAGNAGUL

Dusk was bleaching colour from the eastern slopes of the Dark Iron Mountains, and Gragnagul, Chieftain of the Augrahl clans, was pleased. So far everything was transpiring according to the plan, his plan.

It had not been easy to convince the council to support his invasion tactics. First, he'd needed to negotiate with Barendel, Warlord of the Imbic Nation. That had been unpleasant. The two of them had reached an agreement though, and brought their plan to the human knights of the north plains. Klaud had immediately seen the potential, but still held out for certain concessions which Gragnagul had been forced to agree to. That was to be expected, even respected. Once he'd secured their backing, even the mercurial Oo'vi had been pushed into joining the expedition. The council had thought his plan either genius or madness, and it hadn't been difficult to persuade the others to let him personally lead the invasion force. None of them wanted to risk their necks on the slight chance his idea would proceed as planned.

So now here he was, east of the Iron Ranges with the vanguard of his strike force. Five thousand of his most aggressive troops, and a little over a thousand Imbic, including a hundred of their race's renowned builders.

The humans of Jeranon called the ranges, 'The Dark Iron Mountains'. An overly dramatic name.

After living in the true mountains of his homeland, these snow-capped ranges were nothing to get excited over. To him, or any other mountain Augrahl, they barely even deserved the title of ranges.

Beside him, Barendel was receiving a report from one of his huge workmen as the six-armed Imbic Warlord with the half-cooked-chicken coloured skin of his race toured Gragnagul's camp alongside him.

He wasn't sure what to make of Barendel's visit yet. The Imbic Warlord had arrived in the camp two days ago with a thousand more of his troops riding on the backs of Gareen. The huge reptiles which lived in the southern swamps had always been thought of as useless, but Barendel's people had found some way to train them. Of course, only the Imbic mutations with a semblance of humanoid form could ride them, but that was their problem.

At first Gragnagul had been furious the Imbic warlord had risked revealing their location to the enemy with his visit. The magic barrier which his shamans maintained around them day and night prevented the Jeranonian magi from discovering their location. But it would do nothing whatsoever to protect troops coming or going from being spotted or scried out, irretrievably ending their element of surprise.

When Barendel had ridden in the day before last, Gragnagul had greeted his long-time ally with a bared blade and fifty of his most deadly shamans. Only the warlord's timely announcement that the mounted Imbic were being given over to Gragnagul's command for the duration of the campaign had stopped him from destroying them all on the spot.

He had worked, trained, fought, and risen to power over the course of decades so that he could be in a position to take this chance. He would have killed them all before allowing them to ruin his one opportunity to reclaim the ancient lands of his people due to the tactical ineptitude of the so-called Imbic warlord.

Barendel walked beside him now only because of the courtesy due a full council member, not as an active part of his command.

Gragnagul had to admit though, however inept Barendel might be by Augrahl standards, his people loved him.

Gragnagul had seen Imbic work before, and so knew what to expect when he had set them to constructing the enormous castle. After many laborious phases, their work was almost complete. He had harassed the Imbic builders since the first day of construction, bullying, cajoling, and even having a few of them flogged on general principles. But the truth was he was quite satisfied with the efficiency of the Imbic's master builder and his underlings.

That was until Barendel had arrived. One sighting of their Warlord and the builders had gone into a frenzy, doubling, maybe even tripling their own work rate. That was the other reason Barendel walked beside him now.

If work continued at this rate, Foothold Keep would be ready in just over a phase. The rest of his force would arrive ten to twelve days after he sent word that it was complete. It had been difficult gathering all the stone needed for the monstrous keep. Fortunately, the stripping of several sizeable villages near the foothills of the ranges had garnered enough raw materials to get them started. Once they had added what they could mine from the quarry they had constructed in the cliff behind the keep, the raids had given them a steady supply of stone and slaves to carry out the most dangerous work.

Most of the human wretches had not survived long, but it was of no concern. They had served their purpose in him not having to sacrifice his own troops' health to the hardest, dustiest work.

As the two of them strode around a corner of a tent, a group of loathsome Nostahl were startled into movement by the sudden appearance of the two warlords. Servile creature's akin to the Augrahl in form only, in every way the subrace was inferior, and deserving of their fate. Even their horns were weak, almost as though someone had created a mockery of a true Augrahl.

Those protrusions barely even pierce the skin of their scalps for Orroth's sake!

Besides their other faults, the horrid little pests were not much taller than Barendel's knee, and cowardly to boot. Gragnagul snarled in disgust as the group scattered in a futile attempt to remove themselves from his path. One of them dropped a drink it had been enjoying, a few drops of which splashed onto Gragnagul's boot.

With a roar of fury, the Augrahl Chieftain's blade whistled out of its scabbard and cleaved the insolent creature from neck to hip, causing the others to shriek in terror as they fled.

Gragnagul knew he was not the biggest nor strongest Augrahl in the world. It didn't matter, his shaman enhanced blade would cut through armour or flesh without resistance as though he were cleaving air. The only thing it would not do was slice through an opponent's weapon. The master shaman who had created the blade would not give his leader a coward's weapon. While it would kill without mercy, it was a blade which must still be wielded by one skilled enough to strike past his opponent's guard, as befitted their Chief. Gragnagul had accepted the weapon. He was a master bladesman and there was benefit in being seen to be victorious. He had then slaughtered the shaman for his insolence in giving the weapon an intentional flaw.

The little Nostahl's body fell to the ground in pieces with a dull splat. Gragnagul grimaced at the blue gore that was now dripping from the last two-and-a-half feet of his blade, so he stopped to wipe it clean on the dead creature's clothes.

"You deal with your subjects harshly," Barendel rumbled, stepping around the corpse as the pair continued their tour.

"Hmmph. Their kind are barely worthy to be my subjects. Still, they have a few uses and so are allowed to live, but only at my pleasure."

The pair walked in silence for a time, surveying the nearly completed keep and the organised chaos all around them. The sum of the builders' efforts resulting in the task being completed in what was surely record time.

"I have a message from the council for you," Barendel said eventually. He placed an eight fingered fist into the lining of his wyvern skin robe and pulled out a parchment, handing it over to the Augrahl Chieftain without another word.

It bore the council's seal, and so Gragnagul opened it. He was not afraid of the other council members, but when they used this seal, it was with the combined voice of the four nations west of the Iron Ranges. Nobody ignored that. Not even him. Without his own signature on whatever this document was it was only three of four nations of course. He had to assume since Barendel presented it in person, his name at least would be added to whatever demands were inside, and so Gragnagul read.

'Gragnagul, if you build your Foothold Keep and sack Stonekeep from the rear, know that the council has committed the combined forces of our nations' armies to your attack. If you clear the way through the mountains, send us word and we will march. By the time you read this, we will be at Languish Stronghold with over three hundred thousand warriors. All our nations could muster without compromising our eastern defences. For this to occur, you must send word of your victory within two phases, otherwise our resources here will be depleted, and our armies forced to return home. The council commends your efforts to this point. We feel confident that this will be our time to reclaim the lands east of the Iron Ranges, to which they have denied us for so very long. Do not disappoint us.'

Underneath were the names of the respective leaders of the nations. Barendel, Warlord of the Imbic Nation, Klaud of the Northern Plains, and Arithra of the Oo'vi, who remained as always within her deadly, shifting forest on the westernmost shores of the land.

Gragnagul refolded the parchment and tucked it away under his thick metal armour before smiling to himself. All these long years he had planned for this day, and now that those plans were coming to fruition he was in his element. The other nations had fallen into line as he knew they would. They needed a leader who could achieve the goals they all wanted, namely sacking the Jeranonian's cursed Stonekeep Castle.

That mammoth fortress was the primary reason they had never breached the ranges in full force. They could sneak troops across the border from time to time to raid nearby towns, but the troops they sent rarely made it back unscathed. The Jeranonian patrols, and inhospitable terrain in the ranges had always kept them from attacking in sufficient numbers to hold any territory of consequence. Naval attacks had also been attempted many times over the centuries. Again, it had never been a successful tactic due to the Jeranonian system of watchtowers along both the north and south coasts, which gave them ample warning to prepare. That left the central pass through the ranges as the only genuine option for moving an army the size of the one which was now gathering to the west. Unfortunately that pass led straight to Stonekeep's mammoth defences, which were almost impossible to break. They had taken the fortress on only two occasions in the three thousand years since the Jeranonian's had pushed them out of their ancestral lands. On both occasions, the cursed fortification had held out long enough that the humans had been given more than enough time to marshal their main armies. What western forces had survived those attacks had been driven back soon after, doing significant damage to their enemies' stolen homeland, but holding none.

All that had changed last year though. His spies had reported the humans were fighting amongst themselves as they had not since the time of Eldrik, two thousand years before. Gragnagul had immediately known this would be the best chance they would have in his lifetime to break through the Jeranonian defences. To reclaim and hold at least a portion of the lands east of the ranges. In his wildest dreams he hoped to drive them back down the great stairway, all the way back to the ancient city of Miralthrall. He dared to dream of reclaiming what the humans called the Sammorand Plains, relying on the cliffs above the city to act as a natural barrier between Jeranon and the four nations.

Just as the Iron Ranges now did. He was willing to accept destroying Stonekeep and holding that position as victory, but if he could gain more... It was almost too much to consider. That he be the one who led them home would assure the nations venerated his name for a thousand years to come, perhaps longer.

With that in mind, he set off in the keep's direction, forcing Barendel to follow or be left behind. The Imbic warlord had been waiting to inspect the keep since he'd first arrived. Now that Gragnagul was sure why Barendel had come, it suited to let him do so.

They walked between grey-skinned Nostahl and Augrahl, Imbic mutants which defied description, and steeds of many varieties, though none stranger, or more dangerous, than the huge reptilian Gareen.

Eventually, they made it to the base of the keep, where a large table had been set up. On it were what Gragnagul assumed were the plans for the structure, covered in markings in the Imbic language, which he knew how to read. Most of them were marked as complete, but a final level, along with the towers and defences, were still being finalised. Gragnagul found himself thinking how close they were to their goal; closer than even he had thought in fact.

"Hail Warlord," a hulking Imbic mutation with three arms on one side and a single, oversized appendage on the other, announced as he saw who had come into his work area.

"Hail Joreth," the warlord returned in a booming voice to the Imbic in charge of construction. Joreth was his very brightest engineer, and both of them thumped their chests in greeting.

"How does the building progress?"

The huge engineer turned to consult his plans for a moment before answering.

"Two days ago I would have said five weeks until it is done. With your presence here to spur the builders on, I think it will be more like two."

Two weeks!

"You can guarantee this?" Gragnagul demanded of the huge Imbic.

Even though Joreth was considered a genius by Imbic standards, that didn't mean the massive engineer was much brighter than the average Augrahl. After seeing the brute's work progress each day though, even Gragnagul had to admit that the huge creature knew his trade well.

Joreth thought about it for a long moment, once again checking his plans before answering.

"I can guarantee three, but it will most likely be closer to two so long as the warlord remains."

"I will be here," Barendel confirmed for both of them without prompting. Joreth gave a huge grin, revealing a half row of serrated teeth on the top side of his jaw, and several rows on the lower.

Gragnagul thought furiously.

Stonekeep was a two-week forced march from here, though he intended to use as much stealth as possible, and so a few days would be added to that number. In addition, it would take his main force at least ten days to reach Foothold Keep from the western side of the ranges. He had not wanted to commit the bulk of his troops to the crossing until he was sure this would work. If he sent for them today, the keep would be finished within a day of their arrival. They would have to fight their way through the patrols, but the surprise mass offensive should see the majority make it through to the safety of Foothold Keep. He would allow them a day's rest, then they would march to war.

"I must go," he told Barendel, then turned his back on the two Imbic, who seemed less than interested in his departure.

It seemed like hours before he reached the command pavilion which served as his headquarters until the castle was complete.

Once he had though, he sent for a dozen runners to be brought to him, and waited eagerly on their arrival.

He did not have to wait long, as well he shouldn't. They knew the last to arrive would be flogged, as was his usual practice. As a result, in a little less than two minutes he had his runners assembled. The final arrival was a useless Nostahl who cringed when it realised what was in store.

He had two of his guards haul the pitiful wretch away and proceeded.

"You all know where our army is encamped on the western side of the Iron Ranges. Gather up what you need and leave. Lead them back here, and remember you are not to be taken captive by the Arborii or Terraliv patrols which are now infesting the foothills. If that is unavoidable, chew this," he told them, handing each a small sphere of a dull red colour from a clay jar on one of his tables.

"They have been made by the shamans and will transport you back here. But they are valuable and if I find any of you cowards returning without good reason, I will kill you myself! Remember, we cannot afford for our position here to be discovered under any circumstances. Especially not because one of you oafs valued his own skin above that of every other Augrahl and Imbic in this camp!" he bellowed at them, most of the runners cringing away as he did so.

"Also, whichever one of you reports to my Generals on

the other side of the mountains first will receive a bag of gold once you return with my army. Now get out of my sight!"

The runners scattered and Gragnagul laughed. If any of them were stupid enough to get caught and take the pill, they would meet a gruesome death indeed as the poison destroyed their internal organs. As if he would waste his shaman's time giving such as these an easy escape route when they should never have been caught in the first place!

It was done. He would allow his army to rest for a day when it arrived. Then they would march for Stonekeep Castle and attack as they had never had opportunity to do so before. The best part was that none of it would be possible if the humans had not started fighting amongst themselves. The fools had thinned out their patrols in the Iron Ranges, leaving mostly Arborii and Terraliv to patrol the border. They were both fierce fighters those two races, but there weren't enough of them to account for the entire area of the ranges by themselves. At least, there hadn't been until lately. Thus with some well-placed strikes and the use of every shaman at his personal disposal, his main force had remained undetected as they made the arduous journey across the spine of the ranges and down into the eastern foothills.

Klaud had insisted it was madness when Gragnagul had first brought his detailed battle plan to the council for their approval, as all plans concerning Jeranon were. He had countered by insisting that a bold strike now would have a higher chance of success while their ancient enemy was distracted with its own affairs. In the end he'd convinced them, the council giving its blessing for him to try.

There was little left to do here, so after sculling a mug of thick wine he threw the cup at a waiting Nostahl servant. The creature shied away, but caught the flying piece of crockery without incident, lucky for it, so he headed back out.

There were many preparations left to be made, but he refused to let the excitement of his plans being close to bearing fruit lull him into doing something rash. Too many years of planning had gone into this invasion for him to risk anything interrupting the day which was now less than a turning of the moon away. He smiled, and a pack of Nostahl ran the other way.

'Perhaps they are smarter than I gave them credit for,' he thought as he sought out Barendel back at the Keep, where Gragnagul knew he would still be.

Sending the runners to fetch his army had put him in a good mood. As he approached the Imbic Warlord and his chief stonemason, the two huge creatures looked up from their work. One with fear, the other curiosity at his rare good humour.

"I have sent the runners!" Gragnagul announced as he approached. "The army will be here in ten days' time."

He let that sink in for a moment with the two massive brutes and then turned to address Barendel directly.

"When they arrive, I will let them rest for a day before we march on Stonekeep Castle. Once we leave, Foothold Keep will be vulnerable until we return. My scouts tell me that the closest human force of consequence besides Stonekeep is based nearly a week from here at a city they call Heartland's Gate. That will be the maximum length of time you will have to make Foothold Keep battle ready before they can launch a counterattack. If that happens, you and your lizard things must hold the fortifications until our return. If we lose our base of operations on this side of the mountains, it will only be a matter of time until a lack of supplies drives us back across the ranges, or into the enemy's arms. Then all of this will have been for nothing."

For a moment Barendel looked offended, crossing his six tree trunk arms across his disproportionately vast chest as he attempted to stare Gragnagul down.

"We will hold this place. My people have sacrificed as much as yours for this endeavour Gragnagul, and I sit on the same council you do. It would be wise to remember this before you talk down to me again, little Augrahl."

Gragnagul sneered, his hand twitching in fury. Only his many years of patiently planning this offensive kept it from the sword hilt that was just inches away. He could kill Barendel if he so chose, but to do it now, in front of the others, would force his people into a battle against their own allies. Work on the keep would grind to a halt, and his forces would be reduced, weakening their chances in the real offensive.

Barendel would have to wait. He moved his twitching fingers away from the hilt at last, settling for words instead. Something he was not very good with even at the best of times.

"I will order you, and remind you, of what I see fit Barendel. Just remember who the council has put in charge here. For the duration of the campaign, your people, and even you yourself, will do as I command. If you deviate from my orders by even a hair, I will execute you for treason against the council. Is that clear enough, Imbic?!"

Now it was the Warlord's turn to sneer as he took a step forward, though only one, while Joreth looked on, aghast at what was about to happen. His horrified expression was nothing compared to what it became though when Barendel backed down.

"I will do as you say, for now little Augrahl. But when this is through, your blade and mine will have matters to discuss."

"I look forward to that day," Gragnagul replied, leaving the two massive Imbic to their business before he completely lost his temper.

Stalking away from the pair, this time it was not just Nostahl that ran when they saw him coming. All trace of his previous good mood had now been erased by the insults he'd been forced to swallow. The more so since Joreth had seen him forced to walk away as well.

It was a matter for another time though, he would allow nothing to impede his battle plans. Stonekeep would crumble before him, and before the humans could receive word of the attack and mount a meaningful resistance, his force would move on. They would head directly for the great staircase, blocking the paths that led up the Cloudburst Cliffs from Miralthrall to the Sammorand Plains.

So long as they could hold that point, they could take back almost a quarter of the ancestral lands in one fell swoop. The clans, not to mention the other nations, would sing his praises for as long as memory survived. It was all but assured now, they only needed to avoid detection for another half-moon cycle. The bells at Stonekeep Castle would ring out one last time, warning Jeranon that it was under attack, as they had for uncounted years. Then they would be silenced. He intended to melt those accursed things down to scrap once the castle had been taken. They had heralded the sound of defeat for his people, and the others of the council for almost three thousand years. No more.

'Gragnagul the Cleaver,' that was what they would call him by the time this was over. Then they could move on to the city of Miralthrall and return to their ancient home. None of them knew why they were drawn to that place, only that in three millennia of exile, every single child born to their races had felt the call. The human knights of the Northern Plains were different. They didn't feel the call, but then, they had come later. There was something left unfinished in that place. Something that called to all of them deep in the back of their minds, where it was more an instinctual urge that a lucid thought. He hoped one day to be the first Augrahl through those gates in many, many turnings of the moon. But first he had to eliminate Stonekeep and every human in it. Only then would he be remembered as anything more than another overly ambitious warrior who wasted the lives of their peoples in a futile attack on that impregnable fortress.

He refused to be remembered that way, even if every soldier in his command had to die to prevent it.

CHAPTER 15

NO TIME TO REST

Almost two phases had passed since Sa'rayna allowed Wyll and his men to leave the Wraith Woods alive, if a little the worse for wear. They had found the army's trail at last.

Wyll stopped to examine the latest in a series of camping sites they'd been tracking as they made their way west. He kicked over some campfire ash, revealing the tiniest spark of red glow underneath.

"We've almost caught up," he told the others, feeling the optimistic rush of excitement that for him at least, always accompanied the fruition of an arduous task.

"Check a few of the other fires. This one couldn't be more than a day or two old."

The others spread out, kicking away dead coals to look for signs of warmth or fire itself amongst the ashes. Cale and Tauman found them in good order. Some of the king's soldiers hadn't been thorough in dousing their cook fires when they'd continued their march. The men returned, and the consensus was that the sites were no more than a day old, maybe even from the previous night.

If that's true we should be in sight of the baggage trains by noon, Wyll thought in relief. They could carry out the first part of their mission at last, having the army halt its march. Meanwhile his men would move on to scout out whether

Heramiir's force at Cordova was real, or an illusion designed to throw the king's army off track.

It was midmorning, and the sun had only recently finished burning off the fog of the previous evening. Last night had been chilling, and they'd all struggled to get close enough to the fire to keep their backs warm without burning their fronts in the process.

There was little more to be seen here, and feeling impatient, Wyll ordered his men to mount up. They rode parallel to the path of mulched ground where a hundred thousand men, animals, and carts had turned the ground to mush just a day or so before. The land was quiet here. An army of this size required a vast amount of food. No doubt hunting parties had stripped the surrounding area of its animal life for miles as they sought to supplement the army's supplies. Any creature of consequence cunning enough to avoid them had long ago fled to safer ground.

It was not long after noon when they first caught sight of the troops acting as rear guard for the supply wagons, and only moments after that when the soldiers spotted them in turn. An officer motioned in the distance, and a hundred of the king's men broke formation and turned to ride hard at Wyll and his squad.

Wyll took a moment to dig through his saddle pack and pulled out the scroll containing the king's orders. He held it aloft as he ordered his men to halt, displaying the royal seal.

The regular cavalry troops encircled them before halting. Only once there was nowhere for Wyll and his men to go, did a burly man in a captain's uniform ride into the circle to challenge them.

"State your business," he ordered, as though this were yet another inconvenience to be dealt with.

"Orders from King Erian to General Messand," Wyll replied.

"Hand them over," the captain returned, expecting Wyll to do just that.

"No sir," Wyll replied with a frown. "My orders are to give these to General Messand, and even if you took them, they relate directly to my men and I."

The captain far outranked him, and looked as though he was the kind to try pulling rank even though the mageguard lay outside the normal military chain of command. Some officers would do that he'd been told, not liking the fact that men under their own rank were not subject to their authority. But Wyll was sure the seal on the orders he bore would see him through to wherever he needed to go with no real interference.

The captain rode forward until his horse was next to Wyll's and held out his hand.

"If you are to pass, I must first see the royal seal."

Wyll looked the man in the eyes for a long moment, trying to gauge his intent. In the end he decided it didn't matter if the captain tried to abscond with the orders. What he had told them about relating to his own squad would come to light in any event. Still, it would cause a delay they had little time for, and Wyll only complied reluctantly. He watched the man as he studied the sealing wax. The emblem was red and flecked with gold dust which had been pressed into a rearing, crowned horse in the shape of the king's signet ring.

"All right," the captain allowed at last.

"This appears to be genuine, so I'll let you pass, but you'll be escorted by my men until you've reached the command pavilion. Just to be sure you are who you say you are."

Wyll breathed a sigh of relief as he took the orders back, and once again stowed them in his pack. Meanwhile, the captain called off two of his sergeants and their squads to escort his men up ahead.

Without another word the captain made a circular motion with his hand, ordering his men to follow. The circle parted, freeing them as the rest of the soldiers returned to their place in the rear guard.

"Is your captain always so unfriendly?" Bosric asked one of the sergeants once they were clear of the other troops.

The bald cavalryman stared at the short man for a long moment before deigning to answer.

"Half the magi in Jeranon have turned against us, forcing us into the biggest war in a decade. You are mageguard. There's not a lot of respect for your kind right now. Now follow me, if we ride hard, we should be able to catch up to the General by sundown."

Turning to ride away, the other cavalrymen followed his lead, forcing Wyll and his men to trail after them. He had little choice but to comply, though at enough of a distance to avoid the churned-up mud the cavalry horses were spraying. The day had warmed, and the sun was now beating down from a cloudless sky. Another hour passed, and the bald sergeant called a brief halt so the men could eat their lunch rations. To their right, the vast column of supply trains, infantry soldiers, and support personnel marched in formation every few hundred spans on either side of the churned path beside them.

"Has there been any contact with the enemy?" Wyll asked.

"What do you think? Do we look like we've been fighting?" The sergeant replied as he spat on the ground.

Wyll nodded at the confirmation, rude though it was.

"Stow your armour men," Wyll ordered once they'd taken their rations and returned to their mounts. They'd been wearing the thick leather gear for nearly three phases solid. Enough was enough. There were audible sighs of relief from his men, which elicited a sneer of derision from one of the cavalry soldiers and a raucous laugh from another.

"Shouldn't be much of a fight if this is what's protecting the magi," the laughing man called, bringing more guffawing from the others.

Wyll finished pulling the leather jerkin over his head and stowed it in its place behind his saddle. What he saw as he turned back to the squads was not good. Still on his horse, Bosric was fingering his sleeve, which Wyll knew contained one of the many knives he kept hidden about his person. Sarran's hand was also far too close to his sword hilt for Wyll's liking, and even Seth was sitting at ease, which meant the man was ready for anything.

On the other hand, the men from the cavalry unit had gone quiet, seeming to sense that they'd taken the jest too far.

"I would suggest you control your men, Sergeant," Wyll suggested to the bald cavalryman who stared back at him with open dislike.

"I would. If they were out of line," he returned, his tone matching Wyll's.

Wyll smiled humourlessly.

"Remount," he ordered his own men.

"Sergeant, take your men and return to your unit, we have no further need of your, assistance."

"Nice try, mage lover, but I have my orders, and I intend

to report you for trying to counteract them," the sergeant sneered.

Wyll glanced at his own men, and despite their lack of armour he was proud to see that they all were ready to carry out his orders.

He reached around behind himself and slipped the jet-black blade Sa'rayna had given him from the ivory scabbard which rested across his back. He lay it across the pommel of his saddle, emphasising the fiery runes to the cavalry unit facing him.

"This sword I was recently given as a gift," he told the bald sergeant. The man was eying off the metal, yet completely matt black blade with its three arcane runes as Wyll spoke.

"My orders come from Archmage Tolmarak and King Erian himself, and we have passed through the Wraith Woods to reach here in time to deliver them to General Messand."

He ran a finger across one of the runes, and it glowed a little brighter as he did, though he had no idea why.

The bald sergeant laughed again, though a little nervously now.

"No one passes through the Wraith Woods alive," he said dismissively. "So I call you a liar."

Now men on both sides drew weapons. Not all of them, but enough that Wyll knew he would only get one more chance to make the pompous cavalryman back down without it coming to blows.

"Where do you think I got this? Have you ever seen its like?" He asked. "I was told by the one who gave it to me that a single scratch was all that was needed for it to cause instantaneous death to any creature. I cannot confirm that yet, but I promise you, Sergeant, if you do not obey my rightful orders, you will be the first to know."

The cavalryman was quiet now as he studied the intent, yet confident looks of Wyll's men, and must have decided he had been at least partially in error.

"Even if I believed you, I have my orders," he told them in a surly manner.

"We both know that as a sergeant in the mageguard I can rescind the orders of the regular army up to the rank of lieutenant should I have the need. I have the need," he responded in no uncertain terms.

"Men, put away your weapons. We'll be going on alone."

So saying, he returned the deadly blade Sa'rayna had given him to its exquisite ivory sheath, and his men followed suit.

"Go now, Sergeant," Wyll said.

With another half sneer, the bald cavalryman took his unit and rode back the way they had come, leaving Wyll shaking his head at the man's attitude. He couldn't help but wonder if it prevailed here in the king's camp. Perhaps it was just the officer's opinions filtering down through his men as sometimes happened with headstrong leaders. Still, the bald sergeant at least should think twice about showing such disrespect to the next member of the mageguard he ran across. Otherwise the man would find himself court-martialled in a very short amount of time. In a time of war the penalty for disobeying a rightful order was death by hanging. Not a good end for any man, let alone an officer of the king's army.

"Come on," Wyll told his men. "We've still got a long way to go."

Frowning, Wyll took Socks' reins and set him to a gallop.

After the near disaster with the sergeant's men, he needed to work off some nervous energy. Without his leather armour encasing him for once, the wind of their passage was enough to keep him cool. As he rode alongside the vast column, he searched for any signs of a command presence among them as he went.

As they rode up the line over the next few hours, Wyll couldn't help but be awed at the sheer scope of the surrounding army. On every side men trudged behind those in front, paying little attention to anything but putting one foot in front of the other after phases of solid marching. Unit after unit of cavalry were also flanking the infantry, though they also sat their seats with weary expressions. Wyll had the unmistakable impression that a week of rest whilst he and his men completed their mission would be a welcome respite for most of these men before heading into combat.

About an hour before sunset, the army stopped its slow march, and Wyll picked up speed, eager to be at his destination now that it was so close at hand. His first mission, or at least the first part of his first mission, had been a resounding success, and he felt pride at what his men had accomplished. Not to mention how they had reacted despite the overwhelming odds against them. On and on he rode. The never-ending column of men and animals continued unabated, until just before dusk they crested a low rise and came within sight of the front of the column.

There were two cavalry and six infantry units all camped in front of a large pavilion. The scramble of activity still surrounding it suggested it had only just finished being set up. There was no doubt in Wyll's mind that this was where he would at last locate General Messand.

"Finally," he breathed, though perhaps a bit too loudly

since Cale, who was sitting astride his beige mare to Wyll's left, gave him a slight grin in response.

"Let's do what we came here to do," Wyll said. Their objective being in sight had put him in a somewhat better mood.

The men rode down the rise behind him and he ordered them to halt about fifty spans out from the ring of guards who were surrounding the command pavilion. The guards eyed them wearily, even though his men had approached from within the army itself. Well-trained men, Wyll noted, either that or the apparent division between the regular army and the mageguard at the moment ran a lot deeper than he had suspected.

"Dismount," Wyll ordered before fishing around in his pack for the scroll containing the king's orders. Following his own command, he instructed the others to wait where they were and approached the opening in the tent. Through it he could see warm candlelight peeking through a slit in the canvas. The men encircling the tent observed, but made no move to stop him. However the two guards on either side of the doorway lowered their halberds to bar his way, which Wyll had expected. It was only moments however before a man in a captain's uniform strode up from where he had been discussing some matter with one of the armies' clerks.

"Your business?" he inquired.

"Orders from King Erian to General Messand, Sir," he replied crisply to the man's challenge.

The stout captain had a no nonsense look about him that proclaimed the best way to proceed was to do things the way he expected, and to get on with it.

"Let me see the seal," he replied with no further attempt at conversation.

This time Wyll handed over the document without hesitation. The captain perused the unmarked wax as if he could personally identify a fraud. Wyll had to admit that was entirely possible if he were assigned to guarding the general's command pavilion.

After a long moment he nodded to himself and turned away, and Wyll was forced to call him back.

"Sir, my orders come from the king himself and are to deliver that message to the General. They also relate to my own men, Sir."

The stout captain scrutinised him for a moment, then seemed to decide he was telling the truth. He handed back the scroll and ordered Wyll to follow him inside. As soon as he spoke, the guardsman raised their halberds and a serving man pulled on a rope cord from inside, causing the flap of canvas that was the only visible entrance into the command pavilion, to open.

Wyll wasn't sure what to expect from the man in charge of this campaign. As he entered the pavilion, it was to find a thick carpet spread on the ground. Not a good one for show, but the kind which could get mud on it without anyone caring. It was there to keep the dust and mud away from the maps which covered the table at the pavilion's centre, rather than for any aesthetic value. Around the edges, though not too near the canvas walls of the tent, were a circle of well used brass candelabras shedding light around the structure. Besides that, the tent's only furniture consisted of two stout tables. On the main one in the centre of the pavilion the maps lay. Several men were studying them, marking out distances with various items which Wyll assumed meant something if you knew what you were looking at. On a smaller table to the side was a variety of well spun glass decanters holding a selection of interesting looking drinks. A serving man stood behind it, ready to accommodate the general's guests and staff at any moment. Between each of the candelabras, guardsmen stood, still and silent. Their hands rested upon the hilts of their swords, ready to defend the officers in attendance from attack at any given moment.

The stout captain led the way to the larger table and waited for a few seconds to be noticed. The general was in deep discussion with one of his aide's, and with his back turned did not notice the man standing behind him.

"Excuse me, General Messand, orders have arrived from Aramar Sir," the captain interrupted, gaining the general's attention.

"The courier claims they come from King Erian himself and they do indeed bear the royal seal, whole and unbroken."

"Thank you, Captain," the general replied, dismissing both the officer and his aide with a nod before turning to Wyll and reaching out a hand.

It was not a greeting though, and Wyll placed the scroll in Messand's grip. He waited for the tall but portly man who looked to be well into his fifties, and was losing what was left of his greying hair, to open it.

Messand cracked the wax seal and unrolled the parchment before pacing a few steps away while he read. At first he frowned, then his eyebrows lifted in surprise, and then as he finished the extensive set of orders, he frowned again, this time thoughtfully.

"This changes everything," he said as he walked back to Wyll from where he had been pacing as he read.

"Yes sir, it does," Wyll replied. "With you so close to your objective, the only way for us to reach you in time was to cross through the Wraith Woods. From there we rode in a straight line until we found you. As it is, we can't be more than a week's ride from Cordova as I make it."

"A week's march," Messand corrected him, obviously still digesting the news which had come with the new set of orders. "Your men should be able to ride it in about four days while still avoiding the enemy."

"Sir," the captain who had escorted Wyll into the pavilion interrupted as he returned with an agitated old archmage.

"Archmage Veroneth says he has important information you need to hear."

Messand nodded and the captain once again stepped back.

"General we have a serious problem," Veroneth said so that only he and the general could hear. Of course, Wyll was close enough too, but the mageguard uniform he wore apparently allowed him to be party to the archmage's information as well.

"A few minutes ago every ward we had set in the camp failed, and every effort to re-establish them has been unsuccessful."

Wyll winced.

"You mean we're completely unprotected?" Messand demanded, obviously about to launch into action.

"Sir, Archmage," Wyll interrupted, gathering stares as the two older men seemed to remember he was there.

"Of course," General Messand said to himself as he realised what had happened.

"I'm afraid that's probably my fault," Wyll told them, causing the archmage to frown at him as if he had told them the moon was made of cheese.

"Don't be silly boy. If you had any affinity for the Gift I would sense it in you."

Deciding to keep his explanation brief Wyll laid out the facts for the archmage even though he realised he would probably be punished for his lack of foresight.

"We have just arrived from Aramar, Archmage, with orders from King Erian for the General. To get here in time, we had to cross the Wraith Woods and now we must scout out Heramiir's force at Cordova to determine if it is real or illusion."

"Perhaps you do need to tell me more," Veroneth said in bewilderment.

Thinking of where to start, Wyll decided that the beginning was the best place after all, and did just that.

"It became clear to both the King and Archmage Tolmarak that Heramiir and his inner circle, at the very least, have access to some source of knowledge which the magi of Aramar's college are not yet privy to. They were also receiving reports of a second sizeable enemy army moving along the Laketown Peninsula. These reports, whilst from reliable sources, seemed to suggest that Heramiir has more men at his disposal than is possible. Archmage Tolmarak posited that based on these two facts, either one, or parts of both forces may in fact be composed of illusion and not there at all. The King's orders are to halt the army while we scout out Heramiir's force at Cordova. We will then return and provide you with accurate intelligence as to the true nature and number of enemy soldiers at one of these fronts. We know that at least a portion of Heramiir's actual force is on the Laketown Peninsula, but there was no possibility of reaching there and returning to you in time."

Wyll stopped to take a breath, and Veroneth took the opportunity to speak.

"None of that explains why the wards are down," he said.

"Or how you plan to divine whether these armies are in fact illusion or truth."

"Yes Archmage," Wyll answered, and then begged their indulgence while he went to the door of the pavilion and called out for Cale to bring him the Chalice. The mute soldier did as he was bidden, and Wyll returned to the general and archmage with his prize.

"Of course," Veroneth said as he recognised what Wyll was carrying. "The Chalice of Ajerio."

"The Chalice of Ajerio," Wyll agreed.

"We are to ride as close as we can to Heramiir's supposed encampment at Cordova and see what disappears, and what remains to be dealt with. Then report back to the General. If this army is a fake and the one on the peninsula is real, the King's orders are simple. Reach the fjords below Lake Pristine before Heramiir's forces can cross into central Jeranon, and halt his advance."

"Yes, we certainly can't allow that," the general mused.

"If they cross those fjords, Heramiir will be in position to strike at Midway and cut our supply lines. From there he would have unhindered access to almost all of central Jeranon."

"Those were the King's thoughts as well, sir," Wyll added. "And yet we do not know at this point whether the force on the peninsula is his entire army, or just a few hundred men, or anywhere in between. His entire push onto the peninsula could be a diversion to get the army to do exactly as you said. To try to head him off while he advances from Cordova without serious resistance."

"I agree. Nereth is cunning enough to try such a ploy," Messand concurred.

"Very well, the army will wait here while you carry out

your mission. We could use a few days for the men to rest up and make repairs to their gear before going into combat. Is there anything you need to help you with your mission? A company of men perhaps, or fresh horses, yours must be tired after so long a ride."

"They are a little sir," Wyll agreed. "But they've done right by us so far. Besides, I don't think you could get my men to give them up short of a direct order at any rate," Wyll added with a touch of pride.

"I understand," the general replied, a slight grin tugging at the corner of his lips.

"I might have risen a long way in the last forty years, but I started out in the King's army as a cavalryman myself. Very well, so long as your mounts are all fit, you can continue to use them, but this mission is not to be put in jeopardy because of personal pride. Any man of your squad who wants to use one of our remounts for the duration of the mission may do so. His own horse will be well looked after for when you return with the information we need."

"Yes sir," Wyll replied. "I'll let them know. As for the men, the King thought it best if a small group were to undertake this mission. Just in case we are wrong."

"To minimise losses?" Messand asked, and Wyll nodded in confirmation.

"Captain!" the general called, a new respect seeming to have planted itself in his tone. Even the archmage had looked on approvingly as Wyll confirmed the general's hunch without flinching.

"Captain, see that this man's squad is well provisioned for an eight-day patrol, also with remounts for any man who wants one. And make sure they get a decent meal tonight before they head back out into the field."

The officer who had escorted Wyll into the pavilion nodded, turning to usher him out.

"Also Captain, these men carry a Gift-wrought artefact. They must be billeted at least a mile and a half outside the camp perimeter, or it will interfere with our defensive wards," Veroneth added once the general was finished.

"Yes General, Archmage," the officer replied before motioning for Wyll to follow him outside.

"Oh, and Captain, pass the word that we will not be marching for the next few days. This time is to be used to make repairs to any equipment and to drill the men back to peak performance. I'll follow up with written orders shortly."

"That will be a welcome change for the men, Sir," the captain answered before turning and once again heading for the doorway with Wyll in tow.

Wyll turned to take leave of his superiors, but found them already back in deep conversation and decided not to interrupt them, leaving with the officer instead.

And just like that it was done. They had passed through the Wraith Woods and achieved the first stage of their mission. In the morning they would embark on the second, which in Wyll's mind at least was no less dangerous a portion of the assignment than the one already completed.

"Mount up," the captain ordered. Wyll and his men complied without a word once he had stowed the Chalice back in its place in his packs.

"There is a small watering hole with a copse of trees about two miles to the north. You'll stay there tonight, and I'll have your supplies sent out as soon as I can. Do any of you require remounts for the mission?"

There were some blank looks between the men, and Wyll

explained the general's offer, which they all rejected as Wyll had been sure they would.

"All right then Sergeant, off you go," the captain ordered, though not in an unfriendly manner. Wyll nodded an acknowledgement before using his knees to get Socks moving in the right direction. As soon as they were moving, the captain went about his business. Wyll and his men walked the horses to the edge of camp, where he easily located the copse of trees on a low hill in the distance. Right where the well-informed officer had assured them it would be.

"Come on," Wyll called to his men, and set Socks to a gallop across the flat grassy plain. They would have serious work ahead of them tomorrow, and had narrowly avoided death at the hands of the strange insectile creatures who served Sa'rayna in the Wraith Woods. But as his hair streamed back in the wind of their passage, the only sounds he could hear were the thundering of the horses' hooves. As the sun set off to their left, for right now, for one small minute, Wyll found he could forget all of that, and just be happy to run.

CHAPTER 16

ILLUSION AND TRUTH

Four days had passed since they'd left the king's army, and true to the general's word, Wyll's squad had reached their destination.

The sprawling, unwalled city of Cordova sat hard against the north bank of the Mirallyn River. For all the city's austere beauty, there was little sign of life beyond the normal movements of the people who dwelt within. Heramiir's camp, located more than a mile from the city's northernmost border, was an entirely different matter.

It was hard to make out details at night from this distance. One thing Wyll could see though were rows and rows of tents and pavilions spread out over square miles, and through it all, torch-carrying men scattered like ants. If even a fraction of the men he could see walking patrol and standing guard were real, his task would be all but impossible. Moving his men into position would be the challenging. If those men were real, they would swarm out and intercept his squad before they got close.

"Dismount," Wyll ordered as he walked back into the lea of the small rise which hid the rest of his unit. Even though they were still a few miles away from either the camp or the city, this close to Heramiir's forces, he was taking no chances.

"We'll wait here until two hours before dawn. Then we'll see what's real, and what isn't."

After long phases of hard riding, he could see disappointment on some of the men's faces. After everything they'd been through since leaving the college, they just wanted this mission done with. Although part of him felt the same way, he still had to give tactically sound orders, and so followed it with another disappointment, making a cold camp. Fortunately, there had been a steady cloud cover for most of the day, so the temperature shouldn't drop too much so long as it didn't rain.

Once the tents were set up so they could rest until the appointed hour, the squad had to make do with the dried rations they all disliked. The food was less than appealing, and Wyll grimaced. There was just no way to make the dried strips of cured beef any less, well, dry… at least not without a kettle of boiling water. Wyll smiled vaguely as he remembered a night not too far into their journey when burnable wood had been scarce. Charran had loosened a tooth on the rock-hard dried meat, giving the rest of them a good laugh as he comically persisted with the tough meal, only one side of his mouth able to chew without making him grimace in pain. Still, the man had been hungry enough to manage it, although he now broke the stuff into smaller pieces with his fingers whenever circumstance forced him to consume it.

When everyone had finished eating and doing their other nightly chores, Wyll ordered them to get some rest.

"Kienan and Charran will take first watch, then Bosric and Tauman. After second watch, we'll pack up camp and get as close as we can before first light. I want to hit the edge of the illusion just as dawn breaks. If there *is* anyone down there to chase us, they'll have to shoot into the sun or run us to ground."

No one raised an objection to his plan, so Wyll left it at that. He headed for his tent and went to bed without taking off his leather armour. With Heramiir's army within sight, he was not about to take the chance of being surprised during the night.

He found sleep quickly, the black blade with its fire marked runes resting under his pillow, safe in its ivory sheath for now. It was not the sword, but the woman who had given him the blade Wyll thought on as he left the conscious world.

It seemed an instant later when a rough hand shook him awake.

"Time to go, sir," Bosric merrily informed him as Wyll shook his head to clear it. Bosric left him alone, and Wyll began the now mindlessly familiar task of breaking down his small tent and stowing his few supplies back in his packs. He seemed to have slept on a small rock, resulting in his shoulder being quite stiff. There was even a small bruise he noticed as he felt around for whatever had irritated him.

Most of their gear, along with the pack horses, had been left with the army so they could travel faster. Each man now only carried the essentials, so getting ready took them half the time he was used to. The men who finished first stood around eating flatbread and a wedge of cheese they had divided up. As they completed their own tasks, Wyll and the others joined them, Sarran passing out their shares from the supplies. Once they had eaten, Wyll took Sock's reins and nodded to his men. He was tired of making speeches, and the men all knew what was about to happen. With a sort of silent agreement they set off, walking the horses around the small hill and out onto the open plain. If the men in the camp were real, Wyll knew they would spot his squad within minutes. Tense seconds stretched on, but they drew closer and closer to the monstrous encampment that sprawled across the plain, and no alarm sounded. The night was still dark, and the clouds obscured the half moon, but Wyll knew their luck couldn't be that good. For over an hour they crept slowly closer, even the horses keeping quiet, sensing their masters' moods. Before them the main camp appeared to be sleeping, though torches and campfires were everywhere, and sentries patrolled the edge of the camp, as well as further in.

When Wyll judged they were as close to the camp as they were to the city itself, he ordered the men to mount up. That should put them just outside the chalice's range, he hoped. He had wanted to save the horses' strength in case Heramiir's men forced them to make a quick getaway, and so far it had worked.

"All right," he told them quietly. "We'll get as close as we can if the illusion doesn't lift. Otherwise, once it does, we ride hard at it. Some of those men down there must be real. They'd have to be, to keep the city convinced an army exists if nothing else. Remember what Archmage Volnar told us. If we can use the chalice to nullify whatever's keeping the illusion together, it should be rendered inert. Otherwise, only the parts of it within range of the chalice will go. He also said that the centre of the illusion was most likely where it was being sustained. Given the size of this camp, we will have to ride close to a mile into it before the chalice will reach that far."

Wyll stopped for a moment as he regarded his men. "At any rate, the most important thing is that at least some of us make it back to the General and report our findings."

Wyll thought for a long moment about what they were about to attempt, then came to a hard decision. One he knew should have occurred to him long before this.

"Kienan, return to the hillock where we made camp. I want you to watch from there, just in case."

He left the rest unsaid, but the black-haired musician nodded his understanding.

"Yes sir," Kienan answered. The man was clearly torn between his loyalty to the rest of them, and the knowledge that he was now by far the worst of them with a blade.

"Go now," Wyll told him, not unkindly, but with no room for argument either.

"I'll see you all soon," he returned seriously before dismounting and leading his horse back the way they had come.

"I hope so," Wyll whispered to the man's back as he left, though Kienan couldn't hear.

It wasn't Kienan's fault he was the worst of their squad with weapons, Wyll reflected. Someone had to be, and no one had questioned his courage or commitment. Still, Wyll remembered all too well how he had felt in the Wraith Woods when he'd been forced to leave his men to whatever fate awaited them. Kienan would be feeling that same hollowness now. Wyll said a silent prayer to the Maker, hoping this time turned out as well.

Looking around, he judged they had made better time than he'd expected across the fields between their hillock and the camp. There were perhaps fifteen minutes left until the first grey of predawn would stain the sky behind them. He decided they could afford to wait a few minutes until Kienan was clear, so long as they weren't spotted.

Once he could no longer make out Kienan's shadowy form in the distance, he motioned his men to follow, then nudged Socks into a walk towards the enemy camp. For a long time nothing happened, and an uneasy feeling was starting to build in him as the sky began lightening around them. The sentries patrolling the perimeter appeared to be changing shift now, and Wyll fervently hoped his squad had not been sent on a fool's errand. Surely they were within a mile of the camp now.

Wyll moved Socks up to a canter, and his men followed suit. If the army here was indeed real, they had to get as close to it as they could before those sentries spotted them. The ones going off shift would be tired and inattentive, but those just arriving would be more alert, and far more prepared if this came to a fight.

Wyll was preparing to draw his blade when the first tent shimmered and faded away into nothing. The one behind it went next, along with those around. Suddenly the whole side of the camp was melting as if it were a sandcastle eroded away by a powerful wave.

A shout went up from the camp, and Wyll grimaced. That was all the proof he needed that at least some of those men were real. Fortunately, only a few of the sentries seemed to be of the more substantial kind, and their attention was firmly held on the spectacle of the disappearing illusion. One of the more attentive guards heard the now galloping hooves of their horses and turned. The surprise was evident on his face as he saw Wyll bearing down on him and realised their danger.

There was a twang from Cale's bowstring, and the guard fell before he could raise the alarm, but another saw him fall and raised the cry. Within moments, the few guards who had not melted away with the rest of the illusion were readying weapons and running to intercept them as they advanced.

They were within a hundred spans of the sentry line now, but the guards were spread too thin. Only a single soldier was in position to intercept them as they crossed into the camp. He held a long halberd in his hands as he stood facing them, resolute even though completely on his own. Cale's next arrow took the man in the leg, and he fell, dropping the heavy weapon that could take a rider from his saddle at a blow. Wyll's men rode around him without a backwards glance.

Before them, the illusion retreated in a massive arc, which soon became a circle as they rode further into it. They kept riding, until eventually the tents began to reform behind them, now out of range of the chalice's effect. As it turned out, there were almost no men stationed beyond the border of the massive illusion. By now, he estimated the chalice's effect must be nearing the centre of the illusion. They couldn't go much further or they would risk being cut off from behind. More soldiers, mounted this time, were now riding out from the edge of the city to stop them, but they were still a minute or more away.

In the distance he could see a wide white tent which appeared to be a command pavilion. That had to be his target, Wyll thought as he steered Socks towards it, keeping a close eye on the men coming from the city. There were only a dozen, but they looked like they knew their business, and Wyll wanted to avoid them if he could.

Ahead of him, the lines of tents had receded until the pavilion was almost in range. As they continued to ride towards it, other tents vanished until it was next in line. Wyll smiled when the pavilion remained unchanged despite other tents vanishing beside and around it.

This one was real.

As the chalice's effect reached its midpoint, there was a great swirl of colour all around them. Heramiir's army distorted and scattered into nothing as the whole illusion fragmented, vanishing as if it had never been there at all.

Wyll glanced around, re-evaluating the situation, and was both elated and dismayed by what he found. With Heramiir's fake army dissipated into the morning breeze, his true forces at Cordova were revealed, and Wyll almost laughed. There were perhaps five hundred men either standing around the few square miles where the camp had been, looking greatly perplexed, or else running hard at them. Of the masses of tents, only a few small rows towards the city side remained intact. The pavilion where the artefact which had thrown the king's battle plans into disarray was still erect, but there was precious little else. Wyll took a quick look back at their pursuers. They were still more than a minute away, and he knew what he had to do.

Slowing Socks for a moment to let Seth catch up, he yelled at the man over the rushing wind of their passage.

"Can you hold those men off while I retrieve the artefact?!"

Seth took a quick look at the dozen riders that were by far their closest threat and nodded that he thought they could.

"Good! Tauman, you're with me!" The man had the best horse besides himself, and they sped off towards the pavilion while Seth took the rest of the squad and closed with the enemy riders. They were still quite a way from the single remaining structure, and by the time he and Tauman reached it, they could hear the faint ring of steel on steel.

Seth's group had already engaged their opponents. There was no time to waste.

Wyll brought Socks to a halt, and both he and Tauman dismounted a few feet from the canvas entrance. He had to go in, but he was also sure the pavilion was not completely unguarded, likely by men on either side of the door at the least. Motioning Tauman to take up position outside the opposite flap of canvas, Wyll raised the sword of ages once he had positioned himself. When they were both ready, he nodded. The two men both slashed hard through the fabric and there was a cry of pain from inside. Wyll knew Tauman had hit his mark. His own blade however sailed on through without further resistance. Wyll charged through the gap and bull-rushed the man who had been lucky enough to avoid his attack. Tauman closed in through the doorway, and between them they made quick work of the remaining guard. The soldier danced away and parried his thrust, but a hard blow from the hilt of Tauman's blade to the man's head sent him insensate to the ground. The soldier fell, unconscious, and Wyll ordered Tauman to leave him be. What they wanted was on a pedestal in the middle of the otherwise empty pavilion.

On a four-pronged metal holder sat a perfect sphere of glass, or perhaps crystal. He didn't know whether it looked more impressive when it was active, but with a small shrug he strode over to the object. Since the chalice was in range and an enemy mage was not, he knew no wards protected it. Wyll reached out and took the sphere. He shoved the fist sized artefact into a pocket as quickly as he could.

"Let's go," he said. Tauman was keeping watch outside through the bloodstained rip his sword had made in the pavilion's fabric. Someone had conditioned their horses well while they had been in camp five, and later the grooms at the college had continued those efforts. Both of the now war trained beasts were standing right where they had been dismounted a few moments before. The two men ran over and vaulted up onto their backs before setting off at a dead run. Seth and the rest of the squad were still engaged with the remainder of the enemy unit. Wyll looked around the field. They had perhaps three minutes before a large contingent of light cavalry from the western side of the camp would be within bow range. The sun was cresting the horizon now, and that would make shooting at his men harder. If they couldn't disentangle themselves from this fight before the enemy reinforcements arrived though, they wouldn't live long enough for it to matter.

Seth and the others appeared to have done well. There were five enemy troops on the ground and two more had taken wounds and withdrawn from the fight. His own men still looked reasonably fresh, only Sarran having taken an injury. The older of the brothers had stowed his staff, a predominantly two-handed weapon, in favour of the single bladed axe he preferred for one handed fighting. He was continuing to attack the enemy troops, though not one on one.

Wyll didn't know if it was just luck, or whether Seth had somehow seen them coming. At the last moment he managed to turn his opponent just enough so that Tauman could slash at him as they passed. The enemy soldier tumbled from his saddle as they darted through the fight, hacking at the already hard-pressed enemy forces as they went. Once they were through, Wyll slowed and turned Socks back to the fight, which was all but over. Cale and Charran converged on the last man still mounted and finished him in moments, and Wyll took a second to evaluate their situation. They had perhaps two minutes now until the large force from the west would be on them. They were coming at a dead run, and their horses couldn't sustain that pace for long.

"Let's go!" he called, and set Socks to an easy trot, trying to let their horses recover as much as possible before they had to run again.

When he judged the enemy to be less than a minute away, he kneed Socks to a relaxed gallop. With his men close behind, they headed east, back towards the eventual safety of the king's army. The only thing the enemy had in place which could still stop them were the hundred or more riders still gaining on them. There were twenty or so sentries ahead, all of whom were on foot, but they were not an obstacle. Unwilling to let the cavalry close any further, Wyll rode around the unmounted sentries and left them behind. They continued to chase even though they had no hope of catching up, and Wyll admired their persistence.

Keeping a close eye on the enemy cavalry's progress, Wyll let them gain a little more ground, which made them push their mounts even harder. That was good, so long as they didn't get too close. Their horses must be nearing exhaustion by now, and they would soon have to slow, or kill the animals for nothing.

His men were little more than halfway back to Kienan's observation hillock when he saw with relief that the enemy riders were no longer trying to close. They were now simply attempting to keep up with the squad they were pursuing, and Wyll urged a somewhat renewed Socks to a faster run. His men kept up, and their burst of speed seemed to dishearten the enemy as he'd hoped. Moments later, their leader gave the order to slow their lathered and panting mounts.

A few of them took out bows and fired. The extreme distance, and morning sun in their eyes conspired to only bring two of the projectiles down anywhere near Wyll's men. Neither hit its mark as they stuck fast in the rich soil of a farmer's field.

Wyll smiled and led them on. Once they were out of sight behind their hillock, Kienan re-joined them and reported that the pursuers were still walking their mounts forward. They had expected to catch Wyll and his men at once, and failed. Unlike his squad, who had ridden further, but at a far slower pace, their dead run had used up the animals in one mad dash across their vast camp. It would be hours before they could ride those lathered animals at speed again.

Wyll ordered his men to dismount and walk the horses while Cale bound up Sarran's wound. When Tauman reported that the animals were all tired but unharmed, Wyll returned to the hillock for one last look at their work. What he saw was encouraging. In all, there couldn't have been more than three or four thousand soldiers who had spilled out of Cordova's streets. Aside from their pursuers, most appeared to be infantry, who were now milling in disarray, far too late to do anything about the lightning-fast raid.

Wyll nodded in approval as he returned to Socks. He ordered the men to lead the horses on foot in a fast walk towards the east for now. There was a small stream about half an hour away where they could water the animals once they had cooled a bit.

Without the burden of their riders, the animals recovered well, and by the time they had drunk their fill from the slow-moving stream and eaten a few honeyed oats from the supplies, the animals had recovered sufficiently to be of service again.

Looking back the way they had come, Wyll saw their pursuers were on the move again, though nowhere near as quickly. They had only now cleared the hillock.

His squad had a little breathing room to work with, but that was all, and the king's camp was several days away. Heramiir's men weren't likely to give up, which meant that whoever had the best horses, and most experienced riders, would prevail.

"They're on the move again," Wyll told his men, whose heads, except for Seth of course, swivelled as one back the way they had come.

"We've got a long ride ahead of us. Since there are far too many of them to fight, we'll need to outrun them until we can make it as far as the King's outriders. From there we can find aid, but until then we're on our own. You all know what's at stake here. If we get separated, make your way back to the army any way you can, and report what we've found to General Messand, understood?"

The men all voiced their agreement, and Wyll took a last look back, trying not to frown. There must be at least a hundred men in that party. He would have to use every bit of guile to make sure they couldn't catch up.

"Mount up," he told them, and following his own order, leapt onto Socks' back before taking them to a canter.

The men moved out to flank him in a loose V-formation so the dirt and debris flung up from the other horses' hooves wouldn't hit them as they ran. The sun had climbed a hand-span into the sky now, and it appeared it was going to be quite a nice day, at least weather wise.

Wyll muttered a quick prayer to the Maker that he could keep his men alive until it ended.

*　　*　　*

It was only an hour after nightfall when Wyll looked back over his shoulder and saw a small fire through the thin layer of trees in the distance. The question was, did it mean his enemy had stopped for the night, or was it a ruse? They could be trying to make him think his men safe for the night and stop as well, giving the pursuers time to catch up. Just to be on the safe side, Wyll had the men dismount since it was too dark now for the horses to move at any speed. He made them lead the horses for another hour before coming across a low hill that would hide the light of their fire from prying eyes. Unless their pursuers were on the hilltop right above them of course, but by then it wouldn't matter anyway.

Once they had seen to the horses, they were finally able to rest while Kienan prepared the inevitable reconstituted soup. The clerk had supplied them with 'fresh' ingredients back at the camp and there was coarse bread and even some cheese to go with it. For a brief moment, Wyll felt the tension of the long chase slip away.

There were still too many enemies out there to relax, and Wyll roused himself from the warmth of the fire.

"How many of them do you think there are?" he asked the others, breaking the silence which had hung over them like a fog for much of the day.

"I make at least eighty," Seth told him without hesitation.

No one else disagreed enough to speak up as they lay near the fire, recovering from the day's exertions, so Wyll continued.

"Too many to fight then. Sentries or patrols?" he asked, directing the inquiry to Seth this time. The man had the best grasp of martial tactics out of any of them.

"Sentries," Seth replied, already understanding where Wyll was heading with this line of thought. "They will expect us to be as far away from them as we can get, so they shouldn't make more than a token defence of their camp."

"That was my thought as well," Wyll answered with a slight grin. "Could be a good way to thin out their numbers a little?"

Seth nodded in agreement, and that was enough for Wyll. One day he would have to find out where the man had come by all his military training, since he still wouldn't tell them where he had served. But that was a matter for another time.

Wyll stood, the others watching him with varying levels of apprehension.

"You don't mean to attack them, do you, sir?" Kienan asked. "They outnumber us at least ten to one if what Seth says is true."

"Seth, Cale, Bosric, you're with me," he said, looking Kienan in the eye.

"We are going to see how many of their sentries we can take out without alerting their main force."

"Oh," Kienan murmured, feeling chastened.

"The rest of you will ride for the King's army at first light if we are not back by then. Charran, you'll take the lead."

"Me, sir?" the brown haired staffman asked, surprised to be chosen.

"That's right," Wyll confirmed. "Just get back and report to General Messand, and return the chalice, and whatever that arcane object is that was causing the illusion, to Archmage Veroneth."

"Yes sir," Charran replied, a little too loudly. But then the man had just been granted his first command, even if only by default, and Wyll couldn't blame him for being a little proud. Besides, he had earned it in his training performances back at the college, as well as through his composure during their time in the Wraith Woods. Of course, Seth or Cale, if the man could talk, would have been his first choices. He couldn't spare them though, not if his plan was to have any chance of success.

"All right, gather up your weapons and do what you need to. We'll leave in five minutes, on foot. I want to spare the horses for tomorrow's ride."

The men he'd picked out began seeing to their own needs, and Wyll walked behind a small hill to make a quick privy stop before the mission began. By the time he returned and gathered up his own equipment, the others were waiting.

"Remember, first light. Don't wait," he told Charran, and the large man nodded.

"I won't let you down sir," he answered as he stood.

"Good luck."

"And to you," Wyll replied.

"Come on," he told the men he had singled out. "I make it about four miles back to that fire, and we have little time to lose."

Cale grinned at Seth, and the almost bald man nodded while Bosric began flipping a foot-long knife in his palm, catching the spinning blade unerringly by the hilt. Just as well too, Wyll thought to himself. The man would cut himself badly if he ever missed. Still, Wyll had seen him perform that trick many times before without the slightest problem. That and more. The red-haired maniac was not more than average with a sword, but with his knives, the man was a wonder, and Wyll had never met a more athletically capable man.

He couldn't help a small grin as he set off, the others following on a grassy ground well-lit by the moon. The few trees around them were more just random growth than any kind of true forest. It was a quiet night, and the only noises which accompanied his men were those of natural undertaking. Crickets chirped around them, growing silent at their approach, and the occasional bat flew away on leathery wings to find some place less threatening to hunt its nocturnal prey. There was an eerie kind of beauty to this hushed nocturnal world.

They had been walking for about an hour when Seth called a halt, and the others scanned the area intently. They knew by now that his hearing was better than any of theirs, and he didn't jump at shadows. Wyll moved up beside the man with the bald head, broken only by a topknot of hair, to ask what was wrong. Before he could even take the few steps between them, something huge and black launched itself from a nearby tree.

Seth's reflexes kicked in and he wildly dived aside even as a large knife-hilt sprouted from the creature's neck. The massive shadowy form writhed as it hit the ground, collapsing on the spot where it had intended to strike Seth with its entire weight.

Before either he or Cale even had a chance to react, it was done.

The knife protruding up through its jaw must have pierced its brain to finish it so quickly, Wyll thought.

There was a long moment of unnerving silence once the creature's corpse had settled, every man straining their senses to detect if any more of the beasts lurked above.

"What is that thing?!" Wyll asked the others after a long moment when nothing else stirred. In the dim light under the canopy of thickening foliage, he took a moment to study the now lifeless beast in front of him. Wyll's heart skipped a beat as he studied the disturbing form, which seemed cobbled together from what looked to be several distinct animals.

"It's a baby manticore," Seth said with more surprise in his voice than Wyll had ever heard. The expert swordsman cautiously approached the limp figure. Once he was satisfied it was dead, he rolled the six-foot-long carcass over to extract Bosric's knife. Wiping the blade clean on the creature's hide, he handed it back to the red-headed man. Bosric took it without a word as he too studied the strange looking animal before them. It had the body of an enormous cat, but with a head akin to a goat and the avian wings of a bird of prey jutting out from its back.

"But I've never seen one this far east of the Dark Iron Mountains before. Like the Terraliv, they prefer much colder weather. This is exceedingly strange," he muttered as he continued surveying the lifeless beast before them with an intensity that bordered on obsession.

"And I wish we could study it further," Wyll responded after a moment, more to break Seth out of his strange mood than to get him moving. "But we have a mission to complete."

Wyll had heard about these creatures while he was growing up, but they never ranged as far as the Anchorhead Promontory. Even as far east as the Ice Ranges, they were extraordinarily rare. This might well be the only one he ever saw in person, and Wyll wished the light was better.

"By the way Bosric, well done, that was a *very* good

throw, even for you," Wyll acknowledged. The man's reflexive actions had almost certainly saved Seth from serious injury or death. The six-inch-long, razor-sharp claws which adorned the manticore's feline paws would have slaughtered the man in moments if they had reached their intended target.

"I agree," Seth added. "These creatures are hard to bring down at the best of times, and I have never heard of it being done with a single knife thrust before. So you have my thanks... Look at this!" he breathed, and as the others gathered around, a chill went up Wyll's spine as he realised what Seth had seen.

Underneath the manticore's thick fur was a hardy strip of leather, laced with metal links which wrapped its way around the creature's neck. A thick steel ring joined it at the top.

"This is a collar," Seth announced in consternation. "But that would mean that someone had tamed this creature! That can't be done."

"Well, someone found a way." Wyll returned, trying to bring the man back to the present despite the increasingly odd situation, not to mention Seth's attention, whom he had never seen so distracted.

"If it's the men following us, we have to find out if they have any more of these things, and finish them. Otherwise it won't matter how much we rest the horses; they'll track us from the sky."

"Yes, of course..." Seth agreed, standing and tucking the finely wrought collar under his armour after unlatching its metal link, "The camp shouldn't be too much farther ahead now. We should be careful."

The top-knotted man took a long last look at the creature

before setting out with a furrowed brow, leading the party as usual. Cale, who had kept watch while they examined the creature, brought up the rear.

As Wyll had predicted, it was only another quarter hour before they heard the faint scuffing of footsteps in the nearby brush. Bosric melted away from them without a word to investigate.

There was a soft thud a minute later, and then the muted sound of something heavy being dragged before Bosric came back the way he had left.

"That's one less," was all he whispered as he returned, and Wyll nodded.

"We'll circle the camp, take out as many of their sentries as we can before we're discovered. Let's try to thin their numbers out a little," Wyll whispered to his men, who each nodded their readiness.

"Spread out but don't lose sight of each other," he told them before drawing Sa'rayna's black blade, immediately re-sheathing it as the fiery runes became visible for all to see. Thankfully he still wore the original sword they had supplied him with at camp five in a scabbard on his waist. He drew that instead, though he would have much preferred using the blade Sa'rayna had given him.

It was strange. The sword of ages existed for no reason other than to bring swift, violent death. Yet Sa'rayna had given it to him, and it was all he had of her except for his memories. It made him feel far more connected to a thing made exclusively for killing than he thought he probably should.

It wasn't long before they heard footsteps again off to their left, and this time it was Cale who silenced the sentry, also doing so without raising an alarm. They continued to circle the camp, meeting no further opposition, and Wyll knew they didn't have long until the men they had killed were missed, and an alarm raised. There was a faint wicker of a horse in the distance, and Wyll looked over just in time to see Bosric's grin become a little wider. Seth nodded in approval, a gesture which Cale imitated with enthusiasm. Wyll couldn't help but grin a little as well. If they could chase off some of the enemy's mounts, it would be as good as eliminating their riders from the pursuit, and fewer men would have to die for the result.

Wyll cocked his head in the direction the sound had come from, and his men began moving in the right direction. There was another equine snort, and Wyll moved up ahead of the others to a spot behind a tree where he could finally see their target.

Fifty feet of open ground stood between where they were hiding and the long picket lines. There were four sets of stakes anchoring long ropes to the ground, and about twenty or thirty mounts hobbled to each. Unfortunately, while their pursuers' sentries had been few and lax, there were a dozen men sitting around a campfire on the forest side of their objective. Neither could they circle around to the horses without coming even closer to the main force in the camp.

There was one bit of good news. The men at the fire were not expecting an attack, and were sitting at ease without their armour, though their weapons were close at hand. They were in the middle of eating what appeared to be a late dinner, and Wyll studied the scene before him. There was no sign of other manticores, nor any apparatus for handling them, which of course left several unanswered questions. Did these men even send it in the first place, or did it come from another source entirely? How many more of them might there be out here doing some unknown master's bidding? Had this one escaped some unknown captivity and returned to the wild, or had its abortive attack been deliberate?

Still, after a few more moments of study, Wyll could gather no more useful information, and so returned to the others.

"Can all of you ride bareback?" he whispered, and the others nodded.

"Good, here's what we'll do then," Wyll said, taking them through his plan.

"It's risky," Bosric said with a grin. Wyll could only agree. "I know, but if we can pull it off, we can be free from most of this pursuit and safely back on our way to the King's army by morning."

"All right. Maker's luck to us then," Wyll said when there were no further comments. He drew the black blade from its sheath on his back as he stood, keeping his body between it and the men in the clearing as he did so.

The others also drew their blades. Seth unsheathed his twin Drakheras, the curved blades he always carried with their tiny dart launchers on either side. Cale took out his military issue longsword, and Bosric drew a pair of foot long daggers from his boots, which were almost short swords in themselves. They were a strange collection of fighters, Wyll thought again, and yet somehow they worked well as a unit. He had initially thought they must be stragglers when he had met them back on that first day in camp five. Men too difficult to fit into other units and so chucked together to get them out of the way of the other conventional squads. He now knew he couldn't have been more wrong. The different disciplines each of his men brought to the squad would continue to see them in good stead.

With a last nod, Wyll turned and crept towards the clearing where the men and horses waited.

When he judged enough time had passed that they hadn't seen his approach, he took hold of the tree he was behind and gave it a shake. The leaves rustled enough that the men around the fire stopped their conversation and looked over at where the noise had come from. Wyll prayed the darkness beyond the firelight still hid him. Otherwise this would go very wrong, very quickly. The men from the camp began talking again, so Wyll once again shook the tree. This time the silence was complete until he heard one of them say.

"See, I told you there was something there."

"Who goes there?" one of the men called out, though of course Wyll gave him no response for his trouble.

"Could be an animal?" one of the others suggested, just as Wyll had hoped. He gave the tree another small shake while they were looking straight at him. Surely no intelligent creature would give away their position as blatantly as he just had?

"Come on, let's check it out," the man, who seemed to be a sergeant, ordered some of his companions. Two of them followed him over towards where Wyll was waiting.

He tiptoed back to the next tree as they approached, and then gave it another shake as he did.

"Here dinner, dinner, dinner," one of the soldiers called, earning a hard stare from the sergeant, who drew his weapon and ordered the others to do so as well.

The three men edged past the first tree where Wyll had been hiding, and in doing so left the protective circle of firelight their camp gave off. Wyll rustled the tree he was behind, and the men turned towards him.

The sergeant took a few steps forward and Bosric leapt from the tree branch he'd been perched on. The short man thrust with his knife as he fell, taking the sergeant to the ground with him. The instant he moved, Seth had risen from the shadows beside where the other two were standing.

Not even Wyll had seen where the man had been hiding, but a moment later it was over. The last soldier made a gurgling sound as he slumped to the ground, the merest flitting of a black form announcing Sa'rayna's inevitable presence.

The noise was enough. A moment later, four more of the men by the fire were picking up weapons and striding towards them to see what the commotion had been. The dying soldiers' final cry had not been loud though, and it hadn't concerned the men at the fire enough to raise a general alarm just yet. As the soldiers came towards them, the few remaining troops stared intently into the darkness, standing alert now as they remained behind to guard the horses.

The next four soldiers entered the forest with far less caution than the would-be hunting party. In their haste to locate their commander, they never saw the ambush coming. Wyll stepped out from behind his tree as they passed, and with a steady swing of Sa'rayna's blade took the lead soldier's head clean off. Seth and Bosric took advantage of the enemy's moment of shock to attack from behind. Those men fell. Even as they did, the last remaining soldier recovered his wits and swung at Wyll. His blade connected with the sword of ages, ringing out over the quiet forest, and alerting their enemy that an assault was under way. Seth finished him a moment later from behind but the damage had been done.

"Come on, we'll only have a moment," Wyll ordered as he charged towards the fire, his men in tow. As soon as they broke the tree line, the soldiers by the fire shouted in alarm. One of them dashed back towards the camp, which was only a hundred feet beyond the horse lines.

Wyll, Seth, and Bosric crossed the space between them in seconds and engaged the four remaining soldiers with efficiency. In seconds they were down, and easier than Wyll had expected. They ran to join Cale, who had already snuck in from the side of the clearing to sever two of the horse lines while the enemy was occupied by the fight. Soldiers were boiling out of the tent rows like ants from a kicked nest, and after another few seconds of intense cutting, the third of the thick horse lines was severed. It wasn't fast enough though and Wyll realised they would never finish the task before the enemy overwhelmed them.

"Mount up!" he shouted before vaulting up on to the nearest horse. It fought him for a second, but he took control of the animal and rode it through the mass of horses, shouting and slapping them with the flat of his blade to encourage them to move. His men followed suit, but the brief encounter and the smell of blood from the dead soldiers nearby were not quite enough. The bulk of the enemy soldiers were seconds away, and the horses, while irritated and starting to panic, were not yet ready to bolt.

"Blast!" Wyll muttered as he called at his men to retreat. As their horses started speeding up to a gallop, it was enough to get the rest of the mounts following as they dashed away from the oncoming flood of shouting soldiers. Wyll led his men back to the east along the way they had come. In this darkness and terrain, it would only be minutes before a horse lost its footing and broke a leg, or worse. With the whole enemy contingent on their tails, it was a chance they would just have to take. On either side, trees dashed past, some close enough to scrape branches across him. A low-hanging limb seemed to appear out of nowhere, battering his shoulder hard enough to turn his whole body. More through force of will than anything else, he recovered his balance.

If this continued, there would be worse to come.

It seemed they rode for hours in that timeless state, dodging branches which suddenly appeared to race into their line of sight, and praying their horses didn't stumble. In reality, it couldn't have been more than a few minutes until they reached the small stream which they had crossed on the way to the camp. Wyll saw a low fog had risen around it. It was thin, but it would serve their purposes well. He ordered his men into the stream and dismounted. Many of the loosed mounts had scattered already, and those that hadn't, he and the others encouraged with slaps on the rump from the flat of their swords. In moments they were alone, and Wyll motioned his men north, on foot and upstream, hoping that their pursuers would think they were still on horseback. With this many sets of muddy hoof prints left behind by the scattered mounts, it would be almost impossible to track them on foot up the river.

"Spread out you fools! Find them!" a commanding voice shouted from behind, and Wyll ordered his men up onto a shadowed rock outcropping which overhung the shallow stream. Looking around for cover, he jumped into the branches of a large tree with especially thick foliage. He trusted the darkness to reveal very little trace as to their destination. The others followed, climbing higher through the foliage than a three-storey house, and into the most obscured shadow of its branches. It was only seconds after they had halted their climb that half a dozen mounted men walked their horses deliberately upstream, searching for any tracks leading out of the water.

It was a tense moment for Wyll and his men as the enemy soldiers passed the rock outcropping. Thankfully the deep shadows and natural blackness of the stone were enough to obscure the watermarks from his men's boots. The mounted soldiers missed the subtle mark of their passage, and they continued searching the banks of the river upstream for hoofprints they would never find.

"We'll wait here until they return," Wyll whispered to the others. He was pleased the men obeyed his commands without question, even though they were soaked below the knees and stuck in a tree waiting for enemy soldiers to pass right below them again. Bosric was even grinning, though there was nothing unusual about that.

It was a quarter of an hour later, as Wyll made it, when the sound of splashing footsteps returned, followed a moment later by the soldiers they belonged to. Another few minutes passed as the men continued downstream, and then the angry voice began shouting again, causing Wyll to grin as well.

"You useless scurvy infested dogs! Round up as many of the horses as you can find and get back to the camp. I'll deal with you all later!"

There was a faint sound of galloping hooves, and Bosric chuckled.

"All hail the king of confusion!" he laughed in a whisper, giving Wyll a mocking bow.

"It seemed like a good idea at the time," he returned with a small grin of his own.

"It was a good idea," Seth replied just as quietly. "The plan worked, and we have cut the number of pursuers by at least a third, maybe even half, depending on how many of their horses they can find. We lost no men in achieving this. That is nothing to laugh at, Bosric."

"Who's laughing at him?" the red headed knife man whispered. "I'm laughing with him."

The others continued to give him blank stares.

"Come on, I don't know about all of you, but I think that was maybe the funniest joke I've ever played on anyone. They'll be up all night trying to find those horses. Even if they do, most of them will be too tired to chase us properly tomorrow, or fight us even if they do catch up."

He grinned again, and this time the others did as well. Wyll shook his head at the strange perspective of the world the shortest member of his squad seemed to hold.

Several more minutes had crawled by with nothing but the sounds of the forest and the occasional distant wicker of a loosed horse to be heard. It was time. He ordered the men out of the tree and back across the river.

"All right, be on alert. There must be enemy soldiers all around here looking for their mounts. Let's see if we can't thin their numbers a little more on our way back."

The other men nodded their approval, and Wyll led them out.

So far, everything they had done had turned to gold, so to speak, and Wyll dreaded the day his men took their first losses in battle. But in the meantime, if this kept up, he thought that sometime soon, he might actually start feeling like he'd been the right choice for this command after all.

CHAPTER 17

THE MAD DASH OF A TURTLE

There were still at least fifty men chasing them as they entered a large copse of pines, dense with underbrush, and squeezed together in what was passably a miniature forest.

The pursuing force also couldn't be more than an hour behind.

Given the landmarks Wyll had observed on their way to Cordova, the king's army was at least four hours' hard ride from here. After three days of constant pursuit though, their horses were spent. Pushing the mounts to travel at anything beyond a walk for the next day at least would kill every animal they had, except perhaps Socks. Even if they tried, it was unlikely they could outdistance the men chasing them long enough to reach the army's vanguard. And Wyll was not sure that they should. The moment the enemy caught sight of the king's army, they would send their fastest rider back to warn Heramiir's forces of its position. With a lead that substantial, they would reach the forces at Cordova before they could be intercepted. Whoever was in charge would then send word to Heramiir's main force about the size and position of the king's army, which could disrupt the momentum of the entire campaign.

Yet Wyll didn't know what else he could do. He and his

seven men were no match against the number of troops following, and the information they'd gathered *had* to be delivered to the army as soon as possible.

Leading his men into the dense thicket, Wyll hoped their pursuers would think they were laying some sort of trap and move cautiously through the woods. At the very least, he hoped they would waste time circling around it to see if their tracks came out on the other side. Whether or not the ruse worked, he planned on riding straight on through as quickly as his men could manage.

"Halt and dismount!" a man's voice ordered as its owner stepped out from behind a tree, a loaded and cocked crossbow pointed at Wyll's chest.

Some of Wyll's men drew their swords.

A loud thud accompanied the splintering of wood as a thick quarrel drove itself into a tree next to Cale's head, stopping his men short.

"That's right, I'm not alone," the man said, and Wyll noticed for the first time that he was wearing the green uniform of the king's scouts.

But is he really still on the king's side?

"Your name?" the man asked.

Wyll considered the situation quickly, but could see no way that any of Heramiir's men could know who he was, and so answered truthfully.

"I am Wyll of Grandell, and of the mageguard. These are my men. Now who are you, and why have you stopped us?" he answered, purposely leaving out which faction of the guard they worked for.

The answer seemed to satisfy the scout enough that he lowered his weapon after resetting the safety toggle.

"That's good news. I'm Captain Karloff, General

Messand sent us to locate you. Looks like it was easier than I thought it would be."

Heramiir's men would have had no way to get these fresh troops here ahead of them, making the man's stated allegiance close to a certainty.

"It's about to get a lot harder."

"About an hour behind us there are at least fifty men intent on not letting us return to the general with what we know."

"Yes, we saw the dust trail an hour ago," Karloff replied. "What do you need us to do?"

Wyll thought for a moment as he studied the man who seemed so ready to put himself under Wyll's authority, even though he must be at least a dozen years his superior.

"How many men do you have here?" Wyll asked him.

"Twenty crossbowmen and myself. All infantry," he supplied, competently understanding why Wyll had asked.

There was no chance of getting remounts that could outrun their pursuers' horses then. Not that Wyll would have enjoyed taking that option. It would have meant leaving the scouts in a bad situation when the horsemen checked the small forest. The pursuing force would have to, or risk missing their quarry if they were in fact hiding, waiting for Heramiir's men to pass.

"We're going to have to make a fight of it then," Wyll told the older man.

"Spread the word to all of your men Captain, Heramiir's so called force at Cordova is no more than four thousand strong. The illusion which sustained the rest has been neutralised, and right now they don't know where our army is located, so we can attack them at will. All that stands in the way of taking the city back are those men following us.

They cannot be allowed to escape, to warn Heramiir of our strength and position. This information has to get back to General Messand as soon as possible so he can march on the fjords below Lake Pristine and stop Heramiir's army before they invade central Jeranon."

A slight smile tugged at the corner of the experienced captain's mouth.

"You all hear that?"

There was a chorus of enthusiastic responses, and the captain shouted for one of his men.

"Riley!"

"Here sir," a voice came from somewhere up in the trees.

"Go to ground. If all else fails it will be up to you to get this information to the general as fast as you can, understood?"

"Yes sir," the wiry man replied, scampering skyward into the upper limbs of his tree until even his own men couldn't see him through the thick foliage.

"The way I see it, the men pursuing you won't be expecting us. If you can lead them in here where our bows can pick them off from above, we can eliminate a good number of them before they reach melee range. Do you agree?"

"I do," Wyll returned with a slight grin.

"Good," Karloff replied. "A man with sense. Once you bring them to us, don't stray too far or we won't be able to help you. The trees will be both our ally, and our obstacle in this action."

"Agreed," Wyll returned, "Just don't take too long picking them off. My men are good, but we're exhausted, and we'll be outnumbered six to one on the ground. You'll only have a minute at most before they overwhelm us with sheer weight of numbers."

"We'll have your backs," Karloff replied. "For now, go back to the edge of the copse and dismount as if you are trying to rest your horses before a final dash."

Wyll nodded in agreement at the captain's advice, and turned Socks. His men, though tired, had rallied at the unexpected encounter, and followed without having to be ordered. Wyll smiled to himself, feeling like a real commander for perhaps the first time since being promoted back in camp five. That day seemed a lifetime ago.

"Up!" he heard Karloff call behind him, then heard the remaining scouts who were still at ground level clambering up the surrounding trees to prepare for the coming ambush.

When they were just far enough into the dense copse not to be seen, Wyll ordered his men to dismount and break out some rations. With a strip of jerked meat in hand, he went back to the tree line to monitor the dust cloud which marked their pursuers' position.

It won't be long, he thought as he chewed on the ration and stared out over the plain. The men chasing them were visibly nearer than they'd been a few minutes before. At this pace, Wyll estimated it would be no more than twenty minutes until they reached the small, wooded area where his men were hiding. Returning to his squad, he gave them the news. There was time enough to take some flatbread from his pack and wrap the remaining meat in it. He devoured the meagre meal, and although unsatisfying to the senses, it felt good to have something in his belly all the same. After the hard riding of the last few days, not eating in the saddle was a much-needed pick-me-up.

When he estimated about half the time had passed, Wyll ordered some of their spare goods be unpacked and left out as though they were being caught unaware. He then returned to check on the pursuers' progress. They had reached the copse faster than he'd expected, and were now only a mile away at most. One of the men saw him and gave a shout, which the wind faintly blew to his ears. It was what Wyll had intended, though not just yet. Being discovered left him no choice but to run back to his men as if they had startled him out of his hiding spot. It was now or never. Once he was out of sight behind the tree line, he ordered them to leave the unpacked objects behind and walk the horses further back into the trees. In what seemed only moments, the crash of the enemy horses' hooves on the hard ground and the snapping of branches sounded behind them. Wyll ordered the men to mount up. They moved into a canter, doing their best to avoid the low hanging foliage that was a constant threat to both riders and mounts.

There was a sudden yell behind him, and Wyll knew they'd been spotted. He yelled at his men to flee, doing his best to sound panicked as his men followed suit, breaking formation, though still running their horses in the right general direction. It was only a half minute's ride to where the scouts lay in wait. That was all it took for the superior numbers of the enemy to spread out and flank his men both to the right and left.

Just as the enemy troops were closing in around them, tightening what they thought was a noose, Wyll gave the order to halt. His men reined hard and drew their various weapons even as the first volley of crossbow bolts came plummeting down from the treetops. Over a dozen enemy riders fell at a stroke, including their commander.

For crucial moments Heramiir's men milled about, desperately trying to locate the source of their unseen assailants. Losing their commander had thrown them though, and no orders were forthcoming, giving Karloff's men time enough for another volley. In less than twenty seconds, only two thirds of the enemy riders remained in their saddles.

"Charge!" an enemy sergeant screamed at what were now his men. It seemed to break them out of their confusion, and the now reduced, but still overwhelming unit came charging in at Wyll's men, weapons at the ready.

"Wait!" Wyll called to his men, who were tense but ready. There were only moments until the enemy would close, but Wyll judged there would be enough time for a final volley from on high. As the riders bore down on them, to his vast relief, another volley of shafts appeared in the charging riders, and a third of the remaining enemy fell screaming from their saddles. Those not hit continued their charge across the rapidly shrinking gap.

"Take them!" Wyll yelled, drawing the dead black sword of ages from the ivory scabbard on his back, this time with every intention of using it well. A second later, a soldier was riding past him, slashing down at Wyll's head as he charged. Wyll booted Socks forward and ducked under the blow, cutting a small red line down the man's torso as he did.

There was a flash of black, like a silhouette at the man's side, and he fell from his saddle without ever taking a serious wound. Wyll forced Socks to a gallop in three steps and charged at the middle of the enemy formation, Sarran and Cale behind and on his flanks.

With a tightly controlled blow, Wyll slashed at one man and then blocked another sword with his own. He saw Sa'rayna's black figure from the corner of his eye, and wished he could pay it more attention as a third man took an overhand swing at him. It would have taken off his head if a timely bolt hadn't pierced the man's shoulder, making him lose his grip on the weapon. The sword went flying off into the scrub in a spray of blood and the man's arm limply slapped him in the shoulder. It was all that saved him.

Wyll smashed the man in the head with the hilt of his blade, knocking him unconscious. It wasn't a killing blow, or at least Wyll assumed not since no black shadow darted in to touch the man at his stroke. Passing through the enemy line, he continued a few more steps before reining Socks in and turning him tightly in a circle to meet his next opponent. Cale was engaged with a brute of a man, but looked to be holding his own, while Sarran had been knocked off his horse. The staffman was using his weapon to good effect from the ground, keeping his opponent at shaft's length with ease while a well-aimed bolt finished the rider off. Partially obscured by a large tree, Seth was using his twin blades to desperately engage four of the enemy horsemen, refusing to back away even though he appeared over matched. An instant later, Wyll noticed with a cold sensation that the man was defending the fallen form of Kienan, who was lying still on the ground. Whether alive or dead Wyll couldn't tell, though even from here he could see enough blood for it to have gone either way. Wyll gave Socks a boot and charged at the fight. His other men were all occupied elsewhere, but none of them seemed as hard pressed as Seth right at this moment.

He set Socks to a dead run. As he darted past the men engaging Seth, he lashed out with his blade, taking the right-hand soldier's head off without slowing down. He wheeled Socks in an arc to his left and charged at the man on the other side.

The distraction provided by the unexpected loss of their

comrade was enough for Seth to slay another of the soldiers. Wyll charged in sideways at the two remaining opponents, giving Socks the command with his knees to kick forward as they collided. The blow was true, and the pair of enemy horses stumbled, both their riders thrown unceremoniously to the ground. Before he could even recover his own seat properly, Seth had jumped down from his mount and ended the fight. Each of his curved blades found an enemy soldier before they could recover and continue the fight. Seth looked up.

"Kienan?!" Wyll shouted, the ringing of steel and the singing of crossbow strings accompanying his question.

"I don't know," Seth replied. "I got to him before they could finish their work, but the wound he has already taken does not look good."

Wyll wished he could take the time to help his man, but there was still plenty of fighting going on. The ambush had been highly effective, and they were barely outnumbered now. Unfortunately the main fight had moved out of range of most of the archers, most of whom were obstructed by the dense wall of trees.

A man dropped to the ground beside them, and both Wyll and Seth spun in a reflex that almost ended the soldier's life. Thankfully they were both able to stop, recognising the man as one of Karloff's archers in time.

"I know healing, go help the rest. If he can be saved, I will make it happen."

Wyll didn't like the situation, but knew the man was right. He nodded permission for the soldier to proceed as Seth remounted. The two of them galloped through the dense thicket to where the sound of steel on steel was coming from just out of sight beyond the foliage. Some of the archers were dropping from their tree limbs now, trying to reposition and get back into range of the fight. Wyll took little notice of them since they weren't a threat, and ran Socks past a final tree into a chaotic scene. Men on horseback, and those who had lost their seats, vied for supremacy while the occasional bolt still flew down from above. With the two sides in such close contact, the missiles were as much a danger now to his own men as they were to the enemy.

At a glance he saw Charran was off his horse, his double-bladed staff negating the enemy horsemen's normally superior reach. Tauman had kept his seat, but was holding back. A bloody smear on his left arm told the story, though the man was still doing what he could to ensure the enemy riders couldn't circle behind Bosric and Cale. That pair were being attacked by no less than six of Heramiir's troops. Wyll's men had chosen their position well though. The multitude of skinny tree trunks around them were hampering everyone, rendering the opposing troops' numbers meaningless as they had to make their attacks in turn.

Sarran was nowhere to be seen, and Wyll feared the worst. He pointed his sword at Cale and Bosric to give Seth his orders, and charged over to help Charran with his opponents. The other man didn't hesitate despite the odds, and Wyll couldn't help but admire his courage as Seth plunged into the combat. He took two of the men from behind with his twin blades and then retreated as the others all turned on him, abandoning their previous targets. It was a serious mistake, and Bosric sheathed his sword, pulling a knife from each of his sleeves. He threw confidently, as practised with his left hand as he was with his right. One of his targets fell from his saddle, but the second merely grunted as the small blade sunk into his shoulder, slowing him, but not doing any substantial damage.

Seth was tiring, and still surrounded by the three remaining cavalrymen. Only Cale's timely charge at one of the mounted men stopped him from taking a blow to the back of the head that would have split him from neck to waist. With the circle broken, Seth booted his mount. The horse leapt forward, momentarily moving out of range. Bosric attacked from behind as a distraction, while Cale uttered a wordless scream and engaged the other soldier, separating the combat into individual duels.

Wyll saw most of this as he charged in to help Charran. As he closed with one of the attackers, he launched himself bodily at the enemy horsemen and tackled the man to the ground. Scratching him with the sword of ages as they fell, there was a flash of black that was gone before they'd even tumbled to a halt. Wyll didn't need to look at the body to know the unfortunate soldier's life had been snuffed out in an instant, whisked away to wherever it was Sa'rayna took them.

Wyll shuddered even as he rolled out of the way of the man's horse, which was war trained and trying to stamp on him since he'd just attacked its master. He barely scrambled aside in time. Springing to his feet, he gave it a hard slap on the neck with the flat of his sword. The furious beast snorted in surprise and trotted off into the thicket.

Wyll turned just in time to see Charran throw his staff like a javelin, piercing the chest of a horse that was charging right at him. As its body collapsed, the rider was thrown forward over its head and skidded to a stop at Charran's feet. Without moving even a step, Charran took the sword from the scabbard on his back and ran it through the soldier who was already grasping for his own. The man's body slumped down into the undergrowth, and everything was quiet. Charran, looking around and seeing no further opposition, exhaled heavily, and went to retrieve his staff.

"Sound off!" a clear voice called from high above, and all around them were answering replies of 'All clear!', and, 'That's the last of them!'

Wyll stood there, catching his breath as he took in the gruesome scene around him. A few moments later, the burly form of Captain Karloff swung down from the branch of a nearby tree and dropped to the ground.

"A well-run thing," he commented as he looked both left and right at the surrounding carnage. "Did you lose any men?"

"I don't know," Wyll replied, turning to stride off in the direction where Kienan had fallen earlier in the fight. "Search the woods for any hold-outs or survivors, and take prisoners," Karloff called generally to his men.

"What news?" Wyll demanded of the soldier still ministering to Kienan's wounds. The man turned abruptly, but seeing who was addressing him, motioned for Wyll to come closer.

"Your man took a wound to the chest, it's messy and deep, but it seems to have missed his lungs and heart. If I can keep him alive until we reach the army, most any of the magi should be able to heal it."

"Don't worry," Karloff spoke from behind Wyll. "If anyone can keep your man alive until we re-join the army, it's Corporal Harol here."

Wyll turned, more than a little startled at being snuck up upon this shortly after the fight.

"I didn't hear you following," he said, the adrenaline from the last few minutes keeping his mood tight.

Karloff smiled easily in return. "I wouldn't be much use as a scout if you had, now would I."

Wyll had to agree, though it did nothing to calm his nerves, which still felt as taut as bowstrings after the brief but furious struggle.

"Bosric, get some bandages from the packs and help see to Tauman's arm. Charran and Cale, rig up a stretcher we can attach between two of the horses. I know we're all tired after the last few days, but we still have a job to do. I want to leave within the hour. And somebody find Sarran."

"I'm over here," the big man called from the tree line as he limped back into view. Although he had no visible wounds, the man had obviously been in a serious scuffle. Wyll sighed in relief and nodded to the man.

"How far are we from the army?" Wyll asked as he once again turned back to Karloff.

"About a seven-hour walk. We started out before dawn this morning. I had only planned to use these woods as a shelter for the midday meal when we saw the dust plume from your horses heading straight toward us."

"That's good news," Wyll told him, reassured by the solid response.

"After being pursued nonstop from Cordova, our horses are spent. This was to have been our last rest before we had no choice but to take our chances pushing on to the army. I suspect several of our mounts would not have made it, and their riders would not have fared well under our pursuers' mercies. You have my sincerest thanks Captain. We could not have fought that many men off by ourselves."

"You're welcome Sergeant, though I am curious about

one thing. Several times during the battle I saw you inflict wounds on men with that black blade of yours. They were minor blows, but the men you struck fell over as though the life had been sucked right out of them. Where did you acquire such a unique blade?"

Wyll gave him a small grin as he spotted a small stream among the trees, and felt the sudden need to bathe. He headed toward it, motioning with a small tilt of his head for those of his men who were unoccupied to follow.

"That is a long story, Captain. Suffice it to say that it was presented to me in the Wraith Woods when we passed through them on our way to deliver the King's orders to General Messand."

Karloff just looked at him in minor disapproval for a moment, as if to say that he'd wanted a serious answer. Wyll undid the buckles of his leather armour and removed the breastplate. His shirt followed, and he began drawing up water with his hands to wash away the spatters of blood and gore that still covered him from the short fight. Eventually the captain seemed to decide that Wyll was not making a joke at his expense after all.

The other men began cleaning away the results of the battle in similar fashion, but the tiny stream was little more than ankle deep. Despite their best efforts, none of them could get completely clean. Still, with a little effort they washed away the worst of the blood and gore from both their skin and clothes.

"So what's in there then?" Karloff asked as they worked, still a little uncertain whether he was being made fun of.

"Big insects," Wyll answered before any of the other men could speak.

"As big as a large dog, some the size of a small horse.

They have chitin instead of skin, and kind of look like giant scorpions. They are, however, as intelligent as you or I, and they don't take kindly to visitors."

"You spoke to them?" Karloff asked, his eyebrows climbing his forehead at the unlikely story.

That was why Wyll had wanted to be the one to tell it. He couldn't very well come right out and claim that the Black Lady, the guardian of the next world, had given him a black sword with glowing fiery runes on it. The man would think him a loon, or at the very least a liar and a braggart.

"We had little choice. They can run faster than even a good horse, and they captured us with ease."

"Why did they spare you?" Karloff asked. "From all I've heard, people who go into the Wraith Woods don't come back out."

"I guess we were lucky. Their leader wanted to talk to us, and when she granted us permission to leave, she gave me this sword as a gift."

Karloff's brows furrowed together for a long moment as he thought over what Wyll had said.

"There's more to the story though?" he said, deciding that Wyll was telling him the truth, at least until a point.

"There always is," Wyll replied.

He finished wiping down his armour and replaced it over his shirt, tightening the now familiar cinches over his wet, but somewhat cleaner garment. He did the buckles back up as he stood.

"You said it was a seven hour walk before?" Wyll confirmed.

Karloff nodded.

"Then we should go back to your original plan and have something to eat before we leave."

Karloff grinned and called out for one of his soldiers to break out travel rations. The scouts returned a few minutes later and reported no sign of further enemy troops. For the moment all was quiet, and they ate the light meal together while the stretcher was being finished.

Harol continued to watch over Kienan, having finished bandaging the unfortunate man, who had now regained consciousness. Despite still being in a large amount of pain, he was in good spirits due to the poppy elixir Harol had dosed him with. Probably also for simply finding himself still alive Wyll supposed.

"All right," Wyll said after he'd finished the quick meal. "I assume you were to escort us back to the camp once you found us?"

Karloff nodded but remained silent.

"Good. I would appreciate it if you would take charge of my men for now then," he said loudly enough for all of them to hear.

"Socks is the only one of our horses who is in any condition to continue at more than a walk right now. Even so, I have to get this report back to General Messand as quickly as possible."

"That I understand Sergeant," Karloff replied. "We'll be a few hours behind you, but I'll get your injured man back in one piece."

"Thank you, Captain Karloff," Wyll returned sincerely. "I hope we get the chance to work together again."

"As do I Wyll. Your men fought bravely today, and well. As an officer in the mageguard, if you have need of our assistance, you need only call."

"I'll keep that in mind," Wyll assured him. "But for right now I have to go. The General will not be pleased with this news as it is, and an army the size of the one he now commands will take time to turn around."

"I'll look for you in the camp," Karloff replied before giving him a salute in dismissal.

Wyll returned the gesture and walked back over to Socks. He checked that both the chalice and the other arcane item were still secure, then tiredly mounted the mostly white steed. The brown of his lower legs blended in somewhat with the ground below.

"Seth is squad leader in my absence. But you men are to follow the captain's orders until you return to the camp," Wyll addressed his own squad in a not unfriendly manner.

"Just see that Kienan makes it home alive, and I'll meet up with you later tonight."

Seth nodded, and Wyll knew that if nothing else, he would keep the other men in line. Not that he thought there would be any problems with a captain of Karloff's obvious mettle, and the well-disciplined unit he commanded. It was a far cry from the disgraceful behaviour of the rear-guard contingent they'd run up against when first encountering the army's line of march. This time Wyll had no qualms about leaving his men under the authority of an officer not of the mageguard.

That done, he turned Socks in what he thought was an easterly direction and left the others behind. Once he'd cleared the small patch of forest, he saw he was indeed going the right way, and breathed a small sigh of relief. The last thing he'd wanted was to ride off in the wrong direction in front of such an obviously competent officer, not to mention his own men.

Once the ground flattened out a little, he urged Socks into a canter, and then a gallop. As the trees dwindled behind him, Wyll wondered what he was going to say to the general. The man seemed reasonable, but none of the officers would be happy they had been so effectively deceived by Heramiir's battle plan. Nor that they had been marching all these phases towards the wrong target.

It was late in the afternoon when he caught sight of the vanguard of the army, and another few minutes before he was pulling Socks up in front of some forward sentries who moved to bar his way.

"Your name?" the one in charge asked from the back of his horse.

"Sergeant Wyll of the mageguard."

"Where are your men?"

The soldier looked him up and down, and Wyll realised they must have given the officer his description as the man nodded to himself, satisfied with what he'd seen.

"Coming behind with Captain Karloff's unit. I have information for the General that cannot wait."

"Very well," the sentry nodded before motioning to his men to let Wyll through.

Wyll returned the nod, and led Socks on the final short leg of their journey. It signified the completion of his first mission outside the training grounds of either camp five or the college, and he couldn't help but smile at the fact they had actually pulled it off. They had crossed the Wraith Woods, the first to do so in nine hundred years. If that wasn't enough, they had challenged what could have just as easily been Heramiir's primary force without support. Although they had all suffered injuries along the way, his men were still in one piece. Or at least they would be once Kienan reached the camp and a mage could see to his wounds.

Wyll came to the abrupt realisation that after all these

phases of purpose, he had absolutely no idea what to do after he made his report to the general. He would have to ask Archmage Veroneth for orders he supposed. They would likely involve marching with the army for now, so he wasn't too concerned about the issue as he reached the command pavilion. The same guard captain as when he'd first arrived over a week ago recognised him, and motioned Wyll over.

"Your men?" he asked as Wyll dismounted, handing Socks' reins to a waiting groom.

"Coming behind with Captain Karloff, we sustained some injuries and Socks was the only animal still fit to make an extended run. They should be about three or four hours behind me," Wyll told him as the two of them entered the pavilion. A guard opened the door flap as they approached.

"Life threatening?" the captain asked.

"Yes, but Captain Karloff was hopeful they would reach a mage in time," Wyll responded, very much hoping their resident musician was still hanging in there.

"I'll have a watch put out for them and a mage on alert with the outer sentries," he said as they came to a halt. General Messand was once again studying the maps which covered his table.

"Thank you, Captain, I appreciate that," Wyll replied sincerely, and stood a little straighter as the general noticed them, nodding a dismissal to the captain. The officer saluted Messand and turned without a word, leaving Wyll standing across the table from the general in his now dry, but still bloodstained uniform.

"Report, Sergeant," he ordered, though not in an inhospitable manner.

Wyll gave a small sigh and then broke the news.

"I'm afraid we've been duped. Heramiir has perhaps four

thousand men at Cordova. Where his actual force is I can't tell you, but it isn't there."

For a long moment Messand said nothing, blinking in Wyll's direction as his thoughts turned inward. He then exploded into a flurry of activity, ordering clerks here and there and signing orders which they hurriedly drew up per his commands.

After a few minutes Wyll wasn't sure whether to stay or go, so completely had the general forgotten his presence. He decided to stay until someone at least told him where to go, something he now needed to know since their extended mission was officially over. He would have to seek out Archmage Veroneth if no answer was forthcoming soon. After all, he and his men now fell under the full authority of the mageguard.

Messand abruptly ran out of things that had to be done three days since and called Wyll over, the younger man suddenly glad he'd stayed.

"You've done an exceptional job Sergeant. Is there anything else you can tell me about the encampment, or Heramiir's men?"

"Yes sir," Wyll answered. "The illusion covered several square miles, as though there were many thousands of men living in it. Once dispersed, there were only a few dozen tents and barracks occupied. All of those were located nearest the city, and focused on keeping up the appearance with the city's inhabitants. There were sentries posted around the perimeter, though not enough, and the tent with the artefact controlling the illusion had a few guards. It seems clear they never expected the illusion to be challenged to that extent, or they would have had many more men guarding its source."

"But..?" Messand prompted when Wyll fell silent with a small frown.

Wyll looked at the general for a moment as he thought before answering.

"It just seems strange is all. I mean, that all that thought and planning would go into this ruse, only to be let down by a lack of men guarding the object creating it. Especially when they had plenty of soldiers to spare. The only reason we got away was because most of them were too far away to catch us with their initial charge. Their commander pushed his horses too hard in an all-out pursuit and failed, gaining us enough time and ground to escape."

"So what are you saying?" Messand asked, this time with a frown of his own.

"I'm not sure sir," Wyll replied, knowing that it was an inadequate answer, but not having any other to give.

"Something about it just doesn't feel right though."

"Very well Sergeant, I'll take that under consideration. For now you should report to Archmage Veroneth. Ah, here he is now."

"Yes, I thought it must be you when every ward at this end of the camp went down again."

The elderly man approached Wyll and the general with little sense of humour as he frowned his way towards them.

"My apologies Archmage, but I thought it more important to inform the General of what we had found as soon as was possible," Wyll apologised.

"And right you were," Messand said with a sideways glance at Veroneth. The archmage had raised an eyebrow, about to say something else, but changed his mind as Messand spoke.

"As an officer of the mageguard you must learn to take these things into account. Quickly…"

"Yes Archmage, I will," Wyll replied, trying not to feel offended at the archmage's manner.

"Oh lay off Veroneth, you old bag of wind," Messand told him. The archmage gave him a sideways glance as he shook his head, and Wyll realised these two men had known each other for a very long time.

"What did you find?" Veroneth asked, curiosity winning out in the end.

Messand nodded to Wyll to go ahead, and after a full retelling of the events since they'd left the army a week before, Veroneth looked grimmer than ever.

"So, Heramiir has access to magic that we do not. That is not a pleasant thought," he mused as his fingers stroked his short reddish-grey beard.

"I would very much like to see this artefact that you brought back from his camp. It might offer some valuable clues as to where Heramiir has been learning these new tricks."

Wyll looked to Messand, and the general nodded his approval for Wyll to leave, but then called out as the archmage and sergeant walked away.

"By the way Sergeant, I'm giving your unit a commendation for your actions since you left Aramar. You and your men well deserve it."

"Thank you General!" Wyll replied, surprised and genuinely pleased. "I'll pass on your congratulations to the men."

Messand nodded his approval, and without another word turned back to the map table and the cluster of clerks who were ready to distribute his orders to the army.

It was late in the afternoon now, and Wyll didn't think Messand would give the order to march until first light. After a week-long stay at the current position, the farriers and smiths would have no doubt begun plying their trade during the brief respite. It would take time to pack away their heavy tools along with the Stocks and provisions which would all have to be accounted for. Squaring away the campsites so they could leave early in the morning would be the easy part.

By the time Wyll and the archmage stepped outside the pavilion, the immediate area was already buzzing with activity. Runners were being sent out to inform the rest of the army of the impending departure, and the term 'controlled-chaos' floated to the top of Wyll's mind.

They soon reached Socks, who was still waiting where Wyll had left him, and Veroneth frowned.

"Is that a Rahiri mount?" he asked in obvious surprise, and Wyll nodded.

"His name is Socks," he told the archmage, and now it was Veroneth's turn to nod.

"That's very… appropriate," he said as he looked at the animal's fine coat, which was white all over with the exception that below its knees, the horse was entirely brown.

"Now I see why you felt it necessary to ride ahead of your men. A steed like this would have twice the stamina of any regular horse, and a good bit more speed as well if I'm not mistaken."

"You're not," Wyll assured him as they reached Socks' side. Wyll opened the saddle pack to pull out the chalice, which he had carried all the way from Aramar. Beside it lay the strange artefact which had fooled the king's army into marching in the wrong direction for phases.

"What are we going to do with this?" Veroneth said to himself as he took the chalice from Wyll. Once he had satisfied himself that it was still in its proper condition, he handed it back and took the second artefact, which he studied more closely. The small glass sphere gave away none of its secrets at the archmage's initial inspection.

"This is going to take some time," he muttered to himself before tucking the object away into an inner pocket of his silver-lined, archmagi's cloak.

"In the meantime, I want you and your men to take the chalice and stay on station two miles north of the camp. I'll have a full set of supplies sent out to you by nightfall. For now your orders are to travel parallel to the army while we march. You will continue to keep safe custody of the chalice, since you have done such a superb job of it so far."

"That's all Archmage?" Wyll asked, a little surprised that after all they had accomplished, they were now to be relegated to babysitting a piece of magical equipment.

Veroneth stared at him in disapproval for a moment, but then relented with a frown.

"I don't know you, so you're new to the mageguard. One of those promoted from the training camps if I'm not mistaken?"

Wyll nodded that he was correct, and the red bearded man continued.

"Don't underestimate the importance of this task Wyll. The Chalice of Ajerio is one of the very few pieces of our ancestral homeland of Jeranah which still exists today. Not to mention being an object of great arcane power in its own right. To be blunt, no matter how certain Tolmarak was that you would make it, allowing it to be put at risk by having you take it through the Wraith Woods... Well, that notion displeases me."

His steely expression proclaimed the gravity of his thoughts, as the archmage had examined the chalice once again. When he was done, Wyll carefully stowed it back in its usual place in his saddle bags.

"You're to make sure that it stays out of range of the army for the rest of the march. I'd like our protective wards to stay up from now on. Should the worst occur when we confront Heramiir's army, you are to ride hard for Aramar and take the chalice to safety."

Wyll frowned, about to protest, but Veroneth saw it and cut him off.

"That is a direct order. You will obey it."

"Besides, look around you. There are over one hundred thousand soldiers in this camp, with more on the way, and well over a hundred battle trained magi and archmagi. If things get bad enough that the order I just gave you becomes relevant, one more squad of men in the fray will only lead to more wasted life. Nothing you can do at that point will change the outcome."

Wyll wanted to protest, and he was sure the rest of his men would feel the same way. They had ridden halfway across the kingdom, through the Wraith Woods, and confronted what might well have been Heramiir's main force alone. To be stuck on the sidelines now was the worst kind of anticlimax. And yet Veroneth was right, someone had to look after the chalice. If it was as important as the archmage claimed, Veroneth saw this task as something to be entrusted with, not a method of getting them out of the way. He was also correct in his assertion that one more squad would not even be noticed in this vast mass of men, so Wyll did the only thing he could.

"Very well Archmage, we will do as you instruct," he told

the older man, though still not entirely happy at the prospect.

"I'm so pleased…" Veroneth replied.

"For now, take the chalice outside the camp so we can re-set the wards, again. I'll leave word for your men so they can find you when they arrive."

"Yes Archmage," Wyll acknowledged, then stepped up into the stirrups and vaulted onto Socks' back.

"Good luck," Veroneth said as Wyll turned his mount.

"And to you, Archmage."

He kneed Socks to a tired walk, heading for the north edge of the camp. A quick scan of the area revealed a large rock outcropping suitable for cover, and a campsite where his men would spend yet another night on the road.

SUMMER

CHAPTER 18

NEW ADDITIONS

The day was overcast and cold, and fitted Tolmarak's mood. Dawn of summer was yet to take proper hold, and the morning chill had never really worn off. A blustery wind periodically swept in from the north of the magi's practice range, swaying the treetops as it passed.

He had put off making this decision, but could hold back no longer if he were to obey the king's orders. Missy and Billy were now skilled enough, just barely, to begin more-or-less safely learning more advanced battle magic.

He didn't want to teach it to them. On principal he didn't like the concept, even theoretically, of teaching one as young as Billy to kill. If he'd had any choice at all, it would be years yet before the two younger members of his class ever set foot on the range in this context. The accelerated training of standard spell work the two adolescents had dealt with so far was risky enough. This entire class had been a gamble though, and thankfully his two youngest students had dealt well with its demanding curriculum, killing neither their classmates nor themselves in the process.

He'd been tutoring Jayden and Firerose out here for several phases now. He had added Nadeara to the class a few weeks after the others began, and as of today, the five of them were once again a single cohesive group.

The rest of his students watched as the olive-skinned woman from Avsan concentrated hard on a point at the far end of the charred clearing. It took a full minute of intense concentration, but the dummy, drawn up and fashioned from the ground by Tolmarak's arts, exploded in a violent blast of flame.

A strong, Gift-wrought shield the archmage had placed in front of them before beginning the exercise flared a deeper blue as it protected the class from the flying debris. Where the clay dummy had once been attached to the hard packed earth below, nothing remained except a small, stunted stump.

"Well done, Nadeara. That is exactly how that spell is supposed to operate. Of course, in future you must aim to quicken the effect by focusing your will more efficiently."

"I'll try, Archmage," she agreed with a grin.

She was nowhere near as powerful as Jayden, and was even below Firerose as far as raw strength went, but she was learning. More to the point, she was doing so much faster than any of the apprentices not in their advanced class. No doubt she and Firerose at least would make Mage before another year had passed, as Jayden already had.

I think that will do for you today Nadeara. You seem to have a good grasp of the basics of this spell, so we'll finish up with the newer members of the class."

"As you wish Archmage," she replied politely, then retired to a wooden bench, carved by some unknown mage, and waited for the others to finish the day's final exercise.

"Billy. Let's see what you can do," Tolmarak said as he turned towards the others.

The youngest member of the class came forward, standing nervously in the place Nadeara had vacated.

Tolmarak used the Gift to draw another dummy up from the ground on the far side of the clearing.

There is no excuse for pushing the boy this hard, Tolmarak chided himself for the hundredth time. Under any other circumstances he would have left the eleven-year-old to learn theory and basic spell work as his contemporaries did. He should have the opportunity to learn the various aspects of the Gift in his own time. As one of the five strongest magi recruited the previous year though, Tolmarak couldn't afford to give him the time and space he needed to simply be a child.

For now he seemed to be holding up well, even enjoying his lessons as though it were all some grand adventure with no goal or consequence to follow.

To his mind it probably is, Tolmarak reflected. Yet he couldn't help worrying about what would happen when the boy witnessed an actual battle firsthand, and more, took part. Still, there was little else he could do, especially with the assassin still plaguing the Aramarian magi. His only option was to train Billy as best he could, and hope it was enough to see the boy through what was all too rapidly approaching.

"See if you can do the same thing Nadeara just did," Tolmarak told the boy kindly.

Billy took about as much notice of Tolmarak's mood as his words, which was to say that he saw only what was on the surface. With an affable nod, the youth turned towards the new practice dummy.

There was a long moment of silence as he concentrated on his target. The exercise today was a simple one, though new to most of them. They were to destroy the target across the field with a simple blast of flame. One of the easiest spells to produce for most magi. The trick was that they had to do it without the use of either gestures or incantation.

Jayden and Firerose had done well, and Nadeara succeeded with difficulty. But then, they were also the ones who'd had the most practice with this kind of thing. Tolmarak had tailored his lessons in battle magic to suit each of their growing abilities, and those three had been at it the longest.

The others watched, willing the boy to succeed as he stared across the open space, sweat beading on his brow despite the cool of the day. It was his first attempt at this kind of task, and it would buoy his confidence significantly if he could make the spell work the way he intended.

It was a long time coming, but finally the dummy began to warp. As Billy clenched his fists in concentration, he was rewarded by the sight of the clay seeming to melt and run like wax. Soon only a small mound of clay was left where his target had once stood.

Billy let out an explosive breath that he must have been holding for quite some time. His shoulders slumped, and he placed his head in his hands as though in pain.

"Are you all right?" Tolmarak asked as he placed a steadying hand on the boy's shoulder.

"I'm fine," Billy answered after a minute. "I just made myself dizzy from holding my breath for so long," he sheepishly declared.

Tolmarak chortled.

"Try to breathe next time Billy. It won't affect the spell, but it will make the rest of your life a lot easier, okay?"

"Yes Archmage," the boy replied with a grin, before stepping back so the final student could take her turn.

*   *   *

"Missy, I want you to perform the same exercise Billy just completed," the archmage said as he drew another of the clay dummies up from the Gift-scarred ground.

Missy came forward from her place on the bench to stand in front of the Gift-wrought shield which Tolmarak maintained, and began concentrating on the task. She knew all she could think of was the dummy exploding into flames if she wanted the spell to work right, but she was still new to this kind of thing. A sliver of doubt at her own abilities crept in.

For just a moment she allowed her thoughts to drift. In her mind, a disastrous scene where she messed up the task and set the whole clearing on fire instead of just the dummy appeared of its own volition. Before she could react, other than to yell a strangled warning, something in her mind clicked, and every tree surrounding the clearing burst into a searing inferno a hundred feet high.

*   *   *

Tolmarak reacted instantly, gathering his shield as he realised what was happening, stretching it thinner than he would have liked, but surrounding them all with its protective blue glow. Even with all his experience, he was not quite quick enough to react as the unbearable heat made their skin redden and all their clothes smoulder. Missy stood transfixed, in utter shock at the devastation she was causing as the massive wall of flames immolated the entire clearing.

Tolmarak could already feel his too-large shield weakening under the tremendous assault of the inferno. The desperately thin protective bubble was fully engulfed, and there was time for only a single action before the thin defence collapsed entirely. If he'd had only himself to protect, he could have held out against the raging heat a lot longer. Maintaining a large area shield though had never been one of his talents. Taking a quick step forward, he slapped Missy once, hard across the face, breaking her concentration and dissolving the spell. The Gift-wrought flames began to dissipate even as he felt his shield weaken beyond the point where it could effectively keep the deadly inferno from permeating the mystical barrier.

The air began to heat.

Not a moment too soon, the magical flames winked out around them. The air cleared, at least enough to reveal the entire outer edge of the clearing engulfed in flames where the trees had ignited at the spell's slightest touch.

"You fool girl! You nearly killed us all," Tolmarak shouted as she probed her raw and burned face, still clearly in shock.

Looking around, Tolmarak saw the others huddled together, both Jayden and Nadeara having acted to throw up shields of their own around the group at the bench.

All of them had reddened, burnt skin on whichever side had been facing the clearing, and it was with vast relief Tolmarak saw their injuries extended no further. He'd seen hardened battle magi killed by less than this girl had just accidentally thrown at them.

Clearly he would have to reassess her training.

"I'm... so sorry," she whispered, struggling not to break into tears as she numbly patted down her still smouldering clothes.

The heat outside the shield had all but subsided, but with the trees on the outskirts of the clearing fully ablaze, the range was rapidly filling with smoke and cinders. Tolmarak looked at the surrounding ruins.

"Jayden, Firerose, help me put this out," he said, turning his attention to dousing the burning trees before they started a bushfire that would devastate the entire region. By the time they had finished, Missy was sitting back on the bench with her legs tucked up under her chin as she wept. Nadeara had her arm placed gingerly around the girl, trying to comfort Missy while avoiding touching either her own burns, or the girl's reddened skin as she did.

Once the last of the flames were smothered, Tolmarak looked at Missy for a long minute before turning back to the other students. He couldn't help but sigh.

Despite all their power, or perhaps because of it, he still sometimes forgot just how young this group of students really was. Not for the first time, he wondered about the wisdom of training them to be battle magi at their age and obvious lack of maturity. The king's orders were explicit.

And yet...

"What about the horses?" Billy asked quietly, obviously unsure he wanted to hear that any harm might have befallen his beloved Thunder. Tolmarak had given him the chestnut stallion shortly after Billy had arrived at the college. Growing up as an orphan on the streets of Silvertown in Jeranon's south, the fine animal was the only thing of value he had ever owned in his entire brief life. He loved it.

The question made Missy look up in horror that she might have killed their horses, but Tolmarak put a stop to that before it could go any further.

"The horses are in the other clearing, which is well warded against events just such as this," he announced. "I can still sense the wards, which means they are intact, which in turn means the animals are unharmed."

Billy's shoulders slumped in relief, and Missy hung her head on her knees again as Nadeara gave her a comforting hug, and Tolmarak a stony stare.

Probably because I slapped the girl to break her out of maintaining the spell, he imagined. Perhaps the glower she directed at him was not as unfriendly as it could have been.

Tolmarak frowned back at the young woman until she looked away, then relented with another sigh. He had wanted to accomplish a few more exercises on the way home, but that was unmanageable now. His students had lost their focus, making accidents such as this near disaster even more likely if they continued.

"Jayden," Tolmarak said at last as he finally let what was left of his shield drop. "Before we leave, there's one more thing I want you to do."

He turned back to the range and drew up yet another dummy for Jayden to demolish.

"I want you to destroy the dummy using only spells of air. Proceed."

*　　*　　*

Jayden looked at him for a moment as though he were about to refuse, but then stood and gave a slight shrug instead. He winced at the pain his burns caused, but moved to take his place when Tolmarak once again had the magical barrier back between themselves and the target.

Without resorting to words or gestures, Jayden visualised his intent and sent out a blast of air at the dummy that would have knocked a small barn flat. The target remained unfazed by the sudden gale which had sprung up around it, and he stared at it for a long moment before letting the spell drop.

Jayden frowned at his ineffective attempt. The burnt trees behind the dummy sprang back into their upright positions, throwing off a cloud of ash as the Gift-wrought wind ceased. He crossed his arms as he considered the problem. Tolmarak had made this dummy differently than the previous ones. But was there some trick to destroying it, or was it to test his own superior strength at the same level of difficulty the others were having? Again Jayden gathered his will and struck out at the dummy with as much force as he could muster.

Two of the now blackened trees in his line of fire were bent back far enough to snap in half. They were carried away on the gale, but the dummy itself refused to budge.

Tolmarak sighed as he came over to where Jayden was still frowning at the dummy, and the others waited to see what would happen. Even Missy had stopped crying enough to quietly pay attention.

In all the times they had come up here, this was the first that Jayden had failed to complete a task Tolmarak had set them on his first attempt. He was not impressed.

"What did you do to it?" he asked in confusion. "That blast should have carried it away with ease."

Tolmarak smiled as he answered.

"Quite right. But I made this one different, to point out a flaw in your selection of spells."

"And what would that be?" Jayden returned shortly, his burns beginning to itch.

Tolmarak turned to look Jayden in the eye before replying.

"You are the strongest mage I have ever known Jayden,

but there are times out in the world where brute force will not help you. This is something you have yet to grasp, and yet it is a lesson you must learn before you finish your training. Keep practising on the dummy until every trace is gone. The rest of us are going back to the college once I have attended to their burns, but we will be back at first light tomorrow. You may return once you destroy the dummy, but if I get back tomorrow and it is still standing, I expect you to still be here as well. Understood?"

"Yes Archmage," Jayden answered unenthusiastically.

He had no desire to remain out here all night, but it didn't look as though Tolmarak was going to back down just because he protested. Saving himself the effort, Jayden resigned himself to being out here for a while. At this moment he had no concept how to return the dummy to the clay from which Tolmarak had summoned it.

"Good," Tolmarak said when he saw Jayden wasn't going to argue the point. "There are provisions in the extra pack I brought up, so you shouldn't have too hard a night out here. Just remember, the sooner you complete your task, the sooner you can return to the college. And don't think you can cheat either, I set wards on the dummy, so I'll know if you use anything but air spells on it."

Jayden just looked at the archmage as the old man used his arts to heal the minor burns the others had sustained during Missy's accident, before gathering up his things. Billy and Clarion both came over to say quick farewells before they went to collect their horses. Missy's thoughts were elsewhere. They were all no doubt eager to return to the college and have a hot meal and bath after their life-threatening day of training. He thought Nadeara would have come over as well, but she was too busy helping Missy get ready to leave. The younger girl still too shaken to see to her own things.

He wished he was going with them, but the archmage had set him a challenge. It was something which was getting harder to come by as his powers continued to grow, and he was not about to back down.

"Tolmarak," Jayden called out to the old man as he mounted his grey warhorse. "Aren't you going to heal me before you go?"

Tolmarak turned Wind to face him and shook his head.

"Consider it an object lesson. At some point in a battle one day, you will be injured far worse than this. At that moment, your life will absolutely depend on your ability to set that hurt aside and continue to function despite your injuries. So no, I will not heal you this time."

Jayden wasn't happy with the old man's reasoning, but once again had to admit the archmage had a valid point. He gave Tolmarak a sharp nod.

Without another word, the archmage returned the gesture, then pivoted Wind to lead the others back down the path which would take them back to the college.

As soon as they were out of sight, Jayden sat on the bench to examine his burns. They were painful in a way that a bad sunburn was, but thanks to Tolmarak's almost intuitive reaction time, he wasn't in any real danger. He said a quick thanks to the Maker that he had been able, just last week, to convince Tolmarak he no longer needed the mageguard escort he'd been saddled with for the last two phases. There was no way that anyone weak in, or without access to the Gift could have survived that inferno a moment ago. He found himself shaking at the thought of how easily even more of the protectors, as they called themselves, might have otherwise died just for being near him.

It wasn't until the sounds of the horses had faded that Jayden got up and went to survey the dummy more closely. He needed to make this work. It wasn't that he feared failing in front of the others, they had seen that already. Despite the phases of training, and spending every waking moment together, he still couldn't help but sense that half the time they felt sorry for him. The other half he was sure that they wanted to slap the grief out of him, and strangely enough, only Billy acted comfortably around him. The one thing they all showed confidence in was his power, and he had no intention of losing that small amount of respect by failing the archmage's task.

He knew it was only an accident of birth. That one in ten-thousand random occurrence which made him receptive to the Gift, and then whatever fluke caused it to appear later than most that made him strong. Made him special. Without that, Tolmarak never would have come for him. He would now just be another dead, forgotten victim of Dael's tyranny. Yet if he was to believe the archmage, that same strength was now limiting his view of the world, and somehow needed to be fixed.

Being told the only special thing about you needed to be fixed was less than an enjoyable experience. Lashing out with the Gift, he blasted the dummy from behind with as strong a spell of air as he could muster in case the direction mattered. He realised his mistake an instant too late. As he was blown off his feet by his own spell, he landed ingloriously in the dirt, a good twenty paces back from where he'd begun.

Choking on dust and trembling from the scraping his burned skin took, he groaned at his own stupidity once he'd checked that none of his bones had been broken. After laying on the ground, recovering for several minutes, he looked up at the dummy, which now mocked him as it stood, infuriatingly unaffected by his spell.

Jayden stood with difficulty. His left knee hurt from knocking it in the fall, and his burnt skin still screamed from being grazed in the dirt. It didn't matter. He moved back to his place on the range and thought. Over the next half an hour he sent spells of air at it from every conceivable direction. First, he did it with force, and then as lightly as he could, just in case Tolmarak had been being literal when he said that Jayden's strength could be a hindrance.

As the sun reached the horizon, he took a break and went over to see what the archmage had left for him in the pack. He discovered an oilskin cloth with a slab of cheese and some bread, along with an enclosed bowl containing a thick but cold stew. There was also a large cup which he could fill with water from the surrounding air if he so chose. The remainder of the pack was taken up by a sleeping roll, a blanket, and a pillow. Jayden came to the abrupt realisation that this was going to be harder than he thought. The archmage had meant him to spend the night out here, or at least expected it.

Jayden frowned as he stared at the dummy. He took a large bite out of the cheese and then used the Gift to heat the stew to an appropriate temperature. The intense blaze had sucked most of the moisture out of the air, but with a little difficulty, Jayden managed to fill his cup. He ate the plain but filling meal as he considered the situation.

Night fell as he continued his attempts to decimate the dummy in a variety of ways. Again and again he tried, using every bit of his subtlety and imagination, but eventually, when the moon was high, he was forced to admit defeat. It wasn't that he was giving up, he had simply run out of air spells with which he could try.

Angry with himself for failing, he went over to the pack and pulled out the sleeping roll. By the position of the moon it must be near midnight, and there was nothing else for him to do. He decided to get an early start again in the morning when he was fresher, and hopefully had some new ideas.

Sleep found him easily for once, despite the discomfort of his burns, and though that was welcome, the nightmares that inevitably came with it were not.

He was walking along one of Grandell's beaches. The azure Sea of Dreams stretched out as far as the eye could see to one side, the sheer cliffs from which Rhianna had flung herself dominated the other.

Ahead, he could see her lying on the sand, uninjured, her clothes soaked through as though she had just been for a swim.

He didn't want to go, but his feet carried him closer, just as he knew they would. When he reached her a short time later he sat, looking out at the ocean just as she already was.

"Where am I Jay?" she asked.

"I should be here, but I'm not. Where did I go?"

Jayden just looked at her sadly for a long time before answering.

"You died," he told her softly.

"You died right here," he said again as the truth of where his dreams had forced him to tonight settled upon him.

"Did I?" she replied, as though her mind were focused somewhere else.

"Why can't I let you go?" he asked her dully, not expecting a coherent answer.

She turned to him and smiled sadly, cupping his cheek in

her hand. "You were always my rock, Jay, but now I'm gone, and all that's left of you are pebbles."

Jayden opened his eyes.

With a snarl he pushed the unfamiliar nightmare away. It wasn't her.

It is never her! He shouted in his mind yet again.

Real or not though, she had given him the answer to Tolmarak's challenge. For that at least, he was grateful. It was the first, and only useful thing the incessant nightmares had done for him since Rhianna had been murdered back in Grandell. Yet that anything good, no matter how slight, could come of that… it incited a rage in him beyond anything most men experience in a lifetime.

Looking briefly up at the sky, Jayden stood, gingerly stretching his burnt and scraped skin as the first glow of dawn stained the eastern horizon. He had only a little time before Tolmarak and the others returned for the day's lessons.

Standing back from the practice ground, Jayden erected a shield around himself, as strong as he could form it. He didn't know what was going to happen, and he was taking no chances after Missy's mishap the day before. Calling up the wind, Jayden manipulated the Gift to pick up as much of the loose debris from around the clearing as he could. When he had placed it around the dummy, there was a good-sized pile of stones and burnt tree limbs that made it almost halfway up the target's legs. It should be enough for what he planned. The idea would either work, or it wouldn't.

He created a second shield around the pile, about twelve feet across. It was as large as he thought he could make it while still withstanding the forces he was about to let loose within. Or at least he very much hoped it would.

By the time he was ready, all but the brightest stars had faded from the predawn sky. If this didn't work, Tolmarak and the others would be here before he could think of something else.

Gathering his will, Jayden used a spell of air, and only air, spinning it in a tight loop around the dummy. After a few seconds, the pieces of debris began lifting off the ground, and soon there was a full-blown maelstrom inside the dummy shield. At first there was no more result than that. He maintained the spell though, and the charred wood soon began to break up as it impacted against the dummy and other debris.

Jayden concentrated, making the wind inside the shield spin even faster. The noise of the rocks hitting each other, the wood, and even the dummy became deafening. But soon enough the last of the wood had disintegrated into a fine powder which continued to spin amongst the other debris.

"You're all just pebbles in waiting," he muttered under his breath, using the air spell to smash the debris again and again until it was nothing more than a fine dust. The sky was fully light now he saw, and Jayden knew he had to hurry. Tightening the shield so that it was only three feet wide, Jayden sent the fine debris spinning once again. This time he concentrated on making it scrape around the edges of the dummy as it whizzed along its inexorable path.

A few seconds later, Jayden thought he was on the right track as the target's features began losing their definition. When its nose disappeared into the rush of sand, Jayden knew for sure. But it was taking too long. Tolmarak and the others would be here any minute now, and he wanted to be done by the time they arrived.

Forcing the debris to spin faster still, Jayden concentrated his will on that, and only that, and as he felt the debris speeding up, something strange occurred inside the shield. As the dummy wore down to a featureless stump, the sand inside his shield began glowing from the heat. First it turned yellow, then red, and finally became a white-hot blaze he could feel pushing against his shield. He just needed to hold it for a few minutes longer though, and as he stared into the blaze, he saw with great satisfaction that the dummy had fallen over. What remained of it was running like wax. As the debris and rushing air picked it up and spun it uncontrollably amongst the rest of the wreckage, white-hot spatters of, something, began impacting on his shield.

Gritting his teeth, he forced the wind inside the shield into an ever-tighter pattern. With great effort he managed to stop the stuff impacting on and weakening the shield. As the last traces of the dummy disappeared into the maelstrom, he allowed himself a satisfied smile. He let the wind slow inside the shield until the white-hot ball of, whatever it was, was the only thing left hanging in mid-air.

"Well done Jayden," Tolmarak said from the top of the path that gave entry into the clearing, almost causing him to lose control of his spells in surprise. He hadn't heard the others reach the range, and was a little annoyed that they couldn't have waited another few minutes until the task was complete. But at least he had succeeded.

"What is that?" he asked the archmage, since the man was now present.

"Why don't you cool it and find out. But not too quickly," Tolmarak suggested with a small grin.

Jayden shrugged and did as Tolmarak suggested. The white-hot glow faded back to red, then yellow, and after a few minutes the foot wide sphere began to clear as it approached the temperature of the outside world.

When it was over, Jayden frowned at his creation. He dropped both of his shields and floated it over to rest on the ground near his feet.

As far as he could tell, it was a large glass sphere, clouded, and not exactly round, but glass nonetheless.

"When lightning used to hit the beaches back in Grandell it sometimes left a glass fragment in the sand. This looks a lot like those."

The archmage nodded his agreement.

"The same way your hands get hot if you rub them together long enough, the friction from the debris heated the sand to a temperature near that which lightning would have."

"So that's how glass is made then?" Jayden asked curiously.

"Well, there's more to it than that. But yes, it's made from sand which has been heated to the point where it melts, though of course this is not magic. It is however, one of the many ways in which the Gift can be controlled to create, by a talented artificer, and not to merely destroy," Tolmarak answered. The man had fallen back into his schoolroom lecturing tone, and for a moment Jayden wasn't sure whether the archmage was making fun of him. He decided to let it pass.

"Now, let's see about those burns shall we?" Tolmarak said with a grin. Jayden didn't hesitate, allowing the archmage to work his arts, easing his skin from the painful tightness which had settled over the burns during the night.

Once the archmage was finished, Jayden rolled his

shoulders, appreciating the fact that it no longer hurt to do so as he nodded his sincere thanks.

*   *   *

"All right, now that that's attended to, we can get started for the day. Jayden, Clarion, Nadeara, you three will work on your shields today, I think. I will give Missy and Billy more direct instruction with which you can help me by shielding us from any further accidents."

He said it without looking at Missy, but they all knew why he was being extra cautious after the near disaster from which he had only just healed Jayden.

Missy went red again, and Nadeara reached out a hand to comfort the girl, but Tolmarak stopped her with a firm shake of his head.

"If she does that during a battle, a lot of men will die for nothing. She might even kill herself. She is right to be embarrassed," he rebuked Nadeara, and then turned to address Missy directly.

"At the level of power each of you possess, every spell must be precise, every imagination focused to an exact intent. It is critical that every mage understands the consequences of their actions *before* they take them. I don't say these things to hurt you, nor to put you down Missy. In fact, I would not be so hard on you if you were weaker in the Gift, then the worst that might happen is that you singe off your eyebrows. Not a dignified look certainly, but not as drastic as killing everyone around you through one careless deed. If the King's forces are hard enough pressed that you are called upon to fight in this war, that call will come in the next several phases. If I seem less tolerant of failures from this point forward, please understand that it is not personal. We are all running out of time. I don't want you going into battle without offering the very best chance of survival that I can in our limited time together."

"Won't you be coming with us?" Billy asked as if realising what lay ahead for the very first time.

Tolmarak looked at the young boy with pity before shaking his head.

"No Billy, I am afraid that my duties require that I stay and advise the King. That and lead the defence of Aramar should the worst occur. Not to mention making sure that the college itself continues. Regardless of how many magi we might lose in this conflict," he finished bitterly.

"Oh," was all Billy said, though his disheartened tone made Tolmarak wince. The boy was just too young for this, whatever Erian thought. Once again, he resolved to take it up with the monarch the next time they had a private meeting.

For now though he would continue to teach Billy as best he was able, just in case his old friend refused to let the boy off the hook.

It was a slow day at first, the students performing the tasks Tolmarak set for them with little difficulty, so about lunchtime he swapped them for harder ones. The day continued with a little more frustration, but no disastrous events such as the one the day before.

When the sun began to sink towards the western horizon, he called a halt to the day's proceedings. He was satisfied with their progress as the small group gathered their horses to return to the college, a hot meal, and their beds. Jayden's beige stallion Strider seemed especially glad to see him after being locked in the clearing since the previous morning.

There was grass and water aplenty for the many animals who were constantly being left in there, but sometimes they simply didn't like being alone.

To Tolmarak, the ride back to the college grounds seemed a quick one. He spent the time considering his students and their various levels of proficiency with each of the five powers. He would need to set Nadeara harder tasks soon. The former Avsanian trader had progressed well over the last few weeks, but apart from that, things were little different today than they had been yesterday. Missy had been holding back, which was an understandable reaction, but one for which there was unfortunately no time. Tomorrow he would have to work on getting her self-confidence back on track since she had taken his earlier words to heart far harder than he had intended. By the time they reached the stables, and grooms had come out to take their horses, Tolmarak thought he had the next day's exercises set out in his mind. He followed the others as far as the dining hall, but took his leave of them there. Before exiting, he instructed the staff to bring a meal up to his office, as was his prerogative as an archmage. A relaxing dinner would have been nice, but there was still so much to do.

*   *   *

Jayden sat down at a table with the other students. He was tired after being out on the range all the previous night. As the archmage departed though, strangely enough he felt like sharing a meal with the others, with his friends.

When did I start thinking of them like that?

He would have to leave them of course. There were things he still had to take care of. But for now at least he could sit with them and talk, and even smile now and then, in the rare moments he could forget everything else. Of course, when he did, he always felt guilty afterwards, which Archmage Trellis insisted was contributing to his nightmares. Tolmarak had asked him to make more of an effort to interact with the others a while back. The old man had hinted that it would help to form new connections unrelated to his previous life.

As hard as he had found it at first, Jayden was doing his best to comply. The old man had been right on just about every other subject they had discussed, and at this point he was willing to give Tolmarak the benefit of the doubt.

Due to both their fatigue and the excellent quality of the food, the group shared the simple meal of roast beef and vegetables slathered with a rich mushroom gravy in near silence. He demolished the main meal in short order, along with the large serving of apple pie and cream that was tonight's dessert. As he was about to take the last bite, a messenger arrived at their table, summoning both Firerose and himself to Archmage Tolmarak's private quarters.

Jayden groaned inwardly. After the delicious, filling meal and an uncomfortable night out on the range, all he wanted was to find his bed and sleep until morning, or perhaps the one after that. He thought he might even be tired enough to ward off the nightmares for once, though it now seemed that sleep would once more have to wait.

He shared a look with Clarion, who gave a small shrug. Scooping the last bite of pie from the bowl, he pushed his chair back and stood, motioning for the messenger to lead the way.

Clarion was already standing, and together they followed the young boy up the winding staircase which traversed the outer edge of the conical foyer, before taking a side corridor that led to the archmage's door.

Before the boy could knock, the door opened of its own accord, or seemed to at least, and Tolmarak bade them enter, dismissing the messenger as he did. The boy gave a small bow and left as Firerose entered. Jayden closed the door behind them in a more mundane fashion, and sat in one of the two seats provided.

"I have warded this room against eavesdropping as best I know how, but what we say here must stay between us. If what I am about to tell you gets out, it would devastate the morale of the few remaining magi we have."

Again Jayden shared an uneasy glance with Firerose. From the corner of his eye, she looked enough like Rhianna that his heart skipped a beat. He crushed down the instant of hope that sensation brought with it mercilessly. Rhianna was dead, and Clarion, despite being almost identical physically, was an altogether different woman.

That hadn't happened for phases now, and it made the fury in him rise all over again.

"Yes Archmage," he said a little hoarsely, and Clarion nodded as well.

"I know you tried to do what I'm about to ask you a few phases ago. And I know that I ordered you to focus on your studies instead, but things have changed. I need your help," Tolmarak admitted, bringing Jayden back to his senses.

"I and the other magi in the college, as well as the mageguard and the regular army, have tried every means we know of to catch this assassin. The Maker's awful truth, is that we are no closer to achieving that goal than we were the first day he arrived in the city."

As he finished that statement, the silence in the room was

complete. Tolmarak's blunt admission of failure guaranteeing the two students paid close attention to his next words.

"There are less than thirty magi left in the college at this moment, less than a dozen of them archmagi. We are running out of time to stop this murderer, and running out of magi with which to defend this city. It goes beyond that though. If this assassin wipes us all out, who will teach the next generation how to use the Gift? The entire college could fall, and all the benefits which Jeranon receives from our order, both military and otherwise, would disappear as well. We cannot let that happen, so I need you now to focus your efforts on finding a way, any way, to locate and stop this man. Even more so than you already have. Most of us who are powerful enough to try taking him on, are so set in our ways, so trained in our thinking, that the answer perplexes us. I'm asking you two to focus on this task now specifically because you have not been magi for years or decades. The same lives we have all shared living within these walls do not bind you. I am hoping that your different perspectives might give you some new idea, some spark of intuition that has so far eluded the rest of us."

"So far you are the only mage to survive one of his attacks Jayden, and more, to fight back. And while I commend you on your success, it still means you are on the defensive. What we all need, is a way to take the fight to him. To not be sitting around waiting to be butchered, hoping we can defend ourselves at the last instant. Or somehow overpower a mage who has access to a great deal of powerful magic which we do not yet possess."

"I see," Clarion said once Tolmarak had run out of words. "Is that all?"

Tolmarak sighed. "Yes, that's all. But be careful. If the assassin learns what you are up to, you will both become targets. More than you already are as some of the strongest magi in Aramar at any rate."

"Can you at least give us a place to start?" Jayden asked, feeling a little overwhelmed with the responsibility which had just landed squarely on their shoulders.

"I wish I could, but the whole point of involving you two in this way is to get your ideas, not my own reflected," he told them regretfully. "The rest of us will of course continue our efforts to hunt this man down, but…"

"I understand Archmage, we'll think of… something," Jayden grimaced, trying hard to buoy the old man's spirits, which had flagged noticeably since their return from the range.

"Archmage," Clarion asked as they both stood. "Why now?"

Tolmarak met her eyes for an instant and then looked away.

"While we were out at the range today, the assassin broke into the apprentice's quarters and killed three of our students. The oldest one turned thirteen last week."

Clarion covered her mouth with her hand as though she were going to be sick. For his part, Jayden just felt the old snarl that had become so familiar to him since Rhianna's death crawl back across his face at Tolmarak's grim words.

"I'll find him," he promised hoarsely. "And I give you my word that he will not escape me again, whatever it takes."

"Let's go," Clarion directed, her manner abruptly composed and cold as she began walking towards the door.

"We have work to do."

"We *will* find him," Jayden promised again, then left to

follow Firerose down the hall. He had a sense that with her first step, she had already begun, and he had every intention of being right there beside her.

CHAPTER 19

THE ASSASSIN'S INVITATION

A phase had passed since Archmage Tolmarak had included her in the advanced class, and Missy was feeling a lot more confident about using her powers than she had been in the days after the accident.

She had always been a quick study, some quirk of the mind allowing her to remember everything she read. Tolmarak had assured her it had nothing to do with the Gift, but was a rare talent nonetheless. Even so, since that first disastrous day, she had applied herself even more diligently to her studies. She'd thought she knew what she was doing, thought she had control. If Tolmarak hadn't been there to throw up a shield at the last second though, her friends could have died. It would have been her fault.

The experience, as bad as it had been, had woken her up to what they were truly being trained for.

Thankfully, today's exercises had gone far smoother, some had even been satisfying. She had bested Nadeara in a duel for the first time earlier this morning, under the archmage's close supervision of course. She had even come closer to defeating Clarion than ever before. But then she had made a tree at the far end of the clearing waver as though struck by a heat haze, fading into nothing and stunning them all. She had improved her spell substantially since the night of her conversation with Jayden on the college's rooftop. Tolmarak had scolded her severely when she'd used it in public this morning though. He'd been angry enough that she hadn't been game to admit that she'd been making things disappear for phases. She'd had to backpedal hard, pretending she didn't know what she had done.

Thankfully, Jayden had held his tongue.

From the archmage's reaction, she didn't think the old man knew what the spell accomplished any more than she did. She gave a slight shudder at the thought of that happening to a person instead of a tree, one still half-dead from her previous mishap. Yet she couldn't get the image of it disappearing out of her mind. She was sure that she had sent it somewhere, not destroyed it as some of the others seemed to think. In any event, the archmage had explicitly forbidden her from attempting to experiment with the spell any more than she already had.

She had never been one to leave a mystery unsolved though. So once she was back in the safety of her small room that night, she began making other things disappear as well. She would work out where they went. She needed to know.

She started with a small pile of rocks she'd collected before leaving the clearing, though for some reason she had little success tonight. Only one of them had faded so far. The rest were still right where she had lined them up on the dresser. She would keep trying though. One way or another she would work it out, even with the king's stupid rule about experimentation with the Gift standing in her way.

There was a loud knock at the door. She jumped at the sound, hastily sweeping the small stones into a drawer and closing it before turning to face the only entry into her small apprentice's room.

"Come in," she called.

It was not so late that she had changed out of her daily wear yet, and she was curious who would visit her down here in the apprentice's quarters.

A few seconds went by, and no one entered. She'd heard the assassin was very good at surprising people, but since someone had knocked, she didn't think she was in any immediate danger. And yet…

An envelope slid its whispering way under the door, and the messenger's soft footfalls receded down the corridor without a word being spoken.

Missy considered the sealed square of paper for several moments before erring on the side of caution. She picked it up with an air spell, turning the envelope around so that the front faced her. Written in bold letters in a hand she didn't recognise was a single word, her name.

Curiosity got the better of her. Again with the Gift, she made a few hand motions to concentrate her will, and opened the seam of the envelope, removing the contents. She checked inside for anything else before opening the single folded parchment contained within. It was a simple, unwarded piece of paper, and nothing more than that. Taking hold of the letter with her own hand, she put the empty envelope on the dresser with the Gift, and let the spell fade.

Turning the parchment over so she could read it, Missy's eyebrows rose in disbelief as she read the missive.

Hello Missy.

I have been watching your progress from afar, and both your strength of will and your aptitude for the Gift have impressed me. Thus, I now seek to test your intelligence to complete my picture of you. There is a new day coming to this land, and I wish you to be a part of it. For too long the Giftless have controlled our destiny, making us little better than slaves to their purpose. This old and decaying order is now being swept away. The first steps have already been taken, and more are to follow. You could have a title, lands of your own in this new order, should you wish it.

Magi of your strength are rare, and we would hold you in high esteem in years to come. Though of course you must first complete your training. Think, I urge you, of how much easier, how much more effective that training could be if we were not limited by this ridiculous rule against experimentation with the Gift. A rule which has held us back for generations. It is slowing and dulling our development. It blunts our effectiveness at driving the western nations away once and for all, ending this pointless conflict which has plagued Jeranon for so very long. Think of what the college will offer you as a life. Service, confinement, and then to be sent out on errands for the king and his lackeys to gain their own private ends.

After that, I urge you, think on what you could be, unfettered by these concerns. Should you wish to pursue this line of thought, leave a candle burning in your window tonight and I will contact you again. One further thought. If anyone but I had caught you experimenting on those rocks, it would be enough to have you removed from the college for life and forever banned from using your Gift. You risk being labelled renegade, as you are wilfully breaking the king's law.

P.S. If you leave your room before dawn, or take any visitors, you will not hear from me again.

Missy looked up from the letter, glancing around the room before reaching out to shut the thick curtain which covered her one small window. Heart hammering, she set up a basic delving spell, like the one Archmage Trellis had shown them for basic investigation of wounds. She ran it all around the walls, roof, and floor of her small room. She found no holes, cracks, or any other way someone could physically see inside. The carpet shielded the space below the door, and the frame blocked it from the outside. The window was the only other possibility, although her room was several stories above ground level.

Once she was sure no one could see into the room in the natural sense, she reached out again with the Gift. With a wisp of spirit magic she tried to locate any active wards that might be in her room. She found only the normal background wards she was already aware of, such as the one which kept the college at a certain temperature all year round. Nothing caught her attention, at least nothing she knew how to detect. And yet, someone had been watching her.

Her first instinct was to run out the door as fast as she could, to find Jayden or Archmage Tolmarak and show them the note. It terrified her that the assassin, and it had to have been him, had so effortlessly planted it within her very bedroom. He evidently had free access to the college building.

Forcing herself to stop and think, she reluctantly let go of the doorknob. If she ran, what was perhaps their one chance to learn the identity of the assassin still murdering magi with impunity, would vanish away like mist. And yet if she stayed, he would know exactly where to find her.

She considered the situation for a long time, not liking what she came up with. If she waited until morning and then told the archmage about the note, he would know what to do. He might even want her to set up a meeting with the assassin so they could draw him out and spring some kind of trap.

It wouldn't work though if what Jayden had told her was true, that the assassin had somehow masked his aura so you couldn't feel him coming. Heramiir's assassin didn't have the same problem, giving him ample time to retreat whenever he sensed he was about to be outnumbered. If the others tried to surround him, he would just melt back into the shadows again without ever revealing himself, or pick them off before they even got close.

No, if there was to be any trap here, it was she who would have to set it, and she who would have to spring it. Since the assassin would already expect her, she alone might be able to get close enough to try. Although from what Jayden had already gone through at his hands, she was not at all sure she was strong enough to face him alone.

She folded the note back up, placing it back in its envelope with shaking hands. That done, she unpicked a small section of stitching on her mattress with the Gift, and slid the thin sheet of paper inside, where she prayed no one would find it. If they did, she would be in for some extremely uncomfortable questions.

A half hour later she had still not made a final decision. She was no coward, but intellectually she knew that confronting the assassin herself was madness. Even with the odds against her though, she didn't think she could live with herself if she threw away this opportunity to stop the murders once and for all.

Steeling herself, she took a candle from her nightstand and drew back the curtain to her small window. She couldn't see anyone out there, but that clearly didn't go both ways. Placing it on the sill, Missy lit it with the smallest spell of fire she could make. The top centimetre of wax liquified before she could control it, and she stood back. She would get no sleep this night, despite the exertions of the day. Hesitantly, she went back to practising on her rocks, though at an angle to the window no one outside could see. If she could get this spell right, it might just give her an advantage when she and the assassin met.

That was now a certainty, she realised abruptly. If she tried to get him to meet with her and then didn't show up, he would come after her. Since she'd heard nothing about him trying to recruit magi to Heramiir's side, he would want to keep it that way.

What if some of the other magi have already gone over?

It would explain how the assassin was getting in and out of the college building without tripping the wards. It would also explain how he always seemed to know when a mage was alone, and ripe for attack. She thought furiously.

Who saw me coming into the room just now?

There had been two servants in the corridor. She thought she could remember their faces if she saw them again. There was also a mage, a medium strength apprentice named Tyrone. The man always had been full of himself. Missy had seen him being called down by magi, and even archmagi from time to time since she'd arrived at the college. She imagined an offer such as the one she'd just received would be appealing to such an arrogant man.

Her opinion wasn't proof of course, but she would need to find a way to have him watched just in case.

It all made sense, but none of that explained how the assassin could see into her room. That was the part that frightened her more than any other. From the information it contained, that note had just been written. It hadn't been prepared hours or days before, and only just now been able to be delivered.

That was why she had placed it in the mattress and not just destroyed it out of hand. Since she couldn't determine how it was being done, there was every possibility that he was still watching her every move. It sent a shiver up her spine, but also firmed her resolve. She would make a meeting with the assassin, and she would go to it alone. Telling the others would only hurt her chances to surprise him, not to mention putting her friends in mortal danger on her behalf.

They were all being trained as battle magi to fight in the war which by now must surely have begun. Once again, she said a quick prayer to the Maker that somehow Wyll and his men had made it through the Wraith Woods alive. She had few enough friends here in Aramar that each of them meant a lot to her. The squad of soldiers, mageguard now, she corrected herself, whom they had spent so much time with over the phases before Tolmarak had sent the men on their mission made up a good proportion of them. Wyll's squad was clearly being groomed to make up the core retinue of one or maybe two of the five magi in their class. It was somewhat fitting that even those Giftless soldiers had not been immune to the assassin's ministrations.

She had never liked Marad, the loudmouthed, arrogant giant of a man who had died only a few phases past, but he had not deserved that end. None of those who had fallen did. She would put a stop to it if she could, no matter how dangerous it would be. If she was going to be a battle mage, then she might as well act like it. The butterflies that rose in her stomach knew that deep down she wasn't yet ready. The only alternative was to do nothing though, or to lower her chances of surprising him, and therefore of success, by alerting her friends and enlisting their aid. Either way the killings would likely continue. Even if none of her friends were hurt, she couldn't live with that on her conscience. Not when there was the real chance she could do something about it. All she had to do was master her fear, and keep her wits about her as Tolmarak had taught her to do.

Right now, that meant thinking of Aramar not as a new home, but as a new battleground. Maker help her, by placing the assassin's signal out for him to see, that was exactly what she had just turned it into.

*   *   *

Two more days had passed since the assassin's note was delivered, and yet, no further word had been forthcoming. The class had been out at the range during those days, practising hard, and all of them had shown significant improvement since the advanced classes had begun. Jayden seemed to have broken through his block of thinking that strength with the Gift alone would solve any problem, and was now even deadlier than before. Firerose and Nadeara had both begun using more complex spells with only their minds, and even Billy had progressed to not needing to gesture at targets to blow them up. He was still the least powerful of the group, but the youngest member of their class also seemed to now have the best control over what he was doing. Tolmarak said it was because he was young enough that his child's imagination was still more vivid than that of the older students. It gave him an edge, allowing him to focus his will more efficiently into useful magic. It made sense in the Gift's context. That didn't make it any less frustrating that the eleven-year-old boy could accomplish some of the same spells even better than she could despite being weaker in the Gift. He couldn't blow the top off a hill like she could, but Billy could ignite eight of the practice dummies at once without resorting to gestures to focus his intent. So far Missy could only manage five, not to mention that Billy could keep any number of them quenched while she tried to ignite them herself. She gave herself a pass on that one. Tolmarak had told them early in the lessons that it was far more difficult to imagine something changed, than to focus on keeping it in the state it already existed.

Even so, it was giving her serious doubts about her plan to meet with the assassin. If an eleven-year-old boy could beat her at some things in the Gift, how was she to defeat an assassin who could take out archmagi with impunity?

She owed it to every mage left in the college to try, though she wished she could get some help without compromising her chances of success. No matter what though, she could no longer avoid a confrontation with the assassin. Even if she went to Tolmarak for help. Even if Heramiir's man left her alone until she was the very last mage left alive in Aramar. Even then, she would still have to face him in the end. The only difference would be that all the deaths between now and then would have been for nothing. The only other outcome she could see if she reneged was that he attacked her directly. Probably in her room as he had with so many others, and again she would have to face him alone. At least by going through with the arrangement she would know the time and place of their meeting, and not have to survive an ambush, she hoped.

As she arrived at her room, she opened the door a crack

and reached out with the Gift to check the ward she had placed across the doorway. She hadn't designed it to stop anyone entering, but only to identify who might have crossed the threshold. It seemed undisturbed, save for the servants who cleaned the rooms daily, but then she'd never expected it to catch the assassin. At any rate, she knew who the cleaners were now, so if anything was amiss, she would mark them down as possible accomplices. She entered, closing the door behind her and looking around for any sign of a message. She didn't find one. The room seemed as she had left it, save that the bed had been made, and the furniture dusted. She went over to her mattress, pulled the sheet away from the appropriate corner and reached into the ripped stitching to make sure the note remained undiscovered. Missy felt a chill work up her spine as her fingers closed around two separate envelopes. She pulled the newer one out and opened it to reveal the same handwriting which had adorned the previous missive.

One hour before midnight, behind Jemalar's stables. Be ready to leave Aramar. P.S. Work on your wards.

That was all, but it sent a shiver up her spine. Either the assassin had been in her very room, or else he had an accomplice inside the college who could also cross wards without disturbing them. The ungifted servants would not have even known they were there.

It explained how so many of the magi had been caught unaware in their rooms. They had opened the door for somebody they already knew. It meant that either the assassin had support from at least one Aramarian magi, or else the assassin was himself from inside their own ranks.

Maybe he isn't one of Heramiir's men at all? The assassin

could even be a renegade, murdering under the guise of Heramiir's cause, now that she thought about it.

Missy shook her head to break the chain of thought. It didn't matter. Whether or not the murderer was Heramiir's, whether or not it was for a cause. Whether it was a stranger, or someone she might well have known now for several phases. If she succeeded this night, in a little over four hours, it would all come to an end. This new missive made her nervous. Still, if the assassin thought the meeting was on his terms rather than hers, she dared to hope he would be slightly less on guard.

If everything went as planned, the rest of them would be safe. Jayden would even be free to avenge Rhianna's murder without breaking yet another promise to himself. It made her sad that he couldn't find another way to deal with what Dael had done. By now though she knew there was nothing she could say or do that would change his mind, and precious little in the world which could stop him once he set himself on that course. But that was his battle to fight, and right now she had her own.

She placed both letters back in the mattress, and gathered a few things before heading down to the kitchens for something to eat. She wasn't all that hungry, but she would need all her strength for what was to come. Missy made herself eat something she didn't really remember afterwards, and it filled in some time. The others must have decided to eat later, since none of them were down here, and for that she was glad. If she'd had to talk to them, there was every chance she would lose her nerve and decide not to go through with her plan.

For a while she walked the college grounds, giving a distracted nod whenever she passed a familiar face.

At one point she found herself at the stables. Her beige mare Dasher always gave her a sense of comfort. In the end she couldn't bring herself to ride the horse out to Jemalar's in case all of this really was to lure her into some kind of trap. She doubted that was the case though, or at least, not the primary reason. The assassin hadn't been shy about hitting far more experienced magi than her inside the guarded college walls.

Whatever happened tonight, she had made the right choice. No one else had been murdered since the first note had arrived. Not that the assassin struck every day, but she chose to believe it was because the assassin thought he had weakened Aramar's magi to the point where they might turn on their former masters.

Whether or not it was true, it buoyed her spirits to think she might have already accomplished that much at least, and right now she desperately needed that reassurance.

For a while she considered getting to Jemalar's early to scout the area. That was a futile notion though, since the assassin would sense her coming long before she knew where he was.

No, her only choice was whether to go through with the meeting as planned, hoping for an opportunity to strike, or back out completely. Right now. Of course, she would then have to give the letters to the archmage, and the old man would be furious she had waited until now to do so. It was too late for them to arrange another trap.

The hours passed slowly, but eventually it was time for her to leave. As she approached the front gates of the college yard, wrapped in her black magi's cloak with its white lining, the guard in charge called out a welcome.

"Do you be needin' an escort tonight, ma'am?" The tall

man asked, his casual slur pronouncing him a native of the Sunset Isles.

"No thank you, just out for a quick walk," Missy told the man, who frowned in response.

"As you be sayin' ma'am. Just be sendin' up a signal then if you be needin' assistance."

"Thank you Sergeant," she responded without breaking stride. "I'll be all right."

In truth, the company would have bolstered her spirits, but she remembered Jayden's guilt after one of his escorts had been killed. 'To no purpose' as he had seen it at the time. She didn't want that on her conscience. There was nothing these men could do to aid her tonight. Besides, any deviation from his instructions would likely lead to the assassin refusing to show.

It took her an hour to make her way through Aramar's streets. She reached the main boulevard which led from the docks all the way to the Royal Castle at the city's heart without incident. On the way though, she found herself dismayed to discover that the few citizens still out were simply going about their lives. It was almost as though there were not a civil war on, as if they didn't know or care that magi were being slaughtered not a league from their homes. Well, they would know it soon enough if her plan went as she hoped.

Even if it doesn't, she thought nervously.

Finally, she came within sight of the horse trader Jemalar's and saw a small alley that reached down the side of the structure, fading into the darkness beyond. A brief thought of waiting to catch a glimpse of the assassin as he entered floated unbidden to her mind. Again she reminded herself how pointless that would be. By now, he must already know from her aura exactly where she was. Their unequal footing made her even more uneasy now that she was actually here. Standing out front as though she was trying to get one up on him would only make the assassin more suspicious.

Swallowing hard, she headed towards the dimness of the alleyway, pausing to let a jovial group of drunks pass her by as they headed for some unknown destination. She was a pretty girl, and under different circumstances the young men might have at least called out some unwelcome comments. The white-lined apprentice mage's cloak draped over her shoulders had its advantages. She tried to hide a small smile as the men noticed it and swiftly moved on, singing some raucous ballad as they went.

She turned her attention back to the alleyway. Nothing moved in its shadows. Now all she could do was hope that she had made the right decision and move forward. That, and prepare to bring the strongest Gift-wrought shield she could muster into being at the slightest excuse.

Once her eyes had adjusted to the sudden lack of light, she moved down the long side of Jemalar's stables. She reached the back corner of the building, peering around it briefly before ducking back into cover. Her heart was beating hard, and her hands had begun to sweat.

The back alley was wider than the service lane she was now on, and the moon was lighting it better from high overhead. It gave her a decent look at what lay beyond. There were several carts lined up and fenced in along the horse traders' wall, along with a covered area filled with bailed hay. On the other side of the alley was a blank stone wall from some anonymous business which fronted onto the next street over. Missy began to have second thoughts about this whole idea. Apart from the narrow service-way she now perched at the end of, there were no other visible means of exiting the alley for a hundred spans in either direction. As the moon slunk behind a cloud, the scene faded into a dim jumble of shadows and shapes which she very much hoped were only moving in her own imagination.

She hadn't come this far for nothing though. The assassin almost certainly knew where she was standing, if he was here at all, and it was time to take back some control. With a minor spell of spirit and fire, she lit the alleyway to the brightness of a cloudy day, and stepped forward.

She couldn't see him yet, but Missy was as ready as she was going to be. She had been practising on as many rocks as she could find over the last two days, and it hadn't been for nothing. Almost half of them disappeared as soon as she attempted her spell now. That ability would be her first and best shot at taking him out, since he wouldn't know how to defend against it. She just hoped it worked as she intended. Despite her talent for large scale spells, she was still not sure if she could beat this man in sustained, open combat. In this isolated back alley, if things went poorly, help would never arrive in time.

As she stepped further into the alley, her eyes scanned the rooftops, and what shadows remained, for any sign of the assassin. She had made her way no more than three more steps out into the middle when her light spell died against her wishes.

A voice called out from the abruptly disorienting darkness. "That is far enough, Missy."

The man spoke calmly, but as though he were only a few feet away. Missy spun in fright, attempting to locate the voice's source.

A great feeling of unease washed over her as the moon retreated behind a cloud. She was alone in the alley.

"Show yourself!" she called out to wherever the assassin was hiding.

"Now why would I do that? I brought you here so I could determine whether you are a suitable candidate for the new order. Not so that you could have the chance to identify me."

Her mind spinning, Missy looked around once again, and came up blank.

"I don't need to see your face, just show me where you are. Otherwise I'm leaving."

There was a long moment of silence, then a furtive figure leapt an impossible distance from the roof next door, the cloaked figure landing casually, fifty feet from where she was standing. Missy's breath caught, even at this close distance she couldn't feel an aura, though anyone but a practised mage would have taken serious injury from that drop.

The assassin was of average height for a man, with an unremarkable build that was obscured by his all-encompassing robe. It was impossible to glean any further details in the overcast, and now moonless night.

As Jayden had said, he wore his hood pulled all the way forward to obscure his face, his head remaining bowed in case the moon resumed its nocturnal vigil.

"Trust is a hard-won commodity in my line of work, but since you *did* come alone..."

He was using the Gift to project his voice. Apparently stifling his aura did nothing to affect his other Gift sensitivities.

"I want that title, and everything that goes with it," Missy lied boldly, trying to buy some time to think. He was too far away. She had never tried her spell over such a long distance before, and had no idea what might happen. If there was any opportunity to get closer to the assassin without making him even more suspicious, she needed to take it.

"I see," he responded. "And are you willing to fight for it?"

Missy's spine turned to ice, and she readied her shield.

"Do I need to be?" She replied, taking a step towards him.

"Magi of our talents should always be willing to fight for what they hold dear," the assassin returned slyly. "The question is, how far are you willing to go to see those ends realised?"

Missy casually took a few more steps forward as she answered.

"My parents have never been, and never will be, rich. A title and lands of my own would mean they can spend the rest of their lives in comfort. A far better end than working themselves to an untimely death on our farm to support my brothers and sisters. So yes, I would fight to make that happen."

The assassin nodded, accepting her words as truth, which in fact they were. However, fighting for her family did not equate in her mind to committing treason and murder.

"I believe you," he replied. "But if you wish to be a part of the new order, I require something more of a… commitment, shall we say, to prove your loyalty."

"What did you have in mind?" she asked as she stopped. This was close enough. The spell should work correctly from here.

Suddenly her senses came alive.

At almost the same moment, the two of them looked back in the college's direction. It wasn't their eyes they were using though. The sense of three intense auras approaching them had come into range at what must at least be a run. They might even be on horseback judging from the speed.

"Fool girl," the assassin said, his voice no longer friendly.

"Did you think you could catch me with such a simple trap?"

"This is not my doing!" Missy hissed, her hard won element of surprise now wasted.

"My trap did not involve others."

Before she could react, he launched a ball of flame at her with only his mind. She was ready for it.

Reaching out her hand as if to push it away, she flung the spell she held ready in her mind at him without hesitation. As the fireball hurtled toward her, to Missy's immense relief her own spell shot from her fingertips as intended.

Wasting no time, she erected a shield around herself, but it proved unnecessary. As their spells collided in mid-air, the fireball shimmered out of existence as her own spell intercepted it.

For an instant they both stood there, not entirely sure what had just happened, or what to do next.

An instant was all she got.

Without warning, the assassin used the Gift to leap up onto the adjacent roof and had retreated beyond her line of sight before she could get off another shot.

For a long moment she just stood there, both numb and furious at herself, and whoever had ruined her trap. It would have worked if they had not alerted him to the danger! Now that chance was gone.

For the very first time Missy understood just how powerful her native talent in the Gift was, and smiled unpleasantly. Even the assassin who had killed archmagi with impunity had been surprised at how easily she had nullified his assault. The spell would work from now on, she was sure of it. She just needed to work out what it actually did, whether it transported or destroyed.

The three magi were closing in now, coming for her. She had better come up with a good reason for being out here alone, and for using the Gift within the city itself.

With that in mind, she made one last fruitless scan of the empty rooftops before heading back the way she had come. She strode around the corner and down the alleyway to the main boulevard. At the front of Jemalar's she discovered Jayden, Archmage Tolmarak, and Archmage Trellis just pulling up their mounts.

Seeing her unharmed, Tolmarak heaved a sigh of relief while Jayden smiled amicably in greeting.

"It is dangerous for magi to be wandering alone these days," Tolmarak said. "So what could be important enough to bring you down here without an escort in the middle of the night I wonder?"

"The gate guards?" Missy asked irritably. It must have been they who had ratted her out.

"Performed their assigned duty and informed me when you refused to take an escort with you into the city," Tolmarak reminded her.

She was still furious that they had sprung her trap early, but grudgingly had to concede that the gate guards had indeed done their job. She just wished they hadn't been nearly as efficient. If she'd just had one more minute, all of this might have been over. Still, it was done for tonight, and she noticed Jayden holding the reins of her beige mare Dasher. Without further ado she walked over, took them from him and hoisted herself up into the saddle.

"I just needed a walk."

"I see," Tolmarak replied, not even slightly fooled by her story. "Down a back alley, in the middle of the night?"

"There was a noise. I went to investigate," she returned. The last thing she wanted to tell them right now was that she'd had the chance to stop the assassin, to stop the murders once and for all, and failed.

"By yourself?" Archmage Trellis asked.

"You silly girl, you could have been killed."

"I'm fine," she said shortly, unsure whether she was more offended by the archmage calling her a silly girl, or by Tolmarak suggesting she couldn't handle herself as a mage.

"You need to be more careful Missy," Tolmarak chided her as he shot Archmage Trellis a vaguely annoyed look.

"We cannot afford to lose any more magi, especially one of your strength. I need you to promise me that there will be no more night-time excursions, at least not without a mageguard escort."

Missy sighed. Tolmarak didn't believe her, but he also didn't seem willing to push the issue right now, and that was enough.

"Yes Archmage," she replied in a conciliatory fashion. After all, there was no longer a need to avoid them, now that the assassin knew her true intentions.

"Let's get back to the college," Tolmarak said, and without further words the four of them turned their mounts and began walking up the long, cobbled boulevard. They exited down another street and headed towards the main college building after stabling the mounts. Missy knew she would get no sleep this night. Instead she would spend it wondering whether all her friends would still be alive come morning. Or whether it would be her turn to be found now that she knew something of the assassin's intentions.

The ride back to the college had been a quiet one, with little of interest said or seen. It wasn't until the two archmagi had left them that Jayden turned to her.

"So… What were you really doing down there?" he asked as they returned to the main college building from the stables.

Missy looked at him for a long moment. He wouldn't judge her if she told him the truth. But right now all she could feel was a sense of overwhelming failure. She had let him down, let all of them down by missing her opportunity to end the assassin's threat once and for all.

"I needed to practice that spell," she deflected.

"You can do that in your room," Jayden replied, a little confused.

"I needed to make something larger disappear," she added. "And there was too much risk of being detected here."

Jayden sighed. "You need to be more careful Missy. If you get caught doing unauthorised experiments again, I think Tolmarak is bound by law to punish you."

"I know that!" she replied, her guilt and anger at the nights non-events causing her to snap. "But this was a chance I had to take. I know you don't understand that now, but one day soon you will," she waspishly declared before picking up speed and intentionally leaving him behind.

*   *   *

Jayden just stood there for a minute, confused. Whatever else Missy might be, flighty was not on the list, and the only bit of useful information he ended up taking from the encounter was that Tolmarak had been right. Something here was definitely not as it seemed.

CHAPTER 20

AN IMPERFECT IDEA

Today had been the longest day of Missy's life, helped not at all by a lack of sleep the previous night.

A full day had passed since her attempt to end the assassin's reign of terror, and she had spent the silent hours of the previous night waiting in her room, straining to detect any sign he might have followed her back to the college. Lessons today out at the range had felt safe by comparison. But they had ended all too quickly, and eventually she'd been left with no other choice than to return to her small, isolated room.

She now sat before her mirror, wearing a pale green nightgown. Removing the tangles and snarls which the day's wind and rain had left throughout her long brown hair gave her something else to think about. At least for now. Archmage Tolmarak had gone out of his way to heap praise on her efforts this afternoon at the range. It had only been when she saw the surprised look on Jayden's face that she'd realised he was serious.

'Focus,' Tolmarak had told her, was the most important thing. 'Blowing the top off a hill was fine, but if Heramiir's assassin attacked her, then focus would be everything.'

She'd taken the words to heart, though for reasons other than he'd intended. She still hadn't told him of her humiliating failure the previous night.

Missy knew she'd come a long way in Tolmarak's advanced lessons since that first disastrous day. Whether she had come far enough to hold out against the assassin, now that he knew what she was capable of, was another matter entirely. She'd gotten off easily last night. The assassin had been far more concerned with escaping, identity still unknown, than in trying to cause her serious harm whilst three of the most powerful magi in Aramar raced towards them.

She stood, taking a break from her tangled hair, and placing the old ivory hairbrush back on the dresser. Taking two brief steps, she crossed the width of her small room to stand beside the unmade bed. Under the far corner, slipped into a torn seam in the mattress, the two notes from the assassin still lay, waiting.

She should have burned the first one as soon as she knew what it was, or better yet, given it over to Archmage Tolmarak. Especially considering how her ambush had turned out. Reaching behind the bed, she slipped her hand into the split seam and pulled out the dog-eared pieces of parchment from their now familiar hiding place.

She re-read the short missives, but still couldn't see what else she might have done. She had to tell someone about this whole mess, but the prospect of facing the others, given her complete lack of success, was daunting. At best they would be disappointed, at worst, furious as well.

Maybe I can trust Jayden.

He'd kept secrets for her before, and might even know what to do. Her plan to eliminate the assassin without putting the others at risk now seemed nothing but a child's fantasy. Yet as she looked over the letter a final time, she wondered once more what it would be like to have a title and lands of her own.

Leaning over, she placed the letters back inside the mattress.

She crossed the small room again and picked up the ivory hairbrush. Her mother had given it to her before she'd left home last spring with Archmage Kelta and a recruiting party bound for the capital. Once he'd discovered her talent for the Gift, she'd no longer had a choice. Still, things had turned out as well as could be hoped for, more or less. Since leaving home, she had made new friends and learnt many new skills. Already she could see a promotion to Mage on the horizon, and once that happened she would be in an excellent position to make her family's life a great deal easier.

If I survive that long, she thought grimly as her mind turned once more back to the notes.

Dragging the brush through her tangled hair again, Missy decided to tie it back tomorrow. As much as she preferred it loose, she was too tired from the day's exertions to be bothered removing every snarl and tangle. The only thing that kept her going was the dreadful knowledge that if she didn't proceed, tomorrow it would be far worse. So she persisted with the brush as it pulled its way down the length of her hair. It was that or take a knife to it. Looking at her reflection in the mirror, she chuckled as she imagined what she would look like bald.

'Oh well,' she thought. 'I could use a doormat.'

Pulling her hair around to get a better look at a particularly vicious snarl, Missy glanced in the mirror, and her blood ran cold.

Behind her bed, which she had positioned on the other

side of the room when the assassin had begun attacking magi in their sleep, a tear had silently opened. The stone wall was slowly splitting apart, a crack no more than a finger width appearing near the foot of the bed. She instinctively threw up a shield, completing the spell an instant before her bed erupted in a highly localised ball of red and yellow flames.

Struggling not to scream, Missy ducked around the corner of the dresser and crouched against the wall, out of sight. The fire burned hard for a long moment before the charred remains of her bunk exploded outward. A bolt of raw, Gift-wrought power shattering the wooden frame.

There was a thunderous crash, and the sheer terror and shock of the explosion caused her to lose concentration. Her shield dropped. One of the flying timbers careened off the far wall hard enough to strike her in the midriff, sending her sprawling to the floor. The wind was thoroughly knocked out of her, but in seconds the conflagration died, and the gap in the stonework widened just enough for someone to enter.

Even as she struggled to breathe, Missy pulled her knees up towards her chin, reflexively hoping to stay out of sight of her would be assailant. But the beam had hit her chest, not her head, and she knew that was false hope as her aura would remain constant so long as she lived.

Even as the unbidden thought worked its way through her mind, she worked her lungs furiously, straining to fill them with air that still would not come. A footfall sounded on the other side of the room, but even that was not as disturbing as the twisted aura she could now feel approaching. Not as powerful as Jayden, but darker, and warped in some way that made it infinitely more menacing.

Her heart felt as though it were trying to beat its way out

of her chest. As she finally wrenched in a heaving breath, a footstep fell on the other side of the dresser.

Missy examined her choices as her breath came fast and shallow, and to her horror, realised that the possibilities were far too simple for any kind of plan. She could run, or she could fight. The only door was on the other side of the room, bolted closed. She wouldn't make it halfway there before the assassin cut her down.

"Fight it is," she murmured, still labouring for breath. The tip of a solid workmen's boot appeared right beside the corner of the dresser, and Missy reached out with the Gift, pulling the roof down on them both.

There was a tremendous grinding and a scream from above. Missy flung a shield up around herself just before the first chunks of stone came crashing down onto it. A blue shimmer appeared and was shoved across the room by debris before being buried by rubble and furnishings from the room above.

The assassin had raised a shield in time.

Through the hole in the roof, she could make out a middle-aged servant in a maid's outfit clutching a feather duster in one terrified hand. Missy was reassured when the woman ran screaming from the chamber for help.

Across her own room, the pile of rubble shifted, and the assassin came tumbling out of the debris. The man was shaken, but unharmed. He looked up at the ceiling and scowled. The servant was gone, and he'd been exposed.

With all her strength in the Gift, Missy picked up the huge slab of stone which had crushed her dresser, and flung it at her attacker. He was facing the other way still, and as the stone smashed against his shield, it flickered for a moment. Whether she had momentarily overcome it, or distracted the assassin enough that he had let it lapse for an instant, there was no way to know.

She gestured desperately, turning the air to water around him as he turned back towards her, but her spell wouldn't penetrate the shield he had all too quickly renewed. All she achieved was to soak her already destroyed room, and make the assassin smile. He winked, and the air around her caught fire. Her shield kept the worst of the inferno at bay, but the air inside was heating up alarmingly fast.

Soon it would be too hot to breathe, and Missy knew she had only moments to act.

Pushing her shield outwards, she managed, with considerable effort, to make it span the width and height of the room, and up into the next. She allowed it to lapse behind her. She couldn't concentrate on both directions as she continued to push the barrier forward in a seamless wall that left her plenty of air still cool enough to breathe. The assassin's flame attack faltered. She couldn't quite see his face beneath the hooded robe, but the tilt of his head made him look surprised as he studied the shimmering wall between them.

The sound of running footsteps reached them from the corridor outside. The assassin smiled as he stepped forward to run a finger experimentally across the shining surface, which was taking all her strength now just to maintain. She dared not let him see how close she was to faltering.

"I knew you were special," he said, almost sounding proud of what he'd forced her to do. The assassin took a step sideways and leapt out of her smashed window, disappearing in an instant as gravity took hold.

Shaking, Missy watched him go. A moment later, Tolmarak burst through her door, pushing a deep blue shield before him as he entered, ready to fight. Confronted by an unexpected lack of opposition, he came to a halt and stared in amazement at the shimmering blue wall dividing the room, and the one above it, in two.

"He is gone?" the archmage asked, and when she nodded in exhaustion he let his shield drop, motioning for her to do the same.

A chunk of debris fell from the ceiling with a dusty thud, and Tolmarak motioned her to follow him out into the corridor. Missy complied, her strength sapped away now that she was no longer fighting for her life. Something on the floor caught her eye, and she stopped for a moment to push aside a piece of wooden debris which was half covering her mother's ivory comb. She was surprised to find it had survived the brief attack almost unscathed, if a bit charred on one end. Tucking it away in a pocket, she followed the archmage out into the more stable corridor. She would have to own up to what she had done now that the assassin had followed her back into the college itself. It was not a conversation she was looking forward to at all.

"Are you all right, Missy?" Tolmarak asked once they were safely away from the damaged section of the structure.

There were pounding footsteps from around the corner and Jayden came running full tilt towards them, half a dozen other magi in close pursuit. When he saw Tolmarak had arrived before him, and the threat had passed, he finished his approach at a more reasonable speed.

"I'm fine," she said once the young mage had come properly into earshot.

"Did you..?" Jayden asked, and Tolmarak shook his head in response.

"He was gone by the time I got here. It seems Missy

fought him off all by herself," the old man announced with a slight smile.

Jayden just looked at him for a moment, and then at Missy, who, despite everything, couldn't help but grin cheekily at his surprised stare.

"Looks like you don't get to be quite so special anymore," she told him. She was exhausted from the battles she had fought over the last day and a half. Not to mention the stress of waiting for the assassin to strike back at her. Of course, then there was today's practice out on the range, and a general lack of sleep ever since the assassin's first invitation had been placed in her room. She was suddenly overwhelmed by the urge to both cry in relief and go to sleep at the same time, and then she almost laughed for no reason at all. As she sat down right there in the corridor, all she wanted to do was close her eyes and make this nightmare go away. Fifteen-year-olds shouldn't have to worry about being hunted by assassins.

Even so, she had done everything she could to stop the murderer. She may have failed in that endeavour, but no one could say she hadn't done her best, or that she had been too scared to try. Given that she was still alive to tell the tale, she would take that for a victory right now.

"Believe me," Jayden told her. "Being the only mage to survive an attack by Heramiir's man is a title which I am most happy to be rid of. I'm glad you're all right Missy."

"How did the assassin get into your room?" Tolmarak asked, and all the other magi present went silent as they waited for her answer.

It was written over all their faces. Finally, they would get some more useful information about the murderer who had plagued their small community for the greater part of a year.

Missy thought about it, but not being sure of what spell had been used herself, she decided just to tell them what she'd seen.

"I don't know exactly. I was sitting at my dresser when in the mirror I saw the wall behind me simply part. It was like… like holding a piece of torn paper in your hands and slowly moving them apart to widen the gap, only there was no sound whatsoever. Then, as soon as he had a line of sight, he destroyed my bed with a fire spell before using one of raw power to finish it off. If I had been asleep when he had come… I would be dead now," she whispered. As her mind finally processed the consequences the last few minutes might have had, it hit her hard.

"But you're not. In fact, you fought the assassin off. You beat him, Missy," Jayden encouraged her.

She gave a weak smile in response.

"Maybe. But I think it was more Archmage Tolmarak's aura approaching than anything I did that made him run," she said, turning her attention back to the old man.

"Although I made his shield flicker for a moment," she added with a satisfied grin.

"How?" Tolmarak inquired. "We need to know about any weaknesses we can exploit."

Missy nodded and smiled again.

"I pulled the roof down on him. While he was recovering, I used an air spell and threw the biggest piece of debris I could see at his back as hard as I could. I think even he was surprised by how well it worked," she told them as Jayden laughed out loud.

"That was good thinking," Tolmarak said.

"I'll have to remember that one," Jayden replied. The buoyant mood chilled as they all acknowledged the fact that although Missy had survived, it in no way meant that the attacks had stopped.

"Shouldn't we go after him?" Jayden asked, breaking the sudden silence.

"I raised the alarm before I came," Tolmarak replied. "By now most of the mageguard and nearly every magi not in this corridor are hunting the grounds, though I hold little hope they will find him. Jayden, Missy, you will come with me. The rest of you I want down in the apprentice's quarters, guarding them for the remainder of the night. Just to be sure."

"Yes Archmage," Delinda replied, giving the college leader the title, though she herself was an archmage as well.

"Come on," she prompted the group of remaining magi, and left to carry out the assignment with the others in tow.

Once they were gone, Tolmarak stood while Jayden helped Missy to her feet. The archmage then led them back to the central stairwell of the massive building and up several levels to where his own quarters lay. He stopped only once, to instruct a servant to locate Firerose and summon her to join them in his quarters.

*   *   *

So far, neither Jayden nor Clarion had come up with a useful way to track the assassin since the archmage had assigned them to focus on the task. He hated that, though no one else had done better. It was doubly disheartening for Jayden. While the assassin was free, not only were his friends in mortal peril, but he had promised not to leave Aramar until they were safe.

In his heart, Jayden knew that the time he could keep

that promise was shortening. He wanted with all his heart to do so, but every time he was forced to violence, it became harder and harder to resist the urge to leave this place. Every time he was forced to fight, it reopened the old wounds, and the rage he could never quite quench poured forth anew. It was all he could do not to abandon them all, to leave Aramar and return home to deal with Dael once and for all. He knew it would cost him every friend, every scrap of painstaking progress he had made since arriving at the college to do so. It worried him that that prospect no longer concerned him as it used to. He was not sure why, but in the last weeks since the assassin had murdered the three apprentices, his patience had simply run out. The feeling that he had to act, or forever miss his chance to avenge Rhianna's death had been building in him steadily, unremittingly, until now he could think of little else. The assassin still demanded his attention though. It was the only thing stopping him from sneaking away this very night to do what he now admitted to himself was a certainty. Despite Tolmarak's best efforts to help him let it go, and even the king's threats to declare him renegade. He would execute Dael for his crime. It was only a matter of time.

He knew what Tolmarak was training him for, and that no one else could take on Heramiir alone. That gave him a certain leverage if he acted now, while the king still needed something from him, something only he could give. His father would be ashamed if he knew Jayden intended to use bribery to cover up murder, especially when it was the king who would need to be bribed. Yet he had no choice.

It is justice, he told himself again for the thousandth time, and if no one else was willing to carry it out, he would see it done himself. He wished confronting the king afterwards wasn't necessary, but it was his only chance of having some kind of actual life beyond that day. And a slim chance it was at that, one that assumed he somehow found a way to overcome Heramiir in all his power.

Maybe I'm just trying to convince myself that it will all work out in the end.

King Erian certainly hadn't looked as though he would change his mind when he'd threatened to declare him renegade if he couldn't obey the laws of the kingdom. And yet Jayden knew he would take that chance. When it came right down to it, nothing mattered more than making Dael pay for what he had done to Rhianna. Nothing. Whatever consequences came of that, he would deal with them once the ledger was settled.

The three of them reached Tolmarak's door, and entered once the archmage opened it for them. Before they had even sat down, Firerose also appeared, panting as though she had run all the way up the long, winding staircase. That might even be true since the head of the college had summoned her himself.

"Good. Come in and take a seat," Tolmarak said.

"By now I take it you've heard the assassin made an attempt on Missy's life? Thankfully, she was capable of dealing with the situation," he remarked once she had seated herself.

Clarion's head swivelled, wide-eyed towards the younger girl for a moment, but then took a relieved breath as she realised Missy was unharmed.

"I had heard the assassin had struck again, but not at who, or that she had fought him off," the beautiful red-haired woman replied.

"She was able to keep him at bay until help could arrive, at which point he ran rather than risk capture, as he always seems to do. But to Missy's credit, she is almost without a scratch, as you can see."

"I'm glad you're all right," Firerose told the younger girl with a sincere smile.

"Yes, we all are," Tolmarak interjected. "Now, the reason I have called you two here is to hear for yourselves Missy's account of what happened tonight. It is my hope that it will give you some new insight into the task I set for you," he told the two most advanced members of their class.

*   *   *

Missy looked around at the two older students. Before she had to ask, Tolmarak explained how he had set Jayden and Firerose to look for any way to track the assassin. Or better yet, stop him short once and for all.

It didn't take long for Missy to recount the evening's events, brief as they had been. There was little in her story that she hadn't already told both Jayden and Tolmarak in the corridor near her quarters. When she was done, she sat back in the chair and thought. She didn't want to tell them the rest. She would get into serious trouble when the archmage found out she had squandered perhaps their only opportunity to catch the killer.

"I think we need to focus on how the assassin is choosing his victims. How he always knows when they are alone," Firerose put in after a moment of reflective silence.

Missy sighed, that one question ending any chance she had of honourably keeping her secrets.

"He has spies," she mumbled.

413

The three heads of the other magi in the room turned to regard her in silence.

"That would seem likely," Tolmarak conceded.

"No, I mean he has spies even among the magi themselves. I know who at least one of them is, and there are two other servants I suspect. One of those is a certainty as well, though I'm unsure which."

If there had been a silence in the room before, it was an oppressive one now.

"And you know this how?" Tolmarak asked, his usual calm demeanour on a knife's edge.

"I had best start from the beginning," she told him gloomily.

"That would be an excellent idea," the archmage replied. His usual manner of wise teacher had fled, replaced instead by the authoritative head of the college, and king's advisor, sitting in judgement before her now.

Missy nervously related the events of the last few days to the group. She started with the first note being slipped under her door and left nothing out. She even included her reasons for acting as she had in the hope it might mitigate whatever punishment awaited her for squandering this opportunity. Missy made herself keep talking, recounting event after event until she was blessedly able to stop when she returned to tonight's attack.

When she had told them all she could, she fell silent, waiting for the explosion that she was sure would come. Tolmarak just sat there, watching her unnervingly for long moments as he worked her tale through in his mind.

"I want to be angry at you, Missy," he said eventually. "For putting yourself in danger, for not coming to me with this in the first place, and for not catching the assassin while you had the chance. The truth is, though, I cannot fault your logic. Had you come to me with this information, I would have been compelled to act on it as you said. You were right. It would have ruined your attempt to ambush the assassin, though it seems we managed that anyhow. You saw an opportunity to end this, and even at great personal risk you took it, putting no one else in danger I might add. Your… unauthorised, use of the Gift we will keep between the four of us in this room given the circumstances, agreed?"

He looked directly at Jayden and Clarion, the question a barely veiled command.

The two of them nodded without hesitation, and Missy found herself grateful for the unfeigned support of her two most powerful classmates.

"I should punish you for keeping me in the dark over this, but just this once, Missy, I won't. The simple truth is that you act far more bravely and maturely than anyone else your age I have known for a very long time. I will not discourage that in you. Just don't make a habit of keeping things from me."

"I won't, Archmage," she responded.

"I didn't want to this time either, I just didn't see any other way that my trap would have had as good a chance of working."

"Very well," Tolmarak said at last, apparently believing her, which was good since she had in fact told him the truth. And just like that, the teacher was back.

"Let's move on then," he told them. "Do you have these notes the assassin left you? There might be some other information we can glean from them."

"I'm sorry Archmage, they were tucked into my mattress

for safekeeping. I can't imagine they survived the assassin burning my bed during the attack."

"That is most unfortunate," Tolmarak mused.

"As for these spies, you are to leave them be for now. I will have them watched. Hopefully, they may get careless and give us a clue as to where the assassin might strike next. If they even suspect they are being watched though, they will go to ground. As powerful as you three are, we have people better trained to deal with this sort of thing. Besides, Tyrone would no doubt sense your much larger auras staying close to him. Since he is nowhere near as strong in the Gift, he'll feel you coming long before you're in range of his aura."

*　　*　　*

Jayden nodded in understanding, though knowing Tolmarak was right did nothing to ease his frustration at having to wait while others took up the hunt for Heramiir's man. Meanwhile, Dael was still sitting comfortably in his keep, unaware that his day of reckoning was closing in at a rapid pace.

There was a dull thud from somewhere below, and the cup of tea on Tolmarak's desk, which had long since gone cold during the night's events, shuddered. The milky liquid rippled, and the magi looked at each other for a stunned moment before jumping out of their chairs to run for the door. There was only one thing that would cause the giant structure itself to tremble. As the four magi ran down the corridor towards the central stairwell, a second explosion shook the corridor before silence once again descended.

As they reached the stairwell itself, a plume of black

smoke rose from somewhere below. The glow of orange flames flickered strange shadows across the far wall in accompaniment to shouts from below. Tolmarak hurdled the rail into the grand entry hall. He used the Gift to slow his fall at the very last second, gravity assisting him down to the floor nine stories below, far faster than he ever could have run. Jayden was only a moment behind. Neither Firerose nor Missy were familiar enough with the spell yet to trust their lives to it, and were forced to run down and around the staircase as it entwined the vast hall.

Once Jayden and the archmage had regained their footing, they realised the smoke was issuing from one of the corridors that led to the servants' quarters. Jayden snarled as he realised where this was heading.

"Wait!" Jayden called to Tolmarak, who was already running at a speed that belied his age towards the corridor, a bright blue shield extended before him.

Tolmarak skidded to a halt and turned back to see what had made his young apprentice baulk.

"Missy said that the assassin had spies, two servants and a mage. They must have some knowledge he fears will compromise his identity."

"Go!" Tolmarak snapped. "Tyrone's quarters are on the second floor down the east corridor, the fourth door on the right. I will deal with this," Tolmarak shouted as he began running towards the smoke-filled servants' quarters again. Jayden nodded before looking up at the second-storey balcony and focusing his will. Using both the Gift and his legs to leap up to the target, he was forced to grab at the rail to stop himself falling back to ground level again. With an effort, he pulled himself over the railing and found himself near the east corridor, which Tolmarak's quarters were also part of, several stories above. For now there was nothing amiss, so he took Tolmarak's lead and extended a shield out in front of himself before running towards his objective as fast as he could.

He was almost at the door when the wall in front of him exploded. The doorway, and a good section of corridor ahead, just disappeared as the force of the blast turned everything before it into rubble. Jayden's shield took the brunt of a blast that would no doubt have shredded him, as it had the corridor, if he hadn't been prepared.

As it was, Jayden found himself laying on his back about twenty feet away from where he last remembered being, his head feeling as though he'd been hit by a brick. That might not be too far from the truth, he realised as he groggily noticed that his shield was down.

He had no idea how long he'd been laying there. He could see blood darkening the left arm of his coat, and his ears rang so loudly that he could hear little else. A familiar sensation appeared without warning, a twisted aura that marked Heramiir's assassin as being far too close.

Even in his weakened state, Jayden managed to raise a shield, but it was a sickly, flickering thing, and the assassin would penetrate it with ease. A man in a dark robe stepped out of the destruction, and smiled.

Jayden tried to rally his will, knowing that if he didn't strike first, he was done for. The man's head snapped up. He raised an arm in a reflexive action, drawing a line of blue across himself. The hastily formed shield barely deflected a ball of flame from an approaching mage. The spell reflected off his shield and took out the side of the corridor opposite instead. The assassin snarled and ignored his assailant, launching his attack at Jayden instead. If it weren't for the second shield which sprung up in front of him, blocking the corridor entirely, Jayden knew he could never have repelled the attack. The assassin struck at the shield, sending thousands of needle-sharp ice crystals at it. When he had finished the spell, the solid wall of blue was weaker than before, but held firm. The assassin glanced up at the approaching figures again. His time was running out.

Cursing, he changed tactics and blasted the roof with a spell of raw power. The ceiling collapsed in a spray of dust and debris that was supported in mid-air by the shield. For several moments, the corridor was obscured with debris and dust, which was all he needed to flee yet again. His twisted aura moved away, disappearing to Jayden's senses before he was even out of sight.

The debris above him was abruptly shoved to the side and away before being allowed to fall to the ground. A moment later both Missy and Firerose were at his side, checking on his injuries even before they'd come to a full stop.

"Go after him!" Jayden shouted. "Finish this now."

Clarion nodded resolutely, and without wasting another moment pulled Missy up with her. In moments she had them running after the assassin, Gift-wrought shields at the ready as they rounded the gap in the destroyed corridor wall.

Jayden knew they wouldn't find him there, though. The assassin had no doubt leapt out another window that was too high for them to follow without knowing the appropriate spell. He was going to insist Tolmarak focus on it with the rest of the class tomorrow. Although the archmage had been concentrating on battle magic for the last several weeks, this was one spell that was just too useful to wait. Pulling himself up with his right arm, he saw that a jagged shaft of debris had pierced his left arm straight through. The injury was causing a profuse bleeding that was ruining his coat. Why he cared about that, and why he wasn't in agony, he didn't know as he tried to pull the thin piece of metal from the wound. He cried out in pain as the shaft came free, his nerve ends choosing now of all times to reawaken. It rang out as he dropped it on the floor beside him. Moments later he regained consciousness and found Tolmarak by his side, inspecting the wound. Or at least he thought it had been only moments. He didn't remember blacking out.

Before Tolmarak could heal him, the girls came back into view with frustrated expressions. Jayden knew the assassin had escaped again long before they reported their findings to the archmage.

Tolmarak said nothing as he attended to Jayden's newest wound, and by the time he finished working his arts, the blood had stopped flowing. Jayden knew from experience that he would leave the fine work to Archmage Trellis, who was far more talented in that area of the Gift than even the college leader.

"Come here you two," Tolmarak called, and without preamble both Missy and Firerose knelt beside the two men to hear what he had to say.

"Your two suspects are dead, Missy. What about Tyrone?"

For a moment he didn't think she was going to answer, but after swallowing hard, she did.

"He's in worse shape than his room," she answered, motioning at the shredded corridor in front of them, and the magi's quarters which it had once contained.

"As expected," Tolmarak replied. "And no better than he deserves for helping that murderer against his own people."

Jayden was a little taken aback by the archmage's statement. Until now, the old man had stressed that they needed to capture the assassin. Tolmarak clearly wanted to extract his arcane knowledge before he met his fate at the hands of the king's executioner. The fury in the archmage's voice left little doubt of his sincerity about Tyrone's untimely demise, however. Tolmarak took a deep breath, pulling himself together before continuing.

"It appears obvious that he knew you were aware of who his agents in the college were, Missy. Having failed to kill you tonight, he could not let them live."

Missy looked at the floor for a long moment while the archmage spoke, before looking the old man in the eye.

"I'm sorry, Archmage. If I had come forward earlier we could have stopped this from happening."

Tolmarak gave her a sideways glance and sighed.

"Probably. But right now we have no time for recriminations. Heramiir's agent now feels confident enough to attack magi in the college building itself, in the open, as though nothing we can do will ever stop him. We have to find a way to track him, even without being able to sense his aura, and we have to do it right now, before this happens again."

"I'm sorry Archmage," Firerose apologised. "We have been working on the problem every spare moment, but so far we haven't come up with anything useful. The problem is that he kills most of his victims and leaves without anyone knowing he was even here until a body turns up. The way he cuts through our wards at will, it makes our best scrying techniques useless. Not to mention that having the ability to mask his aura means the only way we can track him is to catch him in the act. To attempt to overpower him like we tried to do tonight. We can't even follow him from the scene of an attack like the city watch might, since he can tell exactly where we are. The mageguard might have more luck with that task, but if he catches them at it, he can kill them at will."

"Jayden?" Tolmarak prompted when the young man failed to add anything to Clarion's report.

For a long moment, Jayden frowned as his eyes seemed to scan the floor beside him, deep in thought. Tolmarak was about to ask him again, but the young mage held up his good hand firmly, stopping his mentor from interrupting. For what seemed like a long time, they waited for him to speak. The glazed look in his eyes abruptly departed, and his head swivelled back up to meet Tolmarak's gaze.

"I think I know how to find him," Jayden told the archmage. "But you are *not* going to like how it's done."

The sound of running footsteps reached them from the end of the destroyed corridor an instant before Captain Ravenburg came sprinting around it from the great hall beyond. He slowed to a quick walk as he approached the group of magi, who were still gathered around Jayden's injured form.

"I'm sorry sir, we couldn't stop him from escaping back into the city," he told the archmage without preamble, though regret was clear in his voice.

"Casualties?"

Ravenburg sighed.

"Twenty-six of the mageguard sir, as well as magi Laurel and Bergstien who were unfortunately returning from the city at the time the assassin was making his escape. They fought bravely sir, but they were not battle trained, and no match for his skill and power in the Gift."

Tolmarak clenched his teeth for a second. It was the only outward sign he gave at his grief at losing two of their more junior magi this night. Not to mention over two dozen of the highly trained men who were sworn to protect them with their lives.

"Can you walk?" Tolmarak asked, changing his point of focus to the injured mage beside him.

"Yeah, I think so," Jayden grunted as he reached out and steadied himself on what was left of the wall with his good arm. He felt light-headed as he righted himself, but as Clarion ducked under his uninjured arm to support him, he managed to stay upright and Tolmarak nodded his approval.

"Send someone to find Archmage Trellis and have her come to my quarters as soon as she has attended to any life-threatening injuries."

Ravenburg nodded to one of his men, causing the soldier to salute and jog back in the direction they had come.

"In the meantime, I want your men to take a head count of every mage left alive in the college. Have them gather in the great hall in one hour. I will address them there."

"Yes sir," Ravenburg replied, and then took his men without delay on the task the archmage had assigned him.

"Come," Tolmarak told the others as soon as the mageguard soldiers were out of sight.

"We have much to discuss, but not until we can make sure it remains private."

It was a long, painful walk up the central stairway for Jayden, but the physical discomfort was nothing compared to having Clarion in such close proximity.

In the year he had been here, he had occasionally shaken one of his classmates' hands, or slapped one of the soldiers from Wyll's squad on the back at a particularly good joke. As she shifted against him, he suddenly realised this was the very first time he'd been in any sort of physical contact whatsoever with the girl who reminded him so much of Rhianna.

He jerked away, unbalancing himself enough to almost fall backwards down the stairs before she caught him again.

For a minute she looked at him, perplexed, then her expression softened to one of sad sympathy. He turned his head away, embarrassed that she'd realised what he'd done. He didn't want to see that from her.

"You still see her, don't you? When you look at me I mean," she asked quietly enough that neither Missy nor Tolmarak, who were now several steps ahead of them, could hear.

"Only when I'm not paying attention," he replied after a long moment. He owed her that much.

"It's just being this close to you. It… brings back things from my past that I've tried very hard to leave behind."

"Do you need additional assistance?" Tolmarak called back at them from above, having noticed that they were no longer following.

"If you would prefer one of the others..?" she offered, giving him a way out of the awkward situation.

Again Jayden looked at her. Even some of her mannerisms were like Rhianna's, but she wasn't her, and that was all there was to it.

"No. No, if you don't mind, I would rather it was you," he told her slowly, unwilling to look her in the eye.

"No Archmage. We'll be with you shortly," Firerose

called back, and Tolmarak nodded before resuming the long walk up to where his quarters lay near the top of the structure.

"Thank you," Clarion said as they began walking again, causing Jayden to look at her inquisitively.

"For not shutting me out," she told him with a small smile.

"I know you have been through some horrible things both before and since you've been at the college. But I truly believe we could be such good friends if you would just give me a chance," she finished with a wince. The words had clearly not come out the way she'd intended, and Jayden realised for the first time that this must be almost as awkward for her as it was for him.

"I am trying," Jayden conceded in a subdued tone as they continued on their way.

"But you have to understand, you look almost exactly like Rhianna in every way, even down to the length and style of your hair. It makes having any kind of bond with you... extremely difficult for me."

They continued in silence for another round of the stairwell before he spoke again.

"I do want us to be friends. But until I return to Grandell and make Dael pay for his crimes, and visit her grave..." He trailed off. "I don't think that I can."

"I understand," Clarion replied slowly. "But if it's all right with you, I will look forward to a day that you can."

For the first time since they had met, Jayden thought that might actually be true.

The rest of their long journey up to Tolmarak's quarters was a little less uncomfortable after that, at least mentally. When they crested the last stairs, it was to find Archmage

Trellis already waiting for them at the head of the corridor where Tolmarak's quarters lay. She ushered Jayden, with Firerose's help, inside, shaking her head when she saw the young mage had once again been injured at the hands of Heramiir's assassin.

"You need to stop getting holes poked in you, young man," she remarked as he sat in one of the chairs in the front office of the archmage's suite.

Jayden couldn't help a strained smile at the comment as Archmage Trellis used the Gift to slice off the little that remained of his left sleeve. Without disturbing the wound beneath, she examined Tolmarak's work while the archmage made sure that no one could listen in on their conversation through means either mundane or magical.

"Now that we can talk privately, Jayden, what was your idea?" Tolmarak asked as he set about making a calming pot of herbal tea for them all to drink while they talked.

Jayden glanced at Archmage Trellis and then back to Tolmarak, who smiled.

"I assure you, anything you need to tell me can also be heard by my sister."

"Your sister?" Missy blurted out, and then looked embarrassed when everyone looked at her at once.

"That's right," Archmage Trellis confirmed.

"We all have family somewhere, do we not? Tolmarak and I just happened to be lucky enough that the Gift sparked in both of us. We came here less than a year apart, a long, long time ago."

"I never thought to look," Firerose added with a wry grin. "But now that I know, I guess you can see the family resemblance after all."

"Which is quite beside the point at this moment,"

Tolmarak broke in, bringing the conversation back to where he wanted it to be.

"How do you propose to track the assassin, Jayden?"

For a moment the room went silent, the others expectant. Archmage Trellis swivelled her head to look at the young mage in glad surprise as she returned to working on his wound.

"It might or might not work," Jayden began hesitantly.

"And either way, I am absolutely certain you are going to hate it."

CHAPTER 21

THE BROKEN STRAW

"Do you really think this will work?" Clarion asked as Jayden finished laying the ward on yet another mage whom Tolmarak had briefly stunned.

A week of stress, mistrust, and sleepless nights had passed since the assassin had attacked the college openly. Time was running out before he would no doubt do so again.

"I hope so," Jayden replied as he studied the man laying sprawled across the floor of Tolmarak's office. "And yet I hope it won't. I mean, I know tracking him this way was my idea, but the more magi we ward like this… The more I can't shake the feeling that we're doing something very wrong."

"I understand," Tolmarak broke in. This was not the first time this question had been brought up over the last week.

"But we still do not know who or where Heramiir's man will attack next. Whether or not we do this, in all likelihood the assassin *will* strike again. At least this way, his next victim's death should be the last."

"I know, but still…"

"Enough," Tolmarak barked as Jayden finished working the Gift on the unconscious man before them.

"The idea might have been yours, but the decision was always mine. Do not forget I have known most of these people many years longer than any of you."

Jayden gave him a flat look.

They were all running on empty after several sleepless nights, but thankfully this time Jayden chose not to push him.

"Yes Archmage," the younger man replied at last, though clearly in spite of his own feelings on the matter.

The boy might still grow into a good man, Tolmarak thought. But he needed to stop taking on a personal responsibility for everything that happened around him. Not that responsibility was to be shunned, but neither were the sum total of the world's problems the boy's doing, or his to fix.

There was a fine line to be walked there. But for now the ward was in place. Tolmarak used another spell, this one of air, to float Kendrick over to the couch until he regained consciousness.

As with the others they'd done this to, it took only moments before his eyes flitted open, and he looked around in confusion.

"What happened?"

"You fainted," Tolmarak lied.

"Unfortunately, you hit your head on the floor when you went down. Here, let me heal that for you," he offered as he moved to the mage's side and deftly worked the Gift. He repaired the scratch, along with the mild swelling the blow had caused when he'd knocked the man unconscious a few minutes before.

"So, as I was saying, your efforts have been well worthwhile, and I thank you for them. One last thing. It is paramount that no one learns you have come to see me."

Kendrick frowned as if he suspected something was amiss. When Tolmarak stood and dismissed him though, the far junior mage had little recourse but to stand and leave after thanking the archmage for his kind words.

They had done it in this manner for each of the magi they had warded so far. The fewer people who knew about the wardings, the less chance there was of the assassin discovering them. Or more importantly, hearing about them from one of his spies before the trap was sprung.

Thanks to Missy they now knew the assassin had some of their own people working for him, and Tolmarak suspected the three the assassin had killed were not the only ones. If any more were proven, they would be punished in due time, but for now they might still serve a purpose if Jayden's plan didn't bear fruit.

It was the middle of the night, and a gale was blowing outside. Loud enough to be heard even this far into the college building, the intermittent crashes of nearby thunder that shook the structure itself did nothing to ease their nerves.

It had been many years since Aramar had seen a storm like this. The last one had seen half of the city flooded, and the great marketplace swept completely away. That had been over thirty years ago, and at the time they had all thought it a freak event that would never again happen in their lifetimes. Tolmarak didn't like being wrong, but the city sewers had filled past capacity hours ago, forcing the driving rain to run freely down the cobbled streets like rivers. The college courtyard itself was already under more than a few inches of water. What was worse, the unrelenting sheets of ice-cold rain coming down outside showed no sign of letting up any time soon.

The three of them had been conducting these meetings with the magi at night for two reasons. First, because it was easier to keep them secret when most of the magi were asleep. But also because the wards were from the spirit school of the Gift, and were easier to manipulate at night. The magi themselves were unaware they were being tagged by the wards, but that was also necessary. A good many of them would not be pleased if they found out what those wards were to be used for.

Tolmarak sighed as he thought again on what they were doing. The others would have the right to be displeased.

After all, for Jayden's plan to work, one of them would have to die.

Not to mention the spell they were using was new, and therefore unauthorised, which made the entire exercise illegal from the outset. Yet what choice did they have?

The irony was not lost on him. To defeat Heramiir's assassin he was being forced to break the same law that Heramiir claimed his entire rebellion was aimed at voiding. Giving them the freedom to explore their abilities and create spells just such as this.

Tolmarak could almost agree with his logic. Heramiir's methods were reprehensible, and only a fool would believe that 'the greater good' was the true reason for everything he had put the nation through over the last year, but still…

"How many more are there?" Firerose asked as Jayden stood and stretched.

Tolmarak walked a few steps and opened the drawer of his desk. He consulted the list, making a mark next to Kendrick's name as he did so.

"We have finished with the archmagi and there are nine more magi to ward before we start on the apprentices, of whom there are currently forty-nine."

Jayden did the math and sighed. They had only been getting through about six magi per night due to the need for secrecy and some amount of sleep.

"Another ten nights of this and I'll be ready to drop," he complained.

Tolmarak smiled slightly and nodded.

"I don't think we'll have to wait that long before the assassin strikes again," he said. "And so far he has targeted the most powerful magi he could get to, except for that one time."

They all fell silent for a moment as they contemplated the attack on the apprentice's quarters just a few weeks gone. It had demoralised the entire college when they'd learned of it. But it had also focused them as never before on finding a way to end these attacks once and for all.

Jayden had promised Missy, and himself, that he would not leave Aramar until his friends were out of danger, but as the weeks dragged on with no hint of resolution, that promise was becoming all but impossible to keep. If this last gambit failed…

He had told no one, but he had moved some of his essential belongings into a pack and hidden them under the hay in the back corner of Strider's stall.

He didn't think Tolmarak would try keeping him here by force, he was a student, not a prisoner, but he wasn't taking any chances either. This way he could leave on the instant if he ever had the need, hopefully before the archmage knew he had done so.

"That's why you wanted to start with the archmagi, because you thought they were more at risk?" Firerose asked.

Tolmarak nodded.

"Not so much because of the title, but because only the most powerful of us ever attain that rank," he clarified, "But yes, for that reason I felt they were the most at risk. That is also why we three were the first to have the wards put on us. If the assassin somehow learns that we have a viable plan to discover him, we would immediately become his next targets. Let us just hope this works."

In theory, Jayden's idea had been simple. To design a new spell of which the assassin had no knowledge, and place it within the bodies of the magi themselves.

Implementing that plan, however, had presented far more difficulty. The new scrying spell they had come up with was supposed to remain inert until activated. He hoped it would avoid the assassin's notice until it was too late. Once the assassin struck, and the magi's body bearing it could no longer function, it would transfer itself to the closest person. The ward would then act as a beacon for any nearby mage to find, announcing their guilt. That was assuming everything worked as it should. Of course, there had been no way to test it. Once transferred to the killer, the ward was designed to insinuate itself into every part of its host's body. In theory the only way for the assassin to rid himself of it would be to cancel out every magical effect at work on himself. Again, in theory, that act should make his aura visible to them all.

Either way they would be able to find him. The college had been working on a similar concept for decades before Erian had ordered them to stop. That lack of success suggested it would be no small matter for the assassin to re-establish the spell even if he figured out how to nullify the ward.

In all honesty their new ward was a useful piece of magic. Tolmarak intended to petition Erian to have it placed on every mage in the country once all this was over. It would mean that anyone who ever killed a mage would be identifiable to any Gift user from then on. Unless they could find someone to remove it of course, but that would require one of the magi knowing it was there in the first place.

After several minutes to allow Kendrick enough time to return to his rooms, Tolmarak once again consulted his list. The next name was a moderately powerful woman named Tarithra who had only been promoted from apprentice less than a phase before. He sent Jayden to bring her to his office.

*   *   *

It didn't take Jayden long to reach Tarithra's quarters. After several knocks and a long wait, a sleepy woman with dishevelled brown hair came to the door, grumpy at having been woken in the middle of the night.

"What do you want?" she asked, looking out along the corridor as if she suspected some kind of trap.

"Archmage Tolmarak wishes to see you," Jayden announced as though he were annoyed to be used as a messenger.

"Now?" she asked sleepily, eyebrows climbing a little at the unusual request.

"Yes, I'm to escort you there," he said again, this time a little less patiently.

If she always reacted this slowly at night, the assassin would make quick work of the newly raised Mage should he ever come after her.

"I'll be out in a moment," she agreed, clearly not

434

understanding why the archmage would summon her at this time of night.

Jayden nodded. She shut the door so she could change into something more appropriate than her nightgown, and Jayden looked around the corridor as he waited. He couldn't help but yawn as he listened to the muted crashing of thunder from outside. The storm was exceptionally strong, and it set his teeth on edge. In all his life he'd only seen one other like it. The one on the night Rhianna had died. Though the way this storm was shaping up, it might even be more violent than the one which had lashed Grandell, if that were even possible.

There was a crash of thunder even louder than all the others, and the building itself vibrated at the impact. It wasn't till a moment later that an icy finger of realisation drew its way down Jayden's spine as he felt an aura wink out, and an extra presence appear several floors above.

That last crash had not been thunder, and his warding had worked.

For a second, the beacon moved away, then plummeted past where he was, and this time Jayden knew what the assassin was up to. Dropping his shoulder, Jayden charged at Tarithra's door and burst through it, causing the half-changed woman to squeal at the sudden intrusion.

Ignoring her, Jayden punched out the glass window of the room with the Gift and leapt through it as he continued his charge into the rain-soaked night. He was closer to the ground than he'd anticipated though, and immediately had to slow his fall. He landed with a great splash in the foot-and-a-half of water that was now immersing the entire courtyard. The darkness, and sheer amount of rain in the air, conspired to restrict his field of vision to twenty spans around him. Of what he could see, the surrounding grounds resembled nothing so much as an eerily shallow lake, black as the night, and tossed by the pounding of the rain. His eyes were useless in this chaos, but the beacon guided him in the right direction.

He had to move fast. If the assassin nullified their ward before he caught up, the man would slip through their fingers yet again. Whichever mage had just died tonight to give them this chance at ending the murderer's reign of terror would have been sacrificed in vain, and that was unacceptable. Every mage in the college would be after that beacon as soon as Tolmarak could rally them, Jayden was sure of that. For now he was alone though, and it was time to hunt.

A sky alive with lightning provided the only illumination. Constant strikes from the inky clouds above cast an intermittent glow as the thunderous rain and wind created troughs and eddies in the already flooded college grounds. As he began to run, Jayden recommitted himself to the task, the assassin's terrorising of the Aramarian magi would end tonight, whatever that took.

As he ran towards the already receding beacon, the shin deep water became a constant irritation. Jayden used the Gift to put a shield up in front of him, sweeping the water aside as he went. The sheer constancy of the pressure pushing against it though tired him all too quickly, and before he was halfway across the courtyard, Jayden was forced to let it go. He'd need to focus once he caught up with the killer, and the constant mental drain of imagining the water dividing before him simply wasn't worth it. He switched to another spell, one he had used before when pursuing this man, and leaped above the water, covering twenty or thirty strides at a step. As he sped up, the rain seemed to intensify, but he could feel himself closing with the beacon. Not quickly, but the distance was shrinking. A flash of lightning, longer than most, gave Jayden a chance to see where he was. Putting that together with the feeling of the beacon in his mind, he imagined the assassin must be at the gates that led into Aramar by now. He had an odd sense of Déjà vu as he saw a red ball of fire sizzle through the night ahead of him. That could only mean the gate guards had tried to halt his progress. They were unsuccessful, and the beacon continued into the city without pause. The man had not even stopped running as he cut his way through their defences.

Who are you?

As Jayden bounded toward the gate, he could see the burnt forms of the guards lying in the deepening water. Reluctantly he chose not to stop and help them. There were many others coming behind him who could deal with these men, but only a handful who might be capable of stopping the assassin if they actually caught up. Jayden knew he was right near the top of that very short list.

Bounding through the gates without stopping, he got a clear look at the assassin as the brightest strike of lightning yet illuminated the street ahead of him. Tonight, the cobbled street more closely resembled a river that flowed between the buildings on either side, though for now at least it was still shallow enough to walk in. The assassin was little more than a hundred spans ahead of him, and as Jayden narrowed even that small gap, he felt the beacon slow and then stop.

He raised a shield in front of himself and slowed as well, walking purposefully towards his target, expecting the man to strike at any moment.

He should have been nervous, or wary, or even excited. As he approached the man who had murdered so many of his comrades over the last year though, all Jayden could bring himself to feel was calm. Tonight, one of them would triumph, the other would die. There could be no other resolution this time.

"Hello Jayden," a Gift enhanced voice called to him from beyond where his eyes could pierce the thundering rain and near total darkness of the night. He could feel the auras of the most powerful magi left in Aramar now at the extremities of his senses. In a moment the assassin would as well. This encounter would be brief.

"Who are you?" Jayden called back, enhancing his voice in the same manner as the assassin.

"My name is Korvith," the assassin called back, and Jayden frowned, not sure whether to believe the man.

"You are surprised I would tell you that?" the disembodied voice continued. "You should not be. Consider that you have now discovered a way of nullifying my advantage over you, therefore whether I escape you tonight or not, my assignment here is over."

"Heramiir sent you?" Jayden called out as he closed the distance until he could make out Korvith's distant form, if that really was the man's name, at the very limits of his vision.

The assassin still appeared only as a vague blur in the night until the lightning flashed again. The grey robed and hooded figure suddenly standing out in stark contrast to the illuminated water rushing past both of them as it tried to find its way to the Camar River below. The man had his hands clasped together, the only part of him showing from the cover of his sodden garments, and Jayden realised the assassin intended to make a stand. With the rest of the magi just minutes behind, this 'Korvith' had only this one chance to remove his most powerful pursuer before being overwhelmed. He was going to take it.

"Yes," the assassin replied, ending phases of discussion as to the man's true purpose. "You should have joined him when you had the chance Jayden. We would have gladly given you Dael, without regret, had you simply sided with your own kind instead of the ineffective king who currently sits the throne."

"Dael's life is mine to take. Not yours to give," Jayden answered with absolute authority, the calmness inside him turning to cold fury as he said it.

Thoughts of Dael were usually enough to make his blood boil, even now, and lose what little focus he had. But tonight, looking at this man who had caused so much suffering amongst their small community, it had the opposite effect. In many ways the assassin was like Dael, he suddenly realised. The man had a great deal of power, but he used it for his own ends instead of aiding the citizens he was supposed to be serving. He also seemed to enjoy the suffering he caused as a matter of course.

"I see," Korvith replied thoughtfully. "Then we come to it at last."

"Yes," Jayden's reply was simple. "We do."

For an instant neither of them moved, and then everything happened at once.

Diving to the ground, Jayden barely avoided being hit with a shower of frozen rain as a flurry of needle-sharp icicles passed overhead. With a motion, Jayden took hold of the shallow river's flow and held it back for a moment. He then reversed the spell with all his might, sending the entire flow crashing through the air. With no way to avoid the sudden wall of water which took up the entire width of the street, the assassin was knocked back several dozen feet. His shield protected him though, and as soon as he was able to, he stood. As he did, Jayden fired off a blast of flame that impacted off Korvith's shield and went careening up into the night, announcing their position for all who cared to see. The two magi didn't even notice as they both fired a bolt of raw Gift energy at each other in the same instant.

The spells collided in mid-air, the detonation blowing out walls on either side of the street. Jayden and Korvith were both knocked off their feet as the surrounding brickwork crumbled with great splashes into the street.

As the incessant rain re-asserted the faux river's flow, inundating the damaged homes, they both struggled to regain their footing. The assassin was faster, and before Jayden could fire off another spell, Korvith had used the Gift to jump up onto the rooftop adjacent, running towards the centre of Aramar as fast as he could.

"Not this time you don't!" Jayden muttered under his breath as he leapt after the man, the beacon once again his only path to follow.

There was no way to know how long it would be until Korvith figured out a means to nullify the tracking spell. He had to hurry. On a night like this, the assassin would need only seconds to disappear for good if he managed to re-mask his aura.

Jayden landed on the rooftop without slipping. He was able to make out the next building and propelled himself across the gap. More lightning flashed through the clouds, revealing the assassin in full flight across the rooftops of Aramar, already two buildings ahead.

Wasting no time, Jayden leapt after him, his feet pounding more steadily than they had any right to across the slippery, slanted tiles. Between each structure lay chasms where darkness and rain obscured the ground below, making it appear as though each alley and yard were a yawning gateway to the netherworld. The lightning played across the sky again and again as he ran. Each time, for just an instant, everything took on an eerie colourless contrast of normality before fading to darkness once more. All the while the drenching rain continued to pour down, obscuring what little vision he might otherwise have had.

Jayden didn't know whether the assassin had a prearranged escape route or whether he was simply trying to stay away from the other magi. At any rate, the others had once again fallen far enough behind that he could no longer sense their auras. His own was more powerful though, and as long as they could sense it, they would eventually catch up. For the first time, Jayden was glad to have his powerful aura, which could be sensed by both allies and foes, from much further away than normal due to his superior strength in the Gift.

A light appeared ahead, and Jayden barely had time to react as a glowing bolt of… something, flew at him. The assassin's aim was excellent, and Jayden only remained unscathed by wildly throwing himself out of its way. As he slid uncontrolled down the slanted roof, he hit his arm hard on a length of sharp guttering, cutting himself above the elbow.

He was forced to use the Gift to halt his descent, and once he'd regained his footing, the lightning showed that he was bleeding again. Something he was getting far too used to these days. It was hard to tell how bad it was this time, the constant rain cleaning the blood off as fast as it could well from his skin. Every drop stung as it hit. With a grimace, Jayden took a moment to heal the worst of it as well as he could. The result was less than ideal, and he tried to ignore the pain as he leapt to the next building, pushing the injury aside and continuing the chase. Korvith had taken advantage as expected, and the beacon was now fainter than before.

Despite his best efforts, Heramiir's assassin was in danger of slipping away yet again.

Jayden clenched his teeth and redoubled his efforts, driven on more by will than stamina at this point, and after several more buildings, felt the distance to the beacon decrease. Lightning flashed, and for an instant he could see his target. Jayden reflexively pounced on the opportunity, firing a bolt of raw energy at his target.

He missed, but not by much. The explosive bolt hit the roof the assassin was still standing on. Jayden watched in satisfaction as he saw the man thrown from the peak before the brilliant flash of lightning once again faded into black.

For a long moment the beacon stopped moving, and Jayden closed the distance rapidly. Korvith had survived the fall, the beacon still active just a few houses ahead. It began moving slowly away.

Jayden smiled grimly. The assassin wouldn't be that easily dealt with. More likely the man was laying a trap for him, trying to make Jayden think he was wounded, and have him rush in for the kill.

Jayden had no intention of being that careless. The assassin had proven himself far too deadly over the last several phases for Jayden to take shortcuts in dealing with him now that his target was finally in range.

He continued jumping rooftops until there was only one more building between where he stood, and where the assassin had fallen to the street.

Jayden jumped down to the yard of the next property with a splash. Korvith would know where he was, there was no getting around that, but the building was blocking the assassin's line of sight. Using it as cover, he splashed his way into the knee-deep rivulet that surrounded the structure, erecting a shield that would keep him safe from whatever the assassin had planned. It also kept the hammering rain off him for a few moments, for which he was grateful.

He stepped around the corner of the large brickwork house, keeping plenty of room between the corner and himself. One ambush via exploding wall had been enough, and no one was near enough to rescue him if it happened again.

A ball of flame flashed past the edge of the building. Curiously, it missed, continuing up into the storm where it was extinguished by the driving sleet.

Perhaps he had been wrong, a small corner of his mind tried to convince him as he continued to advance around the corner. Perhaps the assassin really had been wounded in his wild tumble from the rooftop. Jayden had fallen a far shorter distance and still cut his arm deeply. The sheer coldness of the rain was numbing the wound now. That was good. The saturated material of his sleeve rubbing against it was a painful distraction, one he didn't need right now.

Jayden took another careful step, and finally came into full view of his quarry.

Korvith was lying on the ground, trying to crawl away through at least six inches of rainwater which flowed down the street. His heavy, soaked cloak making him appear little more than a creeping, formless mass in the murky light.

Lightning once again flashed, and Jayden took the instant to study the assassin more closely. He was hurt, but as far as Jayden could see there was no evidence of blood or serious wounds on him, and that made him suspicious. This man had killed so many… Tolmarak wanted him taken alive, but Korvith was far too dangerous to be held long as he was. If the assassin somehow broke free, this entire cycle would start over again.

If what Korvith had said about being finished was a lie, Jayden doubted that his trick of warding the magi themselves would work on the devious man a second time.

Right now, there was no one else in the street besides the two of them that Jayden could see.

He could end it right here and now though. A flick of his wrist, a thought, and Korvith would never harm anyone again. It would mean facing the archmage's wrath, but that was a trivial thing if it meant being free to return to Grandell. To do what he should have taken care of a year and more ago.

He told himself that was not what he was basing his decision on, but in his heart even Jayden knew it was a lie.

He walked forward slowly, his Gift-wrought shield pushing the ankle-deep water ahead of him as he went. When he was little more than a dozen paces away, he stopped. Korvith continued to crawl through the rain. The man hadn't even invoked a protective shield as he pulled himself through the rushing water that covered all trace of the ground beneath. Still the rain hammered down.

Jayden raised his hand to strike, and felt Tolmarak's familiar aura at the limit of his senses. It didn't matter.

A bar of pure white light as bright as the lightning

striking all around them leapt from Jayden's fingers, and in the instant it did so, he realised his mistake. Korvith had never been injured. As he'd first suspected, the man had been biding his time until Jayden was close enough for his own plan to work.

The lightning lashed out from Jayden's fingers. In the instant before it struck, Korvith raised a completely flat shield between them. It not only stopped his spell outright, but reflected much of the energy back at Jayden himself.

The unexpected blow flung him back against the wall of the nearby building as though he were nothing more than a rag doll. His shield held, though it was considerably weakened by his own powerful strike. That blast had been more potent than anything the assassin could have hit him with, Jayden realised in chagrin. Even though Korvith's own shield had absorbed some of the impact.

It took Jayden a second to recover from the blast, which had been intended to finish the unprotected man once and for all. As his eyes readjusted from the sudden brilliance, he heard the assassin laugh while he stood.

"You are a force Jayden Torell, but you have so much still to learn, and no one can teach you as well as Heramiir. That is simple fact. He is the only mage in Jeranon who has your level of power. Tolmarak is a masterful teacher, but not even he has dreamed of the things that could be done with your raw talent. Join the new order Jayden. In time you would enjoy a prominent place in our councils, of that I am certain."

For a moment Jayden wondered how the assassin had learned his family name. It was another distraction he didn't need, and one more reason to deal with the man here and now.

Without answering, Jayden darted sideways, launching a

ball of flame as he moved. The spell hit Korvith's shield flat on once more, but this time the reflected energy sizzled by to his right as it returned. The fireball smashed into the house behind him, blowing a horse sized hole through the wall. The carpet inside briefly ignited before water from the street flooded into the gap, extinguishing the danger in moments.

Korvith nodded deliberately towards him in acceptance, then launched his own attack. Using the Gift, he drew water from the street up into two roughly bipedal monuments, each about twelve foot high and devoid of any distinguishing human features. Reaching into his cloak, the assassin took something from two of his pockets, and with a slight grin hurled one at each at the figures. As the objects entered the huge misshapen towers of water, they began moving on their own accord, and Jayden knew he was in for a fight. The towering columns of water advanced towards him, blocking his view of Korvith, though the mage didn't seem to be trying to flee.

He's waiting for an opportunity to strike while they distract me, Jayden thought as he backed away a few paces.

With frightening speed, both constructs sloshed towards him. Jayden ducked under one of the creatures' arms, which elongated into a tentacle and grabbed at him as he went past, clipping his shield instead.

He launched a fireball at the creature, the intense heat evaporating a hole right through its chest. With an oceanic roar, the thing syphoned more water up from the river at its feet and was whole again within moments.

The second of the creatures had not waited, battering at him tree-trunk thick arms, knocking him off his feet. His shield flared as Korvith launched a blast of power which shoved him halfway through the wall of the next building. His shield took the brunt of the impact, but not all of it, and Jayden was left dazed, shaking his head to clear it. He would have to end this soon. He could handle the assassin, but the two constructs working in concert with him might eventually overpower even his considerable strength. The question was how?

Korvith made to strike again, and Jayden dove out of harm's way as the building crumbled behind him. He hoped there had been no one inside, but didn't have time to stop and check. He launched a blast of flame at Korvith as he rose, not enough to damage the man, but enough to blind him for a moment while he regained his feet. It worked well enough, but the two elemental constructs were still advancing through the shallow street-river, their posture more aggressive than ever. It gave Jayden an idea.

With as much force as he could muster, he used a spell of water to cool the creatures as quickly as he could. For a moment it seemed to work as the creatures slowed and began to freeze. Catching on to what was happening, they began taking up more water from the river, sloughing off the sheets of ice that were forming all around them. With a grimace, Jayden exerted himself and put a low shield in front and on top of the creatures. With difficulty, he held back the driving rain and the river, which was now noticeably higher than when he'd arrived only minutes before.

With great effort he continued to freeze the creatures and maintain his own shield. He couldn't keep up this level of concentration for long. Seeing him stretched to his limit, Korvith hit him with a white-hot bar of flame that almost knocked him off his feet once again. The attack was strong, and draining his shield rapidly, but Jayden gritted his teeth and held on to all three spells. The moment Korvith's attack pierced his shield, it would be over. Until then, Jayden focused all his concentration on the elementals, for critical moments denying them their supply of fresh water. With their reserves cut off, it took only moments for the beings to become glossy and slow once more. Their movement finally halted altogether as they froze solid, despite Korvith's best efforts to break through Jayden's shield.

With a blast of raw power at each, Jayden shattered the creatures into a thousand tiny shards. A well-placed spell of air jerked the two arcane objects towards himself, and he snagged them out of the air as though someone had tossed him a ball. He carefully placed each in a separate pocket within his cloak, just as Korvith had kept them. He had no idea what they were, or how they worked, and he wasn't about to take the chance of carrying them together.

Shattering the constructs while keeping his other spells intact had taken several exhausting seconds, and it was only now that Korvith's flame attack faltered. He stared dumbfounded at Jayden, who turned to regard the assassin, the man who had brutally murdered so many of his comrades over the last year.

"Your turn," was all Jayden said, and Korvith fled before the words had fully left his mouth.

Without a thought, Jayden pursued him up onto the roof and across an alley before a familiar aura appeared in front of him, and then another, and another off to the side. Jayden smiled. Their brief engagement had given Tolmarak time enough to send some magi around beyond the limits of their auras to surround the assassin before he could react.

This is it, Jayden realised with absolute certainty. One way or another, this game of cat and mouse would end tonight, once and for all.

Korvith fired a spell at him, and Jayden took it on his shield without slowing down. He fired back a blast of air which only partially hit its target. Korvith was knocked from his current rooftop, but still hit the street running even with the foot deep water rushing towards the Camar River at the bottom of Aramar's gradual slope. The rain had not slackened at all, and lightning cleaved the sky at a frightening rate. Jayden leapt down and continued chasing Korvith through the streets while the auras of other magi closed in on every side. The assassin ducked out of sight around a corner, though the beacon still shone brightly to his Gift attuned senses. Jayden wondered what the assassin was up to as Korvith came to a complete halt. There were magi all around now, some powerful, others less so, and Jayden realised Tolmarak must have turned out the entire college for this hunt. The closest of the auras were little more than a hundred spans away, though there was still no visible trace of them through the violent summer storm. He would have to act quickly if he were to finish Korvith before they arrived. The beacon winked out.

"No!" Jayden roared as he sprinted towards the corner where the assassin must still be hidden. There was a strange thrumming in his senses, and an aura just less bright than Tolmarak's burned into existence a few spans from where the beacon had disappeared.

Korvith wasted no time, and Jayden saw him leap onto yet another rooftop as he rounded the corner himself. He followed as quickly as he could, knowing that if the assassin could re-establish his masking spell, they would lose this chance forever. There were two magi that Jayden could sense just ahead, and the assassin leapt into their midst. There was a flash from behind the next building, and then the three auras moved off in separate directions, each running as fast as they could. Jayden growled as he reached the street himself. One aura was weaker than the assassin, but the other was so close as to be indistinguishable in power. Both magi had already disappeared into the rain, and Jayden had no option but to choose one of the auras and follow. He chose the one heading towards the city centre as that seemed to be Korvith's goal so far, and ran. The foot deep water hindered his progress until he began leaping through it, doing his best to catch up to the aura he was pursuing. It took him nearly a minute, so fast was his quarry moving. As Jayden finally got a clear line of sight, a silver-lined black cloak was revealed, not a heavy grey robe that was the assassin's normal garb.

"Halt!" Jayden called, using the Gift to enhance his voice far beyond its usual level. He would never have been heard otherwise over the continued barrage of the storm.

The figure did as he commanded, and as it turned, Jayden saw he was chasing a woman.

Kicking himself, he turned and sped back the other way, the other mage hesitating a moment and then following behind. She must have thought he'd been the assassin. It made sense, she and her companion had been attacked, and he had then chased her. Whatever the reason, he could now feel the real assassin's aura, and it was heading straight towards one that was both familiar and disturbing. He ran like he had never run before, leaping further into the air with the Gift, and using a second spell of air to propel himself forward with every stride. It wasn't enough. The two auras converged, and Nadeara would have no chance at taking

Korvith in single combat. He had survived their encounters through his sheer strength, Missy through her remarkable aptitude for shields. Nadeara had no such special talents. She was simply stronger than most magi, though not as strong as Korvith from the feel of their auras, and with none of his experience.

The others were heading in a different direction now, possibly confused as to which aura to follow, as he had been. They would see the Gift being employed soon enough and realise their mistake. He had closed a little over half the distance when the first flash crossed the street somewhere ahead. Jayden snarled. His mistake a moment before was going to cost Nadeara her life if he didn't get there soon. He owed her better than that. She had saved him that first time he had fought with Korvith, arriving just in time to avert a killing blow, and he would not do less for her now.

The ground shook as a building on the intersection crumbled, and still the spells flew. Nadeara was backing away from the intersection even as she desperately tried to keep up her attack. He could feel their auras moving away. Korvith entered the intersection a moment later, approaching his target at a dead run.

With all his power Jayden tried to take control of the surrounding storm, and failed. There was too much of it to concentrate on. Instead he created a single spell, a wide, flat thing that froze the raindrops as they passed though, and pushed it ahead of himself. With a second spell of air, one as powerful as he could envision, he propelled the tiny, pointed projectiles at Korvith in a never-ending stream that temporarily blasted the street clear of the ever-flowing river submerging it.

The spell hit the assassin, and Korvith was knocked sideways by the unexpected attack. Jayden continued his reckless advance as he kept up the violent assault.

Free for an instant of the punishment her attacker was directing at her, Nadeara added a bolt of raw power to the assault, and finally, after many phases of grief and terror at this man's hands, Korvith's shield was overwhelmed by their combined attack.

Jayden propelled himself into the intersection, moving many times faster than the most elite runner. Forsaking the Gift, he swung his fist at Korvith with all the frustration of not being able to stop the man's murdering spree over the whole of the last year.

There was an unmistakable crack from the man's jaw, and Jayden was three bounds past before he could come to a full stop. Korvith splashed down into the rivulet with a thud, his face just inches above water level as he splashed and tumbled to a halt.

Time to end this, Jayden thought as he returned to Korvith's prone form. *Maker knows this man deserves it.*

Jayden flexed his aching knuckles to ensure they weren't broken.

From the corner of his eye, he saw Nadeara bearing down on the two of them. With her arrival, it was now too late for him to end Korvith's life and claim self-defence. He became strangely aware of the freezing rain against his skin, but the cold no longer bothered him as he knelt next to the assassin, who was still struggling to rise. Without even reaching for the Gift, Jayden roughly pushed him down, his right hand remaining on the wounded man's chest to keep him there as he looked into the assassin's eyes.

"You deserve to die," he told the man coldly, leaning over

so he could make himself heard without amplifying his voice through arcane means.

Jayden could feel the auras of other magi closing rapidly on their position. He would have to make his choice soon. He knew Tolmarak's orders regarding this man, but he also knew they were wrong.

"What are you doing Jayden?" Nadeara asked, catching sight of his snarling visage through rain that continued to lash them with unabated force.

Jayden ignored her. Right now there was nothing in the world for him except the man he held pinned on the street, and his decision as to whether the assassin would ever leave this place alive.

Korvith seemed to fully understand his predicament at last, and Jayden saw his eyes grow panicked.

"If you kill me… you will have nowhere else to go… than Heramiir," the assassin gasped through a badly broken jaw.

"So you see… killing me serves no purpose. Join with me now. They could not stop us both… from leaving here," Korvith burbled, having difficulty keeping his mouth clear of water as he spoke what he had to know might be his dying words.

For a long moment Jayden looked at him, knowing the man was probably right. He had no intention of switching sides in the coming war, yet there was something the assassin had said to him, something for which he still needed an answer.

"Heramiir really would have let me kill Dael without reprisal, wouldn't he?"

"Yes. Because it is… justified," Korvith replied slurringly, forcing Jayden to lean even further over so that he could hear the assassin over the ever-present rain and thunder.

"You see. Heramiir considers the spirit of the law… to be of far more importance than its letter. Dael's actions ended that girl's life. Whether she was pushed… or jumped herself… as a direct result of his actions means nothing."

Jayden felt as if someone had clubbed him over the head. A cold, numbing sensation worked its way down his body as he recalled another storm swept night back in Grandell where he had been helpless to put an end to another tyrant's reign.

"How do you know what happened?" Jayden demanded of the man. His brittle, forced composure broke into shards as the old fury rose in him stronger than it ever had. Save perhaps that first moment on awakening in Tolmarak's tent back in Grandell's main square.

For this murderer, of all people, to be lecturing him on morality… It was more than he could process.

The assassin tried to smile, but stopped instantly as his jaw screamed in pain. The man was in agony, and responding to Jayden's questions only because his very life hung in the balance.

"You are the most powerful mage in Aramar Jayden. I made it my business… to know if you could be convinced… to join Heramiir. And how that might be achieved. Join Heramiir. Dael will suffer for his crimes… at your hands alone."

Jayden just looked at Korvith for a long moment as his prone form was illuminated by yet another blinding strike of lightning. Every word the assassin had spoken was true, and it was what he had been telling Tolmarak all along. Dael had committed murder, even if he hadn't physically pushed Rhianna off that cliff.

Yet the man in front of him had killed dozens.

And with his life in the balance, Korvith's final strategy was to attempt turning him by absolving Jayden of yet another murder. One he had resigned himself to committing a long time ago.

Jayden took a deep breath, blinking several times as he finally understood. Whether he became an outlaw tonight, or a few phases from now when he reached Grandell was irrelevant. The remaining magi weren't powerful enough to stop him leaving without a major battle, one he didn't believe Tolmarak would commit them to because of their already diminished numbers. With that inevitable realisation, Jayden felt something inside himself snap. There was no longer any reason to hold back.

"You're right Korvith," he whispered into the man's ear, needing to pull the assassin's head out of the water to do so.

"I will kill Dael. You were also right in that he has committed murder and deserves to die for it. But so have you. Twenty-six magi lie dead at your feet. How much more do you deserve your fate than he does?"

Jayden let the man's head drop back into the water with a thud, and Korvith struggled to rise, knowing his last gambit had failed.

Jayden ignored the man's struggles and called up the Gift, shielding his hand before sending a steady stream of heat through it and into the doomed man below.

"Jayden, stop!" Nadeara shouted from somewhere behind him.

He noticed the sound of footsteps pounding through the rain towards him and felt a surprising resistance on his spell. With a scowl, he cut off the interference by extending the shield until it covered not only himself, but Korvith as well, and continued what he had to do. Dael was nothing compared to this monster he now understood, and the Count of Grandell would die at his hands soon enough. This killer of children deserved far worse. So for Archmage Kelta, for Siara, for Maynar, and especially for the young apprentices this monster had slaughtered on that one terrible night, he stared directly into the assassin's eyes, and continued.

He let the heat intensify as the man's clothes began to steam, drying despite their sodden state. He was forced to raise a second shield between them as Korvith tried to launch a desperate counterattack. The man was too injured and distracted by pain and panic though, and Jayden's defences held fast.

A ball of flame hit his outer shield.

It was nowhere near powerful enough to break through his barrier, and the steam on the assassin's clothes began turning to smoke.

His course was set now, and Jayden refused to allow his focus to be split as Korvith's struggles became desperate. He was no longer fighting back, just simply trying to stem the flames that were igniting on his outer garments. Jayden looked at the man below him as Korvith met his eyes with one last pleading look.

Despite everything, Jayden found himself taking no delight in what he was doing. For phases now, he had wanted this man to suffer, to truly understand why he was being punished. Now that the moment was upon him though, he saw the truth in Korvith's desperate expression. As soon as the man began to burn, he would lose all semblance of coherent thought. It made an agonising death pointless. A cold fury at his inability to ever truly balance the scales to his satisfaction settled over Jayden, and he let the spell go for a moment. He leant even closer, looking the terrified mage right in the eye.

"You should never have come here."

With a massive burst of the Gift, he sent the strongest spell of fire he could manage through his hand and into Korvith's body.

Heramiir's assassin didn't even have time to scream as his flesh convulsed and burst into flame, consuming itself into black and charred remains in less than a second.

Jayden just knelt there for a long moment. A keen sense of unreality took him as he lowered the shields to rid himself of the stench of Korvith's charred flesh. Without the shield's protection, the beating of the rain on the artificial river around him, and the deafening crack of thunder intruded on his world.

So. I am a murderer too, he thought dispassionately. The rain coursed down around him as he knelt next to what remained of Korvith's charred corpse, which hissed and spat as the freezing rain cooled the burnt and broken form.

With a sneer of disgust at himself, Jayden realised he felt no remorse at all as he studied the man he had just executed. A man whom he had already beaten and had at his mercy.

He became aware, in a dim way, that almost all the other magi had arrived, and that they were all looking at him now. Tolmarak, Nadeara, Missy, Billy, and Clarion most of all, staring at him with dismayed gazes that should have been reserved for a stranger found in their homes, one who might at any moment explode into violence. Only this was no ordinary group of villagers standing before him, and the shocked look in their eyes had little to do with fear.

At best those looks could be called wary, and Jayden knew he had just alienated the only group of people in this part of the world he could really call friends. Worse yet, with all of them standing witness to his crime, he had thrown himself out of the College of the Arts for good. He would never be able to learn the skills of the spellcasters who resided there again.

I deserve it. I murdered a beaten man.

With only the slightest flicker of what might have been shame, he realised that he fully intended to do so again. Soon.

Jayden stood, squaring his shoulders. With a look of purest hatred in his eyes, though whether it was for the man he now thought of, or for what he had become, he could no longer tell as the torrential rains continued to pour down around him. Icy cold and completely unfelt.

"Dael," Jayden whispered, and as the cold light grew to a blaze in his eyes, his quiet tone slid between the thundering drops of rain. A far more menacing promise than the loudest raging of the storm.

He was a murderer now, and as soon as he had made that final strike that ended Korvith's life he had declared himself renegade. The college held nothing for him now, and as he stood there, clenching and unclenching his fists in turn, he felt the last piece of the restraint he had worked so hard to achieve over the last year fragment and be carried away with the icy flow of the storm.

As his eyes washed over the others one last time, the magi before him all averted their gaze, or stepped back from the intensity of his. All except Tolmarak, the weathered old archmage returning his frenzied glare with a sad one of his own.

A chill ran down Jayden's spine as he met his mentor's eyes.

One thing remained undone. As the king had once told Jayden the archmage's duty demanded, Tolmarak would have no choice but to hunt him down and execute him like a rabid dog if he couldn't find it in his heart to be loyal. To obey the laws of the kingdom.

So be it, he grimly accepted.

Turning away a moment later, he hoped that for their sakes neither Tolmarak nor any of the others tried to stop him right now. He no longer trusted himself not to strike out at them if they did.

As he began to take a first step, Tolmarak called out, though only a few paces separated the two of them.

"If you do this, there must be a reckoning."

As if on cue, the bell at the centre of Aramar began to toll, and for those few small moments the entire world seemed to hold its breath as the twelve pure notes rose sonorously above the storm.

"You know… I must follow… Wherever you run!" Tolmarak called between peelings of bell and thunder.

He had been wrong a moment before, Jayden decided as he looked back and met the archmage's gaze one last time. It was far more than a measure of distance that separated the two of them now.

"Then come…" he snarled softly through the rain.

Without another word Jayden turned his back, walking slowly away from the only people he might still have called friends in this part of the world. And with hate in his eyes and a coldness in his heart, he strode away into darkness, and the midnight summer rain.

CHAPTER 22

SKIRMISHES AND BITTER SURPRISES

"Flank them. Flank them!" Scout Captain Karloff bellowed at his men.

An enemy soldier rushed at his position, and Karloff hammered him in the head with the wrought-iron butt of his crossbow. The soldier went down in a heap, insensate and out of the fight. He dropped the heavy, ranged weapon and drew his blade. The enemy was pressing them hard, but if his men could keep them distracted long enough for the reserves to set up a crossfire, they might yet prevail.

A horse thundered up behind him, the rider falling limp from his saddle as a crossbow bolt appeared in his side. Karloff ducked around the still charging horse and sought another opponent. That was all too easy as the foe outnumbered them at least two to one. A quarter of his men had withdrawn to set up the crossfire, while still others were doing their best to cover the men already engaged in the hand-to-hand fighting.

A soldier in front of him charged, and Karloff met him squarely. His blade met the other man's high, and he followed it up with a low sweep which took the man's leg off at the knee. There was a scream of pain as the soldier toppled.

Karloff moved on.

To his right, a pair of assailants were overwhelming one of his men and he turned, breaking into a sprint as he tried to reach the group in time. He charged the closest one as hard as he could, leading with his sword. The bold move distracted the second enemy soldier enough that Karloff's man was able to finish him with a deft blow. As soon as the momentum from his charge was spent, he sprung to his feet, taking a second to glance around at the field. They might be outnumbered, Karloff thought, but his own men's discipline far exceeded that of the unit they were fighting.

If they could just hold out for another minute, his men would be in position.

The sun beat down mercilessly now that dawn of summer had arrived. The day hot enough that despite the lack of anything heavier than light leather armour to confine them, his men were tiring more quickly than he would have liked.

"Come on!" he shouted at the young man he'd just helped. Tyler, the man's name was, then took off, racing to intercept an enemy soldier who was also attempting to aid one of his own. This time Karloff couldn't get there in time though, and he let out a guttural growl as his soldier was run through right in front of him. He swung his blade in a huge arc designed to brook no resistance as he met the soldier who had just killed his man. Tyler moved into position from behind, shielding him from the other enemy who was rushing in to help. Karloff's sweep knocked the other man's weapon clear out of his hand, and he ran him through without a second thought before turning to help Tyler with his opponent. There was no need though, and the two men nodded at each other before moving off in different directions to assist yet more of their beleaguered comrades.

There was a twang from somewhere, followed by a thud. The man Karloff had marked out as his next target was thrown back off his feet as a bolt struck him in the chest. Another man fell, and yet another, and the area in front of him was abruptly clear. He turned to find more targets, and was just in time to see a dozen more of the enemy felled by his own unit's fire. There was a brief pause, as his men reloaded the deadly but slow to fire weapons, and into it he shouted for no quarter to be given.

The unit they were fighting was no doubt one of their counterparts, a scouting party sent by Heramiir to assess the size and disposition of the king's army.

It had taken yet another long phase of marching to reach this location since the young mageguard officer Wyll had returned with his warning. But finally the army had almost reached the fjords below Lake Pristine.

Karloff's unit, along with several others, had been dispatched to scout the area ahead and report back with details on Heramiir's force. So far this was the first they had encountered of it, and the captain was not sure what to make of what he was seeing.

If this was a scouting unit, then it was poorly trained and outfitted, not to mention far larger than he would have expected. What that meant, he would let the general decide. Right now, he had more pressing concerns.

Something hit him hard in the head, and Karloff found himself on the ground, stunned by the impact as a rock fell to the earth beside him. The soldier who had flung it was running at him, and as Karloff struggled to get to his feet, a wave of dizziness caused him to fall back to the ground. The grinning man was bearing down on him with frightening speed. As the soldier raised his sword for the strike, he was abruptly shoved sideways as three steel bolts heaved him off his feet, killing him outright. The man's sword fell at Karloff's feet, and he picked it up. It was a good blade Karloff noted, and he knew how to fight with two.

Once more he attempted to stand, this time with more success. When he regained his feet, it was to the singing of bowstrings as his reserves felled almost every other enemy not in direct combat with his troops.

"First squad, close combat!" he called. With a raucous shout, a dozen of his men ran out from their slight cover and drew blades to help their hard-pressed friends who were still outnumbered.

"Second squad, remain on overwatch, if they run, finish them!" he called to the men who had set up the second half of the crossfire so effectively only moments before.

That done, he ran as best he could with his head throbbing and a trickle of blood running down next to his eye, towards his nearest man still in danger.

His old sergeant, Markus, was holding off three opponents at once, and although giving ground, he seemed to be handling the situation.

The seasoned veteran was fast as a viper, and with a well-timed flick of his wrist he had only two opponents. One of the others took a sideways glance at his fallen comrade, and in a blink Markus had run him through as well.

Left to face the sergeant alone, the last enemy soldier tried to run. Markus let him, turning to find a new fight as soon as the other soldier was out of striking distance. There was a twang and a thud, but Markus didn't look back at the dead man who was now sporting a metal bolt through his chest.

"Shall we?" Karloff asked when he'd finally reached the blood-spattered sergeant. Markus shrugged as if to say he had nothing better to do. The two men trotted toward where the final knot of enemy soldiers were converging to make a last stand against his men. Karloff grinned. This would be over soon enough.

"Pen them in!" he shouted to his men, and within a minute the last twenty survivors of the enemy force were a solid knot inside a ring of his own men. The fighting was fierce for several moments as the opposing soldiers seemed to sense the end was near. When Karloff judged it had been long enough, he gave the order.

"Break for fire!" he yelled at the top of his lungs. His well-trained men disengaged instantly, going to their knees in a defensive stance as if this were just another drill in the practice yards. A second later the air was filled with the hum of bowstrings as metal bolts from his reserve unit's crossbows were loosed into the tight knot of remaining troops.

"Charge!" Karloff shouted as soon as the bowstrings went quiet.

The few remaining enemy still standing were no match for his men, who ran at them from every side. In moments it was done. The ringing of steel on steel faded into the quiet of the day as his men stood panting, catching their breath after the pitched battle. Those with wounds took the chance to rest on the dry grass of a hillside now littered with blood and riven flesh.

The smell of fear and bodily fluids was appalling now that there was nothing to take the focus off it, and Karloff wrinkled his nose. This had been a close thing. If the fool of an enemy commander had waited to ambush them for another minute, he might very well have succeeded. As it was, Karloff counted over a dozen of his men slain, and perhaps double that number wounded. Examining his remaining men, it seemed at first glance that most of those who had fallen were newer to his command. Many of them fresh recruits he'd been given responsibility for after defending Wyll's squad against their pursuers last phase.

He shouldn't feel any satisfaction at that, and yet his original core of men had been with him for a long time. It was hard not to feel closer to them than the others.

"Gather up the wounded," he ordered Tyler when his eyes found the competent young man unharmed.

Tyler had only been with Karloff's command for a year, but he'd already distinguished himself as one who would rise through the ranks on the back of his own merit, without the need for noble ties or money.

"Markus, see if we have any prisoners."

He received a nod in reply as the man moved off, not even breathing hard.

Karloff grunted in envy. He was only now bringing his own breathing under control as he continued to survey the field around him. To the east, a small forest perched on the gently sloping hillside before him, not more than a hundred spans away at most. That was where the enemy soldiers had struck from. Thankfully there was no chance of Heramiir's main force being ensconced within, as the whole clump of trees only covered perhaps one square mile.

The target of his search was not to the north, his own unit had just come from that direction. To the west, open plains lay until the Mirallyn River cut a perfectly straight line through the land halfway to the horizon. It was almost as though its course had been made by human hands, not formed over thousands of years by weather and erosion. If Heramiir's army lay in that direction, there would be dust and smoke visible from miles away, but no such signs existed. It was possible his target lay to the east, having already crossed at the fjords. That was unlikely though as the enemy unit they had just fought would have been rear guard, not a scout unit. It almost certainly would have included cavalry who could quickly warn the main force if Heramiir's army was already in front of them.

No, Heramiir's main force would still be south, at least a day's more march if his men didn't have to stop and fight again before they arrived. And if the enemy had not yet completed their crossing at the fjords.

If Karloff were in command of that army, he would have waited until they were ready to cross before sending out his scouting parties and probing beyond the river. That way if they reported it was clear he could move his men without delay. An army of the size General Messand expected would take hours to cross, and reducing that window of vulnerability would be critical.

Whether Archmage Nereth held to that was anybody's guess, but this unit had been a full day's ride from the fjords. It meant that either they were just about ready to cross, or had already begun. Either way he had to report what he'd found.

"Rider!" he called out to one of the three mounted men attached to his unit for this mission. Men who had explicit orders to stay out of any fighting.

"Your map, Sergeant," Karloff instructed without preamble. The man dug in his coat pocket for a second before pulling out an oilskin covered parchment. He unwrapped the material and handed the detailed map to Karloff with a fine charcoal pencil whose marks could be erased either once the mission was over, or in case of imminent capture.

Karloff studied the map for a minute before looking around at the landmarks to confirm their position. He made a small mark at the spot where they had encountered the first signs of the enemy, then handed it back to the sergeant. The officer re-wrapped the map and tucked it back into a large weatherproof pocket inside his coat.

"Take that to General Messand and report what you've seen here. Also tell him I believe Heramiir's army to be approaching or crossing the fjords at this time. We are continuing on to gather more information and leaving our wounded and prisoners in that copse of trees."

"Aye sir," the rider replied with a crisp salute. Karloff returned the gesture, then the man turned his horse and rode north as quickly as his mount could manage.

That done, Karloff looked around for Tyler. He spotted the young man helping a soldier sporting a long gash down his back across to where the other wounded were waiting. With a soft sigh he headed over to the pair and helped Tyler lower the injured man to the ground. The soldier was one of his new ones, and Karloff realised he didn't even know the man's name.

"What's the bill?" he asked as he motioned Tyler to come with him before moving a few steps away from the wounded men so they could speak in private.

Tyler looked around with a grimace.

"Nineteen dead, thirty-one wounded. At least six of them won't make it through the night without the aid of a mage. That aid is unlikely to arrive in time since the army is at least a day behind. Also, of the wounded, more than half of them will have to stay here since they're in no condition to fight, or even march until they're healed."

Karloff looked around at the far too large group of

wounded men and scowled. The butcher's bill was high today, and he was not at all pleased with the result. If his men hadn't performed as well as they had, it would have been much higher still.

"All right, you've done well. Now I want you to take twenty men and scout that small forest. If you sight any remaining enemy troops you may engage, but don't bite off more than you can chew, understood?"

"Yes sir," Tyler replied, and left with a salute.

It would be the young man's first command, he thought as he looked back at the bodies of the slain. Karloff hoped Tyler succeeded. He needed to replace Sergeant Conner, who had died in the initial assault, and although Tyler was young, Karloff thought he might just be the man for the job.

Walking the short distance, he knelt next to the sergeant's body. The man had been with him for almost five years and had been a good friend. He closed the man's eyes and said a quick prayer to the Maker on his behalf. Karloff wasn't much for priests and religion himself, but the sergeant had been, and so he accorded the man what respect he could.

By the time he had finished, Tyler had gathered up his twenty men and begun moving cautiously towards the nearby tree line.

Karloff stood, this time seeking out Markus. It was good to have his second in command back in the unit. An ill-trained horse had broken several of his ribs the same morning they had gone out on the mission to find that young mageguard Wyll's men, forcing the grizzled warrior to remain behind.

Karloff approached the veteran soldier. He and some of the other men were guarding the few captives who had survived the fight, and Karloff looked at the prisoners, trying to feel anything but pity. If he had thought his own men had been bloodied by this encounter, their enemies were far worse off. Of the six who remained alive, three had crossbow bolts sticking out of them in various places, and one had lost his leg and would not last until dusk. Karloff gave a small grimace, knowing he was responsible for that, but also knowing that it had needed to be done. The soldier was unconscious, as was another whom he seemed to remember having beaten over the head with his crossbow earlier in the fight. The final captive was middle-aged and had gashes all over him, but seemed alert despite his wounds. It wasn't until a moment later Karloff noticed the lieutenant's stripes on his uniform under all the dirt and blood.

"That one," he said, and without further prompting Markus had two of the guards haul the lieutenant to his feet, causing the man to gasp in pain.

"I don't know if you follow Heramiir of your own free will, or whether you were forced to it," Karloff told the man. "But right now I am giving you exactly one chance to return to the king's good favour and save the lives of your men. If you refuse, you will all be hung as traitors. Tell me where Heramiir's army is. Tell me its size and disposition, and Lieutenant, tell me now."

The man couldn't even stand. The two guards were the only things keeping him upright, though his straightforward gaze never wavered despite the pain.

"I only joined so that their recruiting parties wouldn't burn my orchards, Captain. My family has to eat," the man said as he looked Karloff in the eye.

"You're a farmer?" Karloff asked, holding off on his other

questions for a moment. He was curious about why this man would be chosen to lead others if his story were in fact the truth.

"Yes sir, I am now. I was a soldier when I was a young man, but it's twenty and more years gone since I left the King's service now, Sir."

Karloff stared at him for a long time. In the end though, he only got the sense that the man before him was telling the truth, and so let him continue.

"These men, I don't know them. That archmage who wears the armour all the time, he had the conscripts split up from their townsmen. Probably to prevent any kind of resistance fomenting, I think. Most of them have never held a weapon before this year though, I know that much."

Karloff felt himself growing ever angrier. He could hear it in the man's voice, see it in his eyes that he was telling the truth. The idea they had just butchered farmers, no matter that they had been attacked first, was repellent. He had to admit though, from Heramiir's perspective it would make sense to keep his best troops with his main force. Scouting was a risky business at the best of times, and even the fact that a scout had not returned home from a mission was a report of a kind.

"Tell me about Heramiir's army. How big is it? Have they crossed the Mirallyn yet?" Karloff prompted, returning to the matter at hand.

"If you give me the information I need I'll see about getting your men's injuries treated."

The man in front of him grunted, then winced in pain at the sudden movement.

"I wish I could, but Nereth kept us away from the army. We were always sent on ahead with orders coming by fast rider. The truth is we never actually saw most of the main force."

By the time the man finished speaking he was sagging between the soldiers, the last of his strength and resolve draining away.

Karloff looked at the man pitiably. He wanted to hate him, to have a simple line in his mind that he was on the right side, his enemies in the wrong. But looking at the soldier, farmer, whatever the man in front of him was, Karloff couldn't help but wonder how he himself would have chosen to assign his loyalties given the same hard circumstances this man had faced.

"Put him down," he said at last, and the two soldiers eased the man to the ground where he hunched over in pain again before looking up.

"I know this much," he said as he began to shiver. "From the dust cloud behind us, we were never more than fifteen or twenty miles ahead of the main force. They should be approaching the Mirallyn by now if they haven't begun crossing it already."

Karloff looked at the man for a moment, measuring those words. Unless the man was an actor worthy of the king's court, Karloff was certain he was telling the truth as well as he knew it.

"All right, secure these men," he told Markus at length, "But see their wounds are treated as soon as our own men's have been attended to."

Markus nodded, the decision not phasing him one way or another.

That task complete, Karloff went back to see if he could help with the wounded. It was his practice to ensure all his men, including any new recruits, were capable of dressing a wound in the field and splinting a broken bone. Having more than one man in the unit capable of performing those duties had paid off for many of his soldiers in the past. He was therefore unsurprised to see the few men who had not gone with Tyler, but survived the fight relatively unscathed, now either standing guard or doing what they could for those who had not been so lucky.

Even so, it was obvious not all of them could be saved, and Karloff felt a moment of sorrow when he saw Kelmar amongst that number. Like Markus and Connor, the man had been with him for years. The gaping hole in his side couldn't be overlooked, and he was glad the man was unconscious. There was little chance he could hang on long enough for a mage to arrive and heal his wounds. By the look of it, that was all that would save him now. Still, two of his men were doing what they could to stem the bleeding, and Karloff nodded his thanks to them for their efforts, futile though they might be.

Most of the others he didn't know very well, if at all, being only new to his command. Losing both Connor and now Kelmar on the same day though, it was enough to dull even his usually steely resolve.

It was perhaps twenty minutes later when Tyler and his squad returned from the tree line with sixteen men in tow.

With a crisp salute, Tyler came to stand in front of him.

"What news?"

"The forest is clear, Sir. We encountered a half-dozen enemy troops acting as minders for their packhorses and supplies, but were able to overcome them without additional losses. I left four men to set up a base camp for the wounded, and inventory the captured supplies."

In all, Karloff was pleased with the young man's report,

though he would have left ten men, not four, to secure the position until the others returned. Second guessing Tyler's very first command decision was not the way to instil confidence in a potential leader however, and so he let it slide, this time. There would be plenty of opportunity to train him up once this mission was over. For now though, Karloff knew he had to continue to the fjords, or as close as he could get to them with the men he had left. Someone would have to stay behind to guard the prisoners and tend to the injured men though, a job he would normally have given to Sergeant Conner.

That wasn't an option however, and Karloff reluctantly admitted to himself that his friend was indeed gone. It felt disrespectful, but he couldn't avoid the fact that as a result, he now needed to replace the competent officer before the mission could continue. Or at least, replace Connor's position in the company at any rate.

Making his decision, he returned to where Connor lay. With great care, he removed the bronze rank insignia from both sides of the man's uniform collar before carrying them back to where Tyler was still waiting.

"Company. At attention!" Karloff called out in his crisp, clear voice.

The men who could walk quickly gathered around, except those attending to the wounded. The survivors of those who were newer to his command followed the veterans' example without a word. This was not the first battlefield promotion most of the unit had seen, nor was it likely to be the last, with the real fighting only now about to begin.

Without ceremony, Karloff stepped up to Tyler, who was standing tall and proud, realising what was happening.

Karloff told him to be at ease and then showed him the bronze pins that marked a Sergeant's rank in the king's army.

"These pins do not bestow honour upon you Sergeant Tyler. Instead, the actions which you take from this day forward will bestow honour upon them, just as the man's who wore them before you did."

"Do you accept this responsibility?" he asked for Tyler's ears alone.

"Sir, I do!" Tyler replied crisply, and from the serious look in his eyes Karloff knew he meant it.

Karloff nodded to himself, knowing he'd made the right choice, even though there were men in his command who had served with him far longer.

"Congratulations Sergeant," he said with a smile, returning the man's salute, then shaking his hand in a more informal manner once he'd attached the pins to the new sergeant's collar.

"All right, listen up!" he called above the men's round of congratulations. "We've got a lot of sunlight left and miles yet to cover, but first we have to get the injured men into the shelter of the trees, and secure the prisoners for the general. I know you're all tired, but let's keep moving, I intend to reach our objective by sunrise. Get to work!" he finished, and then turned to his newest officer.

"I'm leaving you ten capable men. Your first mission will be to guard those prisoners and do all you can to save as many of our men as is possible. When the army catches up, signal for a mage to heal whoever remains."

Tyler looked as though he were about to object to being left behind, but then thought better of it.

"I won't let you down Sir. Or them," he said quietly as the

first of the injured men who could still walk on their own, passed them on their way to the small forest which would be their home for the night.

"One other thing Tyler. I know you don't have to be told this, but make sure that those who didn't make it through the fight get a proper burial. My duty is to complete the mission, so I'm *trusting* you to get this done. I *will* not have our men being food for the crows."

"No sir!" Tyler answered emphatically. "I'll attend to it myself."

Karloff nodded in approval, then motioned towards the forest.

"Lead the way, Sergeant," he said with a tiny smile, and the young man returned his grin.

"Yes sir," Tyler replied, then moved to help prop up one of the injured men, before resuming their trek towards the makeshift camp.

Now that the clamour of battle had been resolved, Karloff had a moment to notice that the small patch of ground they had fought so hard over was quite picturesque. Apart from the actual battle site of course. On this side of the Mirallyn, trees dotted the countryside with thickets at irregular intervals. The occasional large stand such as the one they were about to enter was visible as well.

To the west, the green hills of the Laketown Peninsula were visible in the distance, the river dividing the landscape types like a great silvery knife as it reflected the midday sun.

Leaving a squad behind to guard the wounded too injured to walk, he entered the small forest itself to find that it was mercifully cool. The underbrush was thin and weedy, but the canopy above blocked out just enough light and heat to be comfortable. He ordered the men to construct a few makeshift stretchers for those too injured to walk. It took an hour, but eventually all his men, both living and dead, along with their prisoners were hidden within the tree line. With a last look around, he took his leave of Tyler and gathered what remained of his able-bodied force.

By the time he crossed off the new sergeant and the other men who would stay behind in support, and factored in the casualties from the ambush, the numbers were not good. He had a mere nineteen men still capable of continuing the mission. *Nineteen out of eighty. Plus the two remaining riders.* That attack had hurt them, and truth be told Karloff was unsure he had enough men left to accomplish his orders. It was vital that the general received accurate intelligence on the movements of Heramiir's main force though, and Karloff was determined to make sure he got it. By himself if need be.

"You men, get your gear and follow me. We still have work to do," he called to the others before setting off to the south. Regardless of their fears and the recent combat, his men would continue the mission with the same resolve he carried. They would have Markus to deal with otherwise.

The remaining soldiers followed along sure enough, and for several long hours they trudged south. Dusk made the Mirallyn to the east sparkle as the sun fell, and soon enough every star was shining brightly above.

According to his map, they were perhaps three or four hours north of the fjords now. After allowing a brief stop for a quick cold meal, Karloff ordered the march to resume. On the off chance Heramiir hadn't crossed the fjords yet, he wanted to get into position under cover of darkness so they could monitor the enemy as they approached the small crossing. He was told the fjords were little more than fifty spans wide. It was not much, but it was the only place an army this size could cross the Mirallyn from its mouth at the Sea of Fishes in the south, right up to crescent's bend. He doubted Heramiir would go that way though because of its proximity to Midway. By now the archmage must know it was the king's key staging point in the west.

It was surprising that no one had ever bothered to build a decent bridge across the river here he thought. But then there was little on this side of the Mirallyn worth the effort. At least not until you travelled south beyond the mouth of the river and reached the town of Three Seas on the southernmost tip of the continent. Alternatively you could travel southeast around the Midland Sea towards Southport and Silvertown. Although populous, those regions had little to recommend them in the way of culture or trade since the mines had dried up thirty years past. It was rumoured that another large vein had been found up near the Ice Ranges, but that was a concern for other men.

It was about midnight by the moon's position when he topped a rise and stopped, appalled at the sight before him. Down in the next vale, still on the other side of the river, the opposing hill was ablaze with the campfires of what must be at least a hundred thousand men. Perhaps even a larger host than General Messand had brought with him.

His men were carefully trained though, and had stopped behind him once he halted. Karloff looked back and motioned for one of the remaining riders to join him on foot.

The man joined him at the crest and took in the scene before them with a gasp. The night was clear and dark, but even from here you could hear the faint sound of raucous singing in the distance.

Heramiir's forces looked to have been there for some

time. Either that or they were enjoying a night of reprieve after a hard march, and would begin the crossing at first light. Either way, it was bad. The first rule of warfare was never to let your enemy choose the ground you fought on. With that many men sent against them though, Messand would have no choice but to break them at the crossing. Assuming the king's army even arrived in time to attempt it.

If Heramiir crossed successfully, the two armies would meet on open ground. It would result in a disastrous pitched battle that would cause massive casualties on both sides. Neither force appeared to have the decisive advantage in numbers from what little he could tell in the darkness, and Jeranon's armed forces would be pulverised.

He turned to the scout after they had both spent a minute or more studying the force before them, and gave the man his orders.

"Get back to the General. Don't stop for anything until you've reported what you've seen. Clear?"

The man just looked at him and nodded.

"And make sure it's an accurate account. No embellishments."

He shouldn't have had to remind the outrider of that, but the man was clearly shaken by what he was seeing. The soldier blinked twice, then seemed to come back to himself before nodding again. This time he did it with far more certainty as he took a last look out over the vale where Heramiir's main force was camped. He headed back to his horse before riding out at a gallop, back north the way they had come. Karloff hoped he didn't run into any more of Heramiir's scouts, but he couldn't spare another rider since he only had one man left with a horse. If Heramiir began to cross at first light as Karloff suspected, he would be needed then.

Looking around, he spotted a large rock outcropping on the ridgeline to the southeast where his men could hide from the eyes of the approaching army come sunrise. He motioned them to follow him towards it, quietly.

It took them perhaps another hour to circle around and approach the outcropping from the rear. When Karloff was satisfied they hadn't been seen moving into position, he ordered them all to get what little rest they could.

He couldn't sleep however, not with a hostile army less than two miles away. Several long hours later, as the first fingers of dawn spread across the land, he moved out from the shelter of the outcropping. Being careful not to let his silhouette reveal them to the enemy, he slowly crested the formation.

He breathed deeply and sighed.

He had been wrong the night before, there was not a hundred thousand men down there across the river at all, more like half that again. The king's army would be outnumbered, even with the many magi the general had at his disposal. The one thing Karloff was certain of was that the enemy was led by an archmage of unheard-of power. He had no illusions that after committing treason against his rightful king, Heramiir would stick to the ban on experimentation. The enemy would have some nasty surprises waiting for them.

This would not be a battle easily won, and as hours passed and the morning dragged on, Karloff realised that Heramiir's men were planning on staying put.

As he sent off his final rider, he began to get a terrible feeling in the bowels of his stomach. There was only one reason he could think of for that army not to cross the bottleneck of the fjords whilst they could still do so unopposed.

They wanted to fight, here and now.

Heramiir had chosen his ground.

CHAPTER 23

THE SHATTERED OATH

For over a week now, the army had remained camped above the fjords in the Mirallyn River. Why Heramiir had not ordered them to cross before the king's army arrived, Hassan still did not understand. Heramiir's stated goal for this force had always been to move into central Jeranon where he could subdue the sparse population in this part of the country. They would then move on Midway from both west and south. All this the archmage could have achieved unopposed if he had ordered the crossing when they'd first arrived. Instead, Heramiir had just had them sitting here, waiting.

Hassan didn't like it. The archmage was planning something, but despite his best efforts, Hassan could not divine what that plan entailed.

They had received the reports of first clashes with the king's scouting parties the day before last, and eventually the vast loyalist army had marched into sight on the plains beyond the river.

Hassan had felt numb when he had seen it. Not because of its massive size though, but because the king's forces numbered not more than three quarters of Heramiir's own.

Hassan had realised in that moment that he'd been counting on the king's army having the advantage of numbers at the very least. If the coming battle were not a closely contested thing, there was little his men could achieve. They were only waiting for his signal to turn on their traitorous companions, hopefully turning the tide of that battle. Hassan had known in the instant he had seen the king's force march into view that it wouldn't be enough. He couldn't just give his men orders to change sides. He would have to wait until just the right moment, or his entire command, and most likely their families as well, would not survive the setting of the sun.

The first thing Heramiir had done after Nereth had set his army in position was to order the building of twenty catapults. The engineers had finished them an hour before the king's army had been sighted, and Heramiir had ordered them placed in a line on the overlooking hilltop at the rear of his army. Hassan still couldn't work out why. No catapult ever built could fire far enough to be effective from that ridgeline. Heramiir must be planning to roll them down the hill during the coming battle, or perhaps fire at a point on this side of the river despite his own men currently being located there.

He scowled. Heramiir was up to something there too, and that could only be bad for the king's army, and therefore his own loyal men.

In the distance, a small group of soldiers broke away from the king's ranks, riding towards the river on armoured mounts. One of them held a lance with the white flag of parlay tied to its tip. When the distant figures had reached the narrow stretch of shallow water a few minutes later they stopped, not advancing or announcing themselves in any other way. They were waiting for a response.

Heramiir's own force was stationed well back from the

Mirallyn, out of range of the king's magi. It took some time before Hassan could make out the lone figure riding down the gentle decline to meet the king's envoy on his massive, Gift-altered steed.

Men cleared a path as they saw the archmage approaching. As the rider passed, Hassan spotted the black enamelled plate armour the figure was wearing, and realised that Nereth, not Heramiir, planned to meet the delegation at the fjords.

With a snarl, Hassan ran over and vaulted onto the back of the nearest horse, taking the reins from the soldier who was leading it. He plunged after Nereth, shouting for men to move out of his way as he galloped after the archmage. For Heramiir not to meet with the king's officer himself meant there was no chance of a peaceful resolution this day. Since the archmage had no interest in brokering a deal, Hassan could only assume he intended to attack.

Once he threaded his way through the crowd to the path Nereth had cleared in his wake, the going was much easier. By the time the archmage had pulled in his massive beast down by the river, Hassan had reached the edge of Heramiir's army. He was still a minute away from where the two representatives of the opposing forces were to meet.

Nereth would not be happy to see him, but he could use the excuse that the archmage needed to be guarded whilst in the presence of their enemies. In truth, he couldn't care less if Nereth was killed right there. He desperately needed to know what was said at this parlance though so he could direct his men accordingly. As expected, Nereth looked around and scowled as he heard Hassan's horse close in from behind, and then again as it slowed to a stop beside him.

"Hassan," General Messand said by way of greeting. "I always knew your ambition would take you far, but I never imagined that you would be a willing traitor to the crown."

"Our families are held…" Hassan got out before an invisible hand clamped around his windpipe and squeezed hard enough to cut off anything further. Nereth stared daggers at him for a long time as Hassan squirmed in his invisible grip, his face turning blue from a lack of air. Eventually Messand cut in, his scowl now mixed with some small amount of sympathy as he realised Hassan's, and who knew how many others in Heramiir's army's, predicament.

"Enough Nereth, the secret's already out."

For a long time more, or what seemed like it to Hassan, Nereth's invisible grip continued until he could feel the edges of his vision turning fuzzy and black. Only then did the spell that restrained him finally disappear. He fell from the horse's back as he gasped in breath after massive breath, trying to recover from the Gift-wrought strangulation as quickly as possible.

"Apparently," Nereth replied.

"I suppose you have demands?" the archmage added after a moment.

"You know the King's demands already Nereth," Messand replied. "You cut off the head of the last envoy we sent."

"Yes," Nereth agreed. "They were not acceptable at the time."

"And now?"

"Even less so. We control almost half the kingdom already, and once your force is dealt with, we will move west and claim even more. By the time winter comes I expect we will be no more than a hundred leagues from Aramar itself. So tell me, why should we bow to Erian's oppression for even one more day?"

"Oppression?!" Messand returned, startled at the accusation.

"If by oppression you mean that everything you want for is provided for the magi by King Erian's own coffers, then yes. Or perhaps you refer to the fact that the magi are ordered to maintain a certain number of members patrolling the western border at all times? Do I really need to remind you that for every one of you who puts your life on the line to hold back the western nations, there are at least three hundred regular soldiers, not to mention the mageguard who are doing the same at any given moment. If so, then yes, you should bow to that kind of oppression, though only a coward must be ordered to defend their own homeland!" Messand finished, shaking his head in disgust at the man before him.

Nereth smiled slightly as he regarded the king's general.

"That was a pretty speech. Of course, it changes nothing, and you have yet to provide me a single compelling reason why we should not continue to sweep the king's forces away at our leisure."

Messand looked him in the eye, realising he would get nothing but rhetoric out of his counterpart in Heramiir's regime, and then tried another tack.

"Where is Heramiir, why has he not come down to speak with me himself? Is he too afraid, or too ashamed?"

Nereth smiled coldly.

"If you had sent a mage to treat with us, he might have. In the new Jeranon, men such as yourself simply aren't important enough to be granted an audience with the head of the college."

There was a long moment of silence as the general struggled to speak.

"Then you reveal yourself at last," he replied. "All of that about improving the lot of the people, and correcting injustices to the magi is just lies and propaganda. You simply want power for yourselves."

Nereth's smile became a little meaner as he patted down his frisking mount.

"I had thought you intelligent enough to have realised that from the outset," he replied as he looked the king's general in the eye.

"You have until midday tomorrow to either withdraw your force or swear fealty to Heramiir and the new order. I promise you this though Messand, if your army is still here when the sun reaches its zenith, it will not be when it sets. There is nothing else that need be said."

Turning his oversized mount with his knees, Nereth lifted Hassan off the ground with the Gift and deposited him roughly back on his own borrowed mount.

"Come Hassan, we have a battle to plan."

There was little Hassan could do except hold on to the mane of the horse he'd borrowed, he was having a hard enough time still just drawing in breath. There would be a significant bruise around the whole of his neck by the next day if it had not already begun.

Nereth got his giant steed moving, and used the Gift to whip Hassan's own mount to a canter. He led the animals up towards the top of the slope, past the useless line of catapults and into the tree line where Heramiir's command tent was situated.

Unlike Messand's huge pavilion on the other side of the Mirallyn, Heramiir's was a simple thing of rough canvas. A field commander's tent that could be packed up and moved in minutes if enough men were set to the task.

As they approached, Hassan could see that a pair of magi guarded the door flap. In addition, a ring of mageguard troops circled the entire tent, making sure that no scout or assassin could enter undetected and cause harm to their leaders. Once the two of them had slowed and then stopped in front of the tent, Nereth jumped down from his huge steed and motioned Hassan to do the same.

He slid off with little difficulty, and although still slightly winded, managed not to embarrass himself by falling from the horse's back again.

Once he was down, Nereth led him into the tent without ceremony to find that Heramiir was giving Deshara instructions. That stopped immediately when Heramiir saw who Nereth was leading into his presence.

Without warning, the ground came rushing up around him. Before Hassan could even react, he was encompassed in a hardened mud cocoon fashioned from the ground they were camped on. Whatever secrets Heramiir had been imparting to Deshara were lost to his ears, along with the light. The cocoon was not tight though. As he used his hands to measure the confines of his cage in the pitch blackness, he studied its contours. He had been left enough air in here for a few minutes at least. He assumed that meant Heramiir would release him once he had finished his plotting, and so waited.

His only other option seemed to be to pound his way out of the mud cocoon, but that seemed pointless since Heramiir could just encompass him in another. Besides, he refused to give them the satisfaction of seeing him panic.

As the minutes dragged by and the air inside the cocoon became warm, and then stifling, Hassan began to feel nervous. What if the archmage didn't release him before he ran out of air, or didn't realise how little he had left?

After another few minutes went by, he started to feel light-headed again. He no longer had a choice, he had to break through the cocoon and gain access to fresh air, or this casing would quickly become his tomb. He took a knife from his belt and was just about to begin chipping away the mud when without warning it departed on its own. He was left blinking in the sudden brightness, inches away from Nereth with his knife raised, unintentionally pointing right at the man's heart. The archmage looked surprised for a moment. Rather than attempting to disarm him or move out of the way though, he simply raised an eyebrow as he took in Hassan's now sweat drenched visage.

Hassan's lip trembled in impotent rage as he lowered the knife and re-sheathed it on his belt. He could have killed Nereth right then, had he acted fast enough. It would have meant his life, and no doubt that of his wife and son at the least, and probably many more as well. If it had been Heramiir instead, it might almost have been worthwhile he thought guiltily. He was sure that without the overwhelmingly powerful archmage to lead them, the rest of the rebellion would fracture, and the king's forces could remove the traitors piecemeal. Without Nereth, Heramiir would simply choose another general, and all that he had sacrificed to protect both his own family and those of his men's would have been for nothing. It was too high a price for the death of just one traitor, powerful though he was. Hassan returned Nereth's bland look as he put away the knife, though he offered no more explanation than that.

"I almost ran out of air because of your clumsy spell casting," he accused.

Of Deshara there was no trace, the woman must have left before Heramiir had released him, and Hassan wanted very badly to know what it was they had been discussing. If Heramiir had been worried that he might overhear, it would be something he could affect to his advantage.

Heramiir ignored his words though and turned to Nereth.

"What did Messand have to say?" he asked as he stood from the hard clay chair on which he'd been seated.

In fact, all the furniture in here seemed to have been fashioned with the Gift. The various pieces looked as though they were growing up from the ground as some strange quirk of nature had intended.

"Nothing of note," Nereth replied. "Everything is on schedule."

"What are you plotting traitor?" Hassan demanded of Heramiir. His earlier feeling that something terrible was happening now growing worse.

As one, the two most powerful archmagi in western Jeranon turned their heads to regard him. It was almost as if he were some annoying bug that had just flown within their reach.

For a long moment Heramiir looked as though he were not going to answer, but then a small, cruel smile worked its way onto his lips.

"Very well Hassan, you wish to know what our battle plan is. I will tell you."

*　　　*　　　*

Nereth blinked at Heramiir in surprise, clearly wondering what the archmage was up to.

Heramiir returned to his Gift-wrought chair while Hassan came to stand before him, turning his back on Nereth, who gave no sign of acknowledging the slight.

"I had Archmage Nereth deliver an arrogant ultimatum to the king's general, to surrender by midday tomorrow or we would destroy them. It is a threat I have no intention of backing up," Heramiir told him as if discussing the weather.

"I don't understand," Hassan responded with a furrowed brow.

"Are you saying that all of this is just one giant bluff?"

There was a short bark of laughter from Nereth, the first Hassan had ever heard, and even Heramiir smiled slyly.

"Hardly. You see, Messand is Erian's most trusted general, a man of great intellect and prowess. I knew Erian would send him to lead this army once we attacked. Fortunately for us, the good general is a man who sees every situation as a challenge, a puzzle to be explored and solved. When our deadline passes and we take no action, it will play on his mind. Eventually, sometime after the sun sets and rises again and we still have not attacked or responded to him, he will call his officers together. He will inform them of his new battle plan, thinking us uncommitted, and attempting to seize the initiative. Then, and only then, will we make our move, striking the head from the serpent so to speak."

"The catapults?" Hassan guessed as the bad feeling in his gut intensified. "You've done something to them to make them fire further?"

Heramiir inclined his head in a vaguely respectful response.

"I truly wish you had joined us of your own free will Hassan. You could have been a valuable asset to the new order."

Hassan clenched his jaw against a biting rebuke. In the end he couldn't help but respond though, even though he was being goaded.

"I want no part of your new order Heramiir. I can only take comfort in the fact that you built it on treachery and deceit, for nothing built on such foundations can possibly stand for long."

Heramiir looked at him for a long moment before choosing his own words carefully.

"You had best hope that you are wrong, because in two years, three at the outside, we are all there will be. Jeranon will be under the administration of the new order, and if we fall, the rest of the country will be swept away by the western nations at their leisure."

Hassan gritted his teeth, knowing that if Heramiir managed to win this battle convincingly enough, in all likelihood what he was saying would indeed come to pass.

There had to be some way to stop it. Some way to warn General Messand in time to avoid the lion's share of the king's high ranking and most experienced officers being killed by Heramiir's ambush.

"Now let us discuss your role in all of this," Heramiir continued when he made no response.

"I want nothing to do with this, traitor," Hassan snapped, nearing the end of his patience with Heramiir's calm assumption of authority.

"Nevertheless, you will lead the attack," the archmage replied without missing a beat.

For a long moment Hassan stood stock still, not knowing what to say. He would never have thought Heramiir would place that much trust in him. The idea of leading men against his own king's army was abhorrent to him, and yet the idea held possibilities that unfortunately bore further consideration.

If he did this, his oath to the king would be irrevocably broken. Already, the excuse that Heramiir was forcing him into these actions was wearing thin, even to his own ears. There had to be some point at which he simply said no, despite the consequences. Otherwise he had already become just another of Heramiir's traitorous men.

On the other hand, having the authority to lead the army would give him the best possible chance at turning the tide of battle at a crucial stage, hopefully giving the king's men the upper hand. It was a confounding situation. Perhaps in this one instance, the way he could best serve his king was in fact to break his oath. To lead Heramiir's men into battle against their rightful sovereign. It was an absurd proposition, but if he were going to go through with it, Heramiir could not suspect his motivations until it was too late.

He would need another reason to seem to agree to the archmage's whim, and fortunately there was something he could demand that should draw suspicion away from his real motivations.

"If I do this, I want my family and those of my men released and free to go wherever they choose, whenever they choose. This should be acceptable because you know as well as I do that after this battle neither myself, nor any member of my family will have anywhere else to turn. Regardless of which way the battle goes."

For a long moment Heramiir regarded him, though whether he was searching for a lie or taking his measure, Hassan couldn't tell as he stood unflinching before the archmage's scrutiny.

A long moment passed, and Hassan felt as though he were balancing on a knife's edge, the archmage's next words determining which way he would fall.

Heramiir finally stood and nodded towards Nereth, who began moving towards the door. "Very well Hassan. Lead my men well in the coming battle, and you shall have your reward."

Hassan nodded gravely, surprised, but glad that Heramiir had agreed to the compromise. He had to work hard to keep a victorious smile from sprouting on his face. Once his men's families were free, he could get in contact with Sir Luke. His co-leader of the resistance was based at Seal Cove and his civilian force could begin doing some real damage to Heramiir's holdings. They had focused on intelligence gathering so far, but perhaps it would soon be time for that to change. Even if Heramiir was victorious in the coming battle, his numbers would be severely reduced, and with those thinned out numbers, the resistance would have far more scope to operate.

"Return to your men for now Hassan. I will have orders for you on the morrow."

Hassan clenched his teeth, but nodded his acceptance of the dismissal before leaving the command tent, Nereth only a few steps behind.

"Hassan, hold," Nereth arrogantly ordered as soon as they were through the door flap. He turned to the mageguard captain who was standing near the entry and addressed the officer, who paid keen attention to the archmage's words.

"This man knows our battle plan. Take three men and guard him well. He is not to be left alone until it is complete, not to eat, not to sleep, not to take a privy break. If he speaks of it in part or in whole to anyone including his own men, both he and whomever he speaks with are to be killed immediately."

Nereth re-entered the command tent without another word, leaving Hassan to go about his business, hampered by the men who had sprung up around him at the captain's slightest motion.

Hassan's spirits fell as he stalked past the row of catapults that lined the shallow ridge and made his way down the gentle slope to where his men were encamped. He had been hoping to formulate a plan with Jarl now that he had some idea of what the traitorous archmage was planning. If Heramiir actually had been telling the truth about the catapults, the archmage was likely to order the king's command pavilion destroyed in the initial attack. It was likely he would then have the army create a beachhead on the other side of the Mirallyn before the king's men could react, much as he himself had done at Stonekeep's outer wall just a few phases past.

The memories he had of that day still filled him with loathing, most of all for himself. The men there had been given the opportunity to surrender at least. Somehow Hassan knew that would not be the case here. Anyway, the old general would never give in without a decent fight.

Before today, Hassan had not seen the general for many years, but he had served under him, and couldn't imagine the man changing all that much. Unfortunately it seemed Heramiir had also either met the man, or else gathered sufficient information about his enemy to come up with a dangerously accurate assessment.

The four mageguard troops surrounding him walked in lockstep though as he headed back to his tent, each not more than three steps away in a square formation. As he watched their steely resolve, Hassan couldn't help the sinking feeling that the time for action had somehow passed him by.

Killing them was out of the question. Even if he could manage it, their disappearance would cause far too many questions for which he would have no appropriate answers. Convincing them to leave or turn back to the king were also not viable options. They had been given their orders by a high ranking archmage and they would fulfil those orders or die trying. That was why these men existed, and why Hassan had never joined them, despite being offered a place in their ranks several times over the years.

Unless he could somehow talk to Jarl for a few moments in private, Hassan was suddenly very unsure there was anything he could do to help Messand and his officers without blowing his own cover. He couldn't allow that. It would result in his command being stripped from him, at the least. Not to mention the other consequences that were far closer to home.

For hours more he thought on the problem without any further insight. Somewhere after dusk, he guiltily conceded that if he were to win the war, Messand's survival might be a battle he would have to forfeit, painful though it was to admit. He couldn't risk the entire resistance, not to mention the possibility of swaying the coming battle, for the survival of one man. No matter how important he was.

The mageguard troops had followed through on their orders precisely. With all four of them within hearing range of even a whisper, there was no opportunity at all to act on the knowledge that Heramiir had imparted to him.

It wasn't until near midday the following day though

when it truly sank in just how far ahead of Messand Heramiir was with his strategy.

The king's army was arrayed in a defensive formation on the plains beyond the river, two miles from where Hassan was standing, and ready to meet Nereth's promised attack. Heramiir's men were watching the spectacle closely, donning their own armour and preparing to fight. No orders had come down to assemble though, and so they stayed close by their tents and horses, ready to move at a moment's notice.

It was a long wait in the afternoon heat, and finally Messand seemed to realise that no attack was coming this day. After four hours of staring at each other across the silvery stretch of shallow water, the king's army loosened their formations and return to their camp.

During the whole tense afternoon, no instructions had come down from the archmagi. Hassan couldn't help but wonder whether the lack of communication was a snub to his own men, or to an enemy he knew wouldn't dare charge in whilst they suspected some treachery was afoot.

By sunset the king's army had returned to its campfires, and fresh men had relieved the mageguard troops surrounding him. Infuriatingly, these new troops showed the same grim enthusiasm for carrying out their orders as the previous four. Hassan cursed their efficiency. Not one of the men left their vigil until the relieving soldier had already taken up position. He sighed. Those men hadn't slept last night, they had stood around his little tent, carrying out their duty. He expected nothing less from this new lot.

There would be no chance to warn General Messand of the impending danger. None. The king's officers would just have to weather the attack as best they could. The only thing

Hassan could do was to lead his men well and direct the others until he could change the course of the battle towards the king's favour.

Who knows, it might not even be necessary. The thought gave him the faintest tinge of hope.

Perhaps the king's men will be victorious on their own.

He didn't believe it, not now that he knew something of Heramiir's plan. Tomorrow would tell the tale, one way or another, if Heramiir's predictions remained as accurate as they had been so far.

Hassan went about his business as well as he could manage for the rest of the day. When he entered his tent again that night it was to the sound of boots taking up position almost on top of the very guy ropes of his tent.

It was a long night with little sleep as he once again racked his brain for a way to warn the general in time. He woke the next dawn to find the men still waiting implacably outside his tent, and finally conceded that it was futile. He would just have to do what he could on his own, and hope that was enough to ensure the king's army was victorious this day.

It wasn't long after lunchtime when a summons arrived, and Hassan was escorted back to the command tent by his mageguard shadows. It wasn't until their leader poked his head inside and saw the archmage waiting to talk with Hassan alone that they finally let him be.

Heramiir dismissed the man with a nod, and he left.

"So, you are still alive," he began. "That is good."

"Why have I been summoned from my men?" Hassan snapped a little more strongly that he'd intended, his patience worn after being watched so closely for the last two days.

Heramiir raised his eyebrow at the tone, but otherwise ignored it.

"Messand seems to be gathering his officers to his command pavilion," Heramiir said without preamble.

"You will prepare the army. Make sure they are armed and armoured within a half hour. Deshara will give the order directly into your mind when it is time for you to move. Until then, do nothing to alert the King's forces that we are preparing to attack. Simply pass the word."

"Is that all?" Hassan scowled, wondering why Heramiir had wasted time summoning him to the command tent if that was all he needed to say. Though the part about Deshara touching his mind was an interesting tidbit. As far as he knew that was yet another ability the magi were not supposed to possess. And yet, he'd suspected for some time that Nereth had a way of communicating with Miralthrall far more efficiently than he should. Perhaps this was it?

"That is all Hassan," Heramiir confirmed.

"Just remember what you are fighting for today."

Hassan couldn't help but sneer at the archmage as his eyes blazed in response.

"A traitor who holds innocent women and children as hostages. I won't forget," he promised as he turned to leave the command tent.

"Not after today. If you do your job well," Heramiir called to his retreating form.

Hassan left the tent almost believing Heramiir had meant that, and for a wonder the mageguard soldiers no longer dogged his every step as he re-entered the army. Hassan picked up his pace as he headed back to his men. Perhaps there was still time to warn Messand after all, and yet he would have to be careful. As much as he wanted to save the king's officers from their fate, it was not worth losing the control he'd been given. If the battle went badly for the king's men, Hassan and his unit might be the only thing standing between them and destruction.

For long minutes he tracked his way through the army, passing the word to any officer he found, to ready arms but otherwise wait for his signal. Finally he came to the place where his own men were camped.

As he reached the sprawl of tents that belonged to his own regiment, a sense of deep foreboding overcame him. All around him other units were going about their business, donning armour, and readying weapons. The patch of ground where his men should have been doing the same was empty. The tents and equipment were still there by the hundreds to be sure, and the signs of last night's campfires still smoked, but of men, there were none.

Hassan looked around, his heart leaping in his chest as he moved through the empty campsite until at its centre, he found Nereth waiting.

The archmage was dressed as always in his black enamelled, Gift-wrought plate armour which made no sound. He stood with arms crossed, a tiny smile tugging at the corner of his mouth.

"Where are my men?" Hassan demanded as soon as he reached the archmage.

Nereth smiled in response.

"You don't have any men Hassan. This regiment of Heramiir's army was reassigned to the rear right flank while you were meeting with Archmage Heramiir."

For a long minute it was all Hassan could do not to reach out and try to throttle the traitorous archmage with his bare hands.

Without his core group of loyal men to help him implement his plan, there was little he could achieve in the coming battle. He could still give orders contrary to Heramiir's designs of course. Whether they would be obeyed by the others without his unit acting to prompt them into following was by no means a certainty.

With yet another sinking sensation, Hassan realised there was only one reason Nereth would have given this order.

He knows.

The question was, did Nereth simply suspect his actions, or did he have proof. Either way, he had to play the archmage's game just in case his cover as head of the resistance had not yet been blown.

"Why would you do that?" he asked, even as he ran the situation through in his mind.

Nereth looked at him for a long moment, his expression giving away none of his thoughts before he finally answered.

"I felt it was best to have a unit loyal to the new order on the front line, as this will no doubt be one of the most important battles of the war. Your own unit has fought well and accomplished much for us, but I will risk *no* complications this day."

The emphasis on Nereth's words suggested he was still being watched, even if the mageguard soldiers had been recalled.

"Am I still to command the army?" Hassan asked just as bluntly, trying not to let his despair show.

"Through us, yes, you will still give our orders to the army. But you will have no direct body of men under your command. Instead, each unit will obey your directions, just as you will obey ours."

"I see," Hassan replied, fearing that for the first time, he truly did.

Either Nereth was far more cunning than even he had given the archmage credit for, or else the man had spies in his ranks that not even Hassan knew of. Either possibility was daunting. If Nereth knew enough to take his men away right now, there was every chance the resistance had been compromised as well. He would have to get a message to Seal Cove and warn Sir Luke of the imminent threat.

"I must return to Heramiir now. Get to the front where you will find Captain Sokolov of the mageguard. He will confirm your appointment to the men there and give you the rank insignia of a General. Heramiir tells me that whether that rank becomes permanent depends on your performance today. Congratulations," Nereth said with that mocking grin of his.

"Welcome to the new order."

Hassan didn't move a muscle as Nereth walked past him and headed uphill towards the command tent, his grin having bloomed into a full smile as he did.

Hassan could only stand there, his fists clenched in shame and fury that it could have ever come to this. Across the river, even he could see the king's officers gathering at the huge pavilion General Messand occupied. Officers he now knew for certain he could offer no help at all. Heramiir would make his assault in the next few minutes.

He had failed. He had given his oath to his king when he had been little more than a boy, to protect Jeranon against its enemies.

'My sword and my service until death.'

That was what he had promised, and yet here he was, waiting helplessly for the king's loyal men to be slaughtered in a cowardly surprise attack. One that would no doubt be followed by a full assault on their main force, by an army which he himself directed. And he would have to do it. He would lead that assault and hope for some miracle to present itself so that he could turn the battle to the king's favour.

It was an exceedingly slim hope without his men to back him up though. A single sword thrust from one of Heramiir's loyal men would stop him in his tracks if he was not careful about which orders he gave, and to whom.

He had come too far to back out now though. Any other commander who might lead Heramiir's force this day would do their best to obliterate the king's men without remorse. Despite everything else the archmage had forced him to do over the last year, giving someone that opportunity was something he just could not allow.

Taking a last look around, Hassan walked to his own tent and spent a few minutes donning his armour and strapping his broadsword into its scabbard on his back. He sighed once he was done, and looked towards the bottom of the gentle hill where the forward elements of Heramiir's massive army were encamped.

The sun was bright today, he thought as he started down towards them. A fresh breeze ruffled his hair, and in the high distance a bird called out its raucous song. A sense of disconnection settled upon him as he looked out over the green fields on which the two armies were camped. Between them, the Mirallyn River cut from north to south like a shining silver knife. Of its length, only the shallow stretch at the fjords failed to catch the light as the current tumbled over the frothy stretch of water.

All too soon he reached his goal. The mageguard captain

called the assembled men to order and pinned the metal insignia of a general to his collars. They had been on less than a second when a shout of consternation from one of the men caused all eyes to seek out what had attracted the soldier's attention.

In the distance beyond the river, a great many swirling black clouds had appeared around General Messand's command pavilion. Clouds which appeared oily and thick, and could only ever have been a result of the Gift.

Without warning, each of the clouds spewed forth something bulky and flaming at incredible speed. As they smashed through the walls and roof of the pavilion, a vast pillar of flame and cinders rose like a great mushroom a hundred spans high from the space the king's officers had been occupying just moments before.

Around Hassan, everything went quiet as the men watched, aghast at the sheer power of the spectacle. Hassan could hardly breathe as the king's army began boiling towards them like a horde of wasps whose colony had just been disturbed.

"Take up weapons," Hassan said, and then louder once he realised he was not the only one in shock at what he had just witnessed. "Take up weapons!"

He had received no order yet, but it would only be moments before he did, and after the devastating sneak attack, the king's men would be out for blood. He had to be ready, or he would be dead before he could even try to wring some good from this disaster.

For a year and more he had done everything in his power to avoid this moment. As he heard a woman's voice in the back of his mind urging him to sound the attack, he knew it had all been for nothing. Deshara had given him the order, and after a venomous mental reply he had no idea whether she'd even heard, he had no other choice but to obey.

"We must get to the river and stop them crossing at any cost!" he yelled to the surrounding men. They cheered at his words, but it was as much to summon up their own courage as it was to applaud the idea.

"Pass the word. Forward!" Hassan yelled as loudly as he could. All around him men removed weapons from scabbards and ran towards the narrow crossing in the river, screaming and yelling as they rushed to meet the brown and green coated host of the king's loyal men.

Hassan ran with the rest, though he made no war cry as he did. He met his first man in battle and killed him quickly. But the only thought that went through his head as the loyal soldier's blood splattered across his face, was of how he could ever explain this treachery to his young son Luthor. Or ever again be able to look into the eyes of his wife with anything but shame.

Power. Alcohol. Desire. Each can engender an alteration of perception, causing an individual to act in a manner they might otherwise know is unacceptable, and care not.
Excerpt from 'Musings on consciousness'

CHAPTER 24

VICIOUS INTENTIONS

"Begin!" Heramiir ordered with relish.

Nereth nodded, his face unreadable as was always the case when the Giftless were in sight. He turned in his saddle towards the long line of heavy catapults at the peak of the incline, his black plate armour unnaturally silent as he moved. With a wave, he motioned to the commander in charge of the army's siege weapons that the time had come for the gigantic machines to be loaded.

Nereth could have used a spell to project his voice, but Heramiir noted his general was saving all his strength for the coming fight.

That was good. Even with the extra power the master had given him, opening so many vortices at once would drain his strength quickly. Nereth would be their last line of defence should the battle not go the way they intended.

Along the ridge at various points, though none too near each other in case of a lucky hit by Erian's loyal magi, his top lieutenants waited. Deshara sat at the extreme left of the ridge, her unnerving smile in full force. Even from this distance, she looked ready to hunt. To Nereth's right was Davoor, another of his inner circle who had been part of his plans now for several years. The tall black man sported a bald head, which he took great care to shave every day. Even Heramiir was forced to admit the scowling man on his Gift enhanced steed made for a fearsome sight to any who cared to look upon him.

He had given much thought to the spells the master had taught him before he left, and spent weeks deciding which to use to generate the greatest advantage. As always, though, the outcome of this battle would be significantly better if his opening gambit succeeded.

It was a clear day, Heramiir noted while the catapults were being loaded. The sun had shone throughout, though a cooling breeze was now picking up its pace as the sun sank towards the western horizon. There were perhaps two hours remaining until it set. Hopefully on his victory.

Using the Gift, his lieutenants had been watching intently for hours. Davoor was certain a man who looked like Messand had entered the command tent on the far side of the river a few minutes ago. At this distance though, even his best long ranged attack specialist couldn't be entirely sure it was him. Still, several other officers had entered over the previous half hour, and Heramiir judged they were holding a strategy session on how to best cross the fjords and defeat his forces. They thought they were safe beyond the river, well behind their lines. That far away from the river and the normal range of Heramiir's magi, they should have been right. Not today though, not with the extra strength the master had lent him.

"Catapults ready!" the siege commander called back less than a minute later, once all the weapons had been cocked and loaded.

"Light them!" Nereth returned after sharing a confirming

nod with Heramiir, and in seconds the enormous balls of sawdust and pitch were lit. The time had come.

As the king's army caught sight of the flames springing up on the siege machines' projectiles, activity erupted in the enemy camp.

Heramiir closed his eyes, concentrating his will in the specific way the master had shown him. When he had the spell envisioned, just as he wanted, he applied his will and sent forth a great wave of power. A far greater force than he ever could have managed before the master granted him this boon emanated from him, and the vortices formed in the exact places he imagined them.

Heramiir couldn't help but smile as the spell worked exactly the way he'd envisioned, despite never having tried it before. He took an instant to study the swirling, smoky rings with nothing but darkness at their core. There were two identical sets. The first was grouped around Messand's command tent, the second positioned right in front of each catapult. They were ready to receive their payloads, and both armies stopped for a long moment to stare at the horrifying sight.

An enterprising mage near the king's command tent shot a bolt of energy at one of the inky clouds. The beam appeared on Heramiir's side of the river, emerging from the corresponding vortex. One of his catapults was blasted into splinters as the bolt struck it. The enemy mage didn't seem to have seen where his blast of power had gone though as it disappeared into the vortex. He would never have the chance to find out.

With a last nod to Nereth, his general gave the order to fire. As the restraining cords were released, the catapult arms sprung up, causing the nineteen remaining siege weapons to fire their deadly payloads. The burning cargoes were flung into the waiting vortices, where they were instantly transported to their counterparts on the far side of the river.

The flaming balls held together just long enough to hit the command tent from every side. The burning balls of pitch and sawdust disintegrated on impact, incinerating the structure in instants. In other places they just punched straight through the sides and roof of the structure where the king's officers were meeting.

As the sawdust freed itself from the pitch coating, the substance mushroomed out and up in a fireball a hundred spans high. In moments, all that was left was a burning swath of ground and a plume of oily black smoke where the king's command tent had stood just moments before.

"Reload!" Nereth shouted at the siege commander. Heramiir let the vortices on the far side of the river collapse in on themselves, each creating a thunderclap and rush of wind as it did so. Several nearby soldiers were knocked off their feet, appearing stunned for a few seconds.

He hadn't expected that, but it would be useful later.

The rest of the king's army had overcome their shock, and the closest units were already rushing towards the Mirallyn, armed and armoured, and more than ready to fight.

'Send in the infantry,' Heramiir thought at Deshara. 'The fjords are to be held at all costs, but our men are not to advance beyond them for any reason.'

Deshara turned her head towards where he was sitting on his giant black steed at the crest of the ridge and stared. With a slight shrug, she closed her dark brown eyes and used her particular gifts to send the message out to Hassan with her mind. A few moments later, she reopened them with a predatory smile.

'*He will comply,*' she thought back at him with her unique talent. '*Though he had some not very complimentary things to say,*' she commented while running a hand languidly through her shoulder-length black hair.

Another few seconds passed with no major activity among his ranks, though Heramiir never took his eyes off the battlefield in front of him. As the moments rolled by without any visible action, he couldn't help but wonder if Hassan had chosen this moment to betray him. It would almost be surprising since the lives of the hostages still in Miralthrall would be forfeit.

Another five seconds passed without action, but finally his infantry began moving towards the fjords. They began at a shambling trot, and then sped up to a run as both his own forces, and the king's army, attempted to reach the narrow passage first. Whoever did so would be able to establish a defensive line which their enemies would have to spend many lives to break.

From the other side of the river, a blast of flame came screaming across the intervening space. It wasn't particularly accurate, but with his army still massing, it didn't have to be. It hit the army, killing dozens of his men and injuring ten times that number as it immolated the area around the impact site.

"Davoor, Deshara, that one is yours," Heramiir said as he tried to refocus his spell, opening the corresponding vortices on the far side of the Mirallyn once again. A bolt of what looked to be lightning struck out at him, but Nereth blocked it with a shield he already had in place.

Refusing to allow the near miss to distract him enough that his spell broke, Heramiir blocked out all else, trusting Nereth to keep him safe. With an almost painful intensity of concentration, he was able to make the spell work again, if barely. As the siege commander signalled the catapults' readiness, Nereth once again gave the order to fire.

Nineteen balls of fiery death hurtled out through their respective vortices and smashed into the enemy troops beyond the river, killing hundreds and throwing their rearmost ranks into chaos. The closer troops he could ignore for now, his men would hold them at the narrow fjord long enough for the larger threat to be dealt with.

The king's magi were regrouping now and beginning to fight back, but their response was slow. His ambush had worked, the king's forces were not operating as they should, and a clear lack of unified leadership was apparent in their piecemeal response.

A protective shield began to appear over the king's army in patchwork squares, and Heramiir smiled. At least thirty of the Aramarian magi must be channelling all their strength into making the sections of that shield for it to cover so large an area. In an instant, at least a quarter of the opposing magi had effectively put themselves out of the fight.

It wasn't enough. He didn't just need to win here today, he needed to do so decisively. With a minimum of his own men killed in the process.

Davoor sent out a blast of raw power at the enemy mage who had assaulted them, and Deshara followed it with a storm of razor-sharp icicles. The enemy spellcaster seemed quite talented, and at the last instant a glowing blue shield appeared and took the brunt of Davoor's blast. The impact knocked him off his feet though and Deshara's attack sailed on past, hitting a patch of ground behind the mage without doing any actual harm.

It was hard to tell who it was from this distance. There

were only a handful of magi in Aramar's college who could have so effectively blocked one of Davoor's attacks without warning.

It was probably Veroneth if he had not been in the command pavilion when the catapults had struck, or perhaps Adraam. If Korvith had done his job well, Erian would have kept Tolmarak in the capital to deal with the threat he posed. And to make sure no more of the magi went over to Heramiir's side as well.

His old teacher was not as strong in the Gift as Heramiir was, but the wily old archmage was certainly as ruthless. He tried not to let it show in public, but Heramiir knew him well. The old man had always preferred to work in the background when he needed something done that the others might not agree with. At least, that was how Tolmarak had been during his apprenticeship. He doubted that anything would have changed since his old teacher had returned to Aramar to take the role of king's advisor and leader of the college. But that was twenty years gone now and things could have changed. Tolmarak would be a deadly opponent once they reached the capital, and Heramiir found himself thankful the old archmage was not in command of the force he was now facing.

"Brace!" Nereth shouted.

A large blue hemisphere appeared above them an instant before a bolt of lightning crashed down from a clear sky above, immediately followed by a second and then a third. The mage casting them was strong, and the strain of keeping the shield intact was already showing on Nereth's face. For a moment, the air crackled with electricity, making the hair on his head lift of its own accord. After a long moment of scanning the field, Davoor located the attacker and pointed at the far bank. A needle thin bar of white flame erupted from his outstretched digit and disappeared again almost immediately. It was enough though, and the sky above ceased raining lightning at the same time Davoor attacked, confirming his deadly work with silence.

Deshara nodded approvingly, and the bald archmage grinned in return before returning his attention to the far bank.

There were at least a hundred magi down there that Heramiir could see with his Gift-enhanced sight now that he could once again use the Gift freely. As they had expected, most of the stronger individuals were working on offence. The weaker magi were banding together to form the huge patchwork defensive shield that was, for now at least, covering their troops and keeping them mostly safe from harm.

One of the king's magi took a shot at another vortex, but the angle was off. When the large ball of fire emerged from its counterpart on the ridge, it flew off into the air, missing the catapult behind it.

"I think they saw that!" Davoor called over the distant din of battle. Several of the king's magi were pointing up at the ridge where they now knew that spells could pass through the vortices in either direction.

Heramiir nodded, letting the swirling clouds of blackness on the far bank collapse again, before re-forming them all over the middle of the enemy's defensive shield. To his credit, the siege commander had not been idle while the archmagi were under attack. Seeing that all was ready for the next volley, Nereth gave the order to fire. The catches were released, and the deadly payloads flung through Heramiir's spells to crash into the shield with a grinding clamour. The section of shimmering light they hit simply disappeared, annihilated by such massive physical force. Even he would have had trouble containing that blast, and the far weaker mage below who was responsible for that section of the shield was instantly overwhelmed.

At least half the missiles made it through the gap, striking home before the other magi could readjust the glowing blue roof of protection. Even from his place on the ridge, Heramiir could hear the screams as a gaping swath suddenly appeared in the enemy ranks. At least three thousand men had just been killed outright by those impacts. Many others were severely burned as the searing sawdust and pitch was breathed into their lungs, finishing them, or making them wish it had.

In a way, Heramiir felt sorry for them. Erian had been recruiting, just as he had, and most of these men were not his real enemies. Yet he had no recourse but to go through them to achieve his goals.

Again, Heramiir let the vortices collapse down on the plain, only to make them reappear once the catapults were ready to fire.

As it turned out, the king's magi were ready for them, and as soon as the vortices had formed, they launched attacks of their own. Several went wide. Even so, six more of his catapults were blasted apart by fire, raw power, and combinations of spells that were impossible to distinguish in the brief moment they were in flight.

The sudden destruction of a third of the catapults sent the siege line into chaos. As the survivors struggled to pick themselves up, too many remained on the ground where they'd fallen, dead, or too injured to move. The moment those crews still able to do so had released their payloads,

Heramiir let the taxing spell drop on the other side of the river. He would have to wait until what was left of the catapult crews had dispersed to the remaining machines and taken up their new positions.

The king's magi seemed to take the blunted volley as a sign Heramiir's plans were falling apart. They renewed their attack with vigour, forcing Nereth to order the lesser magi to concentrate on protecting his troops, just as the king's forces were already doing. Surprisingly though, most of the enemy magi's attention was currently directed at the rank-and-file men, and not Heramiir's own spellcasters. They seemed to be trying to clear a space on this side of the fjords so that the king's army could take the field through sheer force of numbers. It all but proved Tolmarak was not amongst them. If he were on the field, all of Heramiir's magi would be under siege, rather than just his lieutenants. As it stood, with the king's magi concentrating on their shield, attacking his troops, or attempting to kill him and his lieutenants, his mid-level magi were operating with near impunity.

A flit of something black darted across his vision, then reared up, ten feet tall and full of teeth and claws. The terrifying creature made a frenzied dash at him before he could react, and Heramiir only recognised the harmless spirit spell for what it was just in time. He sneered. Such a childish trick, but it had distracted him enough that he'd come very close to losing his grip on the master's vortex spell. Once he let that go, the extra power he'd been painstakingly hoarding all this time would dissipate. He would not be able to renew the vortices once it was gone.

For long minutes he held the spell in place on this side of the ridge, his concentration wavering as the catapult line righted itself. It was taking everything he had to focus on the master's spell now, and Heramiir found himself unable to take part elsewhere. His lieutenants made up for it, attacking the enemy magi with gusto and causing chaos in the king's lines almost every time they struck.

His forces were taking losses too, and Heramiir cringed a little every time an aura on this side of the river winked out. Overall, his less powerful magi were holding their own better than he'd expected. Perhaps he shouldn't be surprised. After all, practice on Aramar's range was one thing, fighting for your life on the western border was quite another. It seemed to have given his people an aggressive edge, one which pleased him immensely.

It was hard to tell how many of the opposing magi had been killed. Most of their auras were out of range. Those more powerful were staying well back from the fjords so as not to become immediate targets.

Three more times he was attacked in quick succession while the catapults were reset. Thankfully, Nereth was up to the task of holding the enemy off long enough for his other lieutenants to neutralise the threats as they appeared.

With the enemy's auras out of range, locating the offending targets was a matter of seeing where the spells originated from and attacking the person at its source.

Doing battle this way was a risky proposition, and required a keen eye and excellent reflexes. Too many magi on both sides were being killed after sending out spells and not protecting themselves adequately afterwards, thinking themselves obscured amongst this churning mass of men.

Eventually the catapult line was back under control, the fires from the destroyed engines no longer endangering the other machines or their own payloads. Heramiir nodded in approval.

'Find Veroneth if he still lives,' Heramiir thought at Deshara as he studied the field below. There were bolts of colour and light sizzling through the air in every direction now as the lesser magi attacked and counter-attacked each other repeatedly. Some of them were aiming at the shields above the two armies, others at the opposing magi or even the troops themselves, but Heramiir's purpose had been achieved. The enemy was in disarray, though still fighting well considering they had done so without most of their leaders from the outset. His initial attacks on their rear guard had blocked off their retreat. It hadn't taken them long to realise that since he could reach even their support lines with the Gift, their only way to safety was to go through Heramiir's forces. They were committed to the fight now, which was what he'd wanted all along. If he could disable or kill enough of the enemy magi, this battle might go according to plan to the level that rarely happened once the first blow had been struck. It was a thought that made him smile, though he never stopped scanning the field as he did.

There was a knot of about six or seven magi off on the left flank of the king's army, and once the catapults were in order to fire again. Heramiir took the opportunity and created a vortex right in front of them. As expected, they all turned and fired spells through it, obliterating the catapult and crew on the other side. Another was damaged to the point where its payload rolled off the cup and burned its own machine as the crew retreated from the sudden conflagration.

Unfortunately for the magi below, they failed to see the other vortices Heramiir had opened behind them as soon as their backs were turned. Nereth gave the order, and the twelve remaining siege machines once again fired their deadly payloads.

The magi below disappeared as the flying balls of sawdust and pitch hurtled through them, cutting another swath in the enemy ranks as the projectiles continued to roll.

Heramiir nodded in approval, the attack proving even more effective than he'd hoped.

Unfortunately, things were not going entirely his own way. One of his less experienced magi halfway up the incline exploded in a spray of gore and viscera. Whoever she was, she had been unable to shield herself from the bolt of raw power an enemy archmage had thrown in her direction.

"Two more rounds!" Nereth called to Heramiir, grunting with exertion as he deflected yet another bar of fire up into the cloudless sky, then struck back at the offending mage.

Heramiir nodded his acknowledgement of the siege machines' ammunition shortage and studied the field below. The ground to the rear of the loyalist army was ablaze from his first hits on the command tent. Cinders and pitch seemed to have started the grass there burning on its own. On either flank of the king's army, nothing yet stopped them from retreating at will, and in more than one direction no less. He couldn't allow that if his goals here were to be realised this day.

Eventually, the remaining catapults were loaded again. Heramiir opened the vortices just off the left flank of Erian's force in a straight line not intended to inflict casualties this time, though he hoped that some would result. He wanted to pen them in, from the river to halfway back to where their command pavilion had stood not half an hour before. In moments it was done, but little changed on the field until the final round of burning ammunition was spent a minute later. With the right flank now cut off as well, the situation seemed to finally get whoever was commanding the king's forces' attention.

Heramiir was finally able to let the master's spell drop once the last of the ammunition was spent. The vortices were useless for living beings, and the oily black clouds shrunk into nothing with a loud clap of thunder. His hands remained clenched on his mount's reins for long moments. He closed his eyes, letting his mind drift and allowing the portion which had been holding the spell so firmly in place to return to a more relaxed state.

The apprentice's exercise made him no less exhausted, but with his visual imagination cleared, he was ready to concentrate on other spells. Heramiir took enough time before returning his attention to the battle to turn and give one quick nod of approval to the siege commander. The man had done well given the level of casualties his unit had sustained, and his part in this was now over.

Seeking where best to strike next, he couldn't help but wonder if Veroneth had already been killed in the attack on the command pavilion. He had seen the archmage earlier in the day, but so far nothing the enemy had thrown at them had been powerful enough to have come from the battle hardened archmage. Heramiir was sure he would have been chosen to lead the Aramarian magi all the way out here, assuming that Tolmarak was, in fact, still in the capital. He dismissed the thought. Tolmarak wasn't here. This battle would be going quite differently if he were.

There was fierce fighting for several minutes down by the fjords as the remaining half of the king's magi changed their tactics. Concentrating their attacks on one of his magi after another, they killed several in quick succession, but left themselves more vulnerable in return. As soon as he saw the pattern, Heramiir took more direct action on the offending magi, tired though he now was. Along with Davoor and Deshara, he punished the enemy ranks enough that they abandoned the tactic, once again becoming cautious of revealing themselves in such a manner. But the damage had already been done, and a full score of his magi, including two archmagi, had been ripped apart by the horrifying cascade of destructive spells.

It was enough that the rest of his magi hesitated, their attack flagging as their own casualties mounted.

Down at the fjords, the infantry was doing their best to hold the position, but the king's men were becoming desperate, and fighting all the harder for it. Heramiir knew he would have to divert some of his magi to help if the situation got any worse.

A base rumbling began to issue from somewhere near the river. Heramiir watched in disbelief as a great rent opened in the ground. An ear shattering grinding split the gentle hill on his side of the river with a giant gash into which at least five thousand of his men fell screaming. The hole was not deep, and many of the men would have survived the fall if it hadn't been for the gaping chasm joining with the river. The Mirallyn rushed to inundate the new depression, drowning the tangled men below. Many near the top tried to climb out, but soon, even most of those succumbed as their metal armour made it all but impossible for them to swim.

The whole incident took no more than fifteen seconds, but when the ground stopped trembling, there was a moment of virtual silence on the field. Regardless of allegiance, men from both armies stopped to pick themselves up and stare in horror. Only those in the very front line, who had no time to consider the magnitude of what had just occurred, kept fighting.

Heramiir found his heart pounding as he took in the sight. It was a feeling he was ill-accustomed to as he shouted an order into Deshara's mind.

'Get our least powerful Mage down near the river and find the aura of whoever did… that!'

Very few magi could have pulled off that spell, even had it been one that was sanctioned. In truth, Heramiir had never seen its like, and that worried him. There was at least one extremely powerful mage down there that thought as he did. Who had experimented with the Gift illegally and come up with a battle spell that was highly effective, and unknown to their enemy. He wished he could convert that mage, but right now they were just too dangerous to be allowed to live. Once the mage's aura was located, he would have to take the target out of the fight any way he could. That single attack had cost him almost as many troops as the rest of the battle combined to this point.

In a pitched battle, the casualties to the infantry would have been much higher on both sides. But that was why he had chosen to fight here, where the narrow fjords restricted the actual combat to a space no more than fifty men across. That was also why it was vital that the narrow stretch of water be held and not crossed. That way, his army would receive the minimum number of casualties possible until his magi could finish the king's Gift users and come to the infantry's aid. His army included a heavy complement of cavalry units, of course, but without the ability to flank the enemy or charge in formation, they had yet to be involved.

Their turn would come once the king's routed forces had withdrawn, or been pushed back from the fjords. A proper formation could then charge the enemy, finishing whatever remnants escaped his trap.

In the meantime, piles of the dead were mounting up at the fjords. Periodically they would dam the river until the Mirallyn could reassert its flow with enough pressure to push the obstructions further out into more open water beyond.

The river had turned a sickly red for several hundred spans downstream.

The men in the front line had never stopped fighting, picking themselves up as soon as the ground had stopped shaking and beginning the struggle again without pause. Meanwhile, the king's magi had put up a shield wall on either side of the fjords now as well. It was stopping the men milling on the front lines from firing arrows at each other. The only space they left was at the narrow fjords where the real fight was going on. Heramiir let them keep their wall in place since it would hamper the king's archers as much as it would his. Besides, having the infantry fight and defeat the opposing army through strength of numbers had never been part of his plans this day.

No, he needed those men alive. Defeating the king's main force today would be a monumentally important step towards gaining dominion over the eastern portion of the country. But Jeranon was vast, and he would need most of these men to secure it once Erian had been deposed.

After all, he wanted to rule Jeranon, not destroy it, and for that he would need to leave order in his wake, not chaos. For that to happen, he would require men to enforce that rule, at least at first, and there were only so many to be had. For that reason alone, a pitched battle with the king's army had always been out of the question. The holding action his forces were taking today, in fact, the entire massive army he had brought with him, was merely a diversion. His plan had always been to overawe the mid-level officers who would end up in charge of the king's army after his ambush. To allow his Gift users to take the victory by neutralising their true foe, the Aramarian magi. So far, despite the surprises, events had unfolded more or less as he had hoped. Heramiir eyed the battlefield at the base of the shallow decline even as he shielded himself from yet another Gift-wrought attack. He could brush aside assaults of average power with little difficulty from this range now that he didn't have the master's spell taking up all his concentration. In a way he enjoyed it, since every attack he blunted was one less that could threaten his less powerful magi. magi, who in some cases might have fallen to them.

Heramiir scanned the field for any sign the enemy mage was preparing another deadly surprise for his army, but wherever the mage had gone, Heramiir couldn't see them. Frustratingly, he had no other course but to wait agonising minutes for Deshara's report, and he used the time to begin taking part in the battle itself.

There were perhaps three dozen of the king's magi assigned to offence still fighting effectively down there now. Heramiir wanted to incapacitate as many of them as he could without killing them. It would be difficult from this range. If he were closer, he could have clubbed them over the head with an earth spell, or sealed them in a Gift-wrought barrier of spirit magic that would nullify their powers for a time. Unfortunately, from this distance the people on the other side of the fjords were mere ants to his sight, and even the most powerful archmage's aura was far out of range. For that to change, he would have to move closer. But if he did, every mage on the field would know exactly where he was, and would no doubt all target him at once. Even he couldn't survive that. All he could do was spot the positions spells were launched from with his eyes. It was all but impossible to track the individuals responsible. Heramiir found he would constantly lose them amongst the churning throng of soldiers pressing towards the river, or shambling back through their lines towards the healers' tent. He had ordered that structure off limits to attack, as there would be magi inside seeing to the wounded, or no longer opposing them.

Deshara sent an image to his mind of a mage beyond the river, not a powerful individual, certainly not the one he was searching for, but a target nonetheless. The image was strange though, as if seen from just across the water.

She's linking me into what her scout is seeing...

Heramiir frowned. He hadn't known she could do that.

What else has she failed to mention?

Keeping the image firmly in his mind, Heramiir located the man down by the river and lashed out with a spell of air, clouting the man solidly in the head. The amount of force was off, and the mage went down with a broken neck. A section of the protective shield that covered the king's army went with him.

Heramiir cursed himself for a fool, not understanding what had gone wrong. He didn't make mistakes like that, and could only put the miscalculation down to the strange bond. It was one thing to kill an enemy mage in self-defence, but that man's power had all been going into the defensive shield. He had not been attempting to harm them. He ordered Deshara to find another target.

The scout moved on and soon enough came into range of another loyalist aura, this one far more powerful, which Heramiir pinpointed with his eyes. So, Veroneth had survived his initial assault. The Aramarian archmage was kneeling near the river, attempting to cast a difficult spell while two other magi protected him with shields.

Heramiir thought for a moment before asking Deshara whether she could send the image to Davoor as well. After a moment, the ebony-skinned man nodded as the vision reached him.

"On my signal, incapacitate the two magi guarding Veroneth, I'll deal with the archmage myself."

He didn't know how long it would take Veroneth to complete his earthquake spell again, but he also didn't want to find out under these circumstances. Davoor and Deshara reported their readiness, and Heramiir gave the order without hesitation. In the strange second view, he saw the blue shields drop almost simultaneously as they came under attack from two of Heramiir's most deadly spellcasters. Veroneth's startled expression was satisfying as they fell. Heramiir gave him no time to react, knocking him backwards with a far less forceful spell of air than the one he had previously used. Once the archmage stopped tumbling across the ground like a blown leaf, Veroneth appeared unconscious. Heramiir bound him in bonds of air and then used the master's spirit spell to form a small prison around him, blocking in his powers. It would only hold for a few hours, but that should be enough.

If the sun had already set, the effect would have been stronger, but the power prison was enough to take the deadly archmage out of the fight. With any luck, Veroneth could be made to see reason once he woke to find his army annihilated and all hope of rescue gone. The man was a highly effective battle mage, and Heramiir was loath to lose such a resource. He would need such men in the coming years once Erian had been deposed.

He was nearing the end of his limits now, and a sharp headache had begun in the front of his skull. The magic the master had granted him had worn off when the vortex spell had been completed, leaving him exhausted but with work still to do. Everything since then had been like exercising after three days without food. Bodies and minds could only be pushed so far before they refused to do as bidden. But the battle was far from over. As the scout moved along the river, both Davoor and he disabled what magi the scout could sense in range as often as they could. They were forced to kill some who withstood their initial assault, but Heramiir only did so as a last resort now that another option had presented itself.

The scout mage had nearly crossed the field when the vision turned a blinding red for a moment and dissipated altogether. Heramiir was left nauseous and disoriented for a long moment as he readjusted to the different perspective of his own natural vision. Down near the river, an explosion was just clearing, leaving a black plume of smoke in its wake. That blast had just killed their scouting mage, of that Heramiir was certain.

Further down his own line, Deshara had fallen from her mount and was clutching her head in pain. She was slow to rise from the ground as she tried to shake off whatever horrific experience she had just shared in the dead mage's last moment.

Heramiir took stock as he looked around the field. The spells coming back at his magi from across the river had all but stopped now. Only a few lucky stragglers remained active of the king's magi, those and the ones maintaining the defence for the troops. Those magi would be easily neutralised once his own people no longer needed to concentrate so much on their own defence. The last few of the king's magi actively attacking his forces were too far back from the fjords for another scout to be useful. Besides, as he had already seen, sending them in too close was not a good idea. Especially now that the king's magi seemed to have caught on to what they were doing. Or perhaps they attacked him because they thought it was the scout mage himself who was inflicting so much damage on their ranks. Either way, Heramiir saw no virtue in wasting another of his Gift users in the same way.

"Davoor, I am going to sow fire among their remaining magi. Once they are distracted, strike as best you can."

The big man beside him nodded without taking his eyes from the field.

Beyond him, Deshara had regained her mount. The mind witch looked to still be in a fair amount of pain, but Heramiir was pleased to see she had refocused her attention back on the fjords, where it belonged.

Reaching out with the Gift, Heramiir used the simplest destructive spell he knew. With all the strength he could muster, he immolated the stretch of ground that contained the remaining enemy magi. From this distance he didn't expect the inferno he summoned across the river to crack the Gift-wrought barriers the king's magi would no doubt have around themselves. Anything else nearby would be burnt to cinders in moments.

As the wall of flames cleared, the flickering of blue shields stood out in stark contrast against the black smoke rising from the ground. Davoor struck without mercy, felling four of the king's magi in seconds as their weakened shields gave way under the deadly archmage's assault. Heramiir gathered his remaining reserves for a long minute, and then with a great effort expended the last of his strength to immolate the enemy position once again. The flames spiralled a hundred feet high as they engulfed the area. Everything nearby disappeared into the inferno once again as he sustained the attack for as long as his dwindling strength would allow. He was left exhausted, clinging to his mutated steed for support when his strength finally gave out.

When the flames cleared, Heramiir straightened in his saddle, exhausted from working the Gift on so large a scale from a distance of almost two miles. Even he was not immune to such fatigue it seemed, yet as the secondary explosions caused by Davoor and Deshara cleared, he saw he had accomplished his intent. Only a half dozen of the king's magi had survived the assault in fighting condition. A few dozen mageguard whom the more powerful magi or archmagi had been able to shield were also still standing.

There were grass fires in a hundred places where the outskirts of the inferno had taken hold. In the centre itself, there was only blackened ground, scorched and barren. So consuming had the inferno been that only sporadic smoke appeared here and there where a stubborn plant or piece of armour had somewhat survived the deadly blaze.

"Nereth, continue the assault," he ordered. His general nodded, dropping the defensive shield which had been protecting them both throughout the course of the battle so far. It was time for them to trade rolls. Heramiir had just enough strength left in him to form a small shield around the two of them and their mounts, but that was all, and it wouldn't last long.

The armoured archmage gave a nod to Davoor, which the dark-skinned man returned with an unfriendly grin. The pair returned their attention to the battlefield, launching a punishing attack on the few remaining magi in the group on the other side of the river. Three of them fell to the vicious assault, their defences already stretched to breaking point. Heramiir held up a hand, signalling a change in tactics, and Davoor's shoulders sagged. The threat they posed no longer warranted a full-scale attack. Despite the inherent difficulty it posed, it was time to try incapacitating instead of killing the last of the king's beleaguered battle magi.

It took several minutes, and the last knot of offensive enemy spellcasters fought valiantly, but when they were done, there was an eerie silence on the battlefield. Not that the troops below had halted their mad struggle. With the constant assault coming from the other side of the river coming to a halt, the ridgeline where he stood was no longer in combat. For long moments he scanned the field, trying to find any magi who might be waiting for an opportune moment to strike. After a long minute fruitlessly spent, he knew his spellcasters had done their work well.

There were still many of the less powerful magi down there maintaining the king's Gift-wrought shield, but they were preoccupied, and easily dealt with.

'Deshara,' he thought grimly. '*Order all the magi to attack the shield at the right front flank of Erian's army until it collapses, and move on from there.*'

There was a momentary pause as his mind witch

conveyed the orders 'telepathically'. That was what the master had called it, and then replied.

'We are ready.'

'Proceed,' Heramiir thought back.

A moment later, the better part of a hundred magi across his lines used the advantage of the height their gentle slope gave them to launch whatever attacks they could at the nearest shield. It flickered and died almost quicker than he could see.

Heramiir smiled grimly as hundreds of the king's men who had been relying on its protection were killed by spells intended to destroy the shield, but which had been cast too slowly. Dozens of the spells passed through where it had been just moments before, striking the men beneath.

He had fought many battles over the last decade, against many foes, but rarely had he seen a battle go this well. As his magi struck again, the second section of shield went down moments later with much the same result. A cry went up from the opposing army, and the king's men surged forward, perhaps sensing that this was their last chance for victory.

So far, his men had held them at the fjords, but from his vantage on the hilltop, it seemed that this time his men were having trouble containing the press of the king's army. It appeared their entire force was now desperate to make their way across the narrow stretch of water. It was a sensible tactic. Their only chance of survival now rested on mixing their own lines with those of his men, and they seemed to know it. If they succeeded, his magi would be unable to attack the king's forces en masse unless willing to kill as many of their own troops as they were of the enemy.

His magi effortlessly took a third section of the shield

down. It was enough, and he allowed them to attack the shield randomly as the king's army lost cohesion. Their push across the river was not yielding results fast enough, and more and more of them began to run as they saw their companions being systematically slaughtered. With his own spellcasters able to concentrate on attack now for the most part, it was not long until the entire shield was flickering or down. The few sections which held fast didn't hamper his men. His troops had pushed the king's forces back to the river with what looked, even from this distance, to be nothing more than sheer strength of will. It was time.

'Deshara, give the word,' he ordered his lieutenant. 'Destroy them.'

For the first time in his life, Heramiir saw Deshara smile. Not her usual half feral grin, but a genuine smile of pleasure. It made his skin crawl.

'Your wish is my command, Archmage,' she responded just as silently, but then closed her eyes and focused her will to send out his instructions.

There was a moment of hesitation, as though none of his magi wanted to be the one to begin the slaughter that was about to follow. In the end, Davoor focused his will and called down a bolt of lightning from the clear blue sky onto the unprotected troops below. Earth and men erupted as he struck again and again to ever greater effect. Heramiir nodded his approval, and within instants the rest of his magi had taken up the distasteful task with passion. They wanted this ugliness over with as soon as was humanly possible.

For long moments, his magi sowed utter destruction among the enemy troops, their almost total lack of magical support now leaving them defenceless against the overwhelming onslaught. Thousands died each minute, and it wasn't long before the remnants of their panicked army began to flee in a full rout. There was no plan, no order to it, there was no longer an army. There were only desperate men trying to get away from this place with their lives before one of Heramiir's magi picked them out and decided their fleeing form was next.

One of the king's last remaining spellcasters had damaged the fjords he now noticed. The river there appeared to be uncrossable now, except for one very narrow line where only two or three men abreast could ride at any one time. It was a curious tactic, and he could only assume that one of the Aramarian magi had attempted to block his army from following when they had seen what was about to happen. Perhaps they had been killed before they could finish the job? It would take time to fix that. Operating creative spells underwater was all but impossible. The human imagination was not designed to fully interact with and process that environment, especially with the fouled water blocking their line of sight.

All his years of plotting, scheming, and moving in the shadows were finally coming to fruition. He had taken Miralthrall, the unconquerable city. He had solidified his hold on the Sammorand Plains and much of lower western Jeranon, and now he had routed the king's army in spectacular fashion. They were fleeing for their lives, all but the slowest and injured having reached a safe range from his magi now, though heedless of any kind of good military order. And yet his men had not pursued. There was something happening down at the fjords. He glanced at where his army should now be crossing, and then had to look again as he saw something unexpected.

Down in the narrow stretch of water there was a man. A single man on a horse, fighting with some kind of strange blade, blocking his entire army from passing at the now narrowed fjords. For long moments, Heramiir watched in fascination as the man held his ground no matter how many of Heramiir's troops attempted to dislodge him from his position.

After some time, Heramiir tore his eyes away from the spectacle to share a look with Nereth, who nodded in appreciation. Of all the king's men, this one alone had stayed behind to hold back his forces from overrunning what remained of the routed army.

The man below had no chance of succeeding. No matter how valiant of heart he was, or how exceptional his skills with that blade might be, he would eventually tire and be overrun. He must have known it when beginning this futile action. It was inevitable. But as the first minute passed, and then another, Heramiir began to wonder what strange forces were at work here. No single man could hold off an army, and yet from this distance at least, the warrior looked for all the world as if he intended to do just that.

As Heramiir continued to watch, he saw that although the horseman was tiring, every man who came near him still felt the bite of that blade. He slayed all who came within his reach, so many that eventually there rose a wall of Heramiir's dead men in front of him and his horse. His soldiers now had to scramble over them in an ungainly manner to reach him, making the unknown warrior's task that much easier.

Heramiir studied the scene before him, becoming less and less amused. There was some power at work here beyond the man's sheer skill with a blade. And yet the man had exhibited no use of the Gift that Heramiir could discern. It intrigued as much as worried him.

'If Hassan still lives, order him to attack that man with every soldier at his disposal!' Heramiir thought to Deshara as his troops paused in their fruitless assault for a long moment.

'I want him dead, and the remnants of the King's army overrun.'

Deshara nodded, closed her eyes, and a moment later his army surged forward to finish the fight. The man should have retreated then. Any sane man would have, knowing that he had achieved all he could. Far more than he had any right to, in truth. Instead, the horseman at the fjords turned his mount squarely into their charge and raised his blade. He waited calmly for the first of his opponents to clear the considerable mound of corpses he had created and bear murderously down upon him.

Heramiir nodded in respect for the man. The soldier waited, unyielding whilst the vast press of soldiers rushed over him, covering both the fjords and rider with the living tide of their bodies.

CHAPTER 25

A MAGE OF DARK ASPECT...

Hassan parried an overhead swing with his broadsword, then recovered and thrust at the man who was trying to kill him as rapidly as possible. He didn't connect. The man jumped backwards away from his blade, tripping on a body in the process and falling back behind a wall of other attackers.

As soon as Deshara had given the order he had sounded the charge, but the cursed woman had waited too long. The king's men had reached the fjords first. Whether the delay was to spite him, he had no way of knowing. But the sloppy timing didn't fit at all with Nereth's usual clockwork precision.

It had taken less than a minute to sprint towards the shallow stretch of the fjords and the impending fight. Even so, his men had been confronted by an ever-widening front of the king's loyal soldiers. Men desperate not to lose their foothold on this side of the river. The two armies had met head on in a grinding clash of steel and screams as they attempted to gain control of the narrow crossing. The momentum of their charge was expended in a moment, and it was down to butcher's work now as they struggled to push the king's men back across the river, and stay alive in the process.

On all sides, explosions of Gift-wrought power burst around him, and men in both armies screamed as they died, some in far worse ways than a sword could bring. To make matters worse, archers on both sides of the river had begun shooting across the gap. Hassan had been forced to order a shield wall formed along the waterway wherever there was not direct fighting. The sun beat down on them all, sinking further towards the western horizon behind Heramiir's army with each minute. Its glaring light would be in the loyalists' eyes, giving Heramiir's army the advantage over them in that respect as well.

Another opponent swung at him, and Hassan was forced to kill the man instead of just wounding him. For the fiftieth time this day he cursed Nereth and Heramiir for what they were forcing him to do.

There was no honour in this. He was killing the very men he should have been fighting with, and not only that, but leading others to it as well. Hassan's spirits sank even lower as one of the king's men lifted a sword to strike at him, and the soldier to Hassan's left took the opportunity to skewer the man with his blade.

But perhaps the worst part of it all was that they already seemed to be winning. They were closer to the fjords now than even a few moments before.

By taking away his battalion of loyal men at the last moment, Nereth had all but blunted his plans to sabotage the fight. He was no longer sure how he could affect this day's outcome in any meaningful way.

After everything else he had been forced to do, to betray, since the magi's rebellion, it was too much. For an instant he considered lowering his weapon and letting a soldier who was still loyal to his vows finish him.

The only thing that kept his blade moving was the thought of his wife Sumi and their son Luthor. They would be alone in a hostile city if he didn't return. Or in an even worse situation if the archmage was too displeased with his efforts.

He parried another blow and thrust, blinking away the blood that splattered across his eyes as he ended the life of yet another honourable man.

There was a tremendous explosion behind him, this one close enough to shake the ground and send men flying in all directions. Hassan had to struggle to stay on his feet. A limp body plummeted overhead, thrown by the force of the spell. As it landed ingloriously amongst the tightly packed men at the fjords, Hassan knew that there would be no quarter given by either side this day. One army would emerge victorious, the other would be crushed to the last man.

When the shaking stopped, Hassan was one of the few soldiers in his area who had kept his feet. He took the instant to look around at more than just his immediate surroundings. If he thought things were bad down here at the fjords, it was nothing compared to what was happening on the hill behind him and the plains in front. Explosion after explosion wound its way amongst the ranks of magi on either side of the river. Gift-wrought shields flickered as they were hit. The mage behind them returning the salvo with one of their own, if they were still able. The sky above the armies crackled with magical energy. Beams of fire, light, and the Maker only knew what else, were traded from one army to the other.

Above the king's magi, the swirling black clouds Heramiir had used to obliterate General Messand's command pavilion had now turned their attention to the army itself. Every so often they would slam down burning catapult ammunition on the troops, filling the area with smoke. Otherwise able soldiers fell to their knees in droves, gasping for air if they were near the blast zones. Those within were obliterated by the impacts.

The confusion of losing their leaders seemed to have the effect the archmage intended. Without a unified command structure, the king's magi were attacking a variety of targets. Heramiir's magi seemed more intent on striking down the king's spellcasters than could be said for the other way around. The oily black smoke the catapult shots left in their wake also meant the king's magi had to reposition before they could reacquire their targets.

A few of the king's magi seemed to have worked out what the vortices were. During that last volley they had fired their own destructive spells through the openings, blasting about a quarter of the siege weapons into useless pieces.

Still, Heramiir was winning. If he was going to do anything to change that, it had to be soon. If things continued to progress to where they were given the command to cross the fjords and surround the king's forces, there would be nothing more he could do.

A hulking man appeared in front of him wielding a double-bladed battle axe, and Hassan knew he was in for a proper fight. The giant of a man was holding it with only one hand. In his other, a metal shield which must have weighed as much as Hassan was held firm. The man swung at him faster than anyone his size had a right to, and Hassan ducked back just in time to remove himself from its path.

The enormous man took a quick step forward and bashed him with the shield before he could recover. He found himself laying on his back on the blood-stained ground, head ringing from the blow. The huge man advanced with a look of keen concentration on his face, half an eye on what was happening around him at all times.

The man was a veteran, intelligent too, unless Hassan missed his mark. There would be no tricking this one. For the first time in years, Hassan felt over matched.

"A little help!" He called out, trying not to sound unsure of himself. After all, he was supposed to be a general.

A soldier heard him and charged the massively shouldered man from the side. The king's man swung his axe, taking the unfortunate soldier's head from his shoulders. Without slowing, he turned to ram the full length of that four-foot shield across the body of another combatant, just as he had Hassan. The second attacker fell to the ground and remained still.

The king's man never broke stride.

Out of nowhere Jarl sprang over Hassan, dropping to his knees to avoid the slashing axe blades, and chopping at the enormous man's leg with his sword.

The giant of a man howled in pain, but the thick chainmail greaves he wore kept his leg attached. Still, the blow left a nasty gash where it had penetrated the steel. Soldiers were rushing in from every side now, and after hitting Jarl with the heavy shield, he retreated towards his line. Another soldier feinted from the side while a companion snuck up behind and thrust a blade into his side. The huge soldier stood up very straight against the agony. With a last burst of strength he swung the axe, cutting the man who had stabbed him nearly in half. The sword in his side came free as his attacker died, and he fell bleeding and unconscious to the ground.

"What are you doing here!" Hassan shouted once both he

and Jarl had regained their feet, though still in arms reach of the front line.

"I got… separated, from the rest of the men. Luck that I did by the look of things!" Jarl invoked over the din as he parried another blow.

There was no end to the opponents in front of them, and Hassan was having a hard enough time keeping the enemy from skewering him without carrying on a conversation as well.

Again the ground shook as the catapults fired their burning payloads off to the left of the king's force. Less than a minute later they repeated the process to the right. From the plumes of smoke rising from the debris it looked as though Heramiir was trying to funnel the enemy into the fjords.

It wasn't until he had helped beat back three more soldiers that he noticed that the swirling black vortices which had been plaguing the enemy lines had disappeared. He glanced over his shoulder to confirm that they were no longer at Heramiir's end of the field either. The moment of inattention almost cost him a leg as he was forced to jump wildly to avoid a well-timed stroke from yet another adversary.

Coming down hard, he twisted his ankle and fell. The attacker raised his sword and struck while Hassan attempted to roll away, cursing as he stuck himself on the belt dagger of a fallen man. The swordsman's swing hit dirt behind him. He rolled back off the knife blade, gasping in pain as he grabbed at the man's sword with a gauntleted fist. He thrust towards the soldier's gut with his own broad blade, which was as high as he could reach lying on his back in the soaking mud. The man collapsed with a groan, and

Hassan crab-walked backward as quickly as he could. He dropped his own heavy broadsword, taking a far less weighty blade from one of the dead men that littered this part of the field. As soon as he was no longer in immediate danger, he examined the small wound where the knife had stuck him in the side, penetrating the chainmail cuirass he wore. It was his own fault. If he hadn't hit the point of the blade so hard, it never would have broken through the good steel of his armour. Fortunately the wound didn't seem too bad, and not more than an inch or so deep. It would require a few stitches once the day was done, but for right now he would just have to put up with it.

He tried to lift the lighter sword, testing his movement against the wound and gasping as he felt it tear a little further. The bleeding increased to an unacceptable level.

His time on the front line of this fight was done. Bending down, he used the sword to slice off a strip of a fallen soldier's jacket. He stuffed the material under his cuirass to stem the flow of blood that was now seeping out at a concerning rate, even for him. The knife must have hit more than meat to make him bleed like this.

Holding the cloth tight with his left hand and the small sword in his right, he looked around for the rest of his troops. Unsurprisingly, they were nowhere to be seen amongst the seething mass of men and explosions.

Something pink bolted past his eyes, and before he could react, a space a hundred spans behind him was immolated with flames. The spell had obliterated everything and everyone which had been there a moment before.

This was insane. It wasn't even a battle. There was no evidence of stratagems or ploys being implemented this day. It was simply two armies bringing their full wrath down upon one another and caring nothing for the casualties so long as they won the day. And yet, while Heramiir might be the head of their new power structure, Hassan knew it was Nereth who had planned this engagement. He couldn't shake the feeling that they had not yet seen the archmagi's full design.

For long moments he searched the area with his eyes, trying again to find his men. If they were in position near the rear of the army as Nereth had said, it might be possible to mount an attack on Heramiir's magi themselves. Their chances of success would be slight, and likely very few of them would survive. But if they could disrupt Heramiir's spellcasters, it might free up the king's magi to damage their ranks enough to turn the balance of the battle.

Jarl freed himself from the fray and came trotting back to Hassan's side with a weary look in his eye.

"What are we doing, Sir?" he asked just loudly enough to be heard by Hassan alone.

For a long moment Hassan studied the damage being inflicted on the king's army before looking back at Heramiir's forces. The archmage's army was in slightly more disarray since the king's magi seemed to be focusing more on the common troops than their counterparts were. Yet Heramiir's army still outnumbered them.

Hassan looked over the field a final time before grimly making his decision. It was not what he had been hoping for, not even sound strategy truth be told, but there was no other option. The king's spellcasters were being mauled by Heramiir's battle hardened magi, and unless something changed immediately, this battle was already decided. It was only a matter of time.

"You know where our men are?" he asked Jarl, and the

man he had known for years nodded that he did.

"Take me to them. We must attack Heramiir's magi head on and kill as many of them as we can, regardless of the cost. Our only chance is to hope that the king's army can take it from there.

Again Jarl nodded, though this time his expression was a good deal grimmer.

"I'll do it," he offered stiffly. "If you leave the line Heramiir is sure to find out and suspect you are making a move. I'm not even supposed to be here though, so I doubt anyone will care if they find me making my way back to my assigned unit."

Hassan just looked at his long-time comrade, nodding his agreement. Jarl was right, but sending his men off on a suicide mission without being there himself struck Hassan as the worst kind of cowardice. Yet if the element of surprise were ruined by Deshara breaking into his thoughts at the wrong moment, all their deaths would be for nothing when the magi retaliated.

"Go quickly, old friend."

Without even a nod, Jarl was off, running full tilt towards where the men who had been captured in Heramiir's coup last year were stationed near the rear.

Within seconds Jarl was lost to sight, and Hassan turned his attention back to the fighting. The front had moved, the king's men now pushed back as far as the shallows of the Mirallyn Fjords. Soldiers engaged on both sides were having a hard time keeping their footing as they frantically exchanged blows in the shin deep water.

The shallows were little more than fifty spans across, and at no other point for many leagues in either direction could a man in armour cross the river. It took a moment, but as

Hassan studied the fighting, he realised that this was why he had been ordered not to push beyond them. The archmage must have known how many magi the king could send while maintaining a defence in the capital and surrounds. This entire campaign had been planned to achieve one outcome. Heramiir had stripped Miralthrall and all the other cities he controlled of almost all their battle magi to eliminate that threat. With the bottleneck of the fjords preventing a full-scale charge or flanking action by either side, it wouldn't have mattered if the king had brought five times as many soldiers to the fight. This battle would have progressed in exactly the same fashion so long as the fjords were held and Heramiir's magi could gain the upper hand. A task which they now appeared on the verge of completing.

From somewhere off to his right, there was an ear shattering grinding. For a moment even the front-line combatants were forced to halt their struggle as every soldier on the field was thrown from their feet by the ground's sudden shaking. For several seconds they had no choice but to stay down until the violent tremor subsided. Disturbingly, the Mirallyn sped its pace for several seconds as it rushed to fill some new void no doubt created by the powerful quake. Hassan regained his feet almost as fast as the front-line soldiers in the riverbed, though his side screamed in protest. He held the cloth tight over his wound as he strained to see what had occurred on the right flank of the army.

To his dismay he saw a great rent had opened in the ground on their side of the river, causing a large swath of soldiers in that part of the army to fall into the breach. The river was even now rushing in to cover them before they had tumbled to a halt. A few were stripping off armour in a desperate attempt to swim. Others who had been right at the lip of the rent were helping their nearby companions to dry ground as best they could. After half a minute, he estimated that not more than a hundred soldiers had escaped the spellcaster's trap in a place where as many as four or five thousand must have stood just moments before.

With a shudder Hassan realised just how much the magi had been holding back all these years, or if you listened to Heramiir's line, had been held back. For the briefest of instants he couldn't help but wonder whether Heramiir might be justified in his claims about their skills fading because of the law against experimentation.

Not that it mattered of course. Nothing could justify the wholesale slaughter that was happening across the river now that most of the king's magi had been neutralised. It had been only minutes since he had sent Jarl off, but if the captain couldn't attack Heramiir's spellcasters soon, there would be no point. The enemy magi's ranks were in tatters, though the shield still held above them for the most part. Once they were defeated however, there would be nothing between the rank-and-file men and Heramiir's spellcasters. The entire army would be slaughtered while Heramiir's forces simply held the fjords.

Another minute dragged on, and then another. As explosions continued to pound the ranks on both sides of the river, Hassan was beginning to get a terrible feeling in the pit of his stomach. Less and less of those spells were coming this way, and the time when his men could affect this battle was coming to a close.

Ahead of him at the fjords, the king's men were making a serious push to get across the river. His men should have begun their assault on the magi by now, but as he looked back up the hill, no such activity was forthcoming. Another minute of slaughter passed by, and Hassan's heart beat ever faster as he realised the counterattack would not happen in time.

What had prevented Jarl from carrying out his orders?

He just hoped the man hadn't been killed in one of the random blasts the king's magi were still sending their direction.

Hassan turned, intending to abandon his post as he whispered a prayer to the Maker that he wasn't too late. A figure dressed in black stepped from the crowd as soon as he did, and two others hemmed him in from the sides. They said nothing, but the mageguard troops had eyes only for him. He was left with no choice but to pretend he was surveying the field. He couldn't take all three while injured, and he could hardly ask for aid this time against supposedly friendly troops.

As the incoming fire petered off to almost nothing, Hassan knew the end was here. The slaughter would begin momentarily.

With a resigned wave he sent another company of soldiers into the fray to support those men already engaged in pushing the king's men back across the fjords.

Not even his death would save the king's army now, and at this point Hassan hoped that Jarl had not gotten through. If he had been delayed, he might still try to carry through with Hassan's orders. Then Heramiir would have all the excuse he needed to rid himself of the remaining guardsmen who had resisted his coup.

There was a brief lull in the fighting, almost as if the attackers were not sure what to do next. Or perhaps more accurately, as though Heramiir's magi were catching their breath for one final assault.

Chaos followed.

It took less than a breath for the true scope of Heramiir's power, and that of his lieutenants, to be revealed. The entire hill the king's surviving magi were positioned on blossomed into flames a hundred spans high. Interspersed with the inferno at frequent intervals were explosions of raw power that left nothing living in their wake not already protected by a powerful Gift-wrought shield. Hassan wished he didn't understand what Nereth was about to do.

Before the explosions had even cleared, Hassan could see that the new line of fire at the rear of the king's army would join up with those flanking it on either side in less than a minute. The few magi that seemed to have survived the devastating assault in fighting condition were exhausted and too disorganised to stop it even if given the chance.

A moment later the heat from the blasts reached them down at the fjords as a strong hot wind, a mile from where the king's magi had been stationed. Hassan shuddered.

The resistance he was organising was a joke. There was nothing they could do to confront that sheer expanse of power, no matter how many resources or men he could muster.

As the surrounding flames died with unnatural haste, it seemed some of the king's magi had survived. By dousing the flames though, they once again revealed their position and were struck again and again. The battle was over, Hassan realised sadly, and the soldiers who remained would have no means to defeat Heramiir's magi.

They seemed to know it too as the press of troops at the fjords intensified despite the reinforcements he had sent in.

The king's troops could see what was happening. They knew their only chance now lay in breaking through Heramiir's lines to get to the magi who were decimating their ranks. They made little ground though, and would never make it through Heramiir's entire army alive. Had his troops been with him, even now he could have broken Heramiir's forces at the fjords from behind, creating enough room for the king's men to surge through.

A deep writhing began in Hassan's belly. Jarl hadn't made it through. The man must have been injured or killed.

His plans had failed. The king's army was moments from being subjected to a slaughter on an unheard-of scale, and the time had irrevocably come to choose where his allegiance would lie from this day forward.

He wanted so badly for the king's men to win this battle, to find some way to turn this disaster to their favour. Heramiir and Nereth had planned for this day too long and too well. With the command structure of the king's army obliterated at the outset, and their remaining magi now dead or subdued, the outcome was decided. Only butchery remained, and from the way Heramiir had fought so far, it was unlikely he would hold back once his forces had the advantage.

Every option Hassan had considered, every plan he had made had been countered with precision. Nereth was a tactical genius, but even he couldn't be that lucky. He had to have known. Had to have been informed.

Hassan had served his king his entire life, and it was not too late to fulfil his oath. He could switch sides, die honourably here and now, rather than live as a traitor. It was a selfish option, and he knew it. The lives of the hostages in Miralthrall meant more to him than whatever salve dying that way would bring for his conscience. Besides, if word got back to the archmage that he had betrayed him at the last, it would go badly for those innocents he had done all this to protect.

Hassan looked around desperately. There had to be *something* he could do.

"Help me up there!" he shouted to a nearby soldier as he tried to climb atop a small mound of the dead. The pile was not high, but it let him see over the heads of the men in front. He gripped the cloth tightly against the wound in his side as he mounted the morbid pedestal. The soldier did as he was bid, and in moments Hassan could see the field clearly for the first time since the outset of battle.

What he saw overwhelmed him, any thought of still turning this battle to the king's advantage finally, irrevocably, fleeing.

Beyond the river the entire field was aflame. Columns of oily black smoke from the catapults' projectiles reared up by the dozen, and what had just hours before seemed a vast army had been torn and sundered beyond repair. Already a full half of the king's men were dead or injured, limping or crawling as best they could back to the one massive tent still standing. It was an aid centre where Erian's healers and non-battle-trained magi would be desperately trying to save as many of those men as they could.

Heramiir must have given orders for it not to be hit since nothing else of the opposing army's infrastructure remained. It wouldn't have been out of any sense of compassion though Hassan realised spitefully, but because there were magi in there who were not part of the battle. The archmage was merciless against his enemies, that much Hassan expected. The constant reminders that the magi now stood above every other citizen as some kind of ruling class in this new order were hard to take.

Of the king's magi there was little trace. Perhaps a dozen of any note were continuing to fight back against Heramiir's own Gift users, but they were sorely outnumbered. Most were barely maintaining their own defences, leaving more and more of Heramiir's magi free to attack the king's troops. Which they were doing to devastating effect.

The magi behind him were aiming their attacks towards the rear of the king's army, forcing the opposing troops forward and into the breach of the fjords. The king's men seemed to know that they couldn't harm their true assailants, and as Heramiir's magi continued their butchery, the king's men pushed harder as they became more and more desperate.

Of all things, for a moment he thought he saw a man riding a horse through that tightly-packed throng.

He wanted to do something, anything, but all he could do was watch in horror as the last of the king's magi were overwhelmed in another vast wall of flame.

There was another momentary pause, as for the first time since the start of the battle the sky became clear of brightly lit spells careening by overhead. Hassan bowed his head as he waited for the inevitable hammer to fall.

It didn't take long.

After only a few seconds of silence, dozens of Heramiir's magi attacked at once.

The first segment of the pale blue shield protecting the king's army disappeared instantly under the massive onslaught. The men beneath it fared no better, few of them even having time to scream as dozens of destructive spells enveloped the area in a heartbeat.

Hassan felt hollowed out as a second section of the army's shield met a similar fate only moments later, and then a third. What was left of the king's army was now panicking as they saw their ranks being decimated, especially with no way to strike back at their attackers. Strangely enough they didn't flee, instead pushing at Hassan's line of troops with all the force they could muster. His troops there were now barely holding their ground, and losing more men than the enemy by the looks of their determined bearing.

The king's men had to know there weren't enough of them left to gain the victory, but with a flash of insight, Hassan realised that wasn't their goal. They were trying to mix their own lines with Heramiir's forces, giving them a respite from the arcane slaughter, or forcing Heramiir to attack his own troops. It was a bold move. Had they achieved it earlier they might have caused a serious problem. As it stood, they were simply choosing another method of death by surrounding themselves with the now overwhelming numbers of Heramiir's ranks.

Some attempted to flee from the rear of the army, but none of them got very far once they saw the lines of fire that flanked them had now cut off all retreat. Many of the wounded were still trying desperately to make their way to the healers' tent. Those men were left alone, but any who fled were attacked almost immediately by Heramiir's magi.

"Your orders Sir?" a captain called up at him from a few feet away. Hassan looked at him for a moment before turning away from the scene and stepping off the pile of bodies to sit gingerly on the ground.

"Just push them back and hold them at the fjords Captain. It will be over soon enough," he returned as he pressed the cloth tighter against his wound. The bleeding had slowed to a trickle. The soldier saluted and sent his men to relieve those in the front lines who had been pressed for long minutes now, and were clearly tiring.

Destructive spells continued to sail overhead by the hundreds until finally a great roar went up from Heramiir's men.

"Help me up!" Hassan ordered the soldier who had assisted him before, and whom he had failed to dismiss, he now remembered.

The man did so without hesitation, and Hassan noted in dismay that the king's army was now in full rout. The remaining men, who could still do so, were sprinting headlong away from the fjords in every direction. Each sought one thing, a way through the blistering flames that trapped them in a square mile of land on that side of the river. Many of them seemed to be heading towards the aid tent. It was the only thing resembling a command structure their panicked and terrified minds could relate to in their current state.

With a long sigh, Hassan waited numbly for the mental order to pursue to be issued to him by Deshara, courtesy of her strange gift for conveying her thoughts into other people's minds.

And yet for long moments that order didn't come. He was about to order his men to hold when he saw that not a one of them had yet passed over the narrow stretch of water. The fjords looked different than they had before.

He looked at the river for a long moment before realising that some enemy mage had deepened the crossing point. The area that was usable to a man in armour had been reduced to a little less than two spans wide. That was not the strangest thing though. In the narrow crossing space, a young man sat atop a white stallion. A Rahiri mount if he was not mistaken, with brown lower legs, and was engaging every soldier that came near him with a Gift-wrought blade. The thing was made of a strange black metal, three runes the colour of fire etched into its surface.

It killed at every stroke.

Powerful or not though, the rider was only one man, and Hassan ordered another company into the breach to secure the crossing.

The horseman was a fool to sit there as if he could achieve something with this action. He was obviously trying to buy time for the rest of the king's scattered troops to retreat, though where to Hassan wasn't sure. He silently applauded the young man's bravery, though in the end it would come to nothing. For long moments Hassan watched, mesmerised by the rise and fall of the horseman's blade. Only when he realised that his own men were now having to climb over a pile of their own dead did Hassan understand. This was no ordinary soldier hell-bent on sacrificing himself so that his companions might be granted a few extra seconds to escape.

No, the young man whose slightest scratch with that blade seemed to bring instant death to any it touched seemed to have a far more serious aspect. The stark determination in his eyes and the way he sat astride his mount reeked of confidence. His own men had noticed, and were wavering.

Hassan watched in disbelief as the horseman continued to dispatch opponents with ease despite being clearly tired. Fortunately for the rider, the unsteady mound of dead was hampering the attackers' ability to get within striking distance before he touched them with that devastatingly powerful blade.

'Kill that man and crush the rest of Erian's army,' Deshara's voice rang in his head. Hassan had little choice but to obey, as he would have to from now on. Despite the horseman's bravery, there was nothing left to be gained here today, and no point now giving up all he had sacrificed so much to protect.

With a heavy heart, Hassan raised his voice enough to be heard above the din.

"All units, charge and destroy the remnants of the king's army."

He said it loudly, but with no vigour.

Still, the words had carried well enough, and the mass of Heramiir's army began to move. It started slowly, increasing in speed as the bulk of the men got to the river. He saw the warrior on the horse turn to face the coming onslaught. He raised his black sword high as if in challenge to the oncoming wave of Heramiir's men, who crashed over the barricade of the dead, swarming over him without pause.

Hassan lost the man's form in the crush. As the soldiers behind continued to pour onto the now narrowed fjords, he noticed with a sudden nervous sensation that not one of those who had reached the narrow stretch of water had moved since. None of those behind had continued forward.

His skin crawled.

CHAPTER 26

A WARRIOR LIKE HAS NOT BEEN SEEN...

"We have to do something!" Kienan pleaded over the distant clash of battle. Another blast of hot air reached Wyll's squad, blown their way by a huge explosion closer to the river. From their vantage point on the low hill well to the rear of the king's army, it was obvious things in the valley were not going well.

Down below, at the crossing of the Mirallyn, it was hard to make sense of what was happening. Destructive spells of a hundred colours and shapes slammed into troops on both sides of the river. The shimmering blue of the protective shields above the king's army barely held those arcane energies in check, and occasionally failed as the magi on either side sought to eliminate specific foes.

In the distance, the catapults stationed at the rear of Heramiir's forces were continuing to rain destruction down on the king's men through some arcane means. He had never heard of a spell like it being spoken of at the college, but it was devastatingly effective.

Just as they had during the first moments of Heramiir's ambush on General Messand's command pavilion, the vortices were now taking a heavy toll on the magi of the king's army.

"We have our orders Kienan. We have to protect the chalice," Charran said from behind him before Wyll could take his eyes off the overwhelming scene.

"Besides, the archmage was right," Tauman added, his tone one of hopelessness rather than fear as he waved a hand in the general direction of the battle.

"What possible good could one more squad do compared to that?"

Wyll was forced to acknowledge that all three men had valid points. It was a situation not at all helped by the fact that the king's numbers had visibly shrunk since the outset of battle. Wyll said a quick prayer to the Maker that it only looked that way because the king's men were now bunched up at the mouth of the fjords. The more so since the battle had only started scant minutes ago. Heramiir had achieved complete surprise with his ambush of the command tent. Now it, along with the vast majority of high-ranking officers travelling with the army, were nothing but a smoking patch of scorched ground, ignored by the rest of the battle.

He could see her occasionally, on the outskirts of the fight. A soldier would be killed by an errant spell, or die from their wounds, and she would be there. Sa'rayna, the Black Lady, flitting from one of them to the next and moving their souls on to only she and the Maker knew where.

He couldn't help but feel revulsion at what she was doing, at the ending of so many lives. But if it really was their time, he supposed it wasn't his place to argue. After all, every man on this field would meet that appointed time, even if not for another eighty years or more. It had taken him some time to accept her reasoning. Watching the brutality of the slaughter before them though, Wyll began to see the function she performed in the natural order was in fact as

Sa'rayna had always maintained. It was what must be. If she was not there, if those men were left sundered beyond repair, yet still alive, it would be much worse.

And yet his head could not reconcile that fact with what his heart felt as he looked upon the battle raging a little more than a mile away from where they sat. His men were ready to follow his orders, whatever those might be.

They had all come a long way from their days on the Anchorhead Promontory, even him. Perhaps him most of all Wyll supposed. He still wasn't sure his men were convinced that it was actually Sa'rayna whom he had met with in the Wraith Woods. That death herself had spared them from the insectile creatures which inhabited the forest. He had doubted her at first as well, and had still held deep misgivings following their conversation at Brendan's deathbed. After seeing her down on the field today, Wyll knew he would never again harbour any doubt at all about who and what she truly was.

As the long minutes wore on, it became clear Heramiir's magi were only targeting their counterparts in the king's army. The sustained assault was causing massive damage to the Aramarian spellcasters.

The king's magi seemed to have split their attack. What strategy they were employing, seemed to depend on forcing a breach in Heramiir's blockade of the fjords by attacking the archmagi's troops near the river. They were also assaulting the enemy archmagi further back.

More minutes passed, and through the devastation it was becoming clear that Heramiir's spellcasters were thinning out the king's own at a far faster rate than was happening the other way around. From their vantage point, with time to think, it was obvious where this was all heading.

"They're trying to take down the King's magi completely," Wyll muttered louder than he had intended, and Seth, who was mounted on his horse beside him, overheard.

"If they are successful, it will be a slaughter," the warrior replied in just as quiet a tone before they shared a quick look.

There had to be something they could do to help, but what? The king's army was putting up a good fight from what he could see, they were even pushing past the fjords slightly. But only because Heramiir's magi were ignoring them. The problem was that the fjords were only about fifty spans across and therefore no flanking of any kind was a viable option. Every time a mage tried to create some kind of bridge, they were targeted by their opponents, both magi and archers alike. Nor could the men swim across at any other point due to their heavy steel armour.

Heramiir had planned his entire campaign to unfold exactly this way Wyll suddenly realised. The fake army. The Laketown Peninsula. He had probably even been responsible for word getting back to the king at the time it had. He couldn't have expected them to traverse the Wraith Woods to reach here in time, despite that, they had been too late. Heramiir's deceptions had given him enough time to get his army in place. All of it had been to force this battle, right here on this ground. Even the ambush on the king's officers to disrupt their strategy and cohesion had been pre-planned. Those catapults had already been aligned when the king's army had arrived. All of it had been so that the king's men could be kept at bay with a minimum of casualties to his own troops. The true battle was being waged amongst the magi.

And worst of all, Heramiir's plan was working.

Once the Aramarian magi were neutralised, the rest of the king's troops would be helpless against Heramiir's spellcasters. They would be stuck against the river, unable to push forward, or to retreat in good order. Unless something drastic changed, a slaughter the likes of which had not been seen since the time of Eldrik the Black, two thousand years gone, would soon commence.

The catapults fired again, targeting the open ground on the flank of the army, trying to hem the rest of the king's men into the immediate vicinity of the fjords. Time was running out as more and more of the king's magi were cut down by Heramiir's men. Those still standing were forced more and more to concentrate on their defence as Heramiir's now larger contingent of spellcasters slowly began to overmatch them.

Another few agonising minutes passed as Wyll wracked his brain for any way that his squad could make the slightest bit of difference down there.

Even as he watched, the ground on the far side of the river opened with a great shaking of the earth that even way back here made their horses stumble. Sarran fell to the ground as his mount bucked at the unexpected tremor.

Once he could focus on the battlefield again, Wyll saw that a good swath of enemy troops had fallen into a newly opened chasm. The river rushed into the new gash in the land, drowning the unfortunate men whose armour was too heavy for them to swim to the top. As the ground stopped shifting, there was a moment of almost quiet on the field. It lasted only an instant before the front lines continued their grinding clash of steel, setting the whole scene in motion once again.

The king's magi were all but subdued now. If he was

right, the enemy magi would turn their attention on the troops next. There was nothing his squad could do about it.

Nothing my squad can do about it...

But what about me? Wyll thought as he once again caught sight of the black flicker that marked Sa'rayna's passing.

She would never kill the enemy troops because he asked, he knew that instinctively. But she had said that she loved him, and that she had been alone for a very long time, and he believed her. Maybe that was enough for his half-formed idea to have a chance. A pang of guilt worked its way into his chest. She deserved better than to be manipulated like this, but what choice did he have? If he was wrong about her, he would die along with every other man on the field.

It didn't matter.

Now that he had thought of a way to stop it, he couldn't live with himself if there was even the slightest chance to avoid the wholesale butchery about to begin, and he didn't take it.

There was a massive conflagration at the rear of the king's army, the flames reaching upward a hundred spans into the sky. The blast of heat reached them all the way back here as a solid, scorching dry wave of heat that stripped the moisture from their lungs before it dissipated into the air.

From what he could see, the blast had been every bit as devastating as it looked. Only a few dozen of the king's magi still appeared capable of putting up a fight. If he was going to try this mad plan, he had to do it right now. But it was his plan. His risk to take. There was no reason for the others to meet their deaths alongside him if this terrible idea didn't pan out.

"You men stay here. If I am killed with the rest of the

army, return to Aramar and report to Tolmarak and the king on what you saw here today."

"What are you talking about, Wyll?" Bosric demanded with his usual disregard for rank, the perpetual smile now absent from his face.

"I think I know how to stop this, maybe. But I'm probably wrong, and if I am, anyone who comes with me will die. I won't order any of you into that when I'm not even sure my plan will work. Now follow my orders."

For a long moment, the short, red-haired knife man gave him a measuring look, then executed a perfect military salute any general would be proud of.

Wyll blinked in surprise, then slowly nodded. He untied his saddlebags and let them drop to the ground after removing the Chalice of Ajerio. He tied the artefact to his sword belt with a spare piece of cord attached to the relic's cover.

"All right," he breathed to himself as he worked up his nerve. He exhaled slowly, then booted Socks into a full gallop, aiming at the small group of magi who were all that was left of the king's functional battle line.

It wasn't until he was almost there that he heard another horse and looked back to see Seth riding up hard on his flank. The shaven-headed warrior met his eyes, but didn't so much as nod in his direction. Wyll was grateful for the man's presence, even if he *had* disobeyed orders to be there. Further back, and far more surprisingly, he saw Kienan also struggling to catch up with Socks' far superior speed. Wyll waved the musician back, but he shook his head and rode on. Wyll had the uncomfortable feeling the man was choosing this moment to prove that he was just as valuable a member of the squad as any of the rest of them.

Still, it was a concern that Wyll had no time for. Kienan would just have to look after himself this time if he couldn't follow orders. Besides, Wyll wasn't even sure he would survive the next few minutes himself. He turned back towards the battle without another moment's thought, only pulling Socks out of his dead run as he approached one of the few archmagi left standing.

"I'm busy!" she shouted as a ball of fire deflected off her personal shield. She responded by sending some kind of arcane attack back towards its sender.

"You have to narrow the fjords!" Wyll shouted as more enemy spells were flung in their direction.

"What, why?!" The archmage returned, glancing at him as she launched another attack of her own.

"Orders from General Messand," he lied. With any luck she wouldn't have noticed he had come from the rear of the army, not the medical area where any of the surviving officers must surely be by now.

"It will cost us," she said with a pained expression. "It will take a few moments, and we will not be able to attack during that time."

"It's our only chance!" Wyll replied. The blood of any magi who died performing this action would be on his hands, but what choice was there? There were perhaps a dozen, but no more than twenty, strong magi left fighting on the king's side. They no longer had the numbers to resist effectively. It was a matter of minutes now.

"How narrow do you need them?" she asked distractedly as she protected the four of them from something green that sped their way at an enemy mage's insistence.

"No more than two spans across!" Wyll called back.

The archmage motioned to two other nearby magi and

then nodded her acquiescence. She began concentrating on the fjords for a long moment. Wyll couldn't see anything happen, but after a minute the archmage looked back at him and nodded, her eyes going wide as she did so.

With a desperate wave of her arm, a shimmering blue field sprang up around the four of them as a vast wall of flame encompassed them, engulfing the shield entirely.

In seconds the archmage looked strained to the point of breaking, the intense flames persisting beyond all natural chance. From somewhere in the conflagration they could hear explosions, though nothing was visible beyond the all-encompassing fire that surrounded them. A translucent blue shield that was all that stood between them and the abyss.

The archmage was losing her battle, and the shield shrank inward as her concentration and focus waned.

Without warning, daylight reappeared, and Wyll sighed in relief before an explosion found them and the world turned black.

Everywhere was fire and death as Wyll opened his eyes.

Painfully picking himself up, he looked around and found the archmage who had protected them through that last murderous firestorm. Some of her at least.

Wyll closed his eyes, feeling nauseous at the sight. That death was on his head, but he had no choice but to continue with his mad plan, and hope to the Maker that Sa'rayna would forgive him.

There was no way of knowing how long he'd been unconscious, how long it had been since Heramiir had launched his most recent attack at the remaining line of magi. Or how long he now had to execute his plan.

Pulling himself to his feet, Wyll tried to ignore the ringing in his ears and looked desperately around the immediate area for any sign of other survivors. As he shook off the thick layer of dirt which covered him, he spotted Seth about thirty feet away. The man was also climbing slowly to his feet.

Of Kienan and the other magi there was no sign. In the thick smoke that now covered the area, they might be ten steps beyond Seth, and he would have no way of telling. He could cling to that for the next few minutes, he told himself bleakly.

"Are you all right?!" he shouted over the ringing in his ears. The other man nodded before stumbling off to check on Kienan, whom the thick smoke had now cleared enough to reveal. Wyll sighed in relief, though the man had not yet moved that Wyll could make out.

They were losing this battle. Badly. He'd known it from back at the ridge, but being down here was something else entirely. The sounds of screams and the scent of burning flesh filled the air until it was nearly impossible to think. So far Heramiir's men had not breached the fjords, but it was only a matter of time now that the magi were out of commission. As the smoke cleared even more and he looked up and down the line, there was little in the way of magic being dealt out that he could see. Too many of the king's magi had just met the same fate as the anonymous archmage who had died saving them.

At least the swirling vortices seemed to have disappeared for good. They hadn't just vanished at this end of the field as they had the other times, but up at the enemy siege weapons as well.

Still, without the main force of their own magi to protect the troops, the king's army was taking a pounding from Heramiir's men. Wyll winced as yet another burst of flame came hurtling down from the enemy magi high on the hill above, killing dozens, if not hundreds more of the king's men.

The rest were desperately trying to stay alive, though many were so terrified now that some at the back were beginning to run. To where he didn't know. That last salvo from the catapults had now combined with the blazing lines of flame from that last magical onslaught, cutting off any retreat. One or two of the magi seemed to sense the danger, and were trying to put the flames out, even having some measure of success. It didn't matter. Unless something changed the course of this battle, the king's army would be put to full rout within the next few minutes.

He groaned as he looked out at the seething mass of men.

He could still see her flitting around down there. Sa'rayna. She didn't even have time to appear properly before she had touched the soldier whose time it was. She would then disappear to flit up unseen on the next mortally wounded man, ending his life at a touch.

Back in the glade he had wondered if the inexplicable sense of rightness he had felt around her was some form of enchantment. But it had been phases since then, and despite everything that being the 'Black Lady' entailed, he knew now that he loved her. How that could be, when she was responsible for every life lost down there, he hadn't quite reconciled just yet. It didn't help that she had as much as admitted that she could simply not take these men, even though there would be consequences to that choice.

Well, there always are, Wyll thought as yet another patch of ground erupted in a huge shower of dirt and flying soldiers.

His plan could work. He was almost certain he could stop this, if only he could bring himself to risk his life on that one slim chance.

Not that it isn't already at risk, he told himself sternly, desperately trying to shore up his courage.

"Seth! Seth! I need you man! Where are you?!" he called into the haze of smoke which the wind had now pushed back onto this part of the battlefield.

A moment later the top-knotted warrior appeared out of the smoke as though by magic with a limping Kienan by his side, and Wyll met him halfway.

"We have to keep moving."

"Can you run?" he asked Kienan, and the injured musician smiled.

"No, but you can," he said.

In a dazed condition, he sat on the scorched grass covering the surrounding land. He gave a gasp of pain as he did so, a break obvious in his lower left leg.

Wyll growled to himself. He didn't want to leave his injured man there, even though it was no more dangerous here than anywhere else right now, but there was no more time. If the lines around the fjords broke before he could get there and put his plan into action, it was over.

"Go," Kienan told him, holding his leg against the pain.

"Do what you have to do, Wyll. I won't get in your way anymore."

He smiled sadly and Wyll growled again in frustration before taking off at a dead sprint towards the medical tent.

Where Socks or the other horses were, he had no idea, but sincerely hoped they had made it through unscathed. As he ran further from the point of the attack without spotting them though, he was forced to acknowledge that possibility wasn't likely.

As far as he could tell, no one was giving the army general orders anymore. If any command level officers or archmagi had survived the attack to this point, they would be in the infirmary. That was where he needed to go.

That was what this had been, Wyll realised abruptly, an attack. Not a battle of two sides meeting, but a carefully orchestrated assault by Heramiir's general to lop off most of the king's army's experience and power at a stroke. That one action had left the masses of ordinary foot soldiers and mid-level officers directionless and confused for crucial minutes at the outset of battle. Heramiir must have known that without their leaders they would be no match for his magi and organised forces, and the slaughter at the river was proving him right.

On Wyll ran, struggling to breathe now as he neared the blasted site of the initial attack and passed it. He approached the huge tent, which was set up to receive casualties, though in nowhere near the numbers which were flooding in. As he entered the vast structure and took a smoke choked breath, he was appalled by the sight which confronted him.

Everything was chaos. All around him wounded men lay untended and bleeding, some unconscious and some missing limbs that had been burnt or blown off in the explosions. There were dozens of magi and healers from the herbalists and apothecary's guild all working feverishly on the soldiers, but there was no chance they could get to them all. All the while more men came wandering in, or were carried, filling the tent far past capacity. Almost no patch of floor was visible between the rent bodies of his companions.

Shaking his head to clear it of the horror, Wyll forced himself to focus on what he was doing. He strode to the nearest healer, hating himself for interrupting the woman's tending of an injured soldier, but knowing he had no choice.

"I need to find any of the command personnel right now!" he shouted over the din.

The woman waved a finger in the direction she wanted him to go without taking her eyes off the bleeding patient. Wyll ran. Time was already escaping him, and he silently prayed to the Maker that the men down by the river could hold out long enough for this to work. If it worked.

He plummeted through the vast infirmary looking for any sign of the general or his staff. After a frantic moment of fruitless searching, he pulled himself together and asked the nearest healer.

He lucked out, and the man told him that although badly injured, General Messand had survived. He was being carried outside so he could direct the battle from where he could see what was happening.

Wyll spun on his heel and ran.

When he escaped the tent and all its carnage, he found the general in a cot being carried by four of his men. It wasn't until he reached the group of soldiers though that he caught sight of what a bad way the man was in.

The general's entire left side was burnt and blackened; his left arm gone below the elbow. Despite the crippling pain he must be in, his right eye at least was still focused on the field in front of them. A wet tear was clearing a slow path down his charred and sooty cheek.

"No," Messand murmured when he saw what had befallen the army in his absence. "This is over. We must call a retreat."

"We can't," Wyll told him without preamble as he skidded to a halt beside the injured general. "Heramiir's spellcasters have cut us off and the few magi we have left are being hard pressed just to defend themselves."

"We must retreat," Messand repeated. "Or none of us will last another hour."

"Yes sir," Wyll agreed. "But we cannot leave here fast enough to stop them chasing us down unless Heramiir can be stopped from crossing the fjords."

Messand looked at him with his one good eye as an agonised shudder ran through his body.

"You have an idea?"

"I do sir, but you won't like it."

"Quickly, Wyll," was all Messand whispered in response.

"I had one of the magi narrow the fjords to limit the crossing space and I need the troops to hold at the fjords until I get down there. I will hold the gap until the rest of the army can escape."

Messand just looked at him in consternation with his one good eye for a long moment.

"No one could hold that force alone Wyll, not the greatest blade master who ever lived. I need a plan to save the men from this catastrophe, not boasts," he wheezed.

"Sir," Wyll said loudly enough to bring the general's attention back to him. "I don't have time to explain everything to you now, but I can do this as long as the fjords remain narrowed."

Again Messand looked at him, this time with a little more seriousness.

"I cannot take the chance you are wrong. If Heramiir breaks through the fjords his men will surround us and we will be finished unless we can get these fires under control. The only thing keeping us alive right now is that we are holding those fjords."

"We don't have time for this, Sir. Give the order or we

will all die here today," Wyll told him flatly as a tremendous blast of magical power obliterated the first section of the army's protective shield.

Wyll knew that his time was at an end.

"Don't think to give me orders boy, and for that matter stop distracting me. Restrain him," Messand ordered the men who had carried him out.

Wyll took a step back and drew the Sword of Ages from it sheath on his back.

"I can't let you do that General. It would mean death for every man here."

"Disobeying orders in a time of war is treason, Wyll. I had thought better of you."

"Respectfully sir, this isn't any such thing. Everything I have told you is true. I know you don't have all the information you need to understand this, but right now I must go. If you wish to save your men, make sure those fjords stay narrowed as I suggested, but don't cut them off entirely. I will hold them while you retreat."

The sound of hooves came up behind him, and Wyll looked around, his breath catching as he saw Seth slowing to a halt behind him on a horse that was not his own, and leading a sore looking, but uninjured Socks as well.

"You're serious about this, aren't you?" Messand asked as Wyll backed away from Messand's men and mounted the Rahiri steed after re-sheathing the black blade.

"Just get the men out of here. I'll take care of the rest," Wyll said again, then turned Socks towards the river and galloped out with Seth close behind.

A brief look across to the Mirallyn showed him that Heramiir's men were perilously close to breaking through the crossing at the fjords. He nudged Socks for more speed.

He had to get there before that happened, or even he would be powerless to end this.

"How do you plan to defeat them?" Seth shouted as he managed to bring his horse up behind the worn out Rahiri mount.

"I don't," Wyll called back, leaving Seth to decide whether he was being cryptic or was now too focused on his goal to give further details.

"What do you want me to do?" the shaven headed man called again over the racing wind, as he pushed his own mount hard enough to catch up. There was no way the poor beast could keep that speed up for long.

"Just make sure I get to the fjords, nothing else matters. Once that's done, gather as many men as you can and help organise the retreat!" Wyll shouted back. The ground bucked beneath them at a nearby explosion of Gift-wrought power.

The horses kept their feet, and both of them kept running towards the river, and the confrontation that waited for them there.

It was only seconds before they reached the rear ranks of the king's army. They began pushing their mounts forward through the press, trying not to trample men as they did so, but not having time to stop and make sure.

Wyll had often thought over the last phases that he would like to rise in rank someday, maybe to have a command of his own. He knew that was just foolishness now. At least one archmagi, and many more soldiers, men on his own side, had already died here today through his own direct actions. He could only pray that his plan worked, that those deaths hadn't been in vain. As the two of them barged their way through the press as fast as they could manage, he hoped he could save a lot more of them than he'd put in harm's way. However this ended though, he no longer wanted to lead men into battle, or to be responsible for their lives through his decisions.

With a thunderous crash, a section of the army's shield exploded without resistance. Destructive spells of every kind fountained out from the enemy ranks and tore through its fabric and everything beneath. It was enough to make the ground shake even from this distance, and several men were thrown to their knees. If they went much further, they would be in the line of fire, and there was still something he needed to do if his plan were to have any chance of succeeding.

Pulling Socks to a halt, he took the Sword of Ages from its sheath again. For an instant he desperately hoped that he wasn't putting his faith in something that existed only in his mind. With that last unnerving thought, he took a deep breath, steadying himself as he held it, moving his other hand to within a hair's breadth of the blade.

"What are you doing?!" Seth yelled at him over the screams of the dying all around. Wyll looked up.

"What I have to!" he returned, and then added. "If this doesn't work, take the sword and hold the fjords as long as you can."

"You're going to summon… the Black Lady?" Seth asked. For the first time since Wyll had known him, he noticed a slight tone of what might have been fear in the man's voice. With difficulty he moved his mount closer in towards his commander.

"It's our only chance," Wyll answered with a grim smile.

"It's what must be," he added to himself as he looked back at the matt black blade. Its fiery runes continued to glow, just as they had since the first moment he'd laid his eyes upon the strange weapon.

Sa'rayna had told him it would summon her whenever it cut flesh. She had also told him she would take whoever's soul it did. But then she had also told him that she loved him.

It was a mad gamble, but it was the only chance they had.

"Don't do this Wyll," Seth entreated him. He'd seen what the black blade was capable of back in the forest when they'd met Captain Karloff and his men.

"You're a good soldier, and you have my respect. But not even you can cheat death herself. It goes against all reason and sense!"

"Then have faith," Wyll replied as he looked at his most trusted soldier. "And I will show you something new."

With a wince of pain Wyll slid his arm lightly along the blade, drawing just a few drops of his own blood, and just like that she was there. As beautiful as always, her ankle length black hair flowing in the breeze, her hand outstretched to take the one whom she had been summoned too by the blade.

For the barest instant their eyes met, and in her gaze he saw Sa'rayna's instant horror at whom she had confronted. Consternation replaced it as she saw it was Wyll himself who had made the cut with the black blade.

"No..." she hissed, her lips moving, but barely making a sound.

"Why?"

"I need your help," Wyll told her guiltily. It was asking her to go against everything she was just to not take him right now. He was about to ask a great deal more.

"I have to take you, Wyll. You've given me no choice,"

Sa'rayna lamented as she moved up beside him, her face twisted with a depth of sorrow Wyll would not have credited from just their few brief meetings.

"No, you don't," he returned, suddenly unsure that this had been a good idea after all. "I will come to you, just as I promised. But right now I need your help."

"There is nothing I can do Wyll, even if I wanted to. You know I can't help you defeat these men. If it is not their time I cannot take them."

"And I can't allow the rest of the King's army to be slaughtered without doing everything I can to stop it," he returned. A third section of the shield fell to the combined forces of Heramiir's magi.

Wyll swallowed hard, and then looked the woman he loved, the woman whom he had seen in his dreams all his life, straight in the eye.

"I am going to ride down to those fjords now and stop Heramiir's men from crossing. They will make every effort to kill me, and if you allow them to succeed, you will be alone once again. You can stop them from doing that Sa'rayna, only you."

"Wyll, no! Do not ask this of me. The Maker will not allow it!" she pleaded, seeing the seriousness in his gaze.

Wyll looked at her, hardening his heart because there was no longer any other choice but to get her to agree.

"You said the Maker entrusted this blade to you, to give to me?"

She nodded slightly.

"Then trust that I am doing what must be done with it, Sa'rayna. Everything will be all right, just keep me safe until they stop attacking, that's all I ask," he told her as she looked away. His voice caught on the last as the enormity of what he was asking her to do finally settled in his mind.

The Maker would not allow it, she had said.

The Maker, who had created Jeranon and Jeranah, Avsan and the western nations along with everything else on the world they all shared. The Maker for whom she worked. The Maker with whom she had direct contact.

With a shudder, Wyll pulled himself back to the present. If it were true, if the Maker would not allow this of her, there was nothing anyone in the world could do about it, and his fate was already sealed. But that was only an if, and until it was proven he had no choice but to continue despite the dire prediction.

"Whatever you decide Sa'rayna," he said, pulling her eyes back towards him with his words. "I'll love you anyway."

Not trusting himself to speak further, Wyll booted Socks back to the fastest speed he could reach amongst the press of panicked men. He could feel Sa'rayna's torn gaze on his back as he left her there.

Seth came hot on his heels, then overtook him to help break a trail through the men. More and more of them were now backing away from the fjords, and Wyll knew he had only moments to reach them before this turned into a full-blown rout.

If he couldn't reach the river before that happened, he might well have just lost Sa'rayna for nothing. She hadn't taken him yet though, and that was a good sign he supposed as another shocking display of magical power began running across the shield sections above them in a seemingly random pattern. The shimmering light promising death for any man beneath on the moment the shield sections fell. As the troops below realised what was about to happen, they ran.

He was less than fifty spans from the fjords now. As the first sections of the shield failed, destructive spells tore through anything they encountered. Men all around him retreated in blind panic.

He charged forward into the gap, aiming Socks at the now narrowed fjords where perhaps a dozen men still fought. Those last few either unable or unwilling to disentangle themselves from the front line of the fight.

"Get these men out of here!" he shouted to Seth, and just had time to see the man nod before he rammed Socks into the enemy troop nearest this end of the fjords. The horse's hooves crushed the man's skull with steel shod feet as the war-trained mount kicked ahead to clear the way.

The king's men to either side of the fjords had no choice but to part and allow the horseman room to fight. It was that or risk falling into the deeper water in their steel armour. A certain death sentence. Reluctantly they retreated to the dry land behind him.

If he'd taken a moment to look back, he would have seen Seth giving them orders to retreat, seen them look dubiously at him, and then comply. He had no such moment. From the instant he stepped onto the fjords, enemy soldiers began rushing at him. They saw only a single opponent now standing between them and complete victory, a victory they intended to take.

With a sure sweep of the Sword of Ages, Wyll cut the first man that reached him along the arm. The soldier fell dead at his feet, sliding from the fjords to sink below the water as his armour pulled him under. The next man he took across the cheek and the one after him under the arm, all to the same result.

There was the almost instantaneous flicker of black that

marked Sa'rayna's passage, and then the next soldier would invariably be revealed behind him. As he chopped and cut and parried, an untold number of enemy soldiers massed behind the entrance of the fjords. The moment of truth was near.

He was tiring quickly. The strange metal of the blade he was wielding was no heavier than any other, but with thousands of men lined up to get past him, the situation was hopeless. He had known it from the beginning. Sooner or later he would get tired enough that a thrust would get through, or Socks would miss his footing, allowing an enemy an opening. There were a hundred ways it could happen, he thought as he swung his blade at an oncoming soldier. No matter the details though, the possibilities all boiled down to one thing. His time was coming soon. The only question was, when that moment came, what would Sa'rayna do about it.

She did love him, of that he was sure, but would it be enough to sway her from her commitment to 'what must be?' Ordinarily, he didn't think it would, but after twenty thousand years without speaking to another soul? If it had been him, he would have long since gone mad. She hadn't though, and now that they had found each other, he had to believe she wouldn't just give up on that without a fight.

Perhaps he was a fool, and if so, he was about to be a dead fool, he thought as three more men rushed him together. They skirted the very edges of the shallows to do it. He cut two of them and Socks kicked the third into the deeper water to much the same effect. The effort cost him a shallow gash on his right leg.

For an instant there was a break in the onslaught, and then a man at the far side of the Mirallyn stepped up with a bow and fired.

The shot was aimed directly at his heart, and had it flown true it would have killed him outright. It never launched though. A split second before he fired, the man crumpled to the ground in an all too familiar lifeless manner, the limply released arrow missing by several feet.

Wyll stared at the body of the man for a long second, his heart beating mercilessly in grim hope as more swordsmen rushed onto the shallow bridge to replace him. He had bet his life on the shaky hope that Sa'rayna would protect him. He had always known that she would not take part in the battle itself. By placing himself here though, where the enemy troops had to come within arm's reach of him to pass, he had hoped to use that protection to halt the enemy advance. It was an incredibly stupid risk, but that fallen archer gave him hope that this hadn't all been for nothing.

Again and again he dispatched enemy soldiers who rushed at him across the fjords, needing only to scratch them to take them out of the fight. At some point his exhausted mind noted that there was now a mound of corpses lying between himself and the far bank. Heramiir's men were having to scramble over their fallen companions to get at him, making those soldiers easier targets than they had been before. Yet it still wasn't enough. His sword arm felt like jelly, and even Socks seemed to be tiring from dancing away from sharp blades and kicking men into the river whenever he could.

He had no idea how long it had been, but there was a sudden brief pause in the tide of men. Wyll had a half second to look up at the archmage sitting his giant mount near the remnants of the catapult line before he was forced to turn his attention back to the fight. A wave of men was charging onto the fjords, tired of him slaughtering their companions. They meant to finish him once and for all. He didn't know what was about to happen, but with the few seconds he had left, he turned Socks to face the screaming press of men and raised the Sword of Ages above his head. He would buy as much time for the retreating army as possible, with or without Sa'rayna's help.

In moments they were on him. He had expected them to engage him as the men before had. Instead they rushed him, using the combined weights of hundreds of bodies to shove both him and Socks over, and then under them as they surged forward. Not a few of them fell from the fjords and drowned in the process.

For long seconds Wyll struggled to breathe as he lost his seat on Socks' saddle and was dunked under the water and crushing weight of men in armour. Men who had become unnaturally still he realised with a now familiar chill. Thankfully their momentum had carried him backwards to the very edge of that pile, and pulling himself above the water line with a great effort he coughed out the water he'd inhaled in the fall. Somehow he'd kept his grip on Sa'rayna's sword as he'd fallen. Pulling himself to his knees, he dragged both himself, and it, out of the water. He took three steps forward and stood stiffly atop the backs of the dead men who now covered the entire stretch of shallow crossing.

With a shudder he realised for the first time just what Sa'rayna could actually do, and wondered for an instant whether it might not have been better to let 'what must be' have taken its course. He couldn't have done it though, couldn't have just left them all to die. As he looked out at Heramiir's army, whose front ranks were not more than fifteen feet away, they seemed hesitant now. No doubt they wondered how a single swordsman could have killed so many of their companions in so short a time. The truth they could never know, was that he had only landed killing blows on maybe a dozen of the dead men who littered the surrounding area. The rest he had taken the easy way out and drawn blood. With the Sword of Ages in his hand, scoring a slight scratch on an enemy was as good as lopping off his head, and far less dangerous to himself. So that was how he had fought. Now there were perhaps half a thousand dead men with little evidence of wounds on them lying all around, especially the ones of the unit who had made that last abortive push.

With a tired glance behind him he saw Socks had fallen from the fjords, carried by the enemy's momentum. The horse had swum up to the bank and was shaking the water from himself as he made his way back towards where Wyll was standing.

"Wait there!" Wyll called, not wanting to endanger the superb animal any more than he already had.

Now that he knew Sa'rayna would indeed protect him, he had no more need for the advantage that fighting from horseback had provided. He suddenly couldn't help but grin, making several of Heramiir's soldiers in their front-most rank shy away a step as they began to fear his supposed power.

"Come on, he's on foot now!" someone called from behind the lines of enemy troops, most of whom were now eyeing him with a great deal of trepidation.

Wyll looked at them directly this time and smiled with intent, knowing that it would add to the appearance of the fearsome warrior whose slightest touch slew all before him. The warrior who clearly had unnatural powers that were both deadly and unique. He could see it in their eyes. After that last disastrous charge, they were not ready to try it again just yet, though they probably would still do so when ordered.

"For Miralthrall!" someone else shouted, probably an officer. "Forward, for Miralthrall!"

Looking at each other warily, the front line of soldiers moved forward as evenly as they could. None of them wanted to be the first to face him now.

He set his feet as well as he could on the uneven backs of the fallen soldiers, and waited a few seconds as the men cautiously approached. They attacked as one. Wyll parried the soldier on the left while the one on the right threw himself on the ground and stabbed upwards. It was a move that would have impaled him had the man's hand not gone limp and lifeless just before he attempted the thrust. Wyll used the distraction to scratch his companion, the two of them falling silent at his feet.

"Charge! That's an order!" the officer yelled again, and then stepped out from his troops to lead the foolhardy attempt himself.

Wyll watched as they came at him. Just as the officer was about to strike, Wyll lowered his sword and turned to call Socks back, forcing Sa'rayna to protect him once again. The officer raised his sword for the kill, and fell lifeless to the ground at Wyll's feet as Socks trotted over to where he was. His muscles screamed in protest as he mounted the rahiri steed. He turned back towards Heramiir's army, feeling a horrified numbness that he didn't dare show on his face at the sight which greeted him.

It wasn't just the officer, or the men charging behind him that Sa'rayna had felled this time, but every single man within fifty spans of the fjords.

In a rough semicircle from the end of the shallow crossing, nothing moved, and in the ranks behind them, no sound was made by the men who survived.

Wyll placed his sword across the pommel of his saddle and waited, staring at each man he could see, calmly taking their measure.

A man wearing the rank insignia of a general came forward. He had a wound in his side which he had staunched with a piece of material from some other man's coat. The man looked Wyll up and down for a long moment before inclining his head. If Wyll hadn't known better, he could have sworn that the gesture was more that of a man giving thanks than a general conceding defeat.

"Pull back a hundred spans from the mouth of the fjords!" the general ordered his own troops without taking his eyes off Wyll.

The officer clearly didn't want to anger him, but also wasn't about to be caught off guard either. Wyll couldn't help the momentary sensation that in some unknowing way he had just played into this man's hands.

Regardless of the odd feeling though, he continued to stare back at the general until Heramiir's army had followed his instructions, retreating the specified distance.

A swirling black vortex appeared in front of one of the catapults up in the distance. A rush of air heralded a hole black as pitch and as large as a barn appearing in the sky above him. Its edges were as unfocused as smoke, and it spun like a typhoon out at sea. Wyll stared in trepidation as he held tightly to Socks' reins, willing himself not to run, and hoping desperately that Sa'rayna could stop whatever was about to happen.

Long moments went by as Wyll waited, his very life in

the balance, unable to give up the slightest piece of ground as the swirling maelstrom loomed above him.

Soon Wyll grew uneasy. Why was it still there? Had Sa'rayna forsaken him at last?

As abruptly as it had appeared, the vortex collapsed in on itself with a huge gust of air. Wyll let out the breath he'd been holding, hoping the enemy soldiers hadn't noticed his uncertainty.

He looked around the field for any sign of Sa'rayna, but the flitting darkness that marked her passage was nowhere to be seen. Not even up at the medical tent where the most severely wounded men had been taken.

Somehow he knew she was no longer a part of this. With thousands around the fjords dead, and an even greater number of mortally wounded in the medical tents untaken, 'what must be' had been shattered beyond all hope of repair.

He wasn't sure what he had just set in motion, or whether she would ever want to see him again after he had used her like this today. He abruptly realised he would have to bluff his way through the rest of this day.

If Heramiir's forces attacked again now, then all of this would still be for nothing. At least the fires at the back of the king's army had been doused by the few surviving magi while he had been busy, giving the king's men a clear line of retreat.

Seeing the now marginally ordered lines of thousands of men streaming through the gap, Wyll knew his insane plan had achieved more than he could have hoped.

And yet, while he couldn't bring himself to regret his actions here this day, it was all he could do to stop his face draining of colour as a sudden thought occurred.

He'd accepted from the outset that the cost of his actions

this day might be to lose the woman he loved for good. What he hadn't planned for was that he may well have compromised Sa'rayna's mission to the point where the Maker himself, whom she served directly, might be enraged.

CHAPTER 27

THE GREATER FOE

"Davoor, kill that man," Heramiir ordered as his men down by the river began to back away.

It was unforgivable that someone had given that order, worse if they had not, but Davoor would settle the matter. The tall, ebony-skinned man had been a part of his inner circle for years, and was better than any of them at precision long range attacks with the Gift. It was why Heramiir had the man up on the ridge beside him, looking out for and striking any enemy position doing too well against his own troops.

Davoor nodded his shaved head, and muttered a long incantation before concentrating on the man sitting atop his white horse on the now shrunken fjords below. Gathering the necessary focus, he stretched out his hand to release the spell and fell limply from his saddle. Heramiir stared as the powerful archmage fell, resembling nothing more than a puppet whose strings had abruptly been cut.

Davoor's giant steed bolted away from where its master had just been felled, and even Heramiir's mount backed away a few paces before he could control it. With a scowl, Heramiir dismounted and checked Davoor for a pulse. Finding none, he remounted his steed, equal parts fury and curiosity warring within him as he turned to the catapults.

"Fire on that man!" he shouted, before using up the very last of the strength he had regained during the last few minutes to open one more of the smoky vortices. It would guide the catapult's payload unerringly towards its target. The breach was unstable, and pitifully small compared to the others he had employed to such wonderful effect earlier in the battle, but it would hold for a few moments.

In the distance, what was left of the king's dispirited force was making its wretched way back to their camp, out of range of his magi now for the most part. They would no doubt gather what they needed for a quick dash away from the army that had just routed them, and leave. He surveyed the field and smiled.

It was always hard to tell until proper reports could be obtained, but a quick look at the field told him he had not lost more than about ten, maybe fifteen percent of his men. It meant somewhere between ten and twenty thousand of his troops had been slain, or wounded badly enough that they had withdrawn from the ranks. Compared to the massive disarray the king's fleeing force was in, this had been a crushing victory. It seemed there was but one last obstacle for him to overcome before his triumph was complete. The catapult crew worked as fast as they could, reloading the machine with a ball of burning pitch and sawdust salvaged from one of the siege engines which had been destroyed early in the battle.

To his right he heard the siege commander give the order to fire. Heramiir looked across just in time to see the man who was tugging on the release cord fall bonelessly in the same disturbing manner Davoor had, just moments ago. The cord itself fell back to its resting position, not yet having been fired. One man in the crew, who was nearest his fallen companion and either braver or stupider than the rest, took his place and tried to tug on the cord himself. At the last instant, even as it seemed he would succeed, he also fell lifeless to the ground. The rest of the men backed away from the siege machine as if the lifeless engine had contracted some horrific disease.

"Hold!" Heramiir ordered the siege commander, and the officer gratefully gave the order, though he seemed prepared to go on if Heramiir had so ordered. He would have to reward that young man for his efforts today when this was all done, Heramiir thought again.

At least now Heramiir understood what was happening down at the river. One man on a horse was not enough to make them retreat, but if this were happening there too… With a flash of insight he realised why the king's magi had narrowed the fjords as they had, despite it costing them some of their own. They had created a bottleneck where his men would have to pass within an arm's length of that rider, which none of his troops seemed willing to do any more. From the thousand or more bodies that littered the ground and the river around him, Heramiir now understood why, and suddenly he was sure.

A warrior like has not been seen since the world's foundation.

The thought came unbidden to his mind.

That was what the prophecy had said. Heramiir knew beyond all shadow of a doubt that the man sitting astride his white mount, holding off a hundred thousand men and more with nothing but a black sword in his hand was indeed that warrior.

If that were truly the case, Heramiir had to meet him. He

had always believed that understanding your enemy was the first step to defeating them.

That he fought for the king was no great surprise. After all, the prophecy had seemed to suggest that they would be on opposing sides. Although that left the question of who, 'A boy whose pain shall tear his soul asunder', was. Which side he would be on, or would there be a third player in the events the prophecy alluded to? In truth he was far more concerned with who the 'General whose every thought shall be of betrayal,' was. He thought it might be Hassan, though the man did not permanently hold that rank, at least not yet. Still, it was something he would have to turn his attention to soon. For now though, there was the matter of the extremely dangerous soldier down by the river. Though something seemed amiss. If the warrior could strike so precisely at Davoor and the catapult crews, and if he did fight for the king, why not kill the enemy leader while he was at it? It was a frightening thought, that by some man's will, Heramiir could simply stop living between one breath and the next with absolutely nothing he could do to prevent it. And yet the man had not done so. It made no sense. Heramiir knew that if he had held that same power, Messand would have been his first target. Then regrettably, the supporting magi, at least those amongst them strong enough to be a serious threat.

For a moment Heramiir fancied the figure was looking up the slope at him and his breath caught, but after a long moment nothing happened, and that settled it. If he could be so casually brushed aside by this man, at the very least he would learn the warrior's name.

With that in mind he gave a thought command to his steed, and the huge beast began walking down the slope towards the now deepened fjords. If the warrior continued to deny his men passage, it would take a week to get his army far enough west that it was out of the man's sight. They would then have to loop around somewhere to the north and use the Gift to construct bridges for his men somewhere else.

Heramiir sighed. A week would give the remnants of Erian's army enough time to warn and either evacuate or fortify the towns along the road as they went. It would not stop Heramiir's army of course. Every battle they fought would diminish the number of men he had at his disposal when they made their final assault on Aramar though. With Tolmarak leading its defences, he would need them all.

'*Order the army to hold,*' he thought to Deshara as he guided his mount down the small ridge where the siege weapons were located. He moved through the rows of tents towards the river at a walk. It took almost five minutes to reach the great bulk of his men. They parted as soon as they saw him coming, and Heramiir walked his giant steed in a straight line towards the warrior who still held the small crossing against his army.

Finally he reached the front lines, and as those troops also moved aside, Heramiir saw that the mighty warrior of prophecy was little more than a boy. Surely he was only about twenty years of age, he reassessed at second glance. The confident way he sat his mount and held that arcane sword across the pommel of his saddle had made him seem much older from a distance.

It took an instant, but a shiver of dread worked its way up Heramiir's spine as he saw for the first time what those symbols on the black blade actually were. Doing his best not to let it show, he cringed. They were identical to the powerful set which had been imprinted on the door to the master's chamber. It all but confirmed his suspicions as to the mystery horseman's part in the prophecy. It also made the man in front of him a far more interesting enigma than even he had first suspected. And far more dangerous than a Giftless boy of his years had any right to be.

He needed to know where the boy had found that sword.

"Heramiir?" the boy said, curiosity touching his eyes as he studied the archmage's cloud riven cloak. The artefact was in a frenzy, glowing runes now flashing along its length like even Heramiir had never seen. Perhaps it was the proximity to the sword? He wove his huge steed around the mounds of bodies, those both rent, and many more curiously untouched, which barred the way between his men and the fjord.

Heramiir nodded slightly in acknowledgement when he reached the red stained river.

"And you are?" he prompted when the boy said no more.

"I am Wyll," he said as he looked over Heramiir's steed with distaste, noting the physical mutations which Heramiir's magic had worked in it.

Heramiir was fond of his creations, though he could see why the boy was not, riding a Rahiri stallion as he was. Even for a half-blood, the horse was a good stock. If he'd had access to Arborii steeds like that to augment, he could have made his own mount even more spectacular than he had. Perhaps once Jeranon was under his control, he could pursue that line of research, but that was for another day.

"You clearly have great power Wyll," Heramiir acceded to the young man. "The question is, can you defeat my entire army? Or are you using what power you have to hold this narrow stretch of ground so we cannot pursue the remnants of the King's defeated force?" he mused out loud.

"There is one way you can find out for sure," the rider who called himself Wyll responded as he gave Heramiir a grin that would have done Deshara proud.

Heramiir looked into his eyes for a long moment, gauging his response. He suspected the boy did not have the power to back up his threat, but if that turned out to be true, this Wyll might decide to eliminate the threat of the magi before retreating from the troops. It was too much of a risk when they had such poor information about the extent of his powers. He sighed, they would have to find another way across the Mirallyn, or at least wait until Wyll had gone before attempting a crossing.

"Very well, you have your reprieve Wyll, for now. Take what is left of the King's army and run back to Aramar with your tail between your legs. Make sure you tell them all just how easily we defeated Erian's mighty army today, and that we will be there soon. Tell them if Erian still sits on the throne when we break through Aramar's defences, I will not spare a single man, woman, or child I find within the city walls."

For a moment Heramiir thought he had gone too far as the boy's eyes turned to stone, but he wasn't struck down, and Heramiir was beginning to gain an idea that the boy couldn't. Even so, he'd tested that theory enough for one afternoon.

"Heramiir, take your men and go home. Return to Miralthrall and disband your forces and re-swear loyalty to the King. Otherwise I will come for you, whether you win this war or not."

Heramiir could only smile at that. The boy was powerful, but he was also young enough to be a little naïve.

"My dear boy, look around you. I just won the war," Heramiir told him, failing to keep a little smugness out of his voice.

"What you see before you is not my entire army, and what pitiful remnants of Erian's men survived this massacre cannot hold out against us for long. Neither will they reach Aramar ahead of my force with all their wounded, especially with most of your battle magi dead or injured already. If it weren't for you, my men would already be wiping them from the face of this world."

Wyll looked around, surveying the scene of their crushing defeat as he realised to his dismay that Heramiir had spoken simple truth.

"There is a new order coming to this country Wyll. You could be a part of it if you so choose. I sense no spark of the Gift in you, and yet you clearly have power. You could be an important part of that new order if you so desired."

"And I suppose all I would have to do is become a traitor to the rightful king and fight against him with your men?" Wyll returned. His horse even stamped its brown foot in agitation, picking up its rider's mood.

"That would be my preferred option, yes," Heramiir returned. "But with or without your help, Erian's reign will fall since you cannot be in more than one place at a time, can you?"

From the slight tightening of Wyll's lips he knew that much at least was true, despite the boy's otherwise undetermined powers.

"Think about it Wyll, what good will it do you to hold Aramar if the rest of Jeranon goes over to us as the west already has? Alone and without reinforcements, eventually the people will starve. It will get bad inside the city. First the prices will skyrocket, then crime will soar. After that, animals will mysteriously begin to vanish. If Erian holds out long enough, cannibalism may even come into play. These things have happened in the past. And all the while we will show the citizens that life beyond their walls continues as it always has, only under a different ruler. Before they all die, the citizens of Aramar will tear down Erian's regime themselves and welcome my men, and the food they will bring into the city, as heroes."

Wyll's gaze tightened, and his shoulders slumped a little. The boy was intelligent enough to recognise plain truth when he heard it. That was good.

"That may be so," Wyll conceded after a long moment, "But whether you win the greater war or not, you will not cross this river today. I will not allow you to slaughter defenceless men. Most of these soldiers are too injured to fight against you anymore, and there are not enough magi to heal them all at any rate," Wyll returned. "In time though, many of them will be able to resume their own lives. Even if you are successful in your campaign, you will need them to go back to being farmers, and merchants, and artists if you intend to rule this nation. Or do you simply wish to destroy it?"

Heramiir looked at the young man in front of him with a newfound respect. His words were a test, and yet he had opened his mind to a possibility that Heramiir was certain had not been part of his mindset just moments earlier.

"I agree," Heramiir responded, testing the waters for an opportunity. "And as always, any man who wishes to turn in his sword and live within my domain will be well treated so long as he strives to make an honest life for himself. There is after all, plenty of work to be done before things settle down enough in Jeranon that we can end this war with the western nations once and for all."

"How do you intend to do that?" Wyll asked in guarded surprise as the archmage's words sunk in.

Heramiir smiled.

"I beat you easily enough, didn't I? Rest assured, I already have plans in motion that will aid us to that effect."

"Are you truly arrogant enough to think that the western nations would accept you as their ruler?" Wyll asked him incredulously.

"Ruler?" Heramiir replied with a chuckle.

"I have no intention of ruling the western nations Wyll. I intend to destroy them. Utterly. By the time I am through we will have no need to send troops out to their deaths every single day on pointless patrols that engage with their counterparts in the Dark Iron Mountains. Patrols which all too often come home the smaller for it. This idiotic conflict that has been festering since our ancestors fled the cataclysm and fought the Wars of Founding to carve Jeranon from this unknown land must end. I will see it done before I die. The monarchy has existed for as long as memory can search, but they have lost their way over the last centuries, and now we have come to this. Did you even know our magi used to be better, more skilled, more powerful than our enemies' counterparts? Since the ban on experimentation has been enforced, that has changed. Every generation our enemies caught up a little while we fell behind. Until now we are very much on a similar level. Of course the problem with that is that they have four nations to source their arcane societies from. We have only one, with the Terraliv and Arborii producing almost no strong Gift users over the last hundred years. If we do not change things on our end, or finish this constant warfare before many more generations have passed, we will lose everything. Who rules Jeranon will seem trivial as we once again have to flee our very homes or die where we stand. Look around you Wyll. All that you see here, all that I have done and will continue to do is towards that end. While I am the first to deplore the necessity of it, when five hundred years of peaceful and logical argument cannot coerce the monarchy into doing what is right, what other choice have we left? Jeranon itself has been set on a path to irrelevance and oblivion, and that must change if we are to survive."

When Heramiir was finished, Wyll found himself gripping Sock's reins much harder than was necessary, and forced himself to relax. He wanted to scream at the man in front of him, to strike him down with Sa'rayna's black blade. The Sword of Ages still rested on his pommel, bared in his grip. He dared not attempt it though. Sa'rayna was gone, and even if he could somehow strike a deadly blow at the archmage, killing Heramiir would no doubt bring on another full-strength attack by his forces. If that happened, he would be overwhelmed in seconds, or they would simply work out that they needed only to go around him.

He hated himself for using her like that, and could only beg the Maker not to deal too harshly with her. There were close to thirty thousand men limping back to the camp, or already there. Most of them would be dead by now if he had not done as he had. Despite both his betrayal and its consequences, he was having a hard time as seeing those actions as wrong.

He abruptly found that he had never hated a man more than he did this archmage right now. There must be close on a hundred thousand dead piled around the small pass of the fjords, both Heramiir's own, and the king's. Yet there he sat on his mutated steed, unconcerned with anything but his overall plan.

This must be something of what Jayden feels, he thought uneasily. And yet so far as Wyll knew, no one he loved had died here today.

"The price is too high Heramiir. What good will peace do us if there is no one left alive to enjoy it?"

For a moment the archmage was silent.

"Do you have children Wyll?"

Wyll shook his head but remained silent.

"I see. Well despite your slaughtering of my troops, you strike me as a good man. Too good perhaps for the amount of power you obviously carry. But answer me this. If you had those children, would you give your life if it meant that they would never need to fear when the next invasion would come? If it meant they would never have to be soldiers at all. That they could grow up and live their lives with no more pressing concerns than when to plant the next crop, or whether to take on a new apprentice this season or next? That they could find a partner and grow old together, dying in their beds old men or women surrounded by their family and friends? Because each of them has made that choice," he said, pointing back at his own forces.

"They have taken a stand with us against a noble class too arrogant and self-absorbed to make the sacrifices necessary to ensure our survival. Even now, all western Jeranon stands united to assure our people a future by throwing out this ridiculous ban on experimentation with the Gift. Every one of them has seen, or knows someone who has seen, hard, constant fighting at the front, and all of them want it to end. But most of all, they seek one thing. To ensure that by the time their children tell their own little ones about the coming battles, names like, 'Augrahl raiding party', and 'Oo'vi High Shaper', will be nothing more than tales told around campfires as something we once needed to fear."

"It still doesn't justify, this…" Wyll retorted, motioning around at the blood-soaked field.

They had all assumed that Heramiir simply wanted power. To depose the king and take Jeranon for his own. If what he was saying now were true though, it would make him far more dangerous. It might even make him a hero to the people of the Sammorand Plains, to whom attacks by the western nations were an accepted, if hard, fact of life.

Heramiir gave him a hard stare for a moment before walking his huge mount right up beside Socks and saying quietly.

"Even you, Wyll. Even you are part of the problem. Here you sit, so arrogant on your half Arborii steed, holding back close on a hundred thousand men with nothing but a sword. Why aren't you on the western front? Where are you every day while our people are giving their lives to keep us safe? If even one of your obvious power is too selfish to act in the defence of the poor and the powerless... By your own actions you prove that every step I have taken is justified. Thank you for renewing my zeal."

Wyll gripped the reins, his knuckles white with anger, and again barely restrained himself from striking out. He could kill Heramiir right here and now. At least, he thought he could. The thing was, everything the man had said was true. Jayden's experiences with the nobility were proof enough of that. The part about him was wrong of course, but then Heramiir had no way of knowing how new his relationship with Sa'rayna was, if that even still existed. Or that it was she who had taken his men's lives and not him at all.

It was a different perspective on things which Heramiir held perhaps, but the hard facts were there all the same. As confronting as Wyll found those facts, he couldn't very well kill a man for telling the truth.

"Tell me something," Wyll said as it occurred to him at last. "Why did you send an assassin to kill the Aramarian magi if you want to 'save' Jeranon?"

Heramiir frowned slightly at that. It was perhaps the first subtle sign of remorse he had shown.

"Do you see the men behind me?"

Wyll nodded.

"If all of Aramar's magi had faced us here, our forces would have been evenly matched, and at least half those men would be dead. Even had we won the day, without our now vastly superior numbers the war would have dragged out for more years than necessary. That would disrupt commerce, harvests, and create famine throughout the country as the various armies took whatever they needed from the commoners to re-supply. Even more importantly, the door to the western nations attacking during that time of chaos would be wide open, and I want it closed as soon as possible. All of that I had to measure against the lives of perhaps twenty magi. We lose that number on the border every four to five years already because of the King's pointless commands. A number that will continue to climb as the western nations catch up and overtake us in knowledge of the Gift until they finally break through in force. How long do you think Jeranon will hold against our enemies once those two events occur?"

Wyll grimaced, wishing the archmage wasn't right.

"Even if everything you have said is true, you are talking about something that won't happen for what, a hundred years?" Wyll returned, looking for some chink in Heramiir's logic that would allow him to dismiss the archmage's words as nothing but traitorous lies.

"Yes," came Heramiir's simple reply. "And yet if we wish to change that future for our people, the time to act is now, while we still have the strength to do so."

"You should leave now," Wyll said as he realised what was happening.

"Why now?" Heramiir returned. "I have not had such an intelligent conversation in quite some time."

"That may be, but I don't like what you're trying to do. I am loyal to the King, and I will stay that way."

Once again Heramiir turned his piercing green gaze on the young man in front of him and decided he liked what he saw.

"I don't believe you Wyll," he said so that none but them could hear.

"Would you like my blade to convince you?" Wyll returned, looking Heramiir full in the eye. It was something few people were willing to do, even among his allies.

Heramiir smiled.

"I think you are more like me. A loyal servant of the kingdom, but not necessarily of the king. I think that when it comes right down to it, you will do what is in Jeranon's best interests, not Erian's."

"Leave," Wyll whispered, looking straight ahead and trying not to let the archmage see just how close to the mark he had come. The worst of it was that Wyll hadn't even realised he felt that way himself until Heramiir pointed it out.

"Where did you acquire such an interesting blade I wonder?" Heramiir mused, changing tack to throw the young man off balance.

"Nowhere you need be concerned about," Wyll replied as some kind of commotion erupted in the ranks behind Heramiir.

With a sudden pounding of hooves, another of the grotesque steeds on which Heramiir and his lieutenant's rode into battle came sprinting down towards them at a full gallop. The rider only slowed at the last second, the middle aged yet uncommonly attractive woman riding it beckoning Heramiir away from him in an urgent, almost panicked manner.

Heramiir turned his steed away from Wyll without a word and threaded his way among the bodies to Deshara's mount as quickly as he could. There were few things capable of cracking her composure. He wasn't going to like whatever she had to report.

"The western nations have attacked Stonekeep from the east. I was checking on our forces there a few minutes ago, and the timing was lucky enough that Archmage Forester could give me a proper report. He said that a large force of Augrahl and Imbic had broken through from the rear and the fighting had moved into the north keep. The south was already on fire, and he expected that after extreme losses on both sides, the garrison would be routed within the hour! Worse still, before I lost contact with him, Forester said his scouts had just reported a vast force flying the flags of all four nations heading down the pass."

Heramiir's eyebrows had risen as high as they would go, and his fists were clenched by the time she had finished.

"Why now?" he whispered. "After ten years of near

silence, could they not have waited one more season? From the east you said?"

Deshara nodded.

"How could they get a force big enough to take on Stonekeep across the mountains, and then march on it undetected?"

He thought furiously for a moment and then slammed his fist down on the saddle with a snarl. "Contact Mendacai. Tell him to try scrying the area around the missing villages again."

"Yes Archmage," Deshara deferred, which was always the wise move when he was in this kind of mood.

"What should I tell him to look for?"

"A place where he can't find anything at all unusual," Heramiir snapped.

"A blind spot where an army or... Of course!" he muttered as realisation of just where the missing villages had gone hit him right between the eyes.

"Tell him that there is most likely a fortification constructed with the materials from the missing villages and hidden by arcane means at that position."

Deshara's eyes widened a little but then she closed them, and did as she was told. After a few moments she spoke again.

"He will do as you bid Archmage, and thanks you for the assistance."

"We need to withdraw from this position and move the army onto the Sammorand Plains with all haste. If the western nations beat us to the top of the great staircase, we could lose a third of the country without ever giving them an actual fight!"

Heramiir looked around himself then, a hush seemed to

have grown over the assembled army. He belatedly realised the front ranks had been within earshot of that report.

"I'll take Nereth and the cavalry and leave immediately. You follow behind with the infantry once our camp and stores are seen to, we'll need them once we're on the plains. See to it Deshara," he said in dismissal. The other archmage nodded before riding out at a gallop, calling the troops to order as she did.

Heramiir surveyed the vast scene of carnage that surrounded them for a moment. If only they had received this news a few hours before, the western nations would have twice the fight on their hands that they now would. He sighed. What couldn't be helped had to be dealt with. He turned his mount.

Walking his steed back into the shallow river where Wyll's mount still stood, he saw the boy had also heard the news. That was good, it would save time.

"Take your men to your garrison at Midway, Wyll. Leave whoever cannot travel and fight and come with all haste to Miralthrall. We have larger issues to deal with now than who rules the kingdom."

Wyll looked at him in disbelief for a long moment before shaking his head.

"I don't take orders from traitors," the young man said.

Heramiir nodded to himself, having expected no less.

"If that is your choice Wyll, so be it. But if you will not follow me, then it leaves you with one other to make."

"And what is that?" Wyll returned, not quite believing what he was hearing.

"You already know. We talked about it before," Heramiir prompted in an unfriendly tone.

Wyll thought back for a moment, his eyes never leaving Heramiir's.

"My King, or my country," he bitterly returned when he could no longer ignore the truth.

"Yes."

"The question you must answer is which of them you will choose, now that their needs are in direct opposition. The western nations have broken through our main line of defence. If you choose to continue opposing me, distracting my forces from what we must do, we could lose the whole country. On the other hand, you could choose to do what you know is right. You can join with me and help defend Jeranon against a threat that has plagued it for three thousand years. A threat which shows no sign of stopping until either we, or they, have been utterly erased. But be warned, if you do choose to defend your homeland against this threat, against Erian's orders, then you have chosen my exact path, Wyll. By defending us all, you declare yourself traitor as well, if that is indeed what we are. While I may have instigated this campaign, make no mistake, every man who died on this field today did so because of Erian's pride. If he and his ancestors had allowed us to reach our potential and eliminate the enemies of Jeranon as we should have done centuries ago, none of this would have been necessary."

Wyll sat on Socks' back, feeling dirty to his soul. He had set out from Aramar with such high ideals. Service, duty, loyalty to king and country. But Heramiir was right. The threat from the western nations was too pressing to be ignored. What was left of the king's army was no longer anywhere near large or strong enough to prosecute an effective attack on them, or even on Heramiir's forces. The only other option he could see was that they could sit back and do nothing, hoping that their enemies ground each other down to a more manageable size. Only the thing was, Heramiir's men weren't monstrous enemies bent on their complete destruction. They were brothers, sons, fathers, and uncles of people he probably knew, maybe even of some of the men who were still retreating to the camps in disarray. Having those kinsmen ground down to increase his tactical advantage was not something he was sure he could live with.

With deep loathing, he came to realise that there was only one choice which he could legitimately make. The king would label him a traitor for it, and try to have him hung, but he couldn't ignore a full-scale invasion by the western nations.

If they marched beside Heramiir's men. Never as part of them, he promised himself, but beside. At least Jeranon would be able to field an army that could realistically oppose their enemies in open combat.

This is all wrong, was all he could think as Heramiir waited for his reply.

Fully two thirds of the king's army was dead on the field around him, and most of those who had survived were injured. How was he supposed to convince whoever was in charge of these scattered remnants to join their cause to the very enemy they had just been slaughtered by?

Wyll suddenly found himself wondering whether all this had been worth it.

"Heramiir," Wyll said, hating what he now had to do.

The archmage wisely remained silent, though he nodded for Wyll to continue.

"The last I saw, General Messand was still alive, though

gravely wounded. I don't know of any other high-ranking officer who survived your ambush, and I have no authority to issue any such orders. We will return to Midway and attend the wounded. From there we will march to assist you against the western nations. If I can make the General listen."

Heramiir nodded.

"I was right Wyll, you are a good man. Too good to follow orders without questioning their consequences. I intend to ride hard for the Cloudburst Cliffs with every mage and cavalryman I can muster. Sadly I can spare no magi long enough to heal all your men, but before we leave, I will have them heal your surviving magi. They will then in turn be able to attend to your wounded. I will do this so long as you personally guarantee my people safe passage through your ranks."

"You have it," Wyll agreed. "Send them to me and I'll have them escorted by my own trusted men."

"And where will you be?" Heramiir asked curiously.

"Until your forces have withdrawn from the field, you will be able to find me here," Wyll told him. A mocking grin tried to work its way onto his face, but failed at the last instant.

"I understand," Heramiir nodded, and after a moment of thought extended his gauntleted hand.

"I wish you luck Wyll, but do not take too long."

Wyll stared down at the archmage's hand. He felt hollowed out inside, incapable of taking in any more than he already had.

"It's not time for that yet," he said, his gaze straying back to Heramiir's intense green eyes.

The archmage nodded slightly and let his hand drop.

"I believe in time you will come to see this is the right course, Wyll. Perhaps it was the only one that was ever truly available to men such as we. I'll send those magi to you now," Heramiir said before turning his steed to ride off past the piles of dead men, and back into his own ranks. Already the army was dispersing at Deshara's orders, allowing the few cavalry units seeded amongst them room to move to the rear of the army, following Heramiir's lead.

For long moments Wyll just sat there, motionless, and then at long last did the hardest thing yet he had been called to do all that interminable day. With a single smooth motion, he slid the Sword of Ages back into its ivory sheathe. It was a simple thing, physically at least, but it meant that this battle was truly over. They had lost everything in the process.

There was a shrill, distant cry, and as Wyll looked up into the bright sunlit sky, he was greeted with the sight of a majestically old eagle gliding its way on the thermals far above. It was probably wondering why so many men were gathered beside the shores of this small stretch of unremarkable river.

As Wyll looked back to the east, he saw Seth waiting less than a hundred spans away, and motioned for the man to join him. He couldn't help wondering the same thing again. What had all this been for? A hundred thousand men dead near enough, and the survivors would have little choice but to join Heramiir anyway. It would bring the archmage's numbers back to what they had been at the start of the fight, if not add to them.

"Yes sir?" Seth asked, utter respect in his voice as he waited for Wyll's instructions. Right at that moment Wyll knew he could order this man to do anything, even to charge across the river and attack the archmage himself. He would obey without question. They all would, he realised as he saw identical looks on the rest of his men's faces. When had they joined Seth from their place beyond the medical tent? He would never do that of course. They deserved better, especially after what they had all just been through.

"Heramiir is sending some of his magi to heal our own. See that no harm comes to them, and once they are done, bring them straight back here. Don't leave them alone for an instant."

"Yes sir, is there anything else?" Seth asked.

"No. This is done," Wyll answered tiredly as he saw several of the magi on the opposing hill break away and ride down towards him as Heramiir's grotesque mount reached them in the distance.

"Have you seen any of the other officers?" he asked, his eyes still looking straight ahead.

There was a long pause before Kienan spoke. The man had survived, Wyll was glad to see, but was being supported by Sarran. A mage must have taken a moment to heal his leg. Probably because it was a simple job for them and would get one more man back into the fight, Wyll imagined.

"The initial attack was very well planned. Only a few of the command staff survived the initial blast, and most of them have since died from their wounds. As far as I could tell from a brief trip to the medical tent, no one above captain made it out of there alive. Except for the general, and I'm told that he is unconscious, and the healers can't wake him."

"But I spoke to him before..." Wyll responded, trying hard to care, but failing.

"Yes sir, that was before he was wounded the second time."

Wyll looked down at Kienan in exhaustion and asked the only question he could think of.

"Who is in command then?"

"From what I saw back at the camp, none of the captains wants a bar of this disaster. Many of the men who weren't hurt too badly, especially the newer recruits, are talking about packing up and going back to their homes. With this many dead, who's to know?"

Wyll sighed. He wished he had that luxury, but he couldn't allow what was left of the army to dissipate. Not with what he now knew about the western nations' invasion.

"I have to stay here until Heramiir's army has withdrawn," he told the others. "But I want you to spread the word that I need to address the men as soon as I can. If they will listen," he finished quietly.

"With all due respect sir, they don't need you to talk to them. They need you to lead them," Kienan said quietly.

Wyll just looked at him, numbed by the events of the last hour.

"I'm mageguard, why would they need me?" he asked, not sure whether the musician who had been conscripted against his will was making sport of him or not.

Kienan just stared back at him for a long moment in disbelief. "You and no one else, Sir. I doubt even the general could have held them together as a force after this. Yours is the only name being spoken back at the camp, sir. Every man there knows what you did by now, and I don't think they would take no for an answer, even if you gave it."

"I don't deserve it," Wyll said, watching Heramiir's magi come closer, and thinking on what he'd agreed to, to secure that aid.

"You do, but that's irrelevant," Kienan continued as he shook his head emphatically. "Right now those men are just about as low as men can get and still be breathing. They need something to believe in right now, and since you just saved every one of their lives, and they saw you do it, that means it's you. I don't honestly think they will give you a choice, though the General might have something to say about it when… If, he ever wakes up."

"We can only hope," Wyll said, then gave a long sigh as Heramiir's magi arrived.

If he had to pretend he could be in command of this shattered force, no matter for how short a time, he had best start now.

"These men will escort you to the camp," he told them seriously.

"You will heal all of our magi and any other man you find on the way with life-threatening injuries, then return here with all haste. These men here are under my direct command and will escort you until you return. Do not attempt to leave their side as no one else is yet aware of our deal, and a misunderstanding would not be in anybody's interest. One last thing, you will say nothing about the reason for your withdrawal from this field. Is that understood?"

There were tense nods all around, though some of the magi looked a little surprised.

"There is enough chaos within our ranks at this moment without a mass panic starting. If that happens, what is left of this army will scatter, and you will receive no aid at all against the western nations. There will simply be no army left to give it."

"Understood. We will defer to your direction. On this

occasion," the lead archmage replied before continuing to ride past him and across the field atop his mutated steed, his black enamelled plate armour strangely silent. Wyll's men formed a protective circle around the group as they left.

The eagle had gone now, chasing the sun towards the horizon in hopes of a more peaceful hunting ground, Wyll supposed. He looked once more into the fading light of dusk. Tomorrow would be a new day, with hopes and fears all of its own. When it came, he would have to leave today's horrors in the past and try to move forward.

He was finally alone.

Letting go of Socks' reins for a moment he leant down and covered his face in his hands. Allowing a single tear to trickle down his face, he thought on the mounds of dead bodies lying like driftwood all around. They choked the Mirallyn around the battle site for their sheer number and weight, causing the bloodied waters to pool past their banks as they attempted to reassert their natural path.

Besides perhaps the archmagi Heramiir and Veroneth, he himself was probably responsible for more of those deaths than any other single person on this field. He still dully dared to hope that Sa'rayna would find it within herself to forgive him for forcing her into what she had done to protect him on this most horrific of days. It was one the likes of which he hoped never to see again.

Tomorrow will be a better day though, he promised himself fervently, hoping the desperate vow he had just made to himself would come true. He forced himself to look around at what this pointless power struggle had cost.

It will *be better,* he promised himself again as the sun began to set, casting macabre shadows amongst the piles of the dead. It would be better because *he* would make it that way.

After all, he thought with bittersweet fervour as the groping shadows of the dead began to reach him on the far edge of twilight.

Isn't that what hope is really all about?

EPILOGUE

THE STRINGS OF FATE

The day dawned clear and blue above the windswept plains of Sammorand. Long grasses swayed, and a gentle breeze was driving the clouds west towards the Dark Iron Mountains.

High above the gently rolling hills, an eagle cried out as it scented the drifting smoke still pouring from Stonekeep Castle. She circled away from the flames, passing high over a column of greyskins as she rode the thermals back towards her home in the nearby foothills. As she headed northwest, she passed over the mighty Mirallyn River as it rushed eastward on its never-ending journey. Eastward it flowed, over the Cloudburst Cliffs, into the Star Lake and beyond.

Finally it came to a place where its waters ran red with blood and the bodies of those who had died in that last frenzied attack. On either side of the fjords two armies prepared to march. To the east the king's routed and dispirited forces rallied at their unexpected reprieve. At least enough to see to the wounded, and strike camp before making the long march to Midway.

On the western bank, Heramiir's army was also striking camp, the cavalry having already ridden out at a gallop behind Heramiir's giant steed.

Deshara had stayed with the infantry, her presence giving

Heramiir's troops heart, or at least fear enough to see to the dismantling of the camp. Still, the soldiers threw nervous glances back at the single mounted figure astride his white stallion, the brown of its legs standing just above the sluggishly clogged waterline.

Calm he sat; his dead black blade re-sheathed for now, only its ivory hilt showing above his right shoulder as he held the reins draped across his left hand.

None who had seen the events of that morning unfold had understood the import of what had transpired. But deep underground below the stone-paved streets of Miralthrall, the destroyer felt a tugging, a twisting of a thousand different fates, and knew it was his time.

With a roar that shook the very foundations of the ancient city he pushed at his prison, struggling to weaken the bonds that had held him for aeons. In moments he had expended his strength, but a careful inspection of his cell showed him his efforts had been well rewarded.

He had hoped to find a hole. What he found instead was a weak spot, a place where his power could move more freely through the boundary of the only place he'd known for the last twenty millennia. His time of imprisonment was almost at an end. He would be free. Free to hunt her down, the one the prophecy referred to as 'The power from time immemorial'. Of course, he knew her real name, or at least he had.

It had been so long.

Twenty thousand years, he thought bitterly.

She could have gone a long way in that time, to the edge of the universe even. But he knew she had not, and he would find her. She could not leave this pitiful little world any more than he could be held in this prison forever. It was impossible. It was unquestionable.

It was prophesied.

"Not long now, not long now, Gonna' get out yeah not long now."

For the first time in millennia the Destroyer laughed, and the foundations of Miralthrall trembled at the sound.

HERE ENDS THE INEVITABLE SPRING
BOOK 2 OF THE DESTROYER'S WRATH

ALSO AVAILABLE

THE PATH OF PRIDE

A PREQUEL TO THE DESTROYER'S WRATH

Scan the QR code above for more information!

ALSO AVAILABLE

THE DARK TEMPEST

BOOK 1 OF THE DESTROYER'S WRATH

Scan the QR code above for more information!

Acknowledgements

As always, to my wife and children of course.

To my alpha and beta readers, you all know who you are, and have my appreciation for your work on this latest project

To my cover designer at BRoseDesignz, again, thank you for making the artwork an eye-catching affair that draws in readers all by itself!

Finally, to everyone who has read book one and two of the Destroyer's Wrath (and maybe even the prequel), thank you! Rest assured, there's plenty more to come in **book three of The Destroyer's Wrath**.

THE DAY OF RECKONING.

Coming soon.

Until then. Happy reading.

Regards
N. P. Cooper

About the Author

N. P. Cooper grew up in Melbourne, Australia, and moved to Queensland early in his twenties. He has been writing for most of his life for his own pleasure, but The Dark Tempest marks his first foray into publishing his own work. When not staring at his computer screen, he enjoys spending time with his family and friends, listening to live music, and exploring the local tidal pools with his children.

For more information on N. P. Cooper's upcoming books, appearances, and release dates, visit his website at npcooper.com

FOLLOW THE QR CODE TO
WWW.NPCOOPER.COM

www.ingramcontent.com/pod-product-compliance
Lightning Source LLC
Chambersburg PA
CBHW050058120726
47904CB00004B/1128